The Last Dance

Lisa Selvidge completed a BA in [obscured] at the University of London, with Portu[guese]. [obscured] elling around Asia and teaching English a[s a F]oreign Language for several years in Japan and Russia, she went on to take an MA in Creative Writing (Prose Fiction) at the University of East Anglia in the UK. She subsequently taught at the Norwich School of Art & Design for five years and then at the University of East Anglia where, in 2001, she became the Academic Director for Creative Writing in the Centre for Continuing Education.

In 2004, she moved to Portugal where she is currently living for most of the year. She still teaches online prose fiction courses as well as doing freelance work and running workshops in the Algarve. She is the author of *The Trials of Tricia Blake* (fiction), *A Divine War* (fiction), *Writing Fiction Workbook* (non-fiction), and has edited a collection of writings from seventeen authors inspired by the Algarve, entitled *Summer Times*.

For more information visit www.lisaselvidge.com

Author's note:

I lived in Berlin from 1984 to 1985 and it was a very special place to be in a very strange time. One of my aims in writing this book was to try to capture that unusual moment in recent history. It is not the first time walls have been built (although usually to keep people out, not in), and it will not be the last, but for one country to be split in half, to have its capital city sliced up, and then for each side to be taught to believe in different things, Germany is unique. Peter Schneider writes in *The Wall Jumper*, 'It will take us longer to tear down the Wall in our heads than any wrecking company will need for the Wall we can see.' Since the fall of the Berlin Wall in 1989 it has, not surprisingly, taken twenty years to merge the two Germanys, not only physically and financially, but psychologically. Even today, people over thirty define themselves from the 'old East' or the 'West'. But now there is a new generation which has grown up having never known the Wall. As Johnny says at the end of the book, 'We are all prisoners of our time'. That is true of us all, but particularly pertinent for those caught in a divisive wave of ideological differences.

This is a work of fiction and any resemblance to real people is coincidental. However, most locales are real places in Berlin (such as the Café Swing) or inspired by real places (such as the Kiosk, based on Risiko, a bar in West Berlin in the 1980s). Heidelberger Straße was, indeed, one of the narrowest strips of the Berlin Wall and I believe that the houses on the eastern side were finally demolished in 1985. The events and characters in the novel are fictional but the historical facts about the Berlin Wall are, to the best of my knowledge, true. I have included a bibliography of books consulted at the end of the novel.

Throughout the text I have kept the German 'ß' which is pronounced as a hard 's' and usually transcribed in English as 'ss'.

The Last Dance over the Berlin Wall

To John –
Hope you enjoy!
Best wishes,
Lisa

The Last Dance over the Berlin Wall
Copyright © 2009 by Lisa Selvidge. All rights reserved.

The author reserves the moral right under the Copyright, Designs and Patent Act 1988 to be identified as the author of this work.

Published by **Montanha Books**
montanhabooks@clix.pt

Printed by lulu.com
www.lulu.com

Typeset in point 11 Book Antigua and 11.5 Times New Roman

Front cover image by babaLou
www.babalou.com
Make-up by Alison Kelley

Back cover image by Chris de Witt
http://appropriatesoftware.com/BerlinWall/welcome.htm

PART 1 - 1984

'The border remains a very sensitive area and the East Germans continue to be wary of subversive activities and illegal entries or exits. The authorities are renowned for their Prussian thoroughness, so it would be foolish to try to play tricks.'

Berlitz Travel Guide, 1984

The Watchtower

Klaus continued to watch the white flakes drifting down to the control strip of deserted land when Dietrich's Kalashnikov clattered to the floor behind him.

'*Scheiße*,' said Dietrich.

'Okay?' Klaus asked, picking up his binoculars. It was careless of Dietrich, he couldn't help thinking. Klaus wore his rifle across his chest so he wouldn't drop it.

'Fine,' Dietrich said. 'Except my fingers have frozen.'

Klaus didn't help him; it was bad enough that one of them was rummaging around the watchtower floor. Although, now that it was snowing, only a madman would attempt to cross. Naturally, only madmen and Americans would attempt to cross the Berlin Wall at any time. Between the two 3.4 metre high walls protecting the Deutschland Democratic Republic were rolls of barbed wire and antitank barricades, and the whole area was wired with alarms.

However, madmen did exist. Not here, but other sections of the border had been recently violated. Only a month ago, on 25 December, a man had been spotted near the outer wall in Pankow. He was shot at, of course, arrested and taken to hospital, but later died. He was from the DDR. There had been no incidents so far in 1984 but it was only the beginning of February. Klaus knew he needed to be vigilant, though he dreaded the time he would have to shoot someone.

Only when Dietrich was upright again, with the rifle slung over his shoulder, did Klaus pour some coffee from his thermos flask. He had to admit the heaters under the wooden seats beneath the watchtower windows were not very effective. He took several sips and passed the cup to Dietrich.

'Thanks. It is too cold tonight.'

Klaus agreed even though he liked the cold. It kept him awake, and the snowflakes dancing under the arc lights gave him something to watch, other than rabbits and the occasional nocturnal visitor to an apartment. Some parts of the border were narrower than others and here the houses on each side of the Wall were so close it looked as if you could jump from East to West. But, naturally, you couldn't. The houses on the East marked the border so the apartments on the ground floor were boarded up. Several of the other apartments on the third and fourth floor appeared inhabited though. A pair of trousers hung from the small balcony on one of them. He could easily peer into the windows if he wanted. Not that he did, particularly. Besides, it looked like there had been a power failure in the East and Dietrich was watching the West.

Klaus knew a small percentage of the people in the West were rich, that they could afford things he could only dream of. He had been warned of that. From other watchtowers, he had seen people getting out of large shining Mercedes, arriving home laden with shopping bags from KaDeWe. He had seen their brightly lit rooms, big televisions, sofas and large dining tables with bowls of real fruit even in winter (although his *Postenführer* – the one in charge – had suggested they were plastic). He had seen bookcases full of books and heard telephones that rang.

But he had also seen the true film documentaries about the bright lights, cafés, restaurants, nightclubs and casinos of West Berlin, while people slept in doorways wrapped in newspaper. And he had peeked into apartments without curtains or lampshades, without carpets or rugs, without even beds. Once, he had accidentally focused on one room where five people were living: three men and two women together. They all looked thin and pale. One girl's hair was all knotted and another one had the sides of her head shaved. Maybe she had come out of hospital. He had watched them sharing a cigarette.

He felt some sympathy for these people in the West; the homeless, the unemployed, people existing without the support of the State. After all, they weren't Americans. They were Germans. It wasn't fair how some of them could have so much while others could have so little. It must cause such envy and hatred.

'Dietrich?' he said, letting his binoculars hang around his neck but they banged against his rifle so he picked them up again.

'Yes, Klaus.'

'Have you ever had to shoot anyone crossing from the West?'

'From the West? No.'

Klaus hesitated. Most of them happily talked about shooting and Dietrich seemed quite laid-back. Too laid-back perhaps.

'Don't you think it would be difficult? I mean, you can't blame people for wanting to come to our democratic socialist state, can you?'

Dietrich shrugged. 'It would be strange to jump the Wall from the West. But, we have our orders. It is not about where people want to go, it is about the violation of our border. We don't want to be invaded by Americans, do we?' Dietrich laughed.

his fiery breath which she couldn't name; something that made her hands tremble and her feet tingle. Minutes raced by; hours, days, nights, yet still they didn't let go. Alice imagined them frozen in time, forever. They were made for each other. She was sure.

'And who are you, Alice?'

'I am…' She stopped, unsure.

'What's the theatre company you're involved with?' he asked.

She told him that they were a small group of people from Kreuzberg – at least, she would have liked them to have been.

'Do you act?' she asked quickly. 'I bet you'd be good on stage.'

He smiled and told her he'd done acting at East 15 theatre school but he didn't enjoy it so much. He told her he used to be able to walk on a tightrope as well but he hadn't done that for a while.

'Wow,' she said, suddenly feeling useless. She doubted she could even walk in a straight line, let alone on a tightrope.

'How old are you, Alice?' Johnny asked, looking deep into her eyes.

'Twenty,' she lied. 'And you?'

'Twenty three.'

He was quite a bit older than her then. Six years in fact. Perhaps there was still time for her to be someone. She sighed and drank some Schultheiss and watched the snow falling between the dark buildings.

'Let's go back, Johnny,' Alice said. 'I'm out of cigarettes. And beer,' she said, tipping the last dregs into the snow.

He pulled out another two cans from his leather jacket. Alice clapped her hands in excitement.

'How about five-pence pieces?' she asked, excitedly.

'Five-pence pieces?' he asked, his head resting questioningly to the side.

'Cigarette machines in West Berlin can't tell the difference between five-pence pieces and one Mark coins,' she explained, opening the can.

'Hm,' he said, folding his arms, thinking. Then, as if he had had a brainwave, he put his hand behind her ear and pulled out a five-pence piece. Then another. Then another. Then another.

She counted eight.

A true magician.

They kissed again. And again. The snow blew into the dark doorway, melting on their lips.

outside but she was already flipping towards the door like tumbleweed in high winds.

'Carla!' Johnny called after her.

'I didn't realise she was with you,' Alice said.

'She's not really but I'd better go,' Johnny said, sliding off the stool.

'Wait,' she said. She gave him a friend's address in a squat and shouted after him to bring lots of five-pence pieces but she didn't think he heard her.

After he'd gone, she found a flyer in her pocket for Simple Minds. On the other side it said, 'Thanks. Maybe I will come'. She stared at it in astonishment. How the hell had he done that?

Back in Berlin she'd thought about him almost all the time. She even arranged an apartment in Hermannplatz from a guy who was going to India for a year. It was basic but it had a shower – something most Berlin apartments didn't have – and it cost two hundred Marks a month inclusive. Then she met Tom, an American. She'd been seeing Tom for a few weeks when someone from the squat passed on a Bitburger Pils beer mat from Johnny telling her he'd be arriving at Bahnhof Zoo on February 2nd at 10.30 p.m.. He signed it 'Johnny East'. Wrong side, she thought, laughing to herself. She told Tom that Johnny was coming to stay so she wouldn't be able to see him for a few days. Tom, being a liberal American, was cool about it and said that it was no problem. Actually, he'd said, 'No problem, hon.' Alice wasn't sure if she liked the 'hon' bit.

She was sure Tom would not like the next bit.

'Who are you, Johnny?' she whispered as he pulled her towards him. Snow fell beside them under a street light. They were the only people out.

'A magician,' he whispered. 'I can be whatever you want me to be.' He pulled a row of red handkerchiefs out of her pocket.

Alice gasped in amazement. She laughed and wrapped the handkerchiefs around his neck and pulled him towards her. She wanted him to be with her. He had told her earlier that Carla, the stick-shaped girl, had thrown him out in the middle of the night, that there was nothing between them any more. Her heart slammed against her coat as she looked into his eyes. He tugged gently at the icy clumps of her hair that had frozen outside her astrakhan hat. Snow dripped from her eyelashes as everywhere he touched melted. She clung to his leather jacket, not knowing what to say. As he came closer, she found that they could make their breath clouds disappear. He tasted of paprika, ice and vodka. And there was something else on

She had met him in Gossips a few weeks ago over New Year in London. It was a Goth night and black fishing nets and dark curtains haunted the walls and ceilings while Bauhaus groaned in the background. When the barman slipped her a double vodka and orange, she purred appreciatively and settled down on a stool next to Johnny. She began telling him about Berlin, about how you could buy cheap vodka in Friedrichstraße, in the East, and then get back on the train to West Berlin.

'It's the most alternative city in the world. I mean, can you imagine? A city sliced in half and surrounded by a fucking wall? You know, from West Berlin whichever direction you go, you have to go East. It is bang in the middle of East Germany, the DDR. The Russians control the East and the French, Americans and Brits control West Berlin. It's weird seeing tanks thundering through the middle of a city, but there are so many squats and collectives, so much underground stuff going on. I'm working with a fantastic theatre company. You know, Bowie spends a lot of time there. And Lou Reed. You'd love it,' she said, wiping her nose. 'It's so different.'

He half smiled out of the left side of his mouth and those birdlike eyes stared into hers. Not knowing where to look, her gaze slid down to the bar where she began to shred a Stella beer mat. He offered her a cigarette and lit it for her. She looked over at a stick-shaped girl with dark bushy hair who was glaring at her.

'It could be just what I need,' he said, thoughtfully, before mouthing a smoke ring. 'I'm looking for something new in dance, something radical, something that hasn't been done before.'

'There's a great dance scene. Radical, in fact.' She knew nothing about the dance scene but she was sure it would be. 'I'm going back in a couple of days' time. You should come and visit,' she said. Three times. Well, Bauhaus were loud. He may not have heard her. She didn't mention the fact that she had nowhere to live – she would look for somewhere when she went back.

She found her stool inching closer to his, captivated by this beautiful man. He put his hand beneath her chin and she gazed into those blue eyes. They had stopped flickering. He stared through her as if she were transparent. She closed her eyes, wishing him to kiss her, felt his breath against her lips, and then she found herself dripping wet and the stick-shaped girl yelling at her, and him, that she was a fucking slut and that he was the biggest living piece of shit in London. She was so skinny Alice thought about picking her up and tossing her

Neuköln

Alice laughed as they hid in the shadows of a large wooden doorway of a grit-grey Berlin building somewhere in Neuköln. She thought they were near Peter's apartment but she wasn't sure. They were clutching each other, wanting each other. She slugged more Schultheiss from her can. She had warned him. He was madder than she was. Amazingly mad. He claimed he was a dancer. A dancer who ate fire and juggled. That, in itself, was bizarre. But what kind of man tries to climb the Berlin Wall so he could see some stupid rabbits?

'Are you sure you're not hurt?' she asked, stroking his leather jacket.

'No, I'm not hurt. Are you?' He kissed her gently on the cheek.

She felt her face tingle as she gripped his leather jacket with her freezing woollen fingers and stared into his eyes, trying not to spill beer over him. He had blue irises, a shade lighter than his Mohican, and long, dark lashes. She had noticed them zip from side to side as he was thinking, then they would freeze like a bird locked onto its prey. His nose was Roman, his lips soft and his body was as solid as corrugated iron, as supple as plasticine, and he bounced like a tennis ball. When they had fired flares, he had leapt from her shoulders and rolled onto the pavement, leaving her standing on the table not knowing what to do.

'They could have shot you,' Alice whispered.

'But they didn't,' he said, brushing his face against her stinging eyes. Her eyelashes melted.

Johnny was different from other men she knew and yet she wasn't sure what it was that was different. He was serious, yet he made her laugh. He talked with his hands, yet his face was a blank white page at times. No marks, no freckles, no lines, nothing that told of his life. There were moments when she had no idea what he was thinking. He said he was from London, yet he spoke without a Cockney accent. She'd tried to ask him earlier on the U-Bahn about his past and he told her that his father had run off before he'd even known him and that his mother had died four years ago of cancer.

Perhaps that's what made him different. He was alone in the world. Like her. Just like her. They were perfect for each other. Both outcasts. Paddling outside of the mainstream. Both unique, special, invincible. She slugged some more beer and laughed again.

Both pissed.

his age maybe. She was beautiful but she had a chain of earrings around her nose and ear. They turned to each other and smiled or laughed – he couldn't tell. The fools. They began kissing in the street as the snow started to fall again, like ash, before sinking into the shadows as the patrollers arrived with the Commander.

Dietrich explained what had happened and pointed to the area of the Wall that had been violated. The area was declared safe and the Commander praised their action. Klaus took the opportunity to go and piss against the inner wall while the patrollers were there.

'I wonder what kind of lives they have?' Klaus said, once the patrollers had gone.

'Who knows,' Dietrich said. 'But that's the first time I've ever known someone violating the border from the West.'

Klaus didn't see why Dietrich should be so surprised, but he had to admit the man had looked mad. 'Did you see his hair!' Klaus chuckled.

Dietrich shrugged. 'Don't you watch television? They are punks. That is a Mohican, like the Indian tribes in America.'

Klaus wasn't sure if he saw the connection. 'So? What are they?'

'They are people who believe in anarchy.'

Klaus was going to ask what anarchy was exactly and if the Indian tribes were anarchists but felt he'd asked too many questions. Besides, he knew anarchy involved anti-social behaviour.

'Hey, look,' Dietrich said.

Klaus looked again towards the woman's bedroom. She had put a lamp in the window. For a second, Klaus burned at the thought of her naked behind the window, lying on the bed picking at a bowl of cherries. He imagined himself lying next to her, watching her take the pips out of her mouth. But there in the window above the lamp hung a white banner. On it was written, 'ass holes'.

As Klaus tipped out the last of his coffee, he suddenly felt homesick.

light reminded him of the woman inside. He might as well be on the moon.

The snow stopped but Berlin remained white, unusually bright. Klaus looked up at the moon glaring at him from behind a hole in the clouds. He imagined it to be white, barren and empty like the strip of land below. He dipped his binoculars. On the Western side, a very tall man with blue hair shaped like a crescent moon and wearing a black leather jacket was walking towards the Wall carrying a table. Behind him, a giant woman, in a square fur hat and an old-fashioned, long, black coat, tapered at the waist, followed. She was speaking to him and laughing loudly as they came closer to the border. Klaus thought she spoke English. They could be Americans, although they looked more like Martians.

'Dietrich, look!'

'I see them.'

Dietrich picked up his Very light pistol and went towards the door. The Westerners disappeared from view as they approached the Wall. They looked fairly desperate but they wouldn't, would they?

A black glove appeared on the tubular top of the wall, groping at the lumps of frozen snow. Then it let go of the snow and waved at them. Klaus felt his stomach yo-yo down to his boots and back. How could the man have got up there? There must have been two tables. Or a ladder.

'Hold your fire,' Dietrich said.

Klaus held: they weren't allowed to fire into the West or until the border was violated.

'Shouldn't we alert the patrollers?' Klaus said. Surely this counted as a breach of security? Another glove appeared groping the ice on top of the Wall. Then, slowly, the fan of blue spiky hair appeared, bobbing up above the Wall like a kite.

Klaus aimed his Kalashnikov at the target. A face floated up. A young white face with the sides of his head shaved. Dietrich pressed the button that would alert their Commander and fired his Very pistol above the border. The flare wheezed through the white night. The man shouted and the face tumbled away. For a second, Klaus thought that Dietrich had hit him but then he saw the two giant violators racing away. They stopped at the end of the street and looked back, holding onto each other. The girl put a can of something to her mouth and drank. Perhaps they couldn't see the watchtower, but they were staring straight at him. Klaus looked through his binoculars and saw their pale faces and wild hair under the streetlight. They were young, double checked that there was no movement his side and went to join Dietrich. He focused his binoculars on a bedroom window on the fifth floor to the right of the watchtower. A young woman, early twenties, with dark curly hair down to her shoulders, a pale face, red lips and with long curvy silky legs was standing beneath a naked bulb facing the window. The curtains were open. Either she had forgotten to draw them or… Klaus imagined the alternative as she unbuttoned a long, white shirt.

'Ach, yes…' Dietrich said.

The shirt slipped to the floor where she left it. Standing in only a pair of white lace knickers and bra and dancing up and down, she stretched upwards revealing the dark hair beneath her white arms. Then she folded her arms behind her back and unhooked her bra strap.

'My God,' Klaus whispered.

'Shut up.'

Her breasts were huge. Klaus had never seen anything like them. They were like giant snowballs, smooth, perfectly round snowballs. She was beautiful, a goddess, a beautiful snow goddess whom Klaus wanted to marry. He was sure of it. He ran his binoculars up and down her body, fiddling with the focus, trying to get closer. He fiddled so much the figure that bent over and stepped out of her knickers and emerged completely naked was blurred, but there were two of her. By the time Klaus had got her back into focus he was erect and she was walking towards the window. Klaus didn't know where to look most.

'My God.'

When she got to the window, she stopped and reached across for the curtains. Then, as if she had a second thought, she let go of one side with her right hand and turned towards them and stuck up her middle finger before slamming the curtains shut.

Dietrich laughed while the world slowly collapsed around Klaus. She wouldn't marry him, she would never know him, never meet him. She hated him. It wasn't fair. His erection shrivelled like a popped balloon.

'Isn't she something? Did you see those tits? Imagine. *Scheiße.*'

They both fell silent, both imagining. Klaus didn't trust himself to speak. This sort of thing didn't happen every night and he knew he was lucky, but that didn't help. In fact, it somehow made it worse. His binoculars kept wandering to the West, to Dietrich's side, towards the lit bedroom, but the curtains remained firmly closed. Only a chink of

'Of course not,' Klaus said quickly, wondering why Dietrich was laughing, 'but I mean for the Germans. It must be terrible for them, living in the West.'

'Perhaps, but more people attempt to cross from our side to the West. Why do you think that is?'

'Propaganda, naturally,' Klaus said, repeating what he'd been told. 'They see the Western television which shows the luxury items and the high life of the few and they think that everyone lives like that!' Klaus had never seen Western television until recently as they couldn't pick up ARD or ZDF where he lived.

'I suppose so,' Dietrich said. 'But don't you ever want to see for yourself?'

Klaus knew that this was dangerous territory. He was surprised at Dietrich – unless he was testing him? He must be careful what he said. He didn't want to be reported.

'Well, from what I have seen, no, not really. I mean, perhaps for the day, but I would hate to have to live there. I do not see why anyone would want to.'

They fell silent again and watched the snowflakes spotting the dark buildings on either side of the Wall.

'How long have you been here?' Dietrich asked him.

'Three months. And you?'

'Just over a year,' Dietrich said.

'Where are you from?'

'Leipzig. And you?'

'Dresden.'

'Dresden is a good city. I visited once.'

Klaus liked it but he'd never really been anywhere else before his military service. All his family lived in Dresden. His father was a successful engineer and his mother worked in a nursery. His sister, Olga, was still at school. She was doing very well and it was hoped that she would go to university. She would be the first one in the family. It should be him, really, being the eldest and the boy, but, he had to admit, she was much smarter than he was.

Dietrich whistled.

'Hey, Klaus, a woman is undressing... Come and have a look! A wall stripper!'

Klaus hesitated. Dietrich, as the *Postenführer*, was responsible for their watch, but their Commander would be furious if he found out. And what if it were a trick? Could Dietrich be testing him again? But a wall stripper? He had heard other guards talk about them. He

Sonnenallee

Johnny burrowed his way out of three heavy duvets, aware of a tingling pain in his arm. Clouds sailed from his mouth before vanishing into the cold room. A crack of grey light slithered in from somewhere below where the shutters didn't quite meet. He looked down. He was a little more than halfway between the floor and the ceiling in a stark, impersonal room with a high ceiling, two large windows with folded shutters and bare dirty cream walls. Shadows of clothes lay scattered over a beige leather sofa about five feet beneath him.

He groaned.

His head throbbed and his hair felt like candy floss. He lifted the duvets to the other side of him. Alice was still sleeping, her statuesque body unmoving beneath the quilts, her red and black hair fanned out over the pillow. A row of earrings coiled up around the side of her ear. At rest, she looked so cute and innocent. There were faint traces of freckles, as well as a nose-ring, on her small nose and her cheeks were as round and chubby as a child's. The sides of her lips were blotched with red lipstick the colour of her hair. Her long dark eyelashes, stuck together with clumps of mascara, flickered momentarily.

He blew out more clouds. He hadn't really meant for them to end up in bed together but then neither had he meant to climb the Berlin Wall. Ouch. He rubbed his arm. It must have been the stars in the air. And, of course, she was gorgeous. They had nothing in common but there was something about her. She was strong, attractive, and very different from Carla.

Carla had binbagged him in the middle of Wapping at 2 a.m. on New Year's Day. They had been dance partners at East 15 but they hadn't been getting on. She had wanted a more serious relationship. Then she got upset because he refused to audition for a part in a pantomime. A pantomime? He wanted to change the world of dance, to do something different with his life: something for which he would be remembered. In the middle of that freezing mid-winter night with less than a fiver and two bin-bags, he had to confess he didn't know how.

He had ended up at Penny's, another drama school friend who also lived in Wapping, and stayed there for a few weeks, juggling in a freezing Convent Gardens by day and wondering about Berlin by night. He spoke to Penny about it. 'Then go, Johnny, what have you got to lose? I can lend you some money. There's fuck all here. Thatcher's made sure of that.' She also gave him a Berlitz guide book on Berlin, which she'd picked up in an Oxfam shop, and a small grey canvas rucksack. She was right. There was nothing for him in London. The Arts grants had disappeared together with affordable housing and squats. Wapping was being bulldozed. Even Penny was being evicted.

He had finally thrown his bin-bags down onto the freezing Berlin Bahnhof Zoo platform, flickering under a fluorescent light, last night. As soon as he breathed in the Berlin air, it had felt good. There was no sign of Alice, but an elephant had trumpeted through the emptying station. He smiled – there really was a Zoo in the middle of the city. The night air glittered with tiny ice-stars. As the station clock with broken hands limped towards half-past ten, he decided to put his bin-bags in one of the orange lockers. They contained everything he owned, including his fire-eating equipment, juggling batons, several books on circus and performance, Dostoevsky and Hesse, some performance costumes he had made while at drama school, a photograph of his mother and some clothes. The lockers cost five Marks but, if Alice didn't show up, he didn't want to walk the streets of Berlin with black bin-bags. At the last minute he had stuffed his magic handkerchiefs into his little rucksack.

A few winos slumbered around the entrance of the station, in front of the shuttered up shop fronts. The heavy air was spiced with coal, frankfurters and Marlboro. Johnny followed a flashing naked figure of a woman and a 'Cambio' sign and went into the only bar beneath the railway lines.

'*Ein Bier, bitte,*' he said, speaking his first words of German.

The barman with a large brown moustache nodded and then took what seemed like half-an-hour to pour the Schultheiss out of a large curvy white pump. Two men in leather trousers sat smoking Camels at the bar. Johnny sat by the window on a bar stool and looked at a poster of women dressed in black thongs, red stockings and black shiny boots.

Then someone ran past, wearing a long, black coat, DMs and an astrakhan hat, swigging a litre bottle of something. He knocked back his beer and went after her.

'Alice?'

She swung round, her coat wrapping round her flamenco style.

'Johnny? There you are,' she said, coming towards him. 'I've been looking for you everywhere.' She was clutching a bottle of Blue Label vodka.

They hugged. She gripped him tightly.

'Do you want a beer?' Johnny asked, prising himself free.

'Not here. It's all strip clubs and peep shows. Besides, I have some vodka. Come on. We'll go to Café Swing. Don't you have any other bags?'

He told her he'd put them in a locker and followed her along the wide empty streets away from Bahnhof Zoo, past the line of cream Mercedes parked along the road. Not one of them had the Mercedes symbol on the front.

'See these? Everyone breaks them off,' Alice explained, 'and wears them. To show the fascists.' She laughed again, offering him the vodka bottle.

He laughed, too, swigging vodka. One day though, he suspected, he would have a Mercedes.

It began to snow. They stopped and watched the white flakes dance in front of the Cinzano sign wrapped around the Hotel Belmondo on the corner. A taxi pulled up and an old couple got out. The woman wore a black fur coat.

'I wonder what it's like staying there?' Alice said.

'One day, we'll find out.'

'I doubt it,' Alice replied defiantly, lighting a Marlboro. 'Come on, let's go and see Berlin, the magician's city, sawn in half.'

That sounded good. He couldn't wait to see the Berlin Wall. At that time, he had visions of dancing on the Wall between the truncated corpse of East and West. Alice tucked the vodka under her left arm, held the cigarette in her right and together they ran across a now very white Ku'damm. She was almost wheezing when they reached the other side. She coughed and took another drag of her cigarette. They passed the giant ice cream cone, now snow-flecked, that was on the front of his guidebook, and the black Gedächtniskirche – the old bombed church with its cracked open spire that made it look like a headless dinosaur.

Alice coughed again and threw her cigarette into the snow. 'Give me a Benson's, will you? Marlboro make me cough.'

He laughed and gave her one of his cigarettes. He put his arm around this slightly crazy Amazonian vodka-drinking girl as they passed Wittenbergplatz. She was almost as tall as him.

'Have you been to the East?' he asked.

'Only to Friedrichstraße. To buy vodka.' She winked at him.

He held her tightly, the vodka burning his heart. A cream bus with snowy barnacles stuck to it whined along the street. Number 19. On the outside lane a green and white Polizei van overtook it. The pavements, even the roads and dark buildings that aligned them, had whitened and softened as if icing sugar had been sprinkled over the city. He had an urge to pull her into a doorway out of the snow. She swung round and looked at him out of melting, devoted eyes. He kissed her. She tasted good. Her hands pawed at his jacket. He closed his eyes but he couldn't get rid of the image of the sawn-up city.

'Can we go and see the Wall tonight?' he whispered.

'Okay,' she said, her hands slipping away from his leather jacket. 'But first, let's get a beer. The vodka's nearly finished.'

They drank the rest of the vodka, then crunched to Nollendorfplatz, burning holes in the snow. The big white and blue U-Bahn sign, now also splattered with fat snowballs, grew closer. She took him to the Café Swing, where a waitress with a bald head and a nose-ring served them large Weißbiers at an aluminium table next to a steamed up window. Johnny saw his reflection and checked his melted Mohican wasn't dripping blue: Crazy Colours had a nasty habit of running. He didn't think it had. Next to him a woman with black spiked hair read a magazine. As she turned the page, Johnny saw the bold, black letters – *Zitty*, a city guide. An older guy with dreadlocks sat smoking and writing something into a notebook. Everyone looked very relaxed and at peace with who they were. Salsa music sashayed in the background.

'You're right, it's very different to London,' Johnny said. He felt comfortable, something he never felt in London.

After Alice had burped up the last dregs of the Weißbier, they left the Café Swing and went down the steps by the big white 'U' to the underground station. She wanted to take him to another bar, the Kiosk, which she reckoned was the best bar in Berlin, but he managed to persuade her that the Wall was a much better idea.

'How much is it?' Johnny asked, going over to the ticket machines.

'Two Marks but, fuck it, they don't control at this time of night,' she said.

Johnny wasn't going to argue. Next to the machine was a map of Berlin and the underground network. A thick pink line framed West Berlin. A couple of underground lines crossed under the East. Incredible to think they had divided a city like this.

'I live here, near Hermannplatz in Neuköln,' she explained, her finger squeaking along the plastic cover of the map. 'Here's the Wall. We have to change at Möckernbrücke. We're here – the yellow line, Line 4. We need the blue line, Line 7.'

A two-carriage orange train was waiting at the platform. They had jumped into one of the empty carriages just as the door closed and a recorded voice made an announcement. He sat down next to her on the blue seats. She tried to ask him about his past but he didn't want to talk about it. Today was important. She told him she was from Hells somewhere in Norfolk and was adopted. He didn't ask her about boyfriends. She hadn't mentioned anyone.

They had got off at Hermannplatz and walked down Sonnenallee. A Döner Kebab shop, an Imbiss and a couple of small corner *Kneipes* were still open. Johnny wanted a kebab. He hadn't eaten since a stale sandwich on the ferry. Two Turkish men in fezzes and heavy coats sat and drank coffee, gesticulating widely. Alice chatted in German to the man serving them. Johnny was surprised at her fluency; she'd only been in Berlin a few months. When she wasn't looking he'd bought some more beers from one of the men talking with his hands.

Alice also bought a couple of cans of Schultheiss which she put in her pocket and then they left the shop munching on shredded lamb.

On both sides of the street, the old sombre Berlin houses, four or five storeys high, gazed down at them, their little balconies dressed in white. The roads were quiet, apart from the occasional car slushing through the snow. They crossed several roads and a canal. Alice was telling him again about Peter, the guy who ran the Kiosk, the best bar in Berlin, when he saw it.

'Fucking hell,' he said, and stopped.

A monstrous concrete wall, heavily graffitied, with a piped top, blocked the road. An eerie glow hung above it as the arc lights cast shadows behind, and beyond the shadows loomed the houses in the East, the same as those in the West, but blacker.

'What's the other side?' Johnny asked.

'Big Brother,' she said, lighting another one of his cigarettes. 'He has red flashing eyes which you can see from almost everywhere in Berlin. If we step back, we will see them. And they watch us all the time.'

Johnny thought she meant the television tower that he had seen a photo of in the guide book but he wasn't sure. He was beginning to suspect that Alice may exaggerate a little.

'But what's the other side of the Wall?' he asked.

'No Man's Land, otherwise known as The Death Strip. There are watchtowers situated about every kilometre and they say that it's mined. I don't know if it's true. I saw loads of rabbits from the viewing point at Potsdamer Platz. But maybe they don't set the explosives off.' She sounded bored.

'Let's go nearer,' Johnny said. 'I want to see the rabbits.'

That had been the mistake. He had walked towards the thirteen-foot concrete Wall. Shadows of painted boats on a blue sea sailed across the concrete. He read some graffiti: *Make love, not war, fuck the wall.* Next to it was a drawing of a penis/gun firing sperm or bullets, depending on your perspective. He had to confess then that the rounded top would be tricky to dance on.

'Come on, Johnny, let's go. We don't want to get shot,' Alice said, opening her can of beer.

Then he'd had an idea. He found a small round table on the corner of the street by a closed-up café. She had warned him but he went ahead and put it by the Wall. 'Come on, help me look over.'

'Okay, it's your head.' She put her beer down by the Wall.

He leapt on the table and held out his hand for her but she couldn't get her leg up high enough. He had tried not to laugh as she put her knee on and stood slowly up. She was like a baby elephant.

'What?' she said, aggressively.

'Nothing,' he said. 'Can you lift me?'

'Of course, I can lift you,' she said. 'You can't weigh more than a whippet.'

Touché. He smiled. 'Okay, put your hands together like this.' He indicated that she should make a cradle with her hands so that he could step up. He unlaced his boots. 'I'll stand on your shoulders. Don't worry, if you can't hold me, just say "jump".'

'Okay but they might shoot you,' she said.

He had laughed as he stepped into her palms. It was 1984. You couldn't go around shooting people for looking over a wall. And he had seen over into a white channel of emptiness – for a second. Before they shot flares. Before he had shouted 'jump'. Before he had tumbled to the ground.

He groaned again as he stared at the mucky ceiling.

'Shush!' Alice mumbled from beneath the duvets.

He leant over and kissed her cheek lightly.

'Are you okay?' he asked. Amazingly, she had remained standing on the table, as cool as a cat.

She murmured something and pulled him towards her.

'I need to get a glass of water,' he whispered.

He hoped it wasn't going to be difficult. He didn't want to get into another Carla situation. But a girl who went around with a bottle of Blue Label vodka was hardly likely to get complicated on him. He clambered down the ladder from the high bed and ran, shivering, into the kitchen. He stuck his head under the tap, ignoring the plates engraved with tomato sauce and burnt crumbs. He flew back up the ladder with a glass of water.

He put the glass in her hand. She sat up, drank it all, then leaned over him and threw the glass down onto the chair five foot below. Johnny looked at her as if she were mad.

'What? I wasn't the one who tried to climb the Berlin Wall,' she said, creeping closer to him.

He laughed. 'You have a point,' he said and lay back on a pillow. 'You did very well holding me.'

'Thanks, as I reckon you do weigh more than a whippet.' She huddled up to him. 'God, it's freezing. What time is it?'

'I don't know. I'll put the fan heater on,' Johnny said, trying to free himself. He would like to see some of West Berlin by day.

But she had thrown all three duvets over him and was threading her legs through his. She pinned her cold feet under his calves and began kissing around his belly button, slowly working up to his neck, pressing her breasts onto his chest. He wasn't used to women with large breasts and found himself immediately aroused.

'Don't you want to have sex first?' she whispered, thrusting a condom into his hands.

Sex was fine. He could do with some exercise. But Alice did not want him to be physical. She wanted intimacy, wanted him inside her, hardly moving, wanted him to touch her gently, slowly. She felt good. So good that Johnny wanted to stay there forever. He felt her tremble on top of him. When he came he cried out. Something he had never done before.

Johnny was surprised, mildly annoyed. Even his headache felt better. She rolled off him and asked for a cigarette. He got up and touched the ceiling, then held onto the side of the bed and swung down to the floor. He threw her a cigarette and a lighter, switched the fan heater on, jumped into his jeans and went into the kitchen to make coffee. He unscrewed an aluminium coffee maker and tipped out the mouldy grains and added fresh coffee and water. The fridge contained a carton of milk, some plastic cheese, one tomato and a pot of Kartoffel salad, which, on opening, made his head swivel round involuntarily. Rancid potato salad. Alice clearly wasn't too concerned about domestics.

In between the white patterns on the window, he could make out a tiny square of grey sky and a white courtyard below surrounded by those dark, petulant buildings. Just off the kitchen was a pantry converted into a toilet and shower room, which had been painted in thick white paint, making it difficult to see where the walls ended and the floor began. Or maybe that was the vodka.

'Alice? I'm just going to take a quick shower, okay?' he called through to the main room.

'Sure,' she replied.

He peeled off his jeans and stepped into the pantry. There was a damp towel and he found a Bic razor, but there was no mirror to shave in. His face felt fine – it took him a long time to grow even stubble – but the sides of his head needed shaving. Another time. The steaming hot water ran blue as he washed his hair.

The door opened and Alice appeared, naked, out of the steam, and stood in front of him like a Roman goddess. He stared at her, not sure what to say. She had a beautiful body; tall and strong, with curves that most dancers had to sacrifice.

'Can I come in.'

It wasn't a question.

'Most houses in Berlin don't have showers,' she said, stepping into the shower with him. 'Can you imagine?'

'Mm. What do they do then?' He side-stepped around her to give her the shower.

'There are still bath houses,' she said, putting her hands around his neck.

He was going to tell her that Carla's council house in Wapping only had a tin bath in the kitchen but she was kissing him. He thought he heard someone calling her name at the door, someone with an American accent.

'Shall I get it,' he said, trying to unclamp her arms.

'No, leave it. I'm sure it isn't important,' she whispered, stroking his head. 'It's probably the fascist landlady wanting the rent.'

'I think it's a man's voice.'

'Fascist landlord then.'

Johnny was left gasping again when she finally let him go. By the time he emerged from the shower, she was putting on her coat and coffee bubbled up the coffee pot under the cradling blue flames. It smelled good.

'I'm going to get some bread,' she said. 'Do you want anything?'

'Chocolate,' Johnny said, with the small towel wrapped around him. She stared at his body. 'And eggs for an omelette?'

'Omelette?' She sounded uncertain.

She put on her hat and, looking like a countess, left. The large, wooden door slammed shut behind her and the apartment fell silent. He picked up his jeans and went into the living room to find the rest of his clothes.

Dressed, he sat down on the beige leather sofa and picked up an issue of *Tip* which lay beneath an overflowing ashtray and a couple of dirty glasses but the pages were stuck together. He couldn't read it anyway. He understood enough to work out it was a city guide for Christmas 1983. A man with a red nose, moustache and leather pants playing a guitar straddled the front cover. He put it down. In the corner of the room an old television with tapering wooden legs sat in the corner underneath one of the windows and the fan heater blew tepid air onto a worn-out carpet. Next to the high bed was an off-white ceramic stove which didn't appear to have been used for a while – if at all by Alice. There was no wardrobe so she hung her clothes on the ledge of the high bed, and he noticed an unpacked travel bag on the chair.

He tidied up and opened the shutters. Grey daylight hovered around the dirty windows. Johnny found his watch. It was gone three o'clock. He wasn't going to see much of Berlin today, but he would have an early night and start finding out about dance companies and studios in the morning. Even though dancing on the Wall was out, he had a good feeling that here he would, at last, find what he was looking for. It would be interesting to see what influences the Americans, British and French had on the dance scene here. He checked how much money he had – eighty-four Marks, and eighty pence.

He stretched out until he heard footsteps outside the door.

'Hey,' Alice greeted, holding a red and white shiny plastic bag.

He took the bag from her and they went into the kitchen.

'I think you'll have to magic it,' Alice said.

'Oh, okay.' He emptied the oval sliced black bread, eggs, tomatoes, ham, more potato salad, margarine, a blue box of Teekanne, which he presumed to be black tea, and a lilac bar of Milka chocolate onto the plastic worktops.

She hovered around him, occasionally slipping her arms through his as he made a bland cheese and tomato omelette. They ate it with black bread as they watched pictures of the Space Shuttle Challenger being launched on the grainy television. He thought it strange that they could send people up to into space in rockets and yet they couldn't cure cancer.

Someone banged at the door again.

'Fascist landlord?' he said, smiling.

'Alice?' an American voice boomed. 'It's Tom.'

'Oh, bollocks.' She sighed, and went to the door.

Alice led an older man into the room. He was a couple of inches shorter than her; lean, with dark hair tied back in a ponytail and an earring. A whiff of aftershave trailed behind him.

'Hey Johnny, good to meet you. I came round earlier but you must have been out. I'm Tom. Alice has told me all about you.' He approached Johnny with an outstretched right hand, holding a woollen glove in his left.

Johnny shook his hand, feeling that he should perhaps know who Tom was.

'How you enjoying Berlin?' Tom asked, sitting down on the sofa. He seemed relaxed, unlike Alice, who had fled to the hallway.

'He only got here last night,' Alice called back, 'and already he's been shot at by the guards at the Wall.'

'What did you do to deserve that?'

'He tried to climb it.'

'But it's thirteen foot high! How did you manage that?' Tom's mouth opened slightly as he looked at Johnny.

'I found a table, then Alice gave me a leg up,' Johnny replied.

'Holy shit.'

'Do you want a coffee?' Alice asked him, coming back into the room. 'We were about to go out, actually, but there's time for a coffee, if you want?'

'Gee, thanks, hon. Where are you heading?'

'Johnny has arranged to meet some dancers at Mehringdamm.'

Johnny tried not to look too surprised, although she was so convincing, he almost thought it might be true.

'Oh okay.' Tom sounded disappointed. 'I just wondered what you guys were up to later? There's a party in the Kiosk. It's Stig's birthday.' He turned to Johnny. 'There'll be a couple of American dancers there. A girl from San Francisco and a guy from New York. Maybe good for you to get to know?'

Johnny nodded. Tom did know all about him. So much for his planned early night. But he had a feeling Tom's dancers might be more real than Alice's.

'Okay Tom. We'll see you later.' Alice towered above the sofa.

Tom reached out and touched her leg. 'Any chance of that coffee, hon?'

She vanished into the kitchen.

'Isn't she beautiful?' Tom pulled out a packet of Marlboro and offered them to Johnny. Johnny took one.

'Thanks,' Johnny said, deciding not to answer the question. He had a feeling he could say the wrong thing. He couldn't imagine Alice going out with someone as old as Tom, but the undercurrents were pointing to some story. That should make things easier between them at least.

'Here's your coffee,' Alice said, a little too loudly, coming into the room.

'How long have you been in Berlin?' he asked Tom.

'Almost a year now. It's a great city. Shame about the Germans but, hey, you know.' He laughed.

'What's wrong with the Germans?' Johnny asked.

'Ah, you'll find out. They just need to lighten up a bit.'

'Maybe it's hard to lighten up when you're surrounded by a Wall and occupied by other countries,' Alice said, flicking her lighter.

'Have you been to the East?' Johnny asked, half expecting Alice to set fire to Tom, but she circled the flame round to her cigarette.

'Yeah, several times. But the conventional way via Checkpoint Charlie.' Tom winked at him.

Johnny smiled. Wise guy. 'How was it?'

'Oh, it's far out. They got the best museums and theatres. Kinda depressing though. There's nothing in the shops, no cafés, restaurants, no choice, I guess. And the people look so grim. Makes you realise how lucky we are to live in the good ole capitalist West.'

'What's good about it?' Alice snapped. 'There's people homeless and hungry.'

'Well, democracy is a wonderful thing, hon. We choose our lives.'

'Hardly…'

'I can't wait to go,' Johnny interrupted, trying not to laugh. Alice was about to burst.

'Maybe we can all go to the East together.' Tom looked at Alice, who scowled back.

Johnny smiled and changed the subject, 'Are you working someplace?'

'Not exactly. I'm writing a novel.'

Alice raised her eyebrows.

'What kind of novel?' Johnny asked.

'Crime fiction. Do you read a lot?' Tom asked Johnny.

'Well, I've just read *Crime and Punishment*.'

'What's that?' Alice asked.

'It's a novel by Dostoevsky,' Johnny said.

'Doctor who?'

Johnny smiled to himself; she really didn't know anything. He couldn't believe she was twenty. But then she hadn't been to university or college as far as he knew.

'A Russian writer – Dos-to-ev-sky,' Tom explained patiently.

'Oh. You know it as well. What's it about then?' Alice turned to Tom now, standing in front of him with her arms folded.

'About a man who murders a pawnbroker, an old woman, because he thinks he is better than she is. He believes that extraordinary men have the right to commit crime, go to war, kill men, transgress the law, like presidents.'

'So?'

'So he murders what he calls "a louse". But there is also someone else there, who witnesses the murder so he has to kill her as well. And she was a good person.'

'So?' Alice repeated, frowning.

'So, he finds out he's not an extraordinary man, hon. That's the point.'

Alice smoked her cigarette. Johnny could see her mind at work.

'So, he fucked up,' she said. 'Like presidents do all the time.'

'He doesn't see it like that. He is haunted by his crime.'

'The rest of the book is about punishment,' Johnny said. 'Whether someone can commit a murder and not go insane if he doesn't confess publicly and be punished for it.'

'And does he confess?' Alice asks.

'Yes, he has to. He can't live with himself otherwise. He is sent to prison in Siberia.'

'That's rubbish. I wouldn't.'

Johnny smiled. He tended to agree with her.

'But no one can commit a crime and not be haunted by it for the rest of their lives,' Tom said.

'Politicians do – all the time,' Alice said.

'Yeah but, hon, they're the extraordinary men, they're doing it for a greater good.'

'Bollocks are they. It's the same. They believe they're ridding the world of evil as well.'

'It's not quite the same. There are evil things in this world that we need to fight.'

'Like communism?' Johnny said quickly. 'America's been doing a fairly good job of trying to eliminate communists. Remember the shit that happened in the fifties in America?'

'Sure, I remember McCarthy.'

'Was that for the greater good?'

'It may have put America at risk.'

Johnny laughed. Tom was a jerk.

'What happened then?' Alice said.

'What about Cuba?' Johnny continued. 'The Cuban Missile Crisis?

Tom shifted in his seat, clearly undecided as to whether he should continue. 'Well, I guess that's not quite what I meant but not to worry. I'd better get going.' He drank the rest of his coffee and stood up. 'Hey, I almost forgot, Alice, can I get some buzz for this evening?'

Alice nodded. 'Sure, come into the kitchen.'

'Okay, well, good talking to you, Johnny, and see you later.'

Tom followed Alice into the kitchen. They talked in low voices, but he couldn't make out what they were saying. What the hell was Alice doing with a Republican? She was young but she wasn't stupid. After a few minutes the door slammed shut and Alice came back into the room with some money in her hand, which she put into her purse. Drugs were another thing they didn't share.

'So is the Republican your boyfriend? Or the fascist landlord?' Johnny asked, winking at her.

'You mean Tom?' Alice said, her face blushing. 'He isn't a publican, a boyfriend, or the landlord. He's just a kind of friend. Why? What did he say?'

Johnny laughed out loud. She was serious.

'What?' Alice asked, looking hurt.

'A publican is someone who runs a pub. A *Re*publican is a right-wing American politician – or supporter.'

'Not only,' she snapped. 'Ireland has Republicans.'

Johnny smiled to cover his embarrassment. She was right of course. 'It does, indeed. And lots of publicans. Well, anyway, he likes you a lot.'

'And I like you,' Alice said, coming over and sitting on his knee. She put her arms around his neck, ran her fingers through his flopped Mohican and kissed him.

Johnny laughed. 'I like you, too, but I'm not sure about the Republican boyfriend. Stop, you're tickling me.' He looked at his watch. Half-past four.

'Tom means nothing to me. By the way, do you have that book?' she asked.

'*Crime and Punishment*?'

She nodded.

'Yes, and I have *Notes from Underground* as well.'

'Can I borrow them?'

'Of course. They're in the station. Listen, Alice, I think maybe I'll go out for a while. I need to meet the dancers at – where?' He half smiled with the left side of his mouth, hoping she wouldn't mind.

Alice giggled. 'Sorry about that. I thought Tom would never go if I didn't say something.'

'That's okay, but I do need to go out for a while.'

'Don't you want me to go with you? I can show you around.'

Johnny hesitated. The more time he spent with Alice, the harder it was going to be.

'We could go to see the rabbits at Potsdamer Platz?' she said, almost pouting.

'Another time, maybe. I'd just like to wander around for a bit. You know, get the feel of the place. How about I meet you at the same café we were at last night? Then I could buy you dinner?'

'Dinner?' she repeated, as if the concept was alien.

He hoped she would refuse as he couldn't really afford it.

'Okay, sure. I need to do some stuff, anyway.'

He left the apartment and stepped into the cold stairwell. As he left he thought he heard her mutter, 'fucker' but he may have imagined it.

He sighed. It didn't matter. Last night had been magic, and she was beautiful, but he just knew she would get in the way of what he wanted to do in his life.

The Kiosk

Alice suspected the Kiosk would be packed. People were even drinking outside and it was at least minus ten. The iced-up leftovers from their magical night were now gritty and filthy black, and the sky was too cold and thin to snow again. Ollie's hearse was parked outside. She didn't particularly want to go in. Tom would be there and she knew he would say something to Johnny. Not that she really cared as Johnny was being a complete bastard. He had pulled his hand away when she touched him and insisted on sipping water with his pizza. And to think he had been falling over her last night. Fucker. A shame the guards were such bad shots.

From the outside, the Kiosk looked nothing more than a shop front, boarded up with aluminium shutters. The steel door appeared welded shut.

'Looks like it's closed,' Johnny said.

'Well, it's not,' Alice snapped.

Alice rang the bell and crazy Hermann's eye greeted her through the little spy-hole in the heavy steel door. The door opened and The Clash called out to West Berlin, *Rock the Kasbah*. Alice scanned the familiar faces in the dimmed light of the yellow bar. She was right – it was packed and Nick and JC, two American rock musicians, sat in front of the boarded up window, looking like witches with their long, black spiky hair and black eye makeup. She couldn't see Tom.

'*Guten Abend,* Alice.'

Alice greeted Hermann and introduced Johnny. Hermann, wearing a grey army overcoat and long black boots, nodded to him.

'Hey, Mad!' Peter shouted from across the bar in his Californian voice.

Alice laughed. She wasn't sure if Peter had started calling her Mad because of her name, Madison, or if he thought she was mad. Whichever, she quite liked it. She weaved her way across the black floor, carpeted in melted ice, grit and cigarette ends, to the bar, greeting people she knew on the way. Voices floated on white clouds before mixing into background noise. The shining metal bar was studded with shot glasses with slices of lemon straddling their small rims. Large pots of salt jumped from hand to hand. This was more like it.

Peter strode behind the bar like a pirate swinging onto a ship. He was even taller than she was and had wild dark curly hair, several earrings, and rings on his fingers. The other guy behind the bar, Willi, half Peter's size, dodged about underneath him. She looked around and caught JC's eye and smiled. She had seen him in here several times but she had never really spoken to him. He stared at her.

'Hey, who's your sexy friend?' Peter winked at her.

She turned round.

'Oh. This is Johnny. Johnny, this is Peter.'

Johnny held out his hand. Peter leant over the bar and thrust a tequila into it. Alice smiled. He gave her one as well. She tipped some salt on the top of her fist and passed it behind her to Johnny.

'*Prost!*' Peter called from the bar.

Everyone licked the salt and tipped their heads back. Alice swallowed and squealed, feeling the grin on her face widen like the Cheshire cat's. The Hungarian twins, one with long black backcombed hair and black false eyelashes two inches long, the other with identical but blond hair and white eyelashes, slipped their arms through each other's and toasted each other in Hungarian, arms still linked. *Egészségedre.* Alice tried to say it but she couldn't get past the egg.

'Hey A-leese, you dance?'

A small French girl, Marie – or something beginning with "M" – dragged her into another room at the back. Alice didn't bother looking at Johnny. Peter caught up with her.

'Have you got a line, Mad? I need help, darling. Nice boy, you've brought with you. Needs to loosen up a bit but cute ass.'

'Here.' Alice passed over a small, rectangular magazine wrap.

'Thanks a bunch, darling, I'll catch you later…' He disappeared into the toilet, yelling, 'Emergency!'

Alice danced with the French girl to 'Two Tribes'. She recognised the two dancers Tom had talked about, Sophie and Benjamin. Sophie was short with a marble-white face and thick red lips. She had cropped, almost shaved, hair, a nose ring and wore a leather jacket with tassels, thick tights and cowboy boots. Alice thought she looked too short to be a dancer. Benjamin was taller, black, with dreadlocks bunched together at the back. When the two tribes stopped warring, she went over to speak to them.

'Hi, Sophie, Benjamin? How are you?'

'Pretty good,' Sophie shouted. 'And you?' Like Peter, Sophie had a loud, confident Californian accent, twice the size of her body.

'Good. I'm just gonna get a drink. Do you want one?'

'Sure,' Sophie said.

Alice pushed her way back to the bar, kissing Stig, the birthday boy, on the way. He looked blissfully happy, completely and utterly wasted. Ziggy Stardust leapt from the speakers.

Johnny still sat at the bar talking to the Hungarian twins. They looked like they might eat him.

'Alice, would you like a drink?' Johnny said.

'Beck's,' she said, amazed that he was still talking to her, let alone buying her a drink. Peter thrust a beer in her hand. She took a slug and turned to Johnny.

'By the way, this is Sophie and Benjamin, the dancers Tom was telling you about. They're from...'

'I'm from San Francisco. Benjamin's from New York. Good to meet you,' Sophie said. 'And you are?'

'Johnny. I'm also a dancer. Can I get you a drink?'

His arm brushed against Alice's as he stood up and leant towards the bar. She snapped it away, as if she'd been stung by a wasp.

'Beck's is good,' Sophie said. Benjamin nodded.

'And us,' the Hungarian twins said, simultaneously.

Johnny ordered more beers.

'So how is the dance scene in Berlin?' Johnny asked Sophie, passing round the green bottles.

'What are you into? Classical or modern?'

'Modern, although I have done ballet.'

'Well, let's see. There's the Tanz Tangente studio, which is run by an American, and there's the International Ballet Centrum – they both have workshops and classes in modern dance. We're taking classes at the Tanz Fabrik in Möckernstraße with Louisa Kronenberg – also an American but more radical. I'm hoping to put together a show soon. Maybe you'd be interested?'

'Definitely.'

Perhaps she would go to dance classes as well, Alice thought. She was, at least, tall. She reckoned she had good stage presence. That would show him. She was just about to ask Sophie if anyone could go to the classes when a tequila appeared in front of her. She thought for a minute her magician might be back but Peter indicated that it was from Nick. She went over and clinked glasses with him. JC put his arm around her and said that she was going to be on their next album.

'Do you sing?' Nick asked.

She couldn't sing a note. The tequila tickled her tonsils.

'Sometimes,' she said.

JC whispered if she had any speed on her. She slipped a wrap into his grappling fingers. His dark eyes, blackened by eyeliner, looked into hers as he thanked her, pressing a note into her the palm of her hand. He was cute but, Alice reminded herself, he was a man. And men were fuckers. She made her excuses and left, conscious of JC watching her.

Johnny was in deep conversation with Benjamin about the power of flight or something. Even Sophie looked bored.

Alice cupped her hand around Sophie's ear. 'You wanna line?'

Sophie slid off the stool, quick as an eel, and followed her. Alice grabbed the French girl as well and they all went to the one women's toilet and barricaded themselves in. Alice began to chop up the speed on her small mirror, balanced on top of the cistern. A photocopied black and white flyer for *Serious Drinking* peeled off the wall in front of her revealing a black 'A' in a circle. Someone had written in lipstick, 'Ich liebe dick'.

'Why is it there is only ever one women's loo,' Alice asked indignantly.

Neither of them replied.

Alice turned round. Marie was kissing Sophie. They stopped and looked at her. Marie screamed in laughter and pointed to her and said, 'Your face, your face!'

Alice shrugged, continuing to carve out the lines. Got to be better than fucking schizophrenic men.

'Don't you like women?' Sophie asked.

Alice grunted, rolled up the hundred Mark note that JC had given her and hoovered up a line while Marie caressed Sophie. Alice tapped on the mirror with her lipstick to get their attention.

'Girls!' she cried. 'Do you two know each other?' She sniffed.

'I'm Sophie.'

'My name is Michelle.'

Michelle – that was it. Alice passed the rolled up note to Michelle. Then Sophie. Alice licked the mirror and put it away in her pocket.

'So can anyone go to your dance classes?' Alice asked Sophie.

'Well, they're not really for beginners. Is it for you?'

Alice nodded.

'There are other workshops,' Sophie said. 'I will…'

'Enough dance. You want I kiss you like this?' Michelle said to Alice.

Before Alice answered, the dark pretty face tilted towards her and plunged her tongue into her mouth. She tasted of lime. Alice was aware of someone banging on the door. She didn't know for how long they were in the toilet, but the banging went away for a while. Her fingers were stroking Sophie's velvet head, like a Fuzzy Felt board. The banging turned to thumping and yelling. Alice pulled the string on the toilet and opened the door. They were greeted by the Hungarian twins with folded arms and Einstürzende Neubauten. Peter dashed by and shouted, 'Girls! What have you been doing in there? Really.'

Alice remembered having a beer but couldn't find it anywhere. Johnny was still sat on a stool with whatsisname. His slightly faded blue Mohican fanned out over his head. He had a ring and a jet-black, star-shaped stud in his left ear. And his thigh muscles bulged out of his black sweatpants. He was gorgeous. She sighed. Tom was there, sitting at the bar talking to Johnny. A Japanese guy and Ollie, who drove the hearse, were also sitting at the bar. Johnny and Tom turned to look at her.

'Hi hon, where've you been? Johnny said he hadn't seen you for ages.'

'Toilet. And you?'

'With Hidei. He's from Tokyo but he's just arrived from the States. He's been recording out there.'

'Hi Hidei.'

She bought Beck's and passed them round, still without looking at him. Frankie Goes to Hollywood began to play 'Relax'.

'I'm going to dance,' she said. 'I need to practise.'

'I'll come with you,' Johnny said.

Alice ignored him and went to the back room to dance with Michelle and Sophie. Johnny joined them. Tom followed and stood by the wall, one leg flamingoed over the other, watching, drinking, smoking.

Next time she looked Tom was gone.

As she spun round and sang 'don't do it', Johnny snatched her hand and pulled her towards him. Alice knew then that she really was in love with him. Even if he was bloody Jekyll and Hyde. He pulled her aside where it was almost possible not to be seen. They kissed. Her belly button jumped.

'What's going on, Johnny?' she said.

'I don't know, Alice. I like you very much and… but I don't want to upset things between you and Tom and…'

He continued making excuses about having only just met her and not wanting to invade her life and something about them being different people and wanting different things, not wanting to get involved, but Alice wasn't really listening. So Tom had told him that they were seeing each other.

'It doesn't matter. There was nothing much between Tom and me. I like you, Johnny.'

'I like you too, Alice,' he said. 'Come on, let's dance.'

Stig, the birthday boy, had miraculously reappeared and was swaying in the middle of the dance floor to T-Rex. Sophie and Benjamin were rock 'n' rolling. When Alice danced this time, she felt as if she was spinning on a magic carpet: Johnny, T-Rex, being in Berlin. Blown into another world, a better world. *Dirty sweet and you're my girl.*

'Alice? Can I get something?' Stig mumbled.

Alice slipped him a wrap. Peter appeared behind him and they headed to the loos. Alice wanted a cigarette. Johnny only had a couple of Benson's left, but she took one anyway and, as T-Rex faded, she drifted back to the bar. Nick and JC had been joined by an American band called Black & White. Hidei was talking to them as well but Tom was nowhere to be seen. Johnny joined her.

A woman with dark hair and thick black eyeliner called Frieda was recounting how she had stripped for the border guards. Everyone laughed. Alice didn't see why she would do that. They weren't exactly paying her.

'They shot at us last night,' Alice said.

'Ach, it was you then!' Frieda said. 'You were near me in Neuköln? I see the rocket.'

'Yes, that was us. Is that normal?'

'Nay, not normal, but sometimes, it happens.'

'Do people really get killed?' Johnny asked.

'Naturally. Now is less but every year many people shot.' Frieda took a hard drag on her cigarette and inhaled deeply. 'But how do you get up the Wall?'

'We stood on a table and I lifted him,' Alice said. 'He stood on my shoulders.'

Frieda looked at her. 'You must be very strong. And you must be an acrobat or something?'

Johnny tipped his head from side to side.

'Johnny c'n do anything,' Alice said, noting vaguely that her words were bumping into each other.

'Bet he can't juggle bottles,' said Peter, immediately grabbing two empty beer bottles and sending them spinning into the air. His party trick, Alice had seen him do it before.

'Bet he can,' she said, drinking up her Beck's and giving Johnny the bottle. Several other people did the same.

Within seconds, Johnny had four bottles spinning, Peter still had the two and the bar was full of spiralling green bottles.

'You see, I knew you were a *Spinner!*' Alice called out and laughed. 'Spinner' meant mad.

Peter made the mistake of looking at Johnny and his bottles crashed to the ground.

'*Scheiße.*'

Willi rushed around with a dustpan and brush while Johnny kept on juggling. The whole bar was watching him now. He caught them, one by one. Everyone clapped. Alice thought Peter looked just slightly put out.

'C'n you do five?' Alice asked.

'Five's difficult.'

'How d'you do it?' Alice asked, grabbing a couple of bottles and throwing them in the air. She just about managed to catch them.

'Here you are, darling, use lemons,' Peter said, taking the bottles from her and handing over three lemons hurriedly. 'Don't want any more accidents, do we?'

She took the lemons and Johnny stood behind her. Tom came back into the bar. He looked over at her and Johnny and then went to talk to the band. There was a shadow in his face. Alice concentrated on the three lemons but still dropped them. The blond Hungarian managed to juggle for several seconds. Everyone clapped.

'I need to get some cigarettes,' Alice said, bored. 'Have you got any more five-pence pieces, Johnny?'

He produced four more from behind her ear. She smiled as she went to the door; her magician was back. The cold air almost knocked her over, like stepping into an empty deep-freeze. The street light had gone out and a mist, like a large ghost, hung in front of her. There was no one else on the streets. As she slotted the five-pence coins into the cigarette machine, something grabbed her shoulder. She screamed, swung round and found Tom staring at her with a look in his eyes she didn't recognise. Or like the look of.

'Jesus, Tom, you frightened me.'

'What's going on, Alice?'

'What do you mean?' Alice grasped the tray at the bottom of the cigarette machine and pulled hard. It jerked open, revealing a golden packet.

'You know what I mean. What's going on between you and Johnny? You haven't left him alone all evening and you've hardly spoken to me. Are you sleeping together?'

Alice sighed and took out the cigarettes and slammed the tray shut. So much for American liberalism.

'Yes Tom, we're sleeping together and I like him very much.'

For a moment, Tom didn't say anything. Alice fiddled with the cigarette packet, trying to find the red thread which would undress the box.

'Is that it then? Just like that.'

'Yes.' Alice tore off the cellophane.

'Shit man.' He slapped the side of the machine. Hard. 'I really loved you, Alice.' He turned and walked towards the bridge.

Oh fuck, Alice thought. She hung a cigarette in her mouth, only to find she'd lost her lighter. Fuck. She went back to the bar. Johnny was juggling the lemons, cigarette perched between his lips. People stood around him, watching, talking, clapping. JC put his arm around her, lit her cigarette, and asked her if she wanted to go for breakfast at the hotel. She shook her head regretfully. He wasn't bothered. The twins left with them.

When they'd all gone, there was a hole in the bar. Peter filled it with a green bottle. Ollie came to talk to her and she had a conversation in German she didn't understand. Not that it mattered. Johnny dropped his lemons at last and Peter decided he was going to close up and they would go back to his place for a champagne breakfast.

Alice looked for Michelle and Sophie but she couldn't find them so she got into Ollie's hearse with Peter, Hermann and Johnny. Peter, who was sitting in the front, talked to Ollie about the West German economy while Hermann snorted either speed, or coke, on his knee behind him.

'Hermann, aren't you giving us a line?' she asked, after she'd watched him snort two of the four lines he'd prepared.

Hermann looked up, surprised.

'Wait, we're nearly there, you guys,' Peter said.

Johnny was gibbering about how he and Benjamin were going to start a new innovative dance company. Maybe she could join? Their legs touched. She couldn't wait to curl up with him again.

The hearse stopped at the end of a street cut across by the Wall and they all stumbled out. A grey Berlin morning dazzled the empty street. She saw Heidelberger Straße on the street sign pole.

'This is where we were last night, isn't it?' Johnny asked.

'Yeah, near here I think.'

They all tottered along the side of the Wall, past strange, colourful totem-like faces grinning down at them from the grey concrete. Alice and Peter, laughing, held onto Johnny so that he wouldn't try to jump while Hermann clutched his mirror. They passed through a big wooden door and climbed hundreds of steps. Peter complained about every single one until he reached his converted squat on the top floor. Hot air billowed out as he opened the door.

'Cold sucks,' Peter said, taking off his leather jacket and hanging it on a peg. Scarves and gloves followed. 'Michael organised the heating for us – he's a plumber.'

They all traipsed behind Peter as he showed off his apartment which he shared with Hermann and the plumber, Michael. He had been there for four years.

'We have a spare room if you need it, Johnny?' He winked at him.

Alice felt herself frown. She suddenly felt very sober.

It was a huge five-room apartment with high ceilings, wooden floors and long windows. It was nice, homely, much nicer than hers. In the lounge there was a big dining table next to a warm, white tiled oven. Next to it was a bucket containing coal brickettes. And it overlooked the Wall.

She wandered into the kitchen.

'Isn't he awesome?' Peter said, following her. His eyes roamed over the contents of the fridge.

'Um,' Alice said.

Peter settled on a bottle of Sekt and orange juice.

'Here, Mad. Take this into the sitting room, darling. Glasses are in the cupboard. And ask Johnny to come in. He's promised to help me with breakfast. He seemed to think you wouldn't be much help.'

Alice huffed indignantly, but slunk away from the kitchen with the Sekt and orange juice. Peter was being sarcastic again. She liked him but, sometimes, she wondered if he really liked her or if he just pretended. Whichever, she didn't want to make breakfast.

Johnny was standing at the lounge window, staring at the almost identical houses on the other side of the Wall. Hermann was on the floor in front of his pile of white powder on a mirror, rearranging its contours with a penknife. Ollie sat with his legs draped over a purple armchair reading a copy of *Zitty*, except it was upside down.

Alice put the Sekt and orange juice on the glass-topped coffee table, stained with rings and fallen ash, and joined Johnny at the window. Across the Wall, behind the jaded net curtains, the apartments in the East looked dark, empty, brooding. The ground floor was boarded up. The other apartments looked uninhabited as well, but on one of the alcove balconies there was some frozen washing. A pair of stiff trousers hung above the death strip.

'Peter wants you to help him,' she said.

'Okay. Is that where we were last night?' He pointed to the left.

She could just about see a watchtower if she squashed her cheek to the glass window.

'Yes, I think so,' she said.

'Do you think if those trousers fell down, they'd be shot?' Johnny said.

She laughed.

She stopped laughing when she saw a clown standing at the window of the top floor apartment directly opposite. It had a white painted face, black teardrop eyes and a big, red mouth. A mop of yellow hair stuck up from its head like a miniature corn field.

'Do you see what I see?' Alice asked.

'I do,' Johnny said.

The clown waved to them, slowly, from his elbow, as if cleaning the window. They waved back.

Peter burst into the lounge, flapping his arms. 'Hey, what are you guys doing?'

'Waving to a clown,' Alice said.

'A clown?'

'There's a clown in the opposite apartment over the Wall. Didn't you know?'

The moment Peter came to the window the clown disappeared.

'I can't see anything, darling, although I have seen a young guy there before.'

'It was there, wasn't it, Johnny?'

Johnny nodded, thoughtfully.

'You guys have done too much tequila.'

Peter put a record on that reminded Alice of her parents. She had lied to Johnny when she had said she was adopted, but her parents were so old she might as well have been. Peter grabbed Johnny and the kitchen door closed behind them. She lit a cigarette and continued to stare out of the window but the clown didn't show himself again. Instead, the kitchen door opened and Peter's giant head appeared near the top.

'Mad darling, grab some cutlery and set the table, will you?'

She did as she was told and they all sat down to eat – except Hermann, of course. Johnny sat at the other side of the table from her. She wondered what was wrong this time. She ate a piece of mozzarella and a slice of tomato. She was feeling a bit sick. She drank back the Sekt and burped. Johnny was talking to Peter about combustion engines or something.

As she helped clear up the plates, she asked him if he was ready to go home. She tried to slip her arms around his waist, but he caught her hands and held them.

'Alice, I'm gonna stay here. Peter's got a spare room and has offered it to me for nothing. It's much bigger than your apartment and it makes sense, don't you think?'

Alice's jaw fell. 'Sorry?' she said. A piece of mozzarella churned up her stomach. She swallowed.

'I think it's for the best, Alice. We can still see each other. Let's go to the East one day next week?' He let go of her hands.

'Okay.' She turned and walked out of the kitchen and into Peter.

'Hey Mad, I've got another bottle,' Peter said. She saw his eyes slide over to Johnny.

'Cheers, Peter, but I gotta go.' Alice looked at Johnny, knowing her eyes were thick with tears. She dipped her gaze, thanked Peter for the breakfast, and left. Everyone else was eating, talking, smoking. No one paid any attention as she clicked the door behind her and stepped into the cold. She could hardly think. He was beyond even a fucker. What had his ex said about him? The biggest living piece of shit in London? Add Berlin to that. She should have chucked him over the Wall while she had the chance.

Checkpoint Charlie

'*Guten Morgen, mein Schatz!* Time to go East to see how the other half live in the *Plattenbau* – those beautiful pre-fab blocks that fall down if you lean against them,' Peter called, opening Johnny's door, carrying a mug of coffee. He stopped and gazed at Johnny's half-naked body, poking out of the duvet like a sequoia in a desert. Only his feet were dressed in little black cotton socks. Cute.

Johnny opened his eyes and blinked.

'I've brought you a coffee. I know I need it. But good night last night, darling.'

Johnny had cooked him a candlelit dinner as a thank-you for the room. It was the first night they'd spent together since Johnny had moved in. After several bottles of red wine, he traded The Velvet Underground for his beloved Marlene Dietrich. He seemed to remember they had discussed the possibility of doing a cabaret act together. The idea of him singing on stage while Johnny swallowed fire and juggled lemons almost made him pant. Johnny had told him how much he liked being with him. Peter was convinced it was just a matter of time. Their hands and arms had touched. He put the coffee down, closed his eyes and took a deep breath.

'Are you okay?' Johnny said, yawning, and raising himself onto his elbows.

'I feel like an old dog, darling.' He coughed. He needed to cut down on cigarettes, drugs and alcohol. He kept getting real bad palpitations. Sometimes, he needed to lie down without doing anything for hours and hours until they passed.

'How many bottles of wine did we drink?' Johnny asked.

'I only counted three bottles.'

'And the vodka.'

Peter didn't remember the vodka.

'I had to put you to bed.' Johnny winked at him as he ran his hand through his blue Mohican.

Peter felt something inside his torso thump. He remembered Johnny telling him to lie down. He must have fallen asleep. Ass.

Johnny yawned again, took a gulp of coffee and looked at his watch. 'Shit, it's ten o'clock. We'd better go. I'll just take a quick shower.' He threw off his duvet, got up and headed to the door.

He was completely naked, apart from the socks. Peter tried not to whimper.

'Do we still have to ask Alice?' Peter called after him.

'Yep, I promised her.'

Peter groaned. Mad was great fun and sold good speed but a) she was mad, b) a girl, and c) about sixteen. He had warned Johnny that going to the East was like stepping into a black and white television, and with Mad in tow, it would be more like stepping into a John Wayne Western. Or Eastern. Whichever, they'd probably get their heads blown off. But Johnny was insistent: he felt bad about moving in with him like that. Although it would have happened at some point. Peter was certain of that.

'Are you sure I can't take my fire-eating equipment?' Johnny asked again, as they were about to leave.

'I am so very sure.' Was he mad as well?

They left the apartment just before eleven, dressed in long coats, scarves, trilby hats and gloves. The February Berlin skies were relentlessly grey. Bumps of black snow lined the pavements.

'Be warned, Alice's place is a shithole,' Johnny said.

A shithole was the least of his worries. Peter hoped she wasn't in.

She opened the door almost as soon as his gloved knuckles touched it. Her red and black hair looked like coiled snakes but she was dressed. She blinked black smudgy eyes at them, gripping the side of the heavy wooden door with her left hand.

'Hey Mad. We're going to the East. Are you coming?' Peter boomed. He always spoke too loudly when he was either nervous or sober.

'Hey, Alice, how are you?' Johnny said.

She looked at Peter and then sneered at Johnny. Hell, bad idea.

'Yeah sure, I'll go.' Mad relinquished her grip on the door. 'I've not been to the East yet – except to buy vodka at Friedrichstraße, of course. What's with the hats?'

'They won't let us in otherwise.'

Mad stared at them in amazement and smiled. Peter relaxed a fraction.

'You think they'll let you in like that?' she said. 'You look like the CIA. Or the KGB – whichever. Excuse the mess.' She slunk into the dark sitting room.

Peter and Johnny edged into the kitchen. Peter rolled his eyes in horror at the sink stacked with dirty plates and mouldy knives. Some milk had been left out of the fridge and had mutated into lumpy aliens. Crumbs of pumpernickel, sausage skins, egg whites and an empty tin of Heinz baked beans decorated the cracked plastic work surface. Johnny appeared unbothered and filled the kettle. Some light filtered into the room but the draughty window was filthy. It was foul. Only an English girl could live like this. Even his wife in California hadn't been this bad. Peter made large gestures towards the sink and put a supportive arm around Johnny. Johnny flinched and, shrugging him off, threw away a filter of mouldy coffee. Peter didn't like that flinch and pretended to sulk.

Voices came from the sitting room. Mad was talking to someone. Peter, forgetting his sulk, looked at Johnny in surprise. He hoped it wasn't Tom. He really did not want to spend a day in the East with a straight white stupid, albeit generous, American asshole, as well as a mad English girl.

Johnny poured out the coffee. Mad reappeared, hair and face fixed.

'Who've you got in there?' Peter whispered.

'Oh, you know, a friend.' She smiled.

'Oh well, good for you, darling. Any good?'

'Not your type, Peter. Too nice.'

Peter laughed loudly. Bitch. They drank their coffee – black. Mad brushed her teeth in the bathroom just off the kitchen and emerged tall, stunning, with white teeth and red lips. She put on a leather jacket.

'Maybe another coat would be better, Mad?' Peter said quickly. 'They won't let you into the East wearing leather, or jeans, or anything else that looks even faintly normal. I have been turned away so many times, darling, believe it or not.' Well, only once but she wasn't to know that.

'Are you serious?'

'Mortally. Why do you think we're dressed like this? Johnny spent at least an hour this morning demolishing his Mohican.'

She turned to look at Johnny as if surprised he was still there.

'I thought he looked a bit flat,' she said. 'I'll go and see what I can find.' She went back into the sitting room.

Peter laughed.

'Maybe you two should go without me,' Johnny said.

'No!' Peter shrank away, horrified at the thought. 'Johnny, please don't leave me with her all day. She hates me!'

'It's not you she hates, it's me. I was the one who moved out.'

'I told you we shouldn't have asked her,' Peter hissed.

Mad returned in a long black twenties coat, a green woollen pudding bowl hat, green gloves and a scarf. She carried a book in her hand.

'How's this? Do I look stupid enough? My mother sent me these.' She thrust the book in Johnny's direction. 'Thanks for the loan.'

Peter saw the dark cover: ugh, *Notes from Underground*. Hell, everyone here seemed to like Dostoevsky. A mad dog if ever there was one.

'You look stunningly conservative, darling. It might be an idea to remove some earrings.' Mad had an earful of them. And a nose ring.

'Oh dear, I don't even do this when I visit my parents,' she grumbled, as she took out stud after stud from each ear.

'I thought you were adopted,' Johnny said.

'Yes, but I still call them parents,' Mad said. She managed to intone 'stupid' without actually saying it.

'Okay, passports and money everyone?' he said. 'You'd better leave the book here, Johnny.'

'I'm sure it'll be fine. It's in my bag now.'

'Okay. Don't say I didn't warn you. You haven't got any drugs on you, have you, Mad?'

'Do I look like the kind of girl who carries drugs around all the time?' she said. She checked her pockets anyway and pulled out a magazine wrap.

'Oh,' she said.

Peter longed for a line.

'Do you want some?' she said.

'Well, maybe a tiny-tiny one,' Peter said. What a mad darling.

Mad deftly lined up the fine grains of speed while Peter rolled up a ten Mark note.

'What about Johnny?' Peter asked, seeing she was only doing two lines.

'He won't want one,' she said, dismissively.

'No thanks,' Johnny said, rinsing the cups under the tap.

Johnny was being very strange and moody this morning. Not his usual flamboyant self. Maybe he was tired. Apparently, he went to dance classes every day.

Peter didn't insist and he and Mad quickly hoovered up the white lines. She licked the paper and threw it in the Bolle plastic bag acting as trash can. Then they left the apartment and took Line 7 to Rohrdam. Peter was thankful for the line of speed but even he was getting tired of hearing his own voice. And Mad's. The train announced, *Nächster Bahnhof, Mehringdamm...*

'Why can't we go to Friedrichstraße?' Mad gabbled, as they got off. 'We could get some vodka then.'

'Because it's usually easier to cross at Checkpoint Charlie.'

Peter had never actually crossed at Friedrichstraße. He had tried once, a while back when he first arrived in 1980, but had got lost, and then drunk. Different levels beneath the station created a maze of tunnels, doors, cracked mirrors and blocked exits where East met West. He had found the Intershop on the D-platform at the lowest S-Bahn level without difficulty. The Intershop was run by the East German authorities, which meant you could buy alcohol and cigarettes for almost nothing. As it was supposedly illegal to take them back into the West, the Eastern platform swarmed with alkies. Peter met up with an old West German guy who pointed to the cracked tiled ceiling, claiming he used to live up there with his daughter. Every Saturday night he reckoned he came to the Intershop to be near her, apparently. It was all crazy, of course.

They went up the escalators to Mehringdamm and crossed the station via the glass box bridge. Alice and Johnny still hadn't spoken to each other.

'Okay darlings,' Peter said loudly, stopping on the bridge and holding his hands up. 'I am not spending the day with you two, if you're not going to talk to each other.'

Johnny and Mad stopped and looked at him in astonishment. Commuters rushed by even quicker.

'Why wouldn't we be talking to each other,' Mad said. Her voice could have extinguished the sun if it had been anywhere to be seen.

Johnny went over and put his arms around Mad and pulled a red handkerchief out her pocket. For a moment, Peter thought she was going to strangle him with it but she managed a hurt smile and they made it to Kochstraße in relative peace.

'I need a drink,' Mad said, as they emerged from the U-Bahn into the grey day.

For the first time ever, Peter agreed with her. They went to the Café Adler near the Checkpoint and ordered coffee, brandy and berliners. Only Johnny refused the brandy so Peter and Mad shared his and Peter left the cafe feeling a whole lot better. They passed the small museum dedicated to the history of the Wall and the tourist trade and approached the white sign which read, **You are leaving the American sector** in English, Russian and French. On the Allied Checkpoint Charlie hut in the middle of the road there were the American, British and French flags and a couple of uniformed Americans drinking coffee. Peter cringed when he heard their southern accents. The poor bastards.

'Is this it?' Mad muttered incredulously.

Ahead of them, red and white road barriers and street lamps rose into the grey sky like triffids. They entered the border control hut to be processed.

'Take your hat off,' the controller said politely in German while scrutinising his American passport.

Peter smiled nervously, twiddling the rim. The controller seemed to be examining his admittedly large forehead. Peter felt his eyes roll upwards.

'Do you carry firearms, explosives, books or magazines?'

'No,' Peter said, glad Johnny had not brought his fire-eating equipment. The Brits had a strange sense of humour at times.

Peter bit his thumb nail as Johnny and Mad passed through still wearing their hats. His forehead must have been reassuring enough. They were then all searched. Dostoevsky was quarantined. Best place for him. Fortunately Mad didn't have any more drugs on her. They sat down in front of a portrait of Honecker and were made to wait thirty minutes – even though there were only two other people – to get their passports stamped, pay their five Marks for the visa and change the compulsory twenty-five Marks into Monopoly money. They were told to be back by midnight.

'What happens if we're late?' Mad asked in English, smiling sweetly.

The controller looked at her, his face frozen, and replied in German. 'You will be arrested.'

She must have understood as she didn't say anything but Peter nudged her in the ribs, just in case. He didn't want to spend time in an East German jail because of her. They left the hut and emerged into the East.

'Careful, Mad,' he said. 'This is not a game you know.'

'I know it's not a game. We were shot at the other night,' she said, looking behind her at the Checkpoint. 'This is weird.'

The street was empty except for an old, pale blue Trabant. Behind them they could see bits of the concrete Wall, ungrafittied, a watchtower, and beyond the narrow gap of Checkpoint Charlie, West Berlin glowed like a multi-coloured halo. A tourist bus full of anxious Americans waited to cross.

'I guess no one really comes down here – unless they're crossing the border,' Peter said.

'It's like stepping into a black and white TV,' Johnny said.

Peter looked at Johnny, expecting some acknowledgement but none came. Peter laughed instead and said, 'Yeah, that's what I've always said.' But Johnny still ignored him. Peter snorted.

'There's no advertising!' Mad said, as if having discovered the meaning of life.

'Of course there's no advertising – it's a communist state. There is nothing,' Peter snapped.

'Okay, let's go to some shops. I want to see nothing,' she said, sarcastically.

'Great. We can either go to Unter den Linden which is straight ahead,' he said. 'Or we can head over to the right towards Alexanderplatz? Or we could take the U-Bahn?'

Why had he bothered? Mad wanted to go to Unter den Linden, Johnny to Alexanderplatz. He decided to go towards Unter den Linden, seeing as Johnny was being so fucking uncool.

'That's the U-Bahn station there.' Peter pointed along Mohrenstraße to a smaller, skinnier Eastern 'U'. 'What the Ossis don't know is that Line 6 runs beneath us as well to Friedrichstraße and then up to Wedding and Tegel in the West. It goes through the ghost stations of Stadtmitte, this one here, presumably at a lower level, then Französische Straße, Oranienburger Tor and Nordbahnhof.' Peter was impressed he'd remembered them all. He was fascinated by the way authorities could change physical maps, as well as minds.

'The dark empty stations with only guards with machine guns prowling the platforms with silent Alsatian dogs,' Mad said, marching forward pretending to carry a gun like a mad woman.

'Yep. The stations that no longer appear on the map.'

'I've seen them on the maps,' Johnny said. 'I'm not sure if it was Line 6 but I took the U-Bahn to Pankstraße and it crossed under the East. It was on the map.'

'Only the Western map, darling. The DDR publish maps without the stations. In fact the whole of the West is a blank white space. Period.'

'I want an Ossi map,' Mad whined.

'Surely people wouldn't forget that quickly?' Johnny asked. 'Since 1961?'

'Apparently, they have.'

'What happened in 1961?' Mad asked.

'That's when the Wall went up, you silly ass.'

'I am not a silly ass, you asshole. Let's ask someone – see if they remember where the stations are.'

Before Peter could stop her, she was crossing over the road towards the U-Bahn where a solitary figure was emerging.

'Stop her!' Peter said to Johnny, but Johnny only shrugged. Peter let out a nervous rumble. They just didn't get it. They could easily be arrested for subversion. To say nothing of Mad's murdering of the German language. He heard her from across the other side of the road.

'Entschuldigen Sie bitte. Ich glaube das hier ist eine andere U-Bahn zu Friedrichstraße. Wo ist es?'

He thought he'd better cross over as the woman was shaking her head. This was followed by an admonishing finger telling her that there was no such line. Peter joined Mad, thanked the woman, explaining that they were tourists. The woman hurried away.

'I said they wouldn't remember, you mad Alice,' he growled and strode on ahead. Not for long though as he was soon out of breath. He didn't want an asthma attack.

Johnny and Mad caught up with him. The tourist bus that had been waiting at the Checkpoint passed them, adding a speck of colour to the black and white world.

Unter den Linden, the Eastern icon, was dressed in red, albeit faded. Huge banners hung over the pre-fabricated tower blocks, rippling like drawn curtains in front of an open window. On the long, wide street, the shoppers of the East, dressed in their Russian hats and plastic shoes seemed insignificant. To the left, the Brandenburg Gate occupied a space of its own, proclaiming the edge of the capital of the DDR, monumental, Prussian, untouchable. Its great columns rose above the Wall and on top the four copper horses with their arses to the West, pulled the chariot and the Winged Victory into the East. Tanks dotted the base of the columns and the Wall curved gracefully around it. Behind it, the other half of Unter den Linden stretched into the blank white space of the West.

'Did you know that Hitler planned to hoist the Brandenburg Gate onto a hill so that it would be like the one near the Parthenon,' Peter said, seeing that they were staring in that direction.

'What's the Parthenon?' Mad asked.

Peter hooked up both eyebrows and laughed. She really was ignorant. 'Oh darling, don't you know anything? It's part of the Acropolis, in Athens.'

'Well, of course I know the Acropolis. I've been to Athens.' She folded her arms and walked ahead, away from the Gate and turned her attention to the single item displays of the shop windows. An old couple linking arms joined Mad in front of the display. They all stared into the window.

'Such beautiful things,' the woman muttered as they walked away.

Mad burst out laughing and indicated for them to join her.

'Oh no, what's she doing now?' Peter muttered, smiling at Johnny. He tried to squeeze his hand but as soon as he brushed against his gloved fingers, Johnny snapped it shut.

'Leave it out, Peter,' Johnny hissed. Like a swan. And then walked over to Mad.

'Huh!' Peter stood with his arms folded in the middle of the pavement. Well, wasn't that just charming. One minute they're all over you, the next minute you might as well not be there. Shitty multi-faced Brits. After all Johnny had said last night, how much he liked him, how much he wanted to stay. Yet now, only a few hours later, he was told to leave it out. The arrogant asshole.

'Hey, Peter, look at this!' Mad called out, in between annoying giggles. 'They have beautiful things. And advertising!'

Peter ambled over reluctantly. They were looking in a shop window of cosmetics. Empty boxes of 'Berlin Kosmetik' decorated the inside window ledge. A faded picture of a blue female face and red lacy briefs were stretched out over a rusting metal holder. Once white, now sepia coloured, net curtains lined the display area. In one corner stood an empty bottle of Rotkäppchen. How exciting.

'"Indra" lipstick and red wine,' Mad said.

'That's sparkling white wine,' Peter snapped.

'Why does it say red then?'

'It doesn't. *Rotkäppchen* means Little Red Riding Hood.' He couldn't help sneering.

'Oh. Let's see if we can get some,' she said.

Peter looked pleadingly at Johnny but the motherfucker ignored him and followed Mad into the shop. He waited outside. He wasn't going to act as translator or be subjected to more of her embarrassing German. Besides, even if there was anything to buy, they would never work out how. For most products you needed coupons and for others you needed to buy a ticket.

Peter paced about outside. The roads were quiet except for a few battered buses and Trabbies trundling up and down. Passers-by eyed him askew. Maybe the hat hadn't been a good idea. A couple of armed vehicles, full of grey guards clutching guns, rumbled towards the Gate. Young boys in uniform. One of them caught his eye and stared at him, full of hatred.

Mad emerged, triumphantly brandishing an Indra lipstick and a bottle of Rotkäppchen in front of him. Peter felt the blood drain from his face. It was an act of aggression. Good speed or not, he would never ever go anywhere with her again. As for him. Well, really, fuck his little cotton socks.

Alexanderplatz

Johnny was first off the whirring tram at Alexanderplatz. It crossed his mind that perhaps he should double back and get on again, away from the latest squabble. He really wished he were on his own. He was surprised Peter had wanted to come to the East. He clearly didn't like it and had never been up before 4 p.m. since he'd been staying at his place.

'Well, it is a communist country, I don't see why we should pay,' Alice was saying.

'It's only about twenty Pfennigs,' Peter snapped. 'It's hardly worth the risk.'

'Bloody hell, Peter. We weren't going to be arrested for not having a ticket.'

Johnny lit a cigarette and tried to shut his ears. Peter had already decided he wasn't talking to him which was just fine. Something to do with the fact that he'd rejected his hand on Unter den Linden. Really, he was worse than Alice.

'Never mind, we weren't caught.' Alice skipped towards him. She, at least, was in a better mood now – since he'd told her she was the most fantastic girl he'd ever met. Which was true.

'Hey, where's mine?'

He gave her a cigarette. Peter lit one of his own.

'There's Big Brother,' Alice said, blowing smoke at the red, flashing lights in the grey bowl in the sky. 'I told you about him on the first night.'

She emphasised *first night* just to make him feel bad. He looked up at the tower. So she had meant the Fernsehturm, the Television Tower. It looked to him like a giant eyeball skewered by a long concrete stick, or a flying saucer stationed in the grey sky. He imagined what it would be like to be up there in the sky, above the rest of the world, out of reach of the Wall that divided them. Out of earshot of Alice and Peter. Bliss.

'Which reminds me, how's the play going?' he asked.

'What play?'

'The one you're doing with the group from Kreuzberg?'

'Oh fine. Yes, it's based on *1984*. The idea that we're being watched all the time, just like Orwell imagined.'

He suspected she was fibbing but he didn't say anything. They were waiting to cross the wide, open road with dozens of East Berliners with sour, chapped faces like rotting lemons. Everyone watched them, or only pretended to ignore them. Alice struck up a conversation with someone next to her, a small man in a grey anorak and a woollen hat and scarf. Peter, standing behind him, groaned.

'What's she saying?' Johnny turned round to ask.

'Who knows,' Peter replied dismissively, without looking at him. 'It's almost impossible to understand her German.'

Johnny wasn't so sure. The man was answering her and pointing up towards the Tower and then towards Alexanderplatz. Only when the red round pedestrian light turn to a striding green round man in a bowler hat did everyone cross the road together. The man was still talking, Alice nodding furiously. When they reached the other side, she thanked him and he scuttled off towards the crowds of Alexanderplatz.

'You shouldn't talk to people like that, Mad,' Peter said.

'Why not?'

'You'll get them into trouble. This area is swarming with Stasi. They'll follow him home, arrest him in the night and interrogate him. Then they'll probably shoot him.'

'Oh rubbish,' Alice said. 'You can't get arrested for talking to someone.'

Peter shrugged.

Johnny tended to think that Peter was over-reacting, but he didn't want any more fights. He liked staying at Peter's; he had his own room and pretty much the place to himself during the day. But it looked like it was going to get difficult. Last night, after a couple of bottles of wine, Peter had insisted on dressing up in drag and singing from his four poster bed. He finally sank onto the bed and fell asleep, still clutching Johnny's hand with one hand and a glass of vodka with the other. Johnny had prised his fingers from the glass and his hand, took off his red gown and left him covered up.

Peter was attractive: tall, dark with black curly hair and his deep, sexy Californian voice, but Johnny wasn't interested in getting involved with anyone, male or female. There were so many things he wanted to do with his life. Relationships got in the way. No one seemed to understand that.

'So what did you ask that man?' he asked Alice, who was walking beside him while Peter lurked several paces behind.

'Oh, I asked where the nearest bar was,' she said. 'There's one up there in Big Brother's head and another one here somewhere.'

'The Television Tower would be interesting,' Johnny said. He turned round to Peter. 'Shall we go up there?'

'No. You have to pay and it takes ages. Then when you get to the top there's never any coffee.' He sounded like a dog growling.

Johnny wasn't going to argue, even though they had to spend their twenty-five Marks somehow. This was crazy. They were heading for the fountain on Alexanderplatz.

'So where do you want to go then?' Johnny asked Peter, the temperature in his voice plunging towards freezing. Not that he cared at this point. He'd leave them in the next bar.

'There's a café over there,' he said, wafting his arm across the vast expanse of grey slabs.

'Come on then,' Johnny said. He walked on; either they'd follow or they wouldn't. It was up to them. Several people were gathered around the fountain, watching the water spew out of a collection of giant rigid black petals and stamens. On the round base, psychedelic images were painted on the tiles. But, despite the splashes of colour, the square refused to look anything other than shades of black and white. One building looked like it was encased in a black and white patterned doily, like the ones his mother used to use. Alice caught up with him.

'So is everything all right at Peter's?' she asked.

'For now. I have my own room – and it's rent-free.'

Alice seemed to find that hilarious.

'What about the dance? Are you going to those workshops?'

'Yeah, they're okay, but not overly challenging. Sophie is putting together a show. I said I'd do it but we'll see. I get on well with Benjamin but Sophie and I don't quite see eye to eye.'

'No?'

'No.' It wasn't Sophie's fault. She was a good dancer and she had some great ideas. Perhaps it was because he wasn't sure any more if, ultimately, dance was what he wanted to do. He wasn't finding it as exciting as he used to. Something was missing. It felt restricted. He wanted to fly through a window like Nijinsky. But how? It had all been done.

'What are you going to do then?' she asked.

Johnny didn't reply as something else caught his attention. A crowd had gathered in front of a department store. Someone was juggling next to what looked like a bear. A couple of young girls backflipped in circles, red ribbons trailing around them. Johnny's heart wheeled towards them. This was the first street performance he had seen in

Berlin and, as he focused on the ensemble, his vision turned to colour for the first time in the East. He wished he'd brought his fire-eating equipment. Peter, being paranoid again, had reckoned he would be arrested. Although he had been right about Dostoevsky.

'Oh shit,' Alice said, looking in the same direction. 'There's a bear. Peter, look.'

Johnny didn't wait for Peter's reaction. The crowd reeled him in. The large brown bear, wearing a red collar and muzzle, was walking on its hind legs, handing out leaflets to the people gathered around. It was attached to an old clown with a white face, yellow hair and a red painted smile, dressed in traditional baggy pants and floppy shoes. The people were laughing; no one sure who was handling whom. Every so often the bear pulled on the rope, yanking the clown away from the crowd. The clown pretended to tell the bear off but the bear ignored him.

The girls, dressed in sunset gold leotards and tights and orange ribbons, shone in a grey world. They were both petite, dark, with black eyes decorated with sparkling eyeshadow and a fixed lipsticked grin, somehow intrinsically Eastern. They bent in half, flexible as rubber, and cartwheeled in opposite circles while still spinning the long red ribbons. As they came towards each other, the crowd gasped as it looked like they were going to collide, but they slotted into each other, becoming one crablike creature, dancing in a circle, like a slow spinning top.

'Gee,' Johnny heard Peter muttering behind him. 'Darling, that must hurt.'

The seven-foot bear handed him a flyer but dropped several others. Johnny almost said thank-you and wanted to help him as he fell onto all fours and tried to shovel up the fallen flyers with his paws and muzzle, but couldn't as he didn't have any nails. The clown came over and collected the flyers for him and then pretended to abscond with them. The bear lumbered after him. The clown held up his hands in mock defeat and gave the bear some of his flyers back.

'That's so cruel!' Alice was saying, also behind him.

On the scale of worldwide cruelty, Johnny didn't think it was especially cruel. The bear wasn't starving, its coat was shiny. In fact, it looked in better condition than the clown.

Another younger man juggled batons as he walked calmly around the perimeter of the crowd – five, Johnny noted. Then he exchanged his batons in favour of a couple of hoops and, after juggling them for a minute, held each of them out to the side so that the acrobats could somersault and backflip through them, back and forth, each time higher and higher, like yo-yos. The old clown picked up an accordion and struck a chord. The crowd began to clap. The bear danced round and round with one of the girls, half the bear's size. They held paws and waltzed across the square, Beauty and the Beast.

The juggler extended one of the hoops to one side and the other girl, who looked older, slipped inside it. He then threw both girl and hoop above his head from where she proceeded to sculpt herself into impossible shapes. Completely unperturbed by the laws of gravity, she balanced, upside down on her hands, then split her legs over the juggler's shoulders and danced around the hoop on her hands. She slid her feet onto the hoop and stood up tall, back arched, arms outstretched, while the juggler jigged about beneath her as if she were a bottle of champagne on a silver tray which he was carrying through a swanky restaurant. All the time she smiled as if she were sitting on a swing in a park.

Then it happened. She caught his eye. An expression of bemusement, curiosity even, spread over her face. He gazed back, unable to move. His chest tightened, his legs weakened and his stomach turned upside down. He gasped. This was it. She was the missing something. He was sure of it. She would take him to places he had only dreamed of. She would never get in the way. Johnny smiled at her and for one long second it seemed as if they were the only two people in the world. In that split second, he fell in love with a girl who could defy gravity.

The accordion stopped playing and the bear stopped dancing and the girl slid off the juggler. They all lined up and bowed to rapturous applause. Johnny thought she winked at him. The old clown said something in German and they backed away and began to clear up. The crowd drifted.

Johnny looked down at the flyer. On it was a date: March 1 and a sketch of a circus tent. More than a week away.

'I have to talk to them,' Johnny said. 'Peter, will you interpret?'

'No darling. I don't want to end up in an East German jail, not even for you. Besides, I need a brandy. Alice?'

'Oh fuck you,' Johnny muttered.

'Anytime darling,' he heard Peter say. 'Come on, Alice.'

'Okay, we'll be in the bar over there,' Alice said.

Johnny didn't reply. Fuck them really. They were getting on his nerves. Only interested in sex and drugs. He walked over to the little entourage. As he got closer he saw that their costumes were tatty and dirty. They were putting on layers of clothes on top of their costumes.

'*Guten Tag,*' Johnny said. '*Sprechen Sie Englisch?*'

They looked at him, curious, without saying anything. The old clown shook his head. Her dark eyes pierced his chest. Johnny continued, regardless, telling them his name, how much he liked their performance. She continued to stare at him. He felt naked. The others smiled, nodded and continued to do what they were doing. Maybe Peter was right; maybe he shouldn't talk to them, but he couldn't walk away from her. In a last attempt, he threw off his hat and coat, bent down over an old plastic sports bag and took out the juggler's batons. For a moment, he was afraid the old clown was going to whip them off him, but the clown's attention was drawn to the bear, who began to make a deep crying noise – not unlike Peter last night.

Johnny threw the batons into the air and hoped he could still juggle. The only thing he'd juggled since he had been in Berlin were beer bottles and he'd been so drunk that it was more likely the alcohol that had kept them spinning. Fortunately, the batons flew up in the air, perfectly aligned. He juggled four without any difficulty and then the juggler threw another one at him so he didn't really have much choice. The girls watched, arms folded, draped in fur coats, smiling and giggling.

He dropped them. One by one they bounced onto the large, bare paving slabs of Alexanderplatz. The younger acrobat waved an arm dismissively and she looked away, as if disappointed in him. He gathered them up quickly and tried again. This time, he managed to juggle the five and he was rewarded with a smile. The juggler then threw him another. Johnny had never juggled six before and he knew he would drop them. He caught them rather than face the embarrassment. The juggler, still without speaking, shook his head and took the batons from him and threw all six of them, one after another into the air, as if launching missiles.

Having demonstrated, he gave them to Johnny. The girls were still watching him. Even the old clown glanced over at him. Johnny hadn't felt this much pressure since he had done his performance piece for his exams last summer. Several people idly gathered round. He took a deep breath, relaxed, stood tall, and threw the batons one after another. One, two, three, four, five, six, one, two, three, four, five, six. His hands and body found a rhythm and soon he was juggling the six batons in a wide arc. People clapped but he didn't break his concentration. He sensed the juggler standing near him and he threw three of the batons to him. They each juggled three batons for a few seconds and then in an improvised moment they juggled the six batons back and forth together.

By the time they finished they felt like firm friends. His name was Bodo and he spoke some English. She was smiling at him. She said something to the other girl, but Johnny didn't understand. It didn't sound like German though.

'*Gut, Johnny, gut*. Now we try,' Bodo said.

He dipped into his bag and pulled out a set of gleaming diamond-shaped knives.

'My favourite,' he said, grinning.

The girls groaned. So did Johnny. Maybe they weren't such firm friends. On closer inspection, they were blunted, but they would hurt if he missed. Johnny juggled three; they were smaller than the batons, but the weight was about the same, and the handles were rounded. They were easier than he thought. Bodo pulled out another set and they began juggling together. The crowd gasped at the two men throwing knifes at each other. Johnny tingled with excitement – something he hadn't felt for a long time.

He was so engrossed in their juggling that he didn't notice the three long grey-coated police officers cross the square towards them. No one else appeared to either. They came and stood before Johnny and Bodo, ordering them to *Halt*. Knives crashed to the ground. Johnny couldn't understand what they said but it was clear, from their expressions, that what they were doing was *verboten*. The police officers stood in front of them, arms folded, automatic rifles lodged across their chests. The crowd dispersed into the grey concrete. The old clown spoke calmly to the police while Bodo packed up the knives.

Johnny picked up his coat and hat, expecting to be arrested. It was his fault. He may never see these people again. Bodo zipped up his bag and said something to the girls with his back to the police. Again, Johnny didn't understand. Then, as Bodo stood up he thrust the bag at Johnny, winked, and indicated that he come with them.

One of the police officers, still barking at them, thumped at a document the old clown had given them. There appeared to be some error, but the old clown kept shaking his head and looking sad, as only a clown can. The police officer looked particularly indignant and shook the paper so hard it flew off. The bear, who had been standing at a safe distance behind the clown, lunged at the piece of paper which also happened to be in the same direction as the police. They stepped back in horror and pointed their guns.

'*Nein!*' the old clown shouted, jumping in front of the bear.

The bear managed to pick up the paper and then stood up on his haunches, seven foot in the air, two foot away from the police, flaunting the document triumphantly. The girls could hardly contain themselves with laughter.

The old clown yanked at the bear, who, paper still in paws, backed off. So did the police. They fired some parting threats as the circus folk walked off. Johnny, carrying the batons, followed them. It somehow seemed the most natural thing in the world to do. This is what he had been looking for.

Karl-Marx-Allee

'What in God's name does he think he's doing now?' Peter said, rubbing away the condensation with his glove and peering out of the glass. 'He's following them.'

Alice stood next to Peter as they watched events unfold on Alexanderplatz from a steamed up café. The café smelled of bitter coffee, damp coats and unperfumed cigarettes. Alice was still glowing from Johnny having told Peter to fuck off. With any luck Peter would throw him out. But there would be no need for that now. He was about to disappear into the East forever – without even saying goodbye.

'Do you think we should go after him, Mad,' Peter said, tugging hard at a cigarette.

They had finally got some beers after queuing up for half an hour and were standing at a high table by themselves. Alice was not leaving. Even though Johnny had the Benson's.

'Oh fuck him. Let him be, Peter. If he wants to run away with the stupid circus behind the Iron Curtain, that's up to him.' Alice didn't like circuses. She remembered as a child being taken to the circus by a friend's family and feeling sorry for the animals. And she remembered hating clowns, finding them more scary than funny. Admittedly, the young acrobats and juggler had been good but that poor bear. She was not surprised they'd almost been arrested. What had Johnny seen in them?

'Can I have one?' she asked, picking up his Marlboro.

Peter nodded, clearly distraught. His black curls had been flattened by his stupid hat and his eyes looked red. But everyone in the East seemed to have bad haircuts and looked like they were about to cry so, for once, he didn't look out of place.

'But Mad darling. How can he do this to me?'

'Peter, darling, he did it to me. Remember?'

'Yes, but that was different, you're a girl.'

Alice lit a match. For a second she felt like setting fire to Peter, but she put the cigarette in her mouth and lit that together with her woollen gloves.

'Bugger. Johnny's not interested in you, Peter,' she said, taking off her gloves. The smell of singed wool spiced the bitter café smells.

'That's what you think. He told me just last night how much he liked me. Darling, he even cooked me a candle-lit dinner and... you know.'

'So? He took me out to dinner and we had sex three times in one day.' She probably shouldn't have said that as Peter spluttered on a mouthful of beer and began coughing but he was pissing her off.

Other people, standing up at the bird tables, quietly sipping bitter coffee, glanced at them, mildly disapproving.

'Three times?' Peter blinked several times. 'Are you serious?'

Alice nodded curtly. 'Why do you think I was so upset when he decided to stay at yours?'

'Oh you slapper,' Peter said, pouting. 'I am so jealous.'

'So you didn't sleep together?' Alice asked.

'Not three times,' Peter said, ambiguously, dipping his eyes into the ashtray.

He had charming dark eyes – when he smiled. And he was even taller than Johnny. Shame he was gay, Alice thought. That would have made a nice ending. A highly unlikely one, seeing as he really didn't seem to like her any more. Probably jealous. She knew Johnny, deep down, liked her very much.

She drank some beer and wiped the foam from her lips. Even though they had both been drunk that night in the Kiosk, she remembered every minute. He kept telling her how fantastic she was, how stunningly beautiful, how much he loved sleeping with her, how he wanted to go home with her. They should have gone when he said, but it was she who had wanted to carry on drinking. Not that that was a reason to move out and leave her.

'Well, I guess he fucked us both then,' she said.

But Peter was watching a group of soldiers or police who had come into the café – the same ones who had moved on the circus folk. Their faces were as stone-grey as their uniforms. They stood politely in the queue, but were served immediately.

'What did you say?'

'Nothing.'

Alice sipped more Schultheiss, which tasted different in the East, and suddenly felt sad. She had lost Johnny as well as driven Tom away. She heard he'd gone back to the States. For two whole days, after returning from Peter's that horrible grey morning, she had locked herself in her apartment with a bottle of Southern Comfort, black bread, potato salad and ham. She lay in her high bed, wearing her hat and gloves, swigging Southern Comfort and reading Johnny's copy of Dostoevsky's *Notes from Underground*.

It was the only thing he had left her when he'd shown up during the half hour she was out to collect his stuff. And a note: *Sorry I missed you, Alice. I'm still at Peter's for now and taking lots of dance classes. Thanks for everything and hope we can still be good friends. You are a fantastic girl but please understand that I don't to get involved with anyone at the moment. Let's go to the East together soon.* Bla bla bla...

He didn't come again. No one came, so she lost herself in Dostoevsky's Underground, where she discovered an uncanny resemblance between nineteenth century St Petersburg and twentieth century Berlin. Both were dark, decadent, brooding cities, both challenged common sense and nature: the first had been built on swampland, the other sliced in half and walled up. They were both products of man imposing his will.

From what Alice could gather from Dostoevsky, the pre-twentieth century seemed to have been dominated by God versus science. The Great Debate. Did some great old man with a white beard, sitting up there on a cloud, get bored one day and decide to create the world and then got people to write guide books for him on how to live while he sat and waited in judgement? Or did life evolve over millions of years in conditions just right?

It was fairly obvious to her. How anyone could have ever believed that God was any more real than Superman or Father Christmas she had no idea. She supposed that whatever people were taught as a child stayed with them forever – however irrational. Her parents weren't particularly religious, although her Mum said her birth was a miracle – but that was usually when she was arguing with her father. She remembered singing about Bethlehem and Jerusalem in school assemblies but that was about it – and, even then, she failed to see the relevance to Norfolk. These days, she didn't know anyone who was religious – it was the 1980s, after all.

'You don't believe in God, do you?' she asked Peter.

'Not unless he's six foot tall, has a body like Apollo and carries a leather whip,' Peter said, still watching the officers standing at the bar, drinking their coffee and smoking cigarettes.

So now God was done and dusted, it was communism versus capitalism – state control versus human freedom. This was the new great debate of the twentieth century. Communist states took away freedom and replaced it with security. Just like religion. It was all the same. She nodded knowingly to herself, pleased at having worked it all out. Alice understood the underground man's point that freedom was important but she could also see the beauty of State control: here in the East, people were given jobs, houses, schools. They didn't have to think too much, they didn't have to make choices as there was only ever one. Life was easy. And no one was dying of hunger. Besides, the underground man might be free but he was a miserable fucker. That said, she thought, looking round, so were most of the people in the café. She tried smiling at people but no one smiled back. No wonder Dostoevsky had been confiscated.

'I'm going to have another beer,' Peter announced.

He didn't offer to get her one. Thinking about it, he was more like the underground man.

'Will you get me one too, please.' She gave him some money and he went to stand near the officers.

Outside, Alexanderplatz had returned to grey since the removal of the circus. There was, no doubt, a strange vibe in the East. There may not be hunger, but it was as if the entire East had been spun in a washing machine and left unemptied – with all the colours and laughter washed out. The people, too, were different – just two kilometres away from where she lived and yet they made her feel like an enemy. But she wasn't. On balance, she believed in communism, she believed that everyone was equal, that everyone deserved the same chance in life. It had to be better than capitalism where the rich got richer and the poor stayed poor. She felt like standing up and shouting, 'It's not my fault our governments are fascists!' But then Peter returned with Schultheiss and schnapps. And besides, there was that problem of men being gods and communism replacing religion.

'Good idea, Peter,' she said. 'Cheers.'

They knocked back the schnapps and Alice felt like she'd swallowed fire. Peter drooled after the officers who left the café at last.

'How come the beer's the same in East and West?' Alice asked, holding her glass of beer up.

'I wonder why, Alice? Could it possibly because there used to be a factory in the East and the West?' Peter said, sarcastically. 'Anyway, it's not. This is different. Can't you taste the chemicals?'

Alice slugged the beer. 'Yeah, but they're not bad. Hey, have you read Dostoevsky?'

'Oh God no. Russian literature makes me feels suicidal.'

It had made her miserable as well. But that could have been the Southern Comfort. Whichever, after two days, bored of feeling sorry for herself, she went out and got a job working in a club called Cats.

She knew the owner quite well and he paid her a hundred Marks for taking coats at the door. That's where she'd been until six most mornings. It was funny that Peter thought she had someone in bed: it was only the television. *He* hadn't seemed bothered though.

'So what do you want to do now?' Alice asked. 'Shall we go to the theatre or something?' She knew there was a famous theatre company in East Berlin that she would like to see.

'The theatre? Performances won't start until this evening.' Peter looked for the time. It was three o'clock. 'I don't know. We could see what's on at the Berliner Ensemble and see some Brecht, but you won't understand it.'

'It doesn't matter,' Alice said. That was it, Brecht.

'I still can't believe he left us,' Peter said, drinking up the last of his beer. 'He doesn't even speak German.' He slammed his glass on the table and picked up his hat.

Alice sighed. 'I'm sure he'll find his way back. And if he doesn't, well, with any luck, the lions will eat him.'

Alice put on her singed black gloves. Other people hovered around them ready to perch at their bird table. She opened the café door and stepped straight into Johnny, who appeared from nowhere. Her stomach yo-yoed as she felt his arms momentarily around her.

'Johnny!' Peter yelled behind her, clearly unable to disguise his joy at seeing him. He'd obviously forgiven Johnny for telling him to fuck off.

'Hi guys. We've been looking for you.'

It was then that Alice became aware of the 'we'. Standing outside were two very attractive olive-skinned girls, dressed in long fur coats and hats, and a guy with blond hair and blue eyes. She recognised the guy as the juggler, which must mean that the girls were the acrobats. She smiled down at them, trying to swallow the mouthful of jealousy that was already leaving a bad taste on her tongue. The girls were older than she thought, one was anyway. They were doll-like creatures with beautiful dark eyes, but very small, almost half her height. They returned her smile with laughter – which made her want to slap them.

Johnny introduced them as they moved away from the café. The juggler's name was Bodo and the girls were Natasha and Zoya. Natasha was the older one. Alice didn't think they were very German names.

'You come with us,' Bodo said to Alice in English. 'We go to Ice Bar.'

Alice looked at Peter and Johnny for confirmation. Peter was locked onto Johnny, like a clam to a rock. Johnny was doing his best not to notice and to be friendly to everyone. They all nodded in agreement, whatever the Ice Bar was, and drifted behind Bodo in twos and threes. Alice walked the other side of Johnny.

'So, what happened?' Peter asked him.

'I'm not sure. There was something wrong with their permit. I think I may have got these guys into trouble if they'd known I was a foreigner.'

'Oh really,' Peter said sarcastically.

Johnny hung back to wait for the girls, leaving her and Peter stranded. This was silly. She decided to talk to Bodo as they crossed Alexanderplatz, past the bronze clock branded with all the cities across the world. She spoke in bad German but Bodo was keen to speak bad English.

'I must practise. Please,' he added.

She was going to say that they were in Germany, but his buttery eyes won her over.

'Fine,' she said. 'So what happened with the police?'

'Police? Pah! They say it is forbidden to throw knives.' Bodo sounded indignant. 'We have permit, but they say no knives.'

Alice thought that was fair enough.

'Where's the bear gone?' she asked, changing the subject.

'George very upset. He does not like police. The Professor take him back.'

'George? The bear's name's George?'

'George. Yes.'

'So you do many performances?'

'Performances. Yes. All over the German Democratic Republic. Now we rehearse for summer show.'

'You're a juggler?'

'Yes, I do juggle and I walk the wire.'

'High wire?'

'Yes.'

'Wow.'

They turned onto Karl-Marx-Allee. The rain-stained high-rise concrete buildings blended perfectly into the sky. It was almost impossible to see where one began and the other ended. There were several shops and hotels as well as pre-fabricated apartment blocks. A group of children, dressed in grey uniforms with red neck ties, walking in lines of twos, passed them. A couple of female teachers flanked the rear. One of the children shouted, 'Look out!' Alice wasn't sure for what: an erratic Trabant or them.

'What do you work?'

Alice shrugged. 'Nothing.'

'Nothing?' Bodo sounded surprised.

Alice didn't think he'd understand about selling speed so she told him she did lots of things: working in a bar, nightclub, some acting in films. Bodo nodded but she could see he didn't understand.

'You are very beautiful,' he said.

'Thank you,' said Alice.

The Ice Bar was situated next to the Kino International. They all trooped in, past a man in a grey uniform hovering at the door. Alice thought he was going to stop them, but he almost smiled. Not quite though. The bar was dark and a pianist played in the corner. A few people sat around drinking what looked like ice cream. They handed their coats and hats to a stone-faced cloakroom attendant and received a token and a scowl in return. Alice bet she didn't earn a hundred Marks a day.

'We sit here?' Bodo said.

Alice nodded and sat down on a stool. Johnny sat opposite her while Peter squeezed next to him leaving Natasha to sit on one side of her and Zoya the other. Sandwiched between them, Alice's nostrils were bombarded by a strong body odour. Natasha pulled out a packet of cigarettes and handed them round. Alice took one, trying not to wrinkle her nose. There was a blue rocket on the packet.

'Did you know this was here?' Johnny asked Peter, looking around the bar.

'Yes, of course, everyone knows it,' Peter said. 'Alice, do you want to give Bodo a hand with the drinks?'

'Not really,' she said. 'But I suppose we might as well get rid of our money.' She got up, secretly relieved to give her nose a break, and joined Bodo, but he wouldn't hear of her paying.

'It is very good to meet you. We enjoy to be with you. Maybe you come to our circus?'

'Maybe,' Alice said. 'Will George be there?'

'George, yes, of course.'

There was no way she would go to a circus. As they got back to their table, Natasha was laughing. Johnny was staring at her as if he'd never seen anyone like her before.

'The Russians, they are mad,' Bodo told her.

'They're Russian?' Alice said, surprised.

'Yes, of course.'

'Oh Alice, really, you didn't think they were speaking German?' Peter said bitchily.

'I didn't hear them,' Alice snapped.

Peter looked at Bodo strangely. 'I'm sure I've seen you before,' he said.

'Maybe you see me perform?'

Peter shook his head.

A waiter brought their drinks over – beers for everyone except Zoya. Johnny asked for some extra cups in German. Alice didn't know why he'd done that but she was impressed that he was able to: he'd only been here a few weeks. The waiter frowned sullenly but nodded and went to get some. Alice took a gulpful of beer. It was good.

'Radeberger,' Bodo said. 'It is good DDR beer.'

They all nodded in agreement – except for Peter who said it made him feel like he'd been hit over the head. Alice hoped he'd drink more.

'Was machst du dann in Berlin?' Alice asked Natasha.

Natasha looked at her out of big, dark, smiling eyes and launched into a long explanation of, presumably, what she was doing. She frequently indicated Zoya, who Alice understood to be her sister. Alice nodded, pretending to understand.

'They are the famous Sisters Barovskova!' Bodo declared helpfully.

'What did she say?' Johnny asked Peter, smiling at Natasha.

'Ask Alice,' Peter said.

Alice looked at him, frowning slightly. He was being a pain in the ass. Fortunately, Bodo stepped in again.

'They are on exchange programme from the Soviet Union for one year. They are from the great Moscow State Circus. They learn how to walk the wire.'

'Who teaches them?' Johnny asked.

'The Professor, the clown today. He is the best high wire walker in the world.'

Johnny looked at them thoughtfully. Alice guessed what was coming next.

'Do you think I could learn with him?'

Bodo laughed. 'Of course not.'

'Why not?' Johnny asked.

Natasha also stared at Bodo.

Bodo sighed. 'You have experience?'

'Yes,' Johnny said, challenging.

'How long?'

'I practised for about ten years.'

'Not enough.'

Natasha began a discussion with Bodo, nodding her head furiously. Bodo turned his determinedly from left to right. Zoya, the more serious of the two, sipped her milk shake, or whatever it was, ignoring everyone. She looked about twelve.

Bodo lowered his voice. 'You could perhaps apply for visa to study. Have you ever been in trouble with the police?'

'Yes,' Johnny said. 'Once.'

'Then you don't get visa. We ask the Professor. But you understand, it is forbidden and you must tell no one.'

Peter rolled his eyes and told them that they were crazy. Natasha looked triumphant.

'It will cost you a fortune,' Alice said. 'You will have to pay twenty-five Marks every time you come across. What did you get arrested for?'

Johnny shrugged and said it was nothing much. His mother had been dying, they had no money and, while he was juggling in Convent Gardens a man had walked past with a wallet hanging out of his pocket. Alice nodded sympathetically: she had done far worse.

The waiter reappeared and they all fell silent. He slammed some white coffee cups down on the table in front of Johnny. As soon as the waiter had gone, Natasha took one of the tiny squares of paper napkins which had arrived with the drinks and scribbled something down while Johnny took an eastern Mark coin out of his pocket and showed it to Zoya. Natasha slipped the paper under the table, past her knee to Johnny. Alice didn't see it again but she saw the meaningful look Natasha gave him.

'How often do you train?' Alice asked Bodo.

'Train?' Bodo looked alarmed. 'Now?'

'No, I mean how often do you practise? Rehearse. You know high wire?'

'Ah, practise. Everyday,' Bodo replied, looking relieved. 'We practise for six hours or more.'

Johnny put the coin under the cup and shuffled them around. Without speaking, he indicated to Zoya that she should guess where the Mark was. Her dark eyes spun round the table as they followed the hidden coin. She pointed to the one on Johnny's right. He lifted it up but it wasn't there. Zoya looked horrified and burst into a torrent of Russian. Natasha burst out laughing. The waiter looked over disapprovingly.

Johnny moved the cups slightly towards Natasha and glanced across at her with bursting blue eyes. Alice began to feel sick. Her only consolation was that Peter seemed to have cottoned on as well, and he was looking even sicker. Johnny shuffled the cups forever and Natasha and her sister followed them. So much for him not wanting to get involved with anyone. What bollocks. Everyone wants someone to love. And, preferably, to be loved in return.

'This one,' Zoya said excitedly in English. Johnny looked at her in surprise.

'No, this one,' Natasha said to Johnny.

'You do speak English,' he muttered.

'No, a little. We learn in the school.' She spoke in a thick Russian accent, the 'L's sounding like they'd been drowned in oil.

Natasha chose the correct cup. Zoya shrieked again in horror.

'Anyone want another beer?' Peter said.

'I want orange,' Natasha slurped.

Peter organised more drinks – except there was no orange. Johnny leaned over and promised he would bring some oranges when he came.

Natasha beamed like a kid who had just been promised a new bike.

Alice felt her face slide into a sulk.

Bodo pulled out a small book from his jacket and offered it to her. Alice saw the picture of Lenin on the front and was about to look through it.

'It is for you,' he said. 'Keep it away.' He pointed to her pocket.

Confused, she did as she was told and thanked him. 'Does anyone want to go the theatre?' she asked, changing the subject.

The circus people conferred and shook their heads. Bodo had become nervous. Two men were standing at the bar, watching them. Natasha's birdlike head swivelled behind her to look at them. Her gaze rested there for a moment, before pinging back. The beers arrived and they all clinked glasses and drank:

'To the greatness of the Soviet Union and the friendship between the Soviet Union and the DDR,' Natasha said, grinning happily.

'To the workers of the world!' Bodo said.

'Workers and circuses of the world unite!' Johnny said.

'Communism rules,' Alice said loudly.

'Oh, Mad, really, that's stupid,' Peter growled.

The others looked at her, slightly surprised, but they continued with their slogans.

'To our great socialist life!' Natasha said.

Natasha, Zoya and Bodo finished their drinks, said goodbye, and stood up.

'We must go now,' Bodo said quietly. 'We see you at the circus? It is a beautiful pleasure to meet you.'

He looked at Alice as he said this. Alice looked at Johnny who was looking longingly at Natasha. She resisted the urge to pull Natasha's greasy hair and forced a smile as Bodo waved to her, his forearm swishing like a windscreen wiper.

Then they disappeared as if someone had put a top hat on top of them.

'Well?' Peter exploded, looking expectantly at Johnny. 'What the fuck's going on, Johnny darling?'

But Johnny darling was looking towards the bar where one of the two men had also put down his glass and left. The other one looked like he had eyes in his back. Alice lit a cigarette. The smoke silenced her laughing butterflies. Peter's tightened fist looked ready to punch Johnny. A scene in East Berlin. Excellent.

'You know, I've just realised what I want to do in my life,' Johnny said, finally acknowledging him. He smiled a childish grin, looking from Alice to Peter, defusing Peter's fist. 'What a fantastic place! I'm so glad we came. Thanks guys. Who's for another beer?'

'No, thanks. East German beer gives me a fucking hangover. So what are you going to do, darling?' Peter asked.

'I'm going to be a funambulist!' Johnny declared.

'A fun what?' she asked, hope edging her forward towards him. No doubt Peter would say she was being stupid again but, this time, he didn't say anything.

'A tightrope walker,' Johnny said.

The rest of Peter's fury spilled over into a frown.

Alice leant back and put out her cigarette, disappointed. She'd known that anyway.

'So what now?' Peter asked, deflated.

'Let's get really pissed,' Alice said.

Tierpark

Johnny sprang from his mattress early on Thursday morning after a twelve-hour sleep. He felt good, better than he'd felt for a long time. Today was the day he would begin his new life. As from today, he was going to learn to dance in the air. Yesterday had not been a good day and he'd performed like a wild elephant at rehearsals with Sophie and Benjamin. 'Hey, Johnny, what's wrong with you?' Sophie yelled at him. He couldn't be bothered to explain that he felt dragged down by gravity. Besides, it was more likely the hangover and the fact that he hadn't got home until six in the morning, thanks to Alice and Peter insisting on celebrating their return to the West – after having only just made it to the Checkpoint on time. He'd only had a couple of hours sleep and a part of him had been left behind on the other side of the Wall. He found it hard to concentrate. He couldn't wait to see her again.

He headed for the bathroom, hoping he wouldn't bump into Peter, who'd told him to move out. Johnny had returned from the rehearsal yesterday afternoon, exhausted, to be met by Peter coming out of his bedroom, open armed and naked. It looked like he had only just got home, which was possible as he had left Peter and Alice drinking sambuca with Hassan, the Lebanese owner of the club. Who knows what they'd got up to afterwards. Even while he was there, Peter reckoned Alice had been shagging Hassan in the bottle store. But Peter was a one to talk.

'Come to me, Johnny,' he had said in his husky voice. Johnny liked the fact that Berliners were not inhibited by nakedness but Peter had a habit of hugging him with an erection. Another man growled in German from inside Peter's bedroom, but Peter followed him into the lounge and opened a Beck's with his lighter while Johnny drank his coffee as Peter's erection waved at him unsteadily. Not that Peter seemed to realise.

'Darling, I don't understand why you won't sleep with me?' he whined.

'Peter, it sounds like you've already got one man in your bed.'

'What man?'

His eyes searched the room, a comic gesture that Johnny didn't find particularly amusing. He was too tired for this.

'If you go back to your room, you'll know who I mean,' Johnny said.

'Well, anyhows darling, I want you.'

'Peter. I've just done a three-hour rehearsal. And we were out dancing all night yesterday, remember?'

'Then come and relax with me, darling. Don't you want to?'

'No, Peter. I don't really want to have sex with you. I thought we understood that.'

Peter yelped like a kicked dog. 'Oh fuck you, Johnny, really.' He swigged his beer. 'I think you'd better go. I really do. Pack your bags, darling. Go back to Alice or to that dirty Russian girl. You Brits are full of shit.'

Johnny got up and stood before him. He felt himself shaking.

'Go! Go! Go!' Peter pointed the bottle towards the door, dribbling beer behind the sofa.

Johnny pushed him hard. Peter crumpled to the sofa like a rotten tree, a look of surprise crossing his face. His beer bottle rolled across the floor. He burped and said, 'thank-you, darling.'

Johnny walked towards the door. Peter was out of his head. He shouldn't have pushed him. They needed to talk this through another time – after all, he was happy to pay rent when he got some money. Hassan had offered him work in a nightclub. He turned back to Peter to suggest this but his eyes had already closed, his mouth slowly opening and a noise like a disgruntled sow tripped over his tonsils.

As Johnny went back to his room he heard more snoring from Peter's. The door was ajar. He peered in. There, lying naked on his back, was Hassan. His chunky, short body rose and fell like a blown up paper bag. Beside the bed was a pile of clothes and, on top, a leather wallet. He bent down, opened it and stared. There was a wad of one hundred Mark notes. He hesitated for half a second. Then he took three.

Johnny had gone to bed and slept through until eight o'clock this morning. As he walked towards the bathroom, the toilet flushed. Johnny stopped: he really didn't want a scene with Peter now. But it was Michael, the guy who had put in the central heating, coming out of the bathroom, a towel wrapped round his waist. He smiled at Johnny.

'Morgen,' Michael said. 'Wie geht's?'

'Sehr gut.'

Michael was the only one in the house with a day job so Johnny hadn't seen much of him as Michael was usually up and out before even he was.

Johnny showered. He didn't need to shave; his face looked like a lollipop as Carla used to say. He wondered how she was getting on.

Life with her seemed a long time ago, even though he'd only been in West Berlin just over a month. He was about to shave the sides of his head, but remembered that he should dress conservatively. He didn't want to be turned away, so he trimmed his Mohican and removed his earrings.

By the time Johnny made it to the kitchen, Michael had already cleared up and left. There was some coffee left in the pot which Johnny poured for himself and he sat at the table in the lounge and ate some black bread and ham. Hermann sat on the floor playing with a mirror of speed or something. He had been there for weeks. Johnny didn't speak to him. The guy was wasted.

A red clock with a smiling sun face ticked on the wall. It was ten past eight. He picked up a flyer from SO36 and wrote on the back of it: *Peter, I am going to be out for the rest of the day but here is 100 DM towards bills. I would like to stay for a while longer. Let me know how you feel about this. Johnny.* He then took out one of the three notes, found a used envelope, enclosed the letter and the money, scribbled Peter's name on the front and slipped it under Peter's door. He stood there for a second but couldn't hear anything. It was way too early for Peter. He may still even be out.

Johnny checked his wallet for the coarse Eastern paper napkin on which she had written the time and place and picked up his small rucksack with his dance stuff. He checked the contents: his dictionary would come in useful, as would his small notebook and pen. He flew down the stairs, five at a time, and jogged through the freezing February streets to the U-Bahn, stopping only to buy some oranges for her on the way. He slipped one into his jacket pocket to eat on the train as he waited on the platform of Line 7. He would then need to change trains at Mehringdamm onto Line 6 to Friedrichstraße in the East.

As he passed the ghost stations of Stadtmitte and Französische Straße, the old gothic font danced along the tunnel in the dark. He passed this way every time he went to rehearsals in Wedding but he was still amazed by the gagged and bound stations, patrolled by armed border guards and silent Alsatians. Sometimes even the single electric bulb was off, leaving behind only shadows. He tried to imagine what it would be like to be a guard walking up and down the dark platform. Or up in one of those watchtowers for that matter. To have to shoot people for trying to cross a walled-up street. No doubt they believed they were doing a good job; protecting the East from the corruption of Western capitalism. If he had been brought up in that world then maybe he would too. He couldn't imagine it though. To have to shoot another human being would be a crime. Thank God they didn't have conscription in the UK. At least, here, the West Germans could come to Berlin instead of the army. That wasn't the case in the East though. He waved at the guard in the shadows at the end of the platform. The guard didn't wave back but his eyes followed him as the train disappeared into the black tunnel.

He hit chaos amidst the beer and vodka bottles in Friedrichstraße. Johnny tried to find his way to the DDR but he discovered only mirrors and blocked exits, drunks, guards, police and escalators. There were signs everywhere: **Kein Ausgang, S-Bahn – Wannsee, Verboten! U-Bahn Alt-Mariendorf, S-Bahn – Warsaw.** *Warsaw?* He breathed deeply as he went up another set of escalators but found only an underground S-Bahn platform with an Intershop in the middle.

'Excuse me, how do I get to East Berlin?' he asked the man in the Intershop in German. The elderly man's face was deeply lined as if he had been slashed with a razor, but his blue eyes were ice cold.

'The capital of the DDR is straight ahead, turn right, left, up the escalator and you will see Passkontrolle.'

Johnny followed the man's directions and finally hit the many queues heading towards steel booths with swing doors like execution stalls for animals. Slanted mirrors around the tops of the booths ensured that the controllers could see every part of everyone passing through. There was one long queue full of old Berliners pushing bags bigger than themselves. One woman gripped a coat stand twice her size. Guards were everywhere and loudspeakers crackled out indecipherable words. He asked where he should go.

'Processing queue over there,' he was told abruptly, and pointed towards the Ausländer queue, although that, too, was full of Germans. It was already eleven. She would be waiting now. The door on the booth flapped open and shut as people disappeared into them.

It was his turn. He wasn't feeling so good now. His heart hammered against his chest as the door slammed behind him. A pair of grey eyes burrowed into him. This was worse than Checkpoint Charlie.

'Passport!'

Johnny handed him his black British passport.

'Do you have books or magazines with you?'

Johnny shook his head. He was ordered into a cubicle anyway.

An officer searched his rucksack. Johnny tried to read his face as he rummaged through his dance tights but the man's expression was stone grey. He pulled out his dictionary.

'What is this?'

'A dictionary,' Johnny replied.

'A dictionary is a book. It is forbidden.'

Johnny didn't reply. There didn't seem much point. Then the officer pulled out his notebook. The oranges wouldn't stand a chance.

'What is this?'

'A notebook.'

'What does it say?'

'Read it,' said Johnny calmly.

The man stared at several pages and then rummaged further. His eyes shone as he pulled out the oranges.

'They are oranges,' Johnny said.

'I know what they are. They are forbidden.'

He disappeared with the oranges, his dictionary and notebook. Johnny waited and waited. He realised that he wouldn't be able to do this every week. It was quarter to twelve – he was forty-five minutes late. His new life was going to be challenging. The officer came back - with his dictionary and notebook. Only the oranges had been confiscated.

'Next time, you do not bring,' he said.

Johnny shook his head slightly. His passport was then scrutinised and stamped before he was allowed to exchange his twenty-five Deutsch Marks and waved away.

When he emerged into the Palace of Tears, she wasn't there. He was almost an hour late. His heart fell out of his chest and bounced along the station tiles. He stood motionless in the bustling station, wondering what to do. He pulled out a cigarette, lit it and took several deep drags.

She had probably been here, waited an hour, given up and left. Or, maybe she had never had any intention of meeting him. But why think that? She wouldn't have given him the note telling him that she wanted to see him if she didn't. It was just possible that she had also been held up. He decided to wait half an hour.

He had only just put out his cigarette when a man wearing glasses, dressed in a dark overcoat with ripped sleeves and a long, grey scarf, a woollen hat, sidled up to him, reading a paper. The man rattled his paper, cleared his throat, half turned towards him and spoke without moving his lips.

'Hallo Johnny. Act you do not know me and follow.'

It was Bodo. Johnny followed him through the crowds, turning left and right and left again, into a large store, pausing to look at some newly arrived socks. Next it was the museums. He flew round the Egyptian section of the Pergamon, clearly intrigued by the murals of gods and goddesses.

Johnny was too busy pretending not to know the person he was following to look at anything. Surely he wasn't doing this for fun? Did he think they were being watched? Johnny looked at his watch. It was almost two o'clock; he would never get to see Natasha at this rate. Johnny crept around the mummies and, finally, back out onto the street.

Bodo walked slowly now. Johnny followed him at a distance to the underground station at Alexanderplatz and scooped up a ticket which Bodo dropped. They sat in the same carriage, but at opposite ends of a faded, cranky Eastern U-Bahn. The other passengers eyed him suspiciously. There was something that separated him from these people. He knew it and they knew it.

They got off at the end of the line at Tierpark and boarded a half empty bus outside the station. Bodo sat down, pulled out his paper and began to read again, ignoring him. Johnny sat down a couple of seats behind and stared out of the window. There was a park of sorts nearby but the trees and the grass were grey. Blocks of prefabricated apartments loomed in the distance. Wherever it was they were going, he knew it was forbidden.

The bus bounced and whined over cobbled roads lined with trees, heading further and further away from the city. The road was empty except for an occasional Trabant and soon fields replaced the dilapidated suburban houses. An old plough lay abandoned in an unploughed field. There was no one in sight. They passed several silent villages. They, too, seemed abandoned, but in each one someone got off the bus and disappeared down a ramshackle street. Deserted barns and warehouses with broken windows hunched over the village squares like monstrous vultures. Every so often a curtain twitched. This was weird. Johnny tapped his fingers on the scratched glass of the bus as doubt crept in. How was he going to find his way back? How could he love someone who lived in a world governed by fear, in which you lived in disguise? Peter had warned him. He shouldn't have come. But then he thought of walking above the world and being with her, and his body burned.

The bus came to a final shudder in another seemingly deserted village and the driver switched off the engine. Bodo jumped off and had already disappeared from view by the time Johnny was in the square. He followed the click of Bodo's footsteps down one of the three cobbled roads leading to the centre of the village where there was an old hand pump and a concrete bench. Several houses slumped around, most were closed up. Just as he thought he was entirely alone, an old woman opened a door and called out. 'Shibby!' she screeched. A black cat replied and shot out across the road. The woman didn't even look at him.

Johnny continued out of the village, past some wooden houses with rickety verandas. Where the hell was he going? The cobbled road became a track. As he passed the last building, he spotted Bodo bouncing across the fields towards a large collection of barns, trucks and, for a second, a red cupola poked the grey clouds before disappearing again. There was a solid wooden fence all the way around.

A lion roared and Johnny almost laughed. The circus was in the middle of nowhere. He walked faster, shaking his head, his heart pounding. Bodo waited by a wooden gate.

'Welcome Johnny. I don't think you come. You are late. We miss the bus. That is why we must go to the museum.' He'd removed his glasses and his brilliant blue eyes scanned the fields behind them.

He was about to apologise and explain when Bodo held up his hand.

'*Nein,* I know. But now we must train.'

Johnny crossed the yard with him, past a farmhouse, towards a huge barn. In a paddock to the left, several people were clambering over the Big Top. Large circus trucks lined one side of the fence and several caravans were parked up nearby. They looked lived in, as did the old farmhouse. Grubby kids and dogs jumped over a puddle until someone shouted at them. A man was pointing an arrow at a young boy holding up a gold watch.

'Do you think we were followed?'

'*Na ja,* it is possible,' Bodo said, leading the way into the barn. 'One third of people is spy.'

Great, Johnny thought. They entered a small door which led to a space the size of two tennis courts and as high as a three storey building. Directly in front of him was a warm-up area and weights. To the left was all the aerial equipment. Spotlights shone from the rigging in the roof onto the girl he had fallen in love with.

She was holding balletic positions on a tightrope, which was about five metres in the air and spanned the width of the warehouse. She was concentrating on what the Professor was saying as she slowly slid her legs into a deep split along the wire, her arms held out gracefully.

'Gut, gut,' the Professor said, before she saw him, burst into a fit of laughter and fell from the rope.

A safety line left her dangling in the air like a beautiful spider spinning in vain to reach the other side. Johnny wanted to rush to her and sweep her up in his arms but Bodo was measuring his feet. It appeared they were the same size which meant he could borrow a pair of his shoes. Johnny thanked him as he watched her being lowered. She smiled at him, but the Professor was shouting at her, telling her to do it again. She shimmied up a vertical ladder to the top of the perch and stepped onto the wire as if she was walking on the top of a brick wall. Her dark hair was pulled up into a ponytail and, like everyone else, she wore old tights over a leotard. She was even more beautiful than he remembered. This time she reached the middle of the wire and slid her right leg forward, sitting on her crouched left leg. She lay backwards and let her right leg dangle in the air as the Professor clapped excitedly. She reversed her actions, stood up once more and walked to the other side, where her sister was waiting on the other perch. Everyone clapped, even the shadows in the roof adjusting the rigging.

Johnny slipped his jeans off and his sweatpants on and changed T-shirts, aware that Natasha was blatantly watching him. Bodo handed him some shoes. His heart pounded at the thought he was going to train with these people. He breathed deeply and began to stretch. His muscles had been tightened by the East. Bodo went to speak to the Professor.

Johnny's mouth felt dry. He hadn't really walked on a rope since he was fifteen. One summer, when he was about six years old, his mother had helped him string a rope between the chestnut tree and the metal railings at the back of their East End garden – at the dizzying height of three foot. He fell off it every day for months. Then one day he could walk along it. Just like that. Every day he'd practised for years and had even started juggling balls while standing on it. He couldn't remember why he had given it up. Perhaps he had moved on to 'the awkward age' as his mother used to say.

'The Professor thinks you good at walking. You have experience, *ja*? The balance and strong is good.'

He had been watching him then. Johnny raised his eyebrows at the Professor who nodded. He didn't tell him that it had been almost eight years since he had last walked a rope in the garden.

'*Na ja, gut.* Today we walk the wire.'

More words were exchanged between Bodo and the Professor and then the Professor went over to a trapeze to watch the sisters, who were already upside down on hoops which hung from the rigging.

Bodo handed Johnny a balancing pole.

'Find the centre,' he said. He drew a white line on the floor with chalk.

Johnny jounced the pole, moving it through his fingers, feeling its weight, its shape. It was about two metres long and felt like it weighed about ten kilos. He had never used a pole before, only his arms. He soon found the centre.

'*Gut,*' Bodo said. 'Now walk along this line, one step each. *Wie heißt es?* Foot fingers first.' Bodo wriggled his toes.

Johnny smiled. 'Toes.'

'Toes. Imagine you are in air. Feel you have a rope from your head.'

Johnny did as he was told and walked slowly along the line. It was easy. He didn't falter once. Bodo then dragged out a large object about two metres long and a meter high from a cupboard and laid it on the floor. There was a fine ridge on top about an inch wide and carved in the shape of the wire. What an ingenious way to learn, Johnny thought; much less painful than his rope in the garden.

'Okay, you train here. When you can do this, you can do the train rope over there. Now I go to train.'

Bodo disappeared up to the high wire, leaving Johnny with the block of wood. He took a step forward and promptly toppled off. He tried again, remembering to feel the centre of the balancing pole and to stand tall. He imagined an invisible thread suspended from the roof to the top of his head. His feet curved around the wood and he gripped the rope between his toes in the soft shoes. As a child, he had walked barefoot. He looked straight ahead and walked to the other side. And back. Easy. It was like riding a bike. He wished he had never stopped practising.

'Super!' Bodo called down. 'Now go on the train rope.'

There was a short, tightly entwined rope, like a wire, about a foot off the ground and a couple of metres in length. Johnny slid his right foot onto the rope, expecting to sink down like he used to when he first stepped onto the rope from his base in the tree, but it was taut, strong, strangely solid.

He practised for about an hour before the Professor walked around him and shouted something to Bodo. The Professor disappeared without saying anything to Johnny while Bodo came over.

'Okay, follow me.'

Bodo grabbed his balancing pole and led him to the high wire where Natasha had been training. It was rigged to each side of the wall, which meant that it was about ten metres long and five metres high. Surely they weren't expecting him to walk across that?

'Bodo, don't you think I should try something a little shorter first?' he said, as Bodo made him stand in some chalk by the foot of the ladder.

'*Ja*, of course,' he said. 'But the Professor tell me to do this.'

'I see,' Johnny said. 'He must want to build up my confidence.'

Bodo hunched his shoulders. 'Probably you never want to walk a wire again.'

'That's quite possible,' Johnny muttered, as they climbed up and up the ladder. It was one way of assuring he would never come back.

Bodo reached the perch first and checked the tension on the wire. 'But don't worry, we attach you the safety line.'

A metal line came down and Bodo put a harness on him and attached the safety line. Johnny took a deep breath.

'Okay, do what you did before. Remember toes first, find your centre.'

Johnny stood two storeys high, staring into empty space, and weighed the balancing pole in his arms until it felt comfortable. Then he stepped onto the wire rope like a fish returning to water. The wire quivered slightly beneath the soles of his feet as he slipped forward.

'Super,' Bodo said from down below.

To Johnny, it felt like a miracle. Each step he took discovered a forgotten world. He remembered how it felt to walk on air. His feet slid along the rope, the pole balancing him perfectly. He felt as if he could walk for miles. He stopped in the middle. Bodo called up encouraging comments but he hardly heard them. He had stopped because he wanted to be suspended in space and feel the wire shivering beneath his feet. He absorbed the vibrations and continued, reaching the other side almost in a trance, only half aware of the applause from above and below. He looked down. Everyone had stopped to watch him. Even the Professor clapped.

Natasha fidgeted on the perch, waiting for him on the other side. As soon as he reached her she flung her small arms around his neck and kissed him on the lips. Johnny tasted flavours he had never tasted before. He wrapped his arms around her and pulled her towards him and held her, ignoring the shouts of congratulations from below.

'Walk with me!' she demanded. She shouted something down to the others.

'*Nein,*' Bodo said.

The Professor didn't say anything. Neither did Johnny.

'I stand on you!'

Bodo and Natasha started shouting at each other, but the next thing Johnny knew, a harness came down and Natasha quickly fastened herself. She stood on the edge of the perch and clambered up him like a cat. Her strong toes gripped his shoulders as she stood up. Johnny rebalanced the pole, his centre of gravity now extended. The Professor gave a slight nod. Bodo looked furious.

'Okay, don't move,' Johnny said.

'I don't,' she said.

Johnny gripped the wire with his toes as he stepped forward. Once he'd readjusted his centre to include her weight, he felt her as part of him and he walked to the other side with ease.

Jubilant faces looked up at them as he stepped onto the perch and then they began to all talk at once. Natasha slipped off him and kissed him again.

'Not bad,' she said, 'for beginner.'

He held her in his arms. He had no idea what they were saying down below, but he decided that he would do anything for these people. In one day, they had shown him his direction in life, something that had been staring at him for years but which he had not seen. A dance in the sky, a dance that flew above dance.

'You perform with us,' Natasha said.

It wasn't a question. He looked at Bodo and the Professor. They all nodded.

'Isn't it *verboten*?' Johnny asked.

They all burst into shrieks of laughter, even the Professor.

'Of course,' Natasha said.

'I don't want to get you into trouble.'

'We used to keeping secrets,' Bodo said. 'The Professor says you come again not tomorrow – next day. Saturday. You come early this time. There is a bus from Tierpark at 11.30. The one after is 2.30.'

He had promised to meet Alice on Saturday but she would understand. She might not even remember. She had been very pissed when she had made him promise.

'Okay, thanks. How do I get back?' It was already seven o'clock.

81

'It is dark now. I take you to Tierpark,' Bodo said. 'Then you get the U-Bahn. Where do you live?'

'Near Hermannplatz.'

Bodo raised an eyebrow. For a second Johnny recalled the clown opposite the Wall and was going to ask Bodo if he knew anything about it but Bodo was asking him if that was okay.

Johnny nodded. Natasha stared at him.

'First you must shower. I show you.' She turned to go, expecting Johnny to follow her but the Professor shouted something and she returned, sulkily. Johnny had to leave her under the watchful eye of the Professor.

'How is Alice?' Bodo asked as he led him towards the shower block.

'She's fine,' Johnny said.

'She is very beautiful.'

'Yes, she is.'

'She is model and actress.'

Johnny had serious doubts about Alice's modelling and acting credentials so he didn't reply. Bodo seemed deep in thought anyway.

Johnny showered quickly, leaving Bodo as he went to find Natasha, who was waiting in the dark with her arms folded. Steam poured out the open door with him. They clamped together like magnets.

'I think I'm in love with you,' Johnny said, stroking her dark hair.

She looked questioningly up at him out of her big black eyes.

'Only think?' she said, and smiled.

She pulled him back into the night and they kissed. For the first time that day, he felt as though he was falling. As he tumbled into the welcoming darkness, he thought how strange it was that only a few days ago he had been so determined not to get involved with anyone, and yet here he was, deeply involved. But he knew she was so much more than just anyone; she already felt like an inextricable part of his life. He had never felt so sure about anything before.

'You bring me oranges?' she asked.

Johnny blinked into consciousness and shook his head. 'They were confiscated, taken by Passkontrollers.'

Her face fell and Johnny kissed it until she smiled again.

'It no matter,' she said.

He closed his eyes and they rocked gently in the dark. Something roared behind them. Johnny wasn't sure if it was bad feedback on an amplifier, or a tiger. He wasn't too bothered as nothing could touch him now. He opened his eyes and found himself blinking at a lioness with hungry yellow eyes gazing at him.

'Only Jessie,' Natasha said, looking round.

Jessie stared at them both. Her eyes burned into the night, intelligent and full of sadness.

'You have something for her?' Natasha whispered. 'So she not eat us.'

Johnny thrust his hands into his pockets and found the orange he had forgotten to eat earlier. He was about to sacrifice it to the lion when a loud voice boomed out from the darkness. Jessie turned round to look at her keeper, who was holding out meat on the end of a short pole.

'No, but look what I've found for you,' Johnny whispered, holding up the orange.

Natasha's eyes shone as brightly as the lioness'.

Siegessäule

Alice sang Pink Floyd songs as she struggled to get the key into the chunky wooden door that separated her flat from Sonnenallee. It was normally open. She was back too early; the sky was only just dawning grey. She looked at the key – six inches long, and fat. The keyhole a skeleton in comparison. She bent down and aimed the key at the hole.

'We don't need ... Oh shit!'

She was about to buzz someone but then heard footsteps from the other side. A young woman, about Alice's age, dressed in a long, immaculate pink coat, grey hat and leather gloves, rattled the door open and poked a pram out. Alice stopped singing, looked quizzically at her key and smiled at the woman, trying not to breathe tequila over her. The woman didn't smile back.

'Fuck off then,' Alice muttered as she walked past the bins across the courtyard to the back of the house, the *Hinterhof*. No sense of humour. Then again she doubted she would be smiling if she had to take a baby out at seven o'clock on a Sunday morning. They paid you to have kids in Berlin. It was a trick, of course, but many young people fell for it. Idiots.

Alice opened her door and retreated into her apartment. For once, she was glad to be back and on her own. She checked her wallet: one hundred and forty Marks. A good night. And no Peter or Hassan. Monday had been a great night after the East but she didn't want to repeat it. Hassan was nice enough and had got her a job in the club but he was so sleazy.

The other night – or morning – Hassan decided they were going for a ride in his new Range Rover. As he circled Ernst-Reuter-Platz and then down Straße des 17. Juni, he kept saying, *Alice, du bist so schön...* Alice had laughed and pointed to the sun and the city bursting with colour as people went to work or out shopping; living normal lives. Poking out of the white skeletal trees was the Siegessäule, a gold-winged woman perched on a column, gripping a large ring, or crown, in one hand, and a spear in the other. Her gold dress billowed victoriously in the wind. Beneath her feet, on a viewing platform, people, as small and insignificant as mites, peered over the city. Alice remembered wishing she had her spear as Hassan leant over and touched her leg. *Alice, du bist so schön...* She shouted at him and slapped his short thick fingers. Hassan was about half her height, with a square ugly face and a mole the size of a Pfennig on his cheek, and he had piercing black eyes that had a life all of their own.

'I feel sick,' Peter had said, rolling around in the back.

Hassan pulled over and Peter got out and threw up. Then they had walked though the frozen park, arms linked, laughing, smoking and drinking something Peter had found in the back of the car. Cyclists rang their bells and dogs ran around them. They sat on a bench and watched the water lapping at the frozen banks of the lake. The cold February Berlin air smelled of ashes from the lignite coal bricks that burned in the stoves throughout the city. A lone Imbiss van stood waiting and they ate *Pommes mit Mayo* on a polystyrene plate. Hassan had put his arm around Peter and said: *Peter, du bist so schön...*

She couldn't remember what happened after that.

She went into the kitchen to make a cup of tea. What a mess. She opened the fridge and grabbed the milk carton. She stuck her nose in it. It might be all right. She lit the gas stove and put the saucepan on. Then she flopped into the armchair in the living room. It was dark, only a chink of light bothered to push its way through the crack in the shutters. She thought about opening them wider but it didn't seem worth it.

She let out a deep sigh and inhaled the tequila-scented air. Johnny, Johnny, Johnny. Bastard. He never came round yesterday. He had promised he would come on Saturday and she had waited in all day. They'd had such a great time on Tuesday – once they'd left that smelly Russian tart in the East. He'd swung her round in the streets and they'd laughed together and danced, just like they did when he first came. She could dance, too, she was going to dance classes – she would learn.

Alice stood up and stretched her arms up in front of a narrow and cracked mirror on the side of the high bed. Then she touched her toes and lifted her left leg up with her left hand. Look, she wasn't bad. She could almost do the splits. She just needed to get a bit fitter. She collapsed into the chair again as tears nudged her eyelids. Fuck him.

She pulled out a notebook and began to doodle.

She wished she had wings like the golden woman in the park, then she could fly away. Fly over that bloody Wall and get out of Berlin: that's what she wanted. People had no idea what it was like to live in a city surrounded by a Wall, barbed wire, mines and soldiers with grey faces and guns. To live on an island while a grey war lapped around them. Why else would a government have to pay women to have children? Or encourage West German boys to come to West Berlin instead of serving time in the army?

They all felt free. But they weren't. They were being watched. Always.

Imagine having to live with the knowledge that a city had been cut in half and one half of the population brought up on caviar, champagne and a choice of designer brand clothes, and the other half on potatoes, cabbage, vodka and coarse socks. Imagine being a guinea pig in one of the biggest human social experiments. Half a world here and half a world there. And there was nothing you could do about it.

That's what her play was about. A couple separated by the State, which has sliced up their country to experiment on their people. The couple are forbidden to meet. But they do – in secret, in disguise, until eventually they are caught and measures are taken to ensure that they can never meet again. Twenty years later the State collapses and the countries meet again. So do the couple. Do they still love each other? Do they still even know each other? Can the two worlds ever become one again?

The water bubbled loudly. Alice put down her notebook and plodded to the kitchen to make her tea. Maybe she should leave Berlin, it wasn't a healthy place to be for long. When it was good, it was the best. It was the only place in Europe where American civilians could live, and it was particularly easy for French and British civilians; it was a haven for artists, pacifists, writers and anyone else who dreamed of changing the world.

But when it was bad, it was like being in prison.

Alice drank tea and scribbled in her notebook for hours. It made her feel better, but she still couldn't fill that hole inside her. She looked at Lenin on the cover of the book the juggler had given her. It was a strong image but he looked somehow empty as well. She tried to imagine having a conversation with Lenin. He was an extraordinary man. What were his last thoughts before he died?

'So, Vladimir, after indirectly killing off twenty million people, do you think you've changed the world for the better?'

'Come with me,' he says. He leads her into a yard and shows her broken buckets of giant tomato plants bursting with tomatoes. 'You see. See how healthy they are. And all the same size and shape.'

'Yes, Vladimir, but did you have a right to change the world?'

He breaks one off and hands it to her. 'You tell me,' he says.

Then he hobbles back into his dacha.

She smiled. She had drawn a tomato on the inside cover. She looked at the note Bodo had pressed inside Lenin: *Can I see you again?* Yes, come round for tea tomorrow, Bodo. She doubted she would ever see him again. There was something in the cultural programming between East and West that was more insurmountable than the Wall.

She wasn't sure how her play would end but she reckoned it would take generations to erase the cultural differences. The State had won. The chances of two people loving each other from such different worlds were a million to one – which was why she really shouldn't worry about that little Russian knot in her empty stomach.

Someone knocked at the door and she got up to answer it. It was probably the landlady again, wanting the rent money. She inched the door open and the hole in her stomach swallowed her legs.

It was Johnny.

'Hi Alice, I didn't think you'd be up. Well? Are you going to invite me in?'

Her hand fell loosely from the door.

'I thought you were coming yesterday,' she said at last.

'I'm sorry, I was over in the East training again. I didn't have a chance to tell you.'

'Oh, how was it?' she asked, turning her back on him. She heard the door close behind them.

'It was fantastic.'

'That's good,' she said. The knot tightened.

She went into the kitchen and turned to look at him. His hair was black and his Mohican was growing out. He looked somehow more radiant, confident, happy, healthy.

'Do you want vodka or beer?' she said.

'A coffee would be great. Hey, I'm really sorry.'

She shrugged. 'No problem. Do you take sugar?'

'It wasn't that long ago I was here, was it?' Johnny said, and smiled. 'Please.'

He was just so gorgeous. Alice sighed.

'Hey, are you all right? Have you been out drinking?'

She laughed. 'I'm fine. I've just been up for about twenty hours.'

'I don't how you do it, Alice.'

She shrugged and lit the stove. Johnny wandered into the dark living room.

'Can I open the shutters?' he shouted.

'Sure. Let me find my sunglasses.'

She heard him laugh and that made her feel better. Did that bendy girl make him laugh as well? She went into the toilet and cleaned her teeth and washed her face. She decided against lipstick. When she joined him in the living room he was sitting in her chair staring at her notebook. She snatched it from his hands.

'That's private, Johnny,' she said.

'Sorry, it was just lying here. I like the angel flying over the wall. It's very good.'

'I was just doodling. And it's not an angel, it's a woman with wings.'

'Well, it's a very good doodle. Can I have it?'

'Why?' Alice glowed for a moment.

'Because I think it's good.'

'Sure,' she said and ripped out the page.

He looked at it again for a long time.

'You should go to art college.'

'What for?' She fired the words like missiles.

'Well, one day, you know. I mean what do you want to do? You're not going to stay here forever are you.' It wasn't a question.

'Why not?'

'Because one day I think you'll have had enough. I mean you're not really doing much here are you?'

'I'm doing lots here,' she said.

'Are you? What?'

'I'm living,' she said.

'Yes, but I mean artistic. You need to do something creative and it seems to me that you are very talented. It's a shame to waste a talent. You don't wanna end up like whatsisname, Hermann, do you?'

'What's wrong with Hermann? His life is creative. My life is creative.' She turned her back on him and, taking the notebook with her, went to make the tea, wishing she hadn't said that. What a load of bollocks. But, really, how dare he? Who was he to say she wasn't doing anything here. She was learning German, studying theatre, writing, thinking. Besides, why did she have to be doing something?

She took two cups of coffee into the living room. Johnny sat, relaxed, hands behind the back of his head, one ankle resting on the other thigh, staring at the ceiling. No, she didn't want to touch him.

'Here you are.' She handed him the coffee. For a second their fingers met and the coffee slopped from side to side.

Johnny thanked her and took out a packet of Benson's and offered her one. They lit up.

'So did you hear what happened on Tuesday afternoon after you guys came back?' he asked.

'No,' she said. 'What?'

'Peter greeted me at the door, naked, and then when I turned down his amorous offers and pointed out he'd already got Hassan in his bed, he told me to move out.' Johnny swallowed a cumulus cloud of smoke.

'What did you do?' Alice said, trying not to gloat.

'I left him some money for bills and a note. I saw him yesterday evening when I got back. He didn't say anything about it but he was on his way out. Maybe I'll see him again later.'

'And if he wants you to move out where will you go?' He wasn't moving back in with her, that was for sure.

'I'll find somewhere.' He paused. 'So have you seen Tom?'

'Tom's history,' she snapped. 'I told you that.'

'Sorry, sometimes history repeats itself.' He gave her one of his half-mouth smiles.

'Not with me it doesn't.' She felt herself breathe staccato style. He suffocated her. She needed to change the subject. 'So, how's the circus?'

He began to tell her about crossing into the East at Friedrichstraße the first time, how they had almost confiscated his notebook and dictionary and how Bodo had met him in disguise and taken him on a tour of East Berlin before going to the circus training ground. But she wasn't really listening. He didn't mention *her* though – the rubber Russian girl. Maybe, just maybe, she'd misunderstood the look in their eyes.

'High wire?' she said, as if she had only just heard. 'You can walk on a tightrope – without having practised for years?'

It was like riding a bike, he said. She couldn't imagine how.

'Anyway, Alice, you look like you need to sleep. But you should come to the circus on Thursday. I have a surprise for you. Will you come?'

Alice shrugged. 'Is Peter going?'

'I mentioned it but he said he'd probably be working.'

Alice thought she might be doing the same. It was unlikely Johnny planned to make love to her on a trapeze.

'Bodo wants you too,' Johnny said. 'He asked me to tell you.'

'I see,' she said. 'You're here to ask me on behalf of someone else. Is that it?'

Johnny looked taken aback. 'Not only…'

'Not only?' Alice's voice trembled. Her anger surprised even herself.

'Calm down, Alice. I'm your friend, remember?' Johnny stood up. 'You should get some rest...'

'Don't tell me what to do.'

'Whatever Alice. Here's the address. I would love you to come - and so would Bodo - but it is up to you. Okay?' Johnny wrote something in the Lenin book next to the tomato.

She stood up, looked at him and chased a tear down her cheek with her hand.

'Hey, come here,' Johnny whispered.

She stepped into his arms and he cradled her and stroked her hair as if she were a child. 'I thought we were friends,' he told her ear. She nudged her head into his shoulder and closed her eyes. They stood there, swaying. Johnny kissed her cheek twice. She looked into his pale sky-blue eyes and the next thing she knew they were kissing, deeply, passionately and when they pulled themselves apart, she whispered, 'Johnny, Johnny...'

'I can't, Alice...'

'Come to bed with me, Johnny.'

She felt his resistance crumble.

When she woke he was gone. The shutters were still open and it was dark outside. She must have slept for a long time. She smiled at the ceiling and thanked it. She knew that whatever Johnny said or did no magician's hat could vanish the thread that linked them. It didn't matter how long it took but, one day, he would understand. She climbed down the ladder and shut the shutters and switched on the light. He hadn't left a note. Nothing, except the pencilled location of the circus in her Lenin book: Treptower Park, March 1, 3 p.m.. She looked again at her notebook. He had taken the drawing of the woman with wings hovering over the city wall. He had liked something she had done. One day, he would remember her. Until then she would do anything for him. Even go to the bloody circus.

Treptower Park

Alice could smell it before she could see it. As soon as she got off the train at Treptower Park, the stink of confined animals hit her nostrils. Not for the first time since getting up that morning, she wondered what the hell she was doing. It was freezing cold, the sky concrete grey and East Berlin was even more depressing out here than in the centre. Alice felt alone: alone in a foreign country. And she had no idea what to expect, no idea what the surprise would be.

She could see the red cupola of the circus tent lighting up the grey trees. Several enormous, garishly painted trucks formed a circle around the ground. Through a clown's hoop, she could just about read the words, *The Deutschland Democratic State Circus*. Not exactly Billy Smart's then. Several children with large bows in their hair and polished shoes ran past her, ignoring their parents.

She decided to wander around the neighbourhood for half an hour as she was early, not that there was much to see. Several concrete blocks of houses sprouted out of the cracked concrete roads. Away from the circus, everywhere was grey. Someone should smuggle in some paint, she thought. She passed some state shops. The windows were empty and yet people still queued inside. As she peered at a lonely onion, she felt a shadow behind her.

 She turned round. A young short East German with dark greasy hair and wearing a denim jacket was standing near her. He walked past her but then turned back. She had a feeling he'd been on the same U-Bahn on the way here. He sidled up to her.

'You sell Levi?' he asked in English.

'*Nein danke*,' she said and walked off. But his footsteps followed her.

'Wait a moment,' he said in German.

He asked her if she had money to change. She told him she hadn't.

'Have you books or magazines?' he asked.

No, she hadn't any books or magazines either.

'Shame,' he said. He looked miserable. 'I need some new jeans.'

Alice thought he needed a haircut more than jeans. 'I hate jeans,' she said.

'Why? It is symbol of your country.'

'I don't think so. America perhaps.'

'Not England?'

How did he know she was English?

91

'I guess,' he said in English. 'Your shoes. And you are tall but not fat.'

Alice almost smiled.

'I couldn't afford Levis anyway,' she said. 'They're very expensive you know.'

'But you are rich in the West.'

'No, actually, I'm not rich.'

'Why not?'

'Because I'm not.' Alice smiled sweetly. 'There are many poor people in the West.' The idiot.

'But you have money to travel,' he said slyly.

'No, actually, I work in Berlin, West Berlin,' she added. He was beginning to irritate her.

'Of course. You go to the circus?' he said.

'Yes, I'm going to the circus,' she said

'Then we go together.'

She shrugged and they walked back toward the park. His name was Hans Munster, apparently.

'You know people in the circus?' he asked, again in English.

Alice was about to say she did but she decided it was none of his business.

'No, why?'

'Then why you go to the circus?'

'Why not? Why are you going?' she asked.

He looked confused and changed the subject. 'What do you think of our capital?'

'I think it needs some paint.'

'Paint?'

She couldn't be bothered to explain. She didn't feel like promoting international relations today. She was more concerned about her surprise.

They crossed over into the park. More and more people were heading towards the stink, mainly mothers and young children. An elephant trumpeted in the distance. She really hated to see wild animals perform; it was so cruel, so unnecessary. Oh Johnny. The things she would do for him.

Alice meandered toward the ticket booth. There was already a long queue. In the booth, a clown with a red nose and painted face was selling the tickets. At least they had paint. Hans fumbled in his denim pockets.

'You get me ticket?' Hans asked. 'I do not have money.'

Odd, he offered to change money for her. 'I'm sorry, I don't have much. I spent it in Alexanderplatz.' Alice said. She smiled again.

'Oh, no problem.' Yet still he didn't go.

They got to the ticket booth. Alice was fairly sure it was Bodo but he made no indication that he recognised her. She paid for her ticket while Hans tried to talk his way in, but the clown was not having it, pretending to cry and pulling out his empty pockets. Hans smiled but his lips were tight.

'Maybe I come tomorrow,' Hans said to Alice.

'Okay. Well, good luck getting your Levis.'

'Thank you. I look for you again.'

Alice wasn't quite sure what he meant but she gave him a faint smile. As she entered the Big Top, she turned round and saw Hans walking away. Guilt momentarily stabbed her stomach. She could have easily bought him a ticket. Or given him her ticket for that matter. Fuck it. She didn't like him.

Neither did she like the stinky tent that was quickly filling up. Taped upbeat folk music played from speakers attached to the four columns in the centre. A clown was spinning plates, amusing the kids while they settled down on the wooden benches. Alice sat at the back of the 'Grandstand'. The tiered wooden stand wobbled precariously each time kids ran up and down. In fact the whole set-up looked pretty dingy. In the ring, men and women with dirty fingernails, dressed in black tights and red shirts, ran about checking the rigging and the cage which kept them in, or the audience out. Alice didn't recognise any of them.

Another clown spinning plates came into the tent and headed her way. Please don't come to me, Alice thought. He stopped at the row in front of her and, beaming a big red lipstick smile, offered her a spinning plate. She shook her head but he insisted. She took the plate and, fortunately, it kept on spinning. Everyone around her clapped. He mimed that it was for her and then he pulled out another plate and went to someone else. Alice stopped it from spinning and looked at it. It was plastic and a small dimple in the middle stopped it from rolling off. Not exactly rocket science. On the bottom was a note stuck to it: *I am pleased you are here. Please find me after show. Don't worry, he has gone. We check.*

Alice frowned. Who had gone? And why should she worry? Very odd. And she had a date with a clown. Great. Was this supposed to be her surprise from Johnny? She had no interest in either the abuse of animals or a date with a fucking clown. She got up and started to make her way along the bench but people blocked her way. By the time she got to the end of the row, the tent door was closing. An usher in red and black asked them all to take their seats. She sat down again. The music faded and the few electric bulbs were switched off. Only a few grey shadows crept into the crowded, rank and now eerily silent tent.

And then the drums rolled and a spotlight revealed the musicians in a box above the red curtains. As the band began to oompa-pa, the curtains swung open and the circus ring burst into life. Clowns in Andy Pandy suits with red and yellow shapes sewn to them and acrobats dressed like birds of paradise somersaulted through the now glittering arena. Alice wished she had her sunglasses and some acid. Stars and banners hung in the air, draped on the ground, sailed around the performers. She tried to work out if any of them were Johnny but she didn't think so.

A man with a black top hat and tails entered – the Ringmaster. He wore a big gold watch and brandished a gold stick. He chased the acrobats away and on came prancing white ponies with head-dresses like Mohicans. He ordered the clowns to catch the ponies but they jumped on them instead, rode upside down, back to front and fell off, until the ponies, having had enough of them, bowed to the crowds and disappeared through the red curtains. Everyone, except Alice and the Ringmaster, laughed. The Ringmaster told the clowns they were not funny and ordered them to make him laugh. They proceeded to pull out long hankies and tie and trip each other up. The kids shrieked in delight. The crowd booed the Ringmaster when he sent them off. Alice suppressed a cheer.

A lone elephant lumbered into the ring and stood behind the Ringmaster, who waited impatiently for the next act, hands on hips, occasionally looking at his gold watch. All the kids screamed, 'Behind you!' The elephant wrapped his trunk around him and picked him up. The Ringmaster cried out and tried to free himself. Everyone laughed as the elephant tossed him onto his head and bowed. The Ringmaster ordered that he be put down but the elephant reared up on his hind legs leaving the Ringmaster clinging to a harness the elephant was wearing. The clowns appeared with some carrots and, ignoring the screaming Ringmaster, enticed the elephant out of the ring.

Two acrobats and a podium appeared. The lights went down and several blue-silver spotlights shone on two girls dressed in silver and red tightly fitting lycra. They were the Sisters Barovskova. A hard lump appeared in Alice's throat. It was them. They balanced on top of each other, bent over backwards and their knees touched their heads like little aliens from a distant planet. Ugh. The hard lump slipped down to her stomach. There was no way they could be human. They were more like eels, without bones in their bodies.

She was still reeling when poor George, the bear, and the Professor entered the ring, both on unicycles. The Professor, wearing a scholar's hat, tried to make George sit on a chair to teach him arithmetic but George pretended to fall asleep and then fell off his chair. He got up on two legs, rode round and round, danced to music, juggled balls, laughed at the Professor who fell over the bike, dropped the balls and stumbled when he danced. George was not a bear, Alice thought. He'd been turned into a human in a State experiment. He was more human than anyone, in fact. He made the Professor look like a donkey. Here, nothing was as it seemed. Humans were animals, animals were humans.

A roar sent them both lumbering from the ring. A man, dressed as a gladiator and carrying a long whip, entered, followed by three lions, two females and one male. How macho, Alice couldn't help thinking. What kind of man would want to subjugate the most proud, powerful and beautiful animals in the world? The golden creatures walked listlessly round the ring as if they had lost the will to live. Then they heaved themselves onto podiums and yawned. One of the lionesses roared. The lion trainer looked worried for a second and asked only the other two to perform. It was only when the lion trainer held up a hoop that Alice realised that he had rounded hips and soft eyes. He was, in fact, a she. A very muscular, powerful she with scars on her arms and legs but, irrefutably, a she. The lump crawled back up her throat.

The lioness still refused to move. The lion trainer went up to her and tried to tempt her down with a piece of meat, then with her whip, but the lioness swiped a paw at her. The crowd gasped as the trainer jumped back, quicker than any cat. From then on she ignored the lioness and the lioness ignored everyone until the end. Then, without any prompting, the lioness jumped off the podium and roared at the Grandstand. Alice was glad she hadn't taken any acid. The lioness joined the others, glancing at the trainer as if to say, 'I told you I wasn't going to do it'.

An interval followed and the circus folk scurried around dismantling the cage and setting up rigging and a safety net. Alice recognised the Ringmaster, now dressed in the standard tights and red shirt, shimmying up a ladder, like the other riggers. She realised that all the performers were also the ushers and riggers. A spotlight fell on a couple of aerial acrobats hanging upside from some ropes. Still no sign of Johnny though. A clown came to offer her a toffee apple. It was Bodo again. He winked at her.

'You like?' he whispered.

Alice wasn't sure if he meant the show or the toffee apple, but she nodded anyway. He beamed at her, then disappeared into the crowd, presumably selling toffee apples. Alice still wanted to go but, unless she feigned illness, it would probably be very rude. Besides, she still wanted to know what her surprise was. She sat and ate the toffee apple, listening to more folk music and watching the aerialists.

The second half opened in the sky. Slick, colourful but wingless birds flew through the air. She was fairly sure that the two girls were Natasha and her sister. Despite the lumps in her stomach, now glued together with toffee, she could watch this all day. If only circus were just this. No wonder Johnny liked the horrible bendy little alien.

The aerialists were chased away by the Ringmaster who then dismissively introduced an older performer with six dogs. The Ringmaster demanded money from the man but he had only empty pockets. In the meantime, the dogs jumped through hoops, chased each other in circles and figures of eight and ran across a beam in the centre of the ring about a metre off the ground. When the Ringmaster ordered the man away, the dogs tried to bite the Ringmaster's coat tails, making the kids howl with laughter. Then they began to sing. One little white dog stood on his hind legs and held a stick in his paw as he sat the other dogs in a line in front of him and conducted their howling. The Ringmaster yelled at them to be quiet. Another dog appeared from somewhere with a placard which said, **Equality to All!** And another, **No More Rent!** Even Alice laughed. Were they taking the piss? Soon all the dogs were running round with placards in their mouths. Then the drums rolled and for a second the lights went out to be replaced by a single spotlight.

A slightly older man entered the ring with a bow and arrow. The Ringmaster dragged a young boy in the middle of the ring and put an apple on his head. Alice wondered where they got the apples from. The sharpshooter split it with a single arrow. Calls came from the crowd for the Ringmaster to put an apple on his own head but he had disappeared. The boy produced the Ringmaster's gold watch, to the delight of the kids, and the sharpshooter hit it with an arrow, triggering an alarm. The Ringmaster ran back into the ring, punching the air with his cane, but he was overtaken by a juggler on a unicycle, juggling hoops.

Alice held her breath. Was it Johnny? No, Bodo again. A couple of the dogs returned, this time carrying balls in their mouths which they deposited on a podium and then disappeared for more items for him to juggle. He was good, juggling everything: hoops, batons, balls, knives. He even juggled with his feet. He climbed up onto the beam and juggled there. Every so often the sharpshooter shot an arrow into one of the balls and Bodo would look around, confused.

The Ringmaster demanded that he be removed. A hoop came down and lifted him up, legs akimbo. He was deposited onto a lower perch some twenty feet above the circus floor. The focus was once again in the sky where a spaghetti junction of high wires spanned the tent like a spider's web. Bodo, holding a balancing pole, began to walk up one of the high wires to the next perch. As he was about to reach it he suddenly slipped backwards, all the way back down. Alice gasped.

A female silver aerialist tumbled out of nowhere down a rope and balanced on a perch. Alice couldn't tell if it was one of the Russians or not. And then another one, a man, landed on a perch opposite. Was it Johnny? It was hard to tell with all the make-up. He stepped onto the top wire and somersaulted. Wow. He couldn't do that. The wire shook precariously and Alice found herself gripping the wooden seat. Then, in the middle he stopped and lay down. The Ringmaster looked up horrified as the tightrope walker lay on a silver thread high up in the cupola – but then he got up slowly and glided across to the other side. The applause was thunderous. Even the Ringmaster nodded in approval. It was then that Alice recognised that the Ringmaster was the Professor, the same man they'd first seen with the bear in Alexanderplatz. What talented people.

The high wire act was not yet over. The young girl stepped onto the man's shoulders. Surely not. She must have glue on her feet. He stepped onto the wire again, slowly this time, holding the balancing pole. A collective gasp seemed to empty the tent of oxygen. Alice could feel drops of sweat bursting onto her forehead. As he approached the centre of the wire, the girl put one hand onto his head and sculpted herself into an arabesque shape. She glided like a bird of peace slowly through the beam of light. The drums rolled again as they approached the other side. Then they dived like shooting stars down onto the safety net.

It was then that Alice felt the blood drain out of her heart as she realised that it was, indeed, Johnny and with him, the bendy Russian girl. What a surprise.

The Big Top

Applause thundered in his ears as he somersaulted down to the safety net. He could hardly believe it – his first circus performance at twenty-three. If only his mother could see him fly through the air now. Maybe it was a smaller step from cabaret to circus than from cabaret to modern dance. Maybe it was in his blood after all. Natasha was right next to him; he could almost reach out and touch her. They hit the net and, simultaneously, bounced upright and somersaulted forward again. As he flew through the air, he wished he could keep on rolling through space forever. Perhaps that's how it is when you die. You just keep on rolling through dark space towards a brighter and brighter light.

They landed again and gently bounced until they could stop and bow to the noisy crowd and to each other. He could feel his skin glistening. His muscles shone. Natasha winked at him before turning back to the audience, a huge grin across her face. Below them acrobats and clowns somersaulted, balled up, laid out and twisted, round the ring, each taking a bow. Bodo tumbled down on a rope wrapped round his leg. Ponies cantered around the outside, George was on a unicycle and the Professor bowed solemnly until he was once again whipped up by Oscar's trunk and placed on top of the elephant's head. For a moment, the ring was chaotic, yet orderly, larger and greater than life.

He should have run away and joined the circus years ago as a kid. Once, when he was very young, he did try to run away but he was brought home again in a police car. His mother had told him when he was older that the police had found him trying to get on a bus in Hackney to America. They would laugh together about it. He could never have left her really.

Johnny lapped up the applause, feeling happier than he had ever felt before, privileged to be a part of this ingenious spark of life. The drums rolled again as he flipped backwards off the net and ran forward. The ground felt clumpy, uneven after space, and Johnny almost stumbled. Natasha reached out for his hand and they ran together. All the performers now stood in a semi-circle and bowed to the clapping and cheering audience.

Johnny smiled up at the memory of his mother and, as he did, spotted Alice, tall and beautiful, looming above the children, mothers and the few men in uniform. He was surprised but pleased she was here. At least, there would be one friend who had witnessed his inaugural steps across space. Who knows when he would get the opportunity again. He knew that it would be too risky to continue to perform with them. Bodo had already told him that someone had been tracking them. But he didn't care. Tonight was his to remember forever.

The performers tumbled out of the ring, waving their goodbyes. The bright lights were extinguished and the hum of the generator swallowed the music. As soon as Johnny got out of the tent and felt the cold, dark air slap him round the face, he turned round and picked up Natasha. She wrapped her feet around his thighs. He spun her round, laughing, smiling, kissing.

'You are great,' she said, planting big kisses all over him.

Bodo came up, sweat dripping into his blue eyes, and congratulated them before muttering that he was going to find Alice. One by one, the circus passed by to tell them how exciting their new act was. Zoyenka came up and hugged her sister. She nodded at Johnny and told him that they were very good. Natasha whispered something to her and her sister looked angry and shook her head. Natasha spoke sternly and she sulked away into the dark. Johnny looked questioningly at Natasha but she just laughed. The Professor approached, hugged and patted him on the back. He said something to Natasha.

'What did he say?' Johnny asked when he had gone.

'He say that it is the greatest high wire act he saw. He sad you not come with us.' A small tear burst out of her eye but she quickly wiped it away.

'We'll work something out,' Johnny whispered. He didn't have a clue what but he wasn't going to ever let her go.

Alice arrived with Bodo. She threw her arms around him, telling him he was fantastic. She looked at Natasha and half smiled. He didn't see what Natasha did but he felt her arm around his back pulling him towards her. She whispered that they could go back to her caravan, her sister would stay guard. Bodo was telling Alice that she could go and visit Leah and the lions while he got washed and then, maybe, they could all go back to his apartment.

'Great,' Alice said.

Only Johnny registered the sarcasm. He knew that Alice didn't like the performing animals but surely the afternoon had been worth it.

'We'll be back in a minute, Alice. I need to take a shower. Okay?'

For a moment, she looked confused and he could feel her gaze drilling into him as he followed Natasha. He felt bad but Bodo would look after her. Bodo was in love with her.

'Who is she?' Natasha asked as they crossed the circus ground with their arms wrapped round each other.

'Alice? You met her the other day.'

'But who is she?'

'She's a friend.' He pulled Natasha towards him and tried to kiss her, to reassure her, but Natasha tensed up. He shouldn't have slept with Alice the other day, but she was so hard to resist – she was so beautiful and she felt so good. But it had made him feel so bad afterwards. Even though they both knew it didn't mean anything. Natasha wriggled away and looked up at him out of her dark, now serious, eyes. A light from a caravan hit the glitter on her face and made it sparkle like a polished diamond.

'But you like her?'

'Yes, I like her of course, she's a friend.'

She still stared at him, searching his face, as if waiting for something.

'I do not think it possible to have such a beautiful friend.'

Johnny shrugged. He could smell the salt on her arms, the paint in her hair, the powder on her face. He could feel the smooth skin beneath the wet silver leotard. He could taste expectation in the air between them. She was probably right and it wouldn't happen again.

'Then I won't be her friend,' he whispered.

She kissed him. Johnny lifted her up and carried her to the steps of the caravan as Zoyenka opened the door. He put her down and they went in. A small light on the table cast yellow shadows. The caravan smelled of the girls, their clothes and make-up decorated the floor. Zoyenka said something to Natasha before scowling at Johnny and opening a window on the other side of the caravan. Johnny thought she was letting in some air and thanked her. But she snaked her way through it. Natasha laughed at him.

'Why the window?' he asked.

'So no one see we alone. She come back in thirty minutes. The Professor not like that I like you.' She laughed her mad little laugh. 'Quick, quick!'

She pumped some hot water into a bucket and put some towels on the floor and lay on them with her leotard half off. He unpeeled the other half. She was naked underneath. He watched as she washed her small body sculpted out of muscle, tendons and shadows.

'What?' she said.

He shook his head and got undressed. She was not at all embarrassed or shy. But then, why should she be. He had touched every part of her body – almost. He stood naked in front of her. She pumped some more water and passed it to him, then lay on the bottom bunk and stared at him.

They curled up together but, whereas in the air they could anticipate each other's every move, here on earth, Johnny found himself fumbling around her. They bumped knees. They were like starlings at sea.

'Let's put up wire,' Natasha said.

They laughed and fumbled again. She jumped on top of him and gripped him tightly as if she were on a fairground ride. He felt his way slowly inside her small body. Her muscles squeezed him until he thought he would break into a million pieces. 'I love you,' he whispered.

They lay back with bruised knees. Natasha clambered around on top of him as if he were part of the bunk bed and reached down for a packet of cigarettes with a blue rocket on the front. They lit up. The rough Soviet tobacco lashed his throat. As he coughed, she rippled with his body.

'I want to be with you forever,' Johnny said.

'Maybe you live in our great Soviet Union?'

'Maybe,' Johnny said. He would do whatever she wanted. 'What's it like where you live?'

'We live next to great city – Odessa. Most beautiful city in the world.'

'What do your parents do?'

'My mother hero mother,' she declared proudly.

'What do you mean?'

She said it in Russian which didn't help. Then she explained that her mother had ten children and in the Soviet Union mothers receive a special award, particularly if they worked in a coal mine as well. Johnny didn't know if she was serious or not. She was laughing again. She laughed even more than Alice.

'And your father?'

'He was performer for Bolshoi but he ... how you say? Break his leg?' She turned on her side and brought her knees up to show him. 'Now he Communist party official.'

Johnny raised his eyebrows. Not quite what he'd expected. He had always imagined circuses to be family traditions, gypsies, not daughters of Communist party officials. It was good for circus in general but didn't think it bode too well for him.

'How is London?' Natasha asked.

'Big, grey, dirty, cold, pretentious.'

'You not like it?'

Johnny blew smoke rings. 'No, I don't like it.'

'Many people without house or work?'

Johnny smiled. 'Many.'

'I know. They tell us. You return?' Natasha asked. Ash fell from her cigarette onto his arm.

'No,' he said. 'Not unless you come with me.'

'How?' She massacred the butt of her cigarette on a saucer.

It would be difficult, Johnny had to agree. Particularly with a Communist party father.

'Then I don't go back.'

'But London your home.'

'I have no one there,' Johnny said, stroking her hair.

'Your family? Mother and father?'

'My mother died of cancer three years ago and I don't really know my father. And no brothers or sisters.'

Natasha was silent as she searched his face.

'Sorry,' she said.

'It's okay,' he whispered.

He believed in the present and not the past. But tonight his mother seemed to be with him, reminding him. He could still see her wasting away in front of his eyes on a hospital bed in the living room. They sent them home when there was no hope. He had tried to do all he could, shopped and cooked for her – not that she'd eat much. He'd held her hand and told her stories and she'd tell him to go out, to live his life and sometimes he would. But he drifted and, at that time in his life, he didn't know what he was doing. He'd juggled in the park, taken dance classes, hung out in Covent Gardens. It was during this time he had been arrested for pick-pocketing and the police phoned his mother on their recently-installed telephone. When he got home with some shopping, she was sitting up in bed, her bald head wrapped in a blue and white polka scarf, red lipstick smudged across her thin lips. She patted the side of her bed with an arm as fragile as a dry stick and he perched next to her and took her hand. Her fingers were black.

'Johnny,' she said. Her voice was as brittle as her hand. 'I'm sorry I haven't given you more. To survive in this world sometimes you have to do bad things, but never do them when you don't have to.'

His mother hadn't been one for advice so he remembered this.

'It is true that in the West many broken families?' Natasha asked.

'Yes,' said Johnny. 'It's true.'

'You have much sadness,' Natasha said, kissing him.

He pulled her even closer. 'You make me happy,' he whispered.

'But soon I go on tour.'

'Then I come with you.' Perhaps he could persuade the Professor to take him with them. He would defect. Then they would get married. He had never wanted to marry anyone – he had never seen the point – but now he wanted to marry Natasha more than anything in the world.

The window clicked open and Zoyenka climbed noisily back into the caravan. She said something in Russian and both she and Natasha burst out laughing. Zoyenka stood in front of them, staring, and turned up her nose as she sniffed the air. Natasha slapped her on her leg and said something. They both laughed again.

'Bodo waiting,' Zoyenka announced in English. 'He has vodka.'

Alice would be pleased, Johnny thought. Natasha scrambled off him, leaving him naked. Zoyenka continued to stare, as if trying to understand her sister's attraction to him. Johnny stared back. She was only fifteen, but already she was a fraction taller than her sister.

'You stay here,' Natasha said to her. 'You too young.'

An argument broke out in Russian. Zoyenka glared at him. She had a mean glint in her eye at times. He closed the door behind them and they made their way across the hard, glittering, frozen earth. Oscar trumpeted into the night: an eerie sound in a moonlit park in East Berlin.

They found Bodo and Alice with Leah, the lion trainer. Alice was holding her hand firmly over her mouth and nose. Leah was in the cage with Jessie, who was lying down on thinly spread straw, her tail idly flickering. Jessie lifted her golden head to see the new visitors, but then dropped it again to the floor. Leah talked to her in a soothing voice in a language Johnny had never heard before. He was about to ask what it was but Natasha put her hand over his mouth and shook her head. Jessie lifted her head again and yawned, her dagger sharp teeth silhouetted against the cage. Bodo indicated that they should go and they all moved slowly away from the cages and the caravans into the park. Natasha gripped his hand and whispered that she loved him. They stopped near a bench and sat down while Bodo opened the bottle of vodka and passed it to Alice, who had plonked herself the other side of him.

'Where the fuck have you been?' Alice hissed, gulping down vodka. 'Yuck! That tastes like petrol.'

'Sorry Alice,' he said quietly, smiling at her, trying to defuse any tension. 'We went back to the caravan.'

'I won't ask what for,' she snarled.

He shrugged. He really shouldn't have slept with her on Sunday – not only had Natasha sensed something but Alice couldn't handle it.

'What is wrong with Jessie?' he asked Bodo, taking the vodka.

'We don't know,' Bodo said. 'She has been like that since last week. Leah is very concerned.'

'It's probably because she's cooped up in that small cage. Wouldn't you be ill?'

No one replied to Alice. Johnny suspected they didn't understand what she said and he couldn't be bothered to argue with her. She was right about the vodka though. He passed it to Natasha who tipped it back without flinching.

'Shall we go to my apartment?' Bodo said. 'It is still early? I think it is safe. There is no one else watching us. We have not seen any more Hans this evening.'

Bodo had told him briefly about the Hans incident.

'Maybe it would be safer to go to a bar,' Alice said.

'No, there are always spies in bars.'

'Then let's go to yours,' Johnny said. It would be interesting to see where Bodo lived when not with the circus. 'Do you think the Professor would come with us?' Johnny wanted to talk to him.

'No, he must go back for something.'

'Do you live alone?'

'Yes, my mother was taken by the Stasi. She never come back.'

'I'm sorry, I lost my mother, too,' he said, suddenly. 'Cancer.'

'Then they die the same. The Stasi are the cancer of this country.'

Johnny laughed dryly. Did he really want to live in a country that had cancer? He had enough of that in his life. But, perhaps, Odessa was different.

They set off through the park. Bodo lagged behind with Alice. Johnny put his arm around Natasha and kissed her on her cheek, her neck. He wanted to ask her to marry him but Alice screamed. They stopped and looked behind.

Alice was pointing into the night. Bodo put his arms round her to comfort her.

'What is the matter with your friend?' Natasha said.

'I don't know,' Johnny said, tugging on Natasha. He thought Alice was just demanding attention. Then he thought, once or twice, that they were being followed but, every time he swung round, the park was empty except for the trees.

'Did you see something?' Bodo asked, coming up to him and handing Natasha the bottle of vodka. 'Alice say she see something.'

'No, nothing,' said Johnny.

'I think we are followed,' Bodo whispered to him. 'Don't look behind you. And please don't scream,' he said to Alice.

'Can I have the vodka then,' she said, snatching it out of Natasha's hands.

Heidelberger Straße (West)

Peter tipped the last few mouthfuls of beer down his throat and yawned noisily as the credits to *Planet of the Apes* rolled up the black and white television screen. What a great cinematic moment – the Statue of Liberty sunk into a beach. And they were so cute, those apes. Much cuter than most of the humans who drank in the Kiosk. He wished he had been in that film. He wished he had been in any film. He wished he were a star. That was one thing that bugged him about Johnny: Peter knew one day he would be famous.

'*Na ja, was für eine Scheiße,*' Michael said, getting up from the chair. '*Wie spät ist es? Ach Scheiße.*'

'It's only about eleven. Get us another beer, will you?' Peter asked. 'It's so hot.'

'Ach Peter, you need a slave,' Michael said. 'Already I carry the crate up for you.'

'I know, darling. Are you offering?' Peter laughed.

He stretched out on the sofa, revealing his hairy legs from beneath his silky crimson dressing gown, and admired his new black furry slippers. He had bought them at a stall at the freezing cold flea market on Sunday morning on his way home from the Kiosk with the Hungarian sisters and Hamit, a Turkish guy he knew. He seemed to think they'd all bought some but couldn't quite remember. He couldn't quite remember a lot of things lately.

Hermann sat on the floor, still slicing up his mini mountain of speed on its mirror base with a pen knife. It looked like he was trying to reproduce a model of the Statue of Liberty poking out of the white grains – as in the film. He was completely insane.

'Hermann, what are you doing? You've been playing with that speed for about a month now. Admittedly there is less of it.' Peter laughed, not expecting an answer and, fortunately, didn't receive one. Hermann could either be deathly silent, or rant for hours.

'Johnny is out very late,' Michael said, returning with three beers.

'Cheers. He's performing in a circus, in the East,' Peter said.

Michael laughed. Peter couldn't be bothered to elaborate. With any luck Johnny wouldn't come back. Peter couldn't quite remember what had gone on last week after their great day out in the DDR. He had vague memories of drinking sambuca with Hassan in Cats, and being in a park with Alice – of all people – and Hassan, but that was all until he had woken up on the sofa. He remembered very clearly then standing up and taking two shaky steps towards the window where he saw a naked – and extremely well endowed – man standing at a window on the other side of the Wall. But perhaps it was a deeply buried sub-conscious fantasy. The strange thing was the man had looked a little like the East German juggler they'd met, Bodo. He remembered that Alice and Johnny claimed they had seen a clown there. Confused, Peter had stumbled back to his bedroom to be greeted by Hassan, naked, on his bed, then rushed to the bathroom and vomited.

Johnny had left him a strange note asking if he could stay a bit longer, together with some money. Peter tried to speak to him about it on Sunday night but Johnny closed his bedroom door. Maybe he'd had a bad rehearsal, or maybe it was because of what Peter had said last week. Peter didn't care. Johnny was an asshole. He'd invited him to the circus but fuck that. Peter had told Johnny they'd all be sent to Siberia if they were caught but he didn't seem to want to listen. He bullshitted about having found his purpose in life. Peter had to accept that Johnny wasn't interested in him. Maybe a shag still wasn't out of the question but even that wasn't looking likely. His only consolation was that he wasn't interested in Mad either. The Russian rubber doll seemed to be favourite at the moment and Peter had a feeling that wouldn't last for long either. A relationship with a man who had 'a purpose' was doomed.

Peter glanced at the window but there was only darkness. He should close the blind. Such a shame to block out the possibility of seeing a naked man but, if it had been real and it were Bodo, he dreaded to think what may happen. They'd probably try to cannonball themselves across or something. Peter decided to close the blind, then picked up his tobacco from the coffee table. He would have one last joint before bed.

'Hey guys, *prost!*' Peter said, and clinked bottles with the other two. It was an age since the three of them has spent an evening in together. Actually, it was probably the first time.

Peter was trying to take it easy. His chest pains and palpitations had forced him to go to the doctor's yesterday. The first thing she (typical) asked him was what drugs he did, how much he drank and how much he smoked. When he told her (less rather than more) she reckoned he was lucky to be alive. She said that if he wanted to reach thirty he would have to cut down radically on drinking, smoking and drugs. Then she'd prescribed him a Ventolin inhaler. More drugs. Super. He was already addicted.

He lit the joint and inhaled deeply.

'How do you get on with Johnny?' he asked Michael.

Michael shrugged.

'He's trouble,' Hermann said, holding his knife up.

Peter almost choked on his joint. Poised, with a knife in his hand and a pile of speed in front of him, he knew who he thought was trouble.

'Um,' Peter said, laughing, half offering his joint to Hermann. Hermann didn't normally smoke joints but he didn't want him to start ranting.

Hermann hesitated before taking it. 'It's not my problem,' he said, swallowing smoke.

'What?' Peter asked hesitantly.

'Your beautiful Johnny.'

Peter looked at Michael who opened his arms, hunched his shoulders and tilted his head as if to say that it was not up to him to comment.

'He is arrogant, you know, thinks he's better,' said Hermann, and took another deep drag.

This was about the longest conversation he'd ever had with Hermann. He had a point – except Hermann was crazy.

'Can I have my joint back please? Yeah, he's arrogant. But that's because he's awesome. Such a cute ass.'

'That is his problem,' Hermann said, passing the joint back to Peter.

'*Na ja*, maybe.'

'I think he's here,' Michael said, turning his head towards the hall.

Peter listened. There was someone outside the door. Thank God he'd closed the blinds. At least there couldn't be any surprise waves from naked clowns or jugglers. A girl's giggle charged into the hall.

'Ah hell,' Peter muttered. 'Mad Alice.' He rearranged his dressing gown and sat back down on the sofa.

'I think I have to go to bed,' Michael said.

'Good idea, Michael darling. I might come with you.'

'Not tonight thank you, Peter,' Michael said, smiling as he walked by him. 'I have enough pipes to fix tomorrow.'

'You son-of-a…,' Peter called after him just as Johnny and the awful Alice walked into the lounge. She was drunk as well. Then again, when wasn't she? Peter gulped back his beer. Johnny came into the living room while she fumbled with the door in the hall, trying to close it.

'Hi Peter,' Johnny said, touching his shoulder as he walked past towards the kitchen.

'Hi darling,' he said, trying to ignore his tingling shoulder. 'How did it go?'

Johnny stopped and looked down at him. 'It was fantastic, really fantastic.'

'What, so you actually performed?'

'Yeah, a high wire act. It was just great. I loved every second.'

He sounded delirious. He looked awesome. His black hair stood up boyishly. Dark eyeliner lingered around his blue eyes. Peter wrapped his dressing gown around himself again. Mad was still trying to close the door.

'Far out,' he said, before taking a deep breath and shouting, 'Mad, leave it!'

'Shame you didn't make it,' Johnny said.

'Yeah really. Afraid I have to take it easy for a few days. Otherwise I might have come.'

'Why? Are you okay?' He sounded concerned.

'Yeah, I'm fine. Just exhausted. Hey, there's some beer in the fridge if you like.'

'Cheers Peter,' Johnny said, and glided into the kitchen.

'Bloody door, you should get that fixed. Hi Peter. Nice dressing gown. You look like a ladybird,' Mad almost shouted as she thundered into the room. 'Hi Hermann!'

Hermann looked up at her and nodded.

'Hi Mad,' Peter shouted back. A ladybird. Really. She should be shot.

'Hey, no need to yell like that,' she said. 'You missed a real treat this afternoon at the circus. Johnny carried that little Russian...' She lowered her voice and mouthed *"tart"*, '...across a wire this wide.'

She indicated with her thumb and forefinger how thin the wire was – except her estimate opened and closed like a goldfish's mouth. She held out her arms and tried to walk across the floor in a straight line but, predictably, wobbled over. Peter remembered then she'd been so drunk the other night at Cats she'd fallen flat on her ass while dancing with Johnny.

Johnny came back with a couple of beers and threw one at Mad, who, amazingly, caught it. He fell gracefully into the armchair and hooked his legs over one arm. Peter noted that Johnny hadn't even said hello to Hermann. Mind you, it was easy to miss him as he blended into the wooden floor.

'Yeah?' Peter said. 'Were they good?'

'Brilliant,' Mad said, sitting down next at the other end of the sofa, nearest Johnny. 'Johnny was fab. But the poor lions and elephants and bears and things. It's horrible…'

Peter looked at Johnny while Mad continued to rant about the circus. Johnny's eyes were shining but vacant as if he had gone out and left the lights on. He had to give her credit for tenacity. She wouldn't let go – even when the Russian *tart* was miles ahead.

'Well, there's no need for it is there?' Mad said.

'Mad darling, there is so much cruelty in this world. I don't think you know half of it.' Peter laughed, and then coughed. He felt a twinge in his chest. He coughed again and reached for his inhaler.

'Oh dear, you sound crap,' Mad said.

Peter wanted to kick her off the sofa but he wheezed deeply, waiting for the sweet dry oxygen, or whatever it was, to circulate.

'Ah fucking joints,' Hermann said. He got up from the floor, picking up his powdery city of New York.

'Where you going?' Peter asked.

'Sleep. Fucking joints make me sleep,' he said. 'Goodnight.'

'Goodnight Hermann,' Peter said.

'*Tschüss!*' Mad trilled.

Hermann left the lounge and went to his room for the first time in about a month. Mad drooled after the mirror in his hand. Johnny's face was still a blank.

'So they didn't arrest you then, Johnny?' Peter asked.

Johnny blinked. 'No, but someone approached Alice this afternoon. The circus folk got rid of him but then Alice and Bodo reckoned we were followed later tonight… So I guess I'm not going to be doing any more shows.'

Well, really, what did he expect? Peter wondered what would happen to the rubber doll. Mad would be pleased, although she didn't look it.

'Hey you gonna make me a joint?' Mad tapped his leg from the other side of the sofa. 'Shame Herbert's gone.'

'Hermann,' Peter said. 'And watch your dirty boots on my legs.' She could at least have taken them off.

'Hermann,' she repeated. 'I know that.' She burped.

'So, why do you think you were followed?' Peter asked as he began to roll another joint.

'You remember Bodo? The juggler we met in Alexanderplatz?' Johnny said.

111

Peter nodded his head slowly, thoughtfully, dreading what was coming.

'Well, he reckons he's seen the guy Alice met hanging around the centre and he's fairly sure he works for the Stasi. He's not sure if he is actually one of them or if he's just working for them.'

'Bodo's the one who gave you a book on Lenin, wasn't he?' Peter asked Mad. Too loudly.

She nodded but she didn't seem excited. Then again, it was impossible to be in love with two people at the same time. Peter licked the joint and passed it to her to light. He hoped she wouldn't stay for long. He could go to bed but the thought of leaving her alone with Johnny in his apartment was horrifying.

'So what did you do after the show?' he asked.

'Johnny disappeared and left me for hours with Bodo and some tigers,' she said.

Johnny shook his head. 'A lioness. It wasn't for hours. Anyway, you had a nice time, didn't you?'

'Very nice. The lion lay there groaning and Bodo told me how much he liked me and asked me if he got to the West would I go out with him.'

She really was a bitch. She had men buzzing round her like flies around a sow.

'What did you say?' Peter asked automatically.

'I said no.'

'Oh Mad, that's not nice now.'

'Why?' she said sharply. 'I don't want to be responsible for someone getting shot.' She blew out hash clouds.

'Yeah but you've spoiled the man's dreams.'

'Well, why should he have dreams? Mine are all spoilt.' She didn't look at Johnny but you didn't need a psychologist to know who it was aimed at.

'You're not the only one, darling,' Peter muttered. 'But you could leave him some hope, the poor man. We're not the ones living under a fascist regime.'

'It's not fascist, it's communist.'

'Really Mad? I think you'll find it's the same thing,' Peter said. 'The people are not allowed to leave, they have no freedom, they are constantly indoctrinated. I don't know if you've noticed but there's a goddam Wall out there – to keep them in.'

'So? Everyone is guaranteed a job, a home and security. Bodo told me that, as a circus performer, he would be provided with the state pension after thirty-five if he wants. You wouldn't get that in England. Even less so in America. Besides, it's what the people want. If they wanted to change it, they would.'

'Have you not been in the food shops? Or the *Plattenbau*? Would you like to live in a world with empty shelves and buildings made out of cardboard? Why do you think Bodo wants to come to the West.' Peter laughed. She was just a kid.

'Yeah, well, to see me. Everyone wants what they can't have.'

'I think that's a bit naive, darling.'

'Why?' she challenged. 'I bet he would hate it if he lived here.'

Peter groaned. He really couldn't be bothered to have this conversation with a drunken English girl. Johnny had closed his eyes again, his legs drooping along the wooden floor, his hands cradling the back of his head. Traces of white make-up glistened around his eyebrows.

'Can I have my joint back, Mad,' Peter said. It was nearly all gone. 'Do you want any, Johnny?'

His pale blue eyes opened. He shook his head slowly. 'No thanks.'

'You agree with me, don't you, Johnny?' Mad said.

'What?'

'That life is good in the East.'

'It's okay. There are some good things about it. I guess it's what you're used to.'

Peter groaned and tugged at the last bit of hash in his joint. Not him as well. 'So what else did you do out there in the wonderful East?' he asked.

'We had a bottle of vodka eventually when Johnny came back with … what's-her-name. Everyone was saying how great he was. But they're going on tour soon or something, aren't they, Johnny? In April or something. For six months.'

'Yeah.'

'Where they going,' Peter asked Johnny.

'Eastern Europe,' Mad replied. 'DDR, Hungary, Czechoslovakia… They want to take him with them but they can't really – not unless he defects.'

'Oh well, there's an option,' Peter said. 'Seeing as you guys like the place so much.'

'And then we were going to go back to Bodo's cos he's got an apartment in the centre, quite near the Wall I think he said, but as we were followed out of the park Bodo said we'd better not. So we left them at the station and came back.'

'Oh poor Mad. Did the commies spoil your fun,' he said, chuckling, before realising that she'd said Bodo lived near the Wall. The fantasy really could be real.

'Fuck off, Peter. I wasn't looking for sex. I had sex on *Sun*day, thank you.'

'That was five days ago, darling.'

'Four actually.'

Johnny yawned. 'I'm going to bed. I'm exhausted and I've got a dance rehearsal tomorrow.'

'Oh don't go, Johnny,' Mad whined. 'Let's have another beer.'

'No, I can't, Alice. I can hardly feel my legs.'

Mad got up from the sofa and sat down next to him on the arm of the chair and began to thump his thighs, presumably in an attempt at massage. Peter couldn't help but laugh.

'Ouch, Alice,' Johnny said, brushing her aside. He got up and stretched. His muscles billowed beneath his shirt as he moved. He turned round and faced the window.

'Actually, I'm about ready to sleep as well,' Peter said, turning his laugh into a yawn. He didn't think Mad would take the hint but it was worth a try.

'What a shame you've got the blind down,' she said, joining him near the window. 'We can't wave to the clown now.'

'What clown? You were hallucinating darling.' Fuck her. Why did she have to remember.

'I wasn't. Johnny saw it too. Thinking about it, there are a lot of clowns in East Berlin,' she said, peeping through the wooden slats of the blinds.

'Perhaps that's because the city's a circus,' Peter couldn't resist saying, beginning to clear up the beer bottles. 'Grab those for me, will you, Mad?'

She didn't pay any attention. 'Can I open this?'

'No, I'd rather you didn't. Michael's just fixed it.'

'Well, goodnight all,' Johnny said. 'Alice, you'll be okay getting back, won't you?'

The blinds snapped shut and she swung round to face Johnny but he wasn't even looking at her.

'Sure,' she said, cool as ice. 'Don't worry about me.'

Johnny left the room and went into the bathroom. For a moment, all fell quiet. Peter still held the bottles as Mad, holding back tears, stared at him. Almost feeling sorry for her, he half opened his arms, two bottles in each hand, and she immediately stepped towards him, slipped her arms around his back and rested her cheek on his shoulder. Her breasts nuzzled his chest. She smelled of girl sweat and vodka. The latter he could cope with. The beer bottles clinked as he rubbed his thumbs up and down her back.

She whispered, 'He's such a bastard.'

'Let me take these bottles into the kitchen and I'll get us another beer,' Peter found himself saying. 'Okay?'

She nodded and, sniffing slightly, sat down in the chair. He took out another couple of beers from the refrigerator. Now he was left with a blubbering Mad Alice. But he was itching to know what Johnny had done to her. He scurried back into the living room.

'Here you are, darling. So tell me what happened?'

She sniffled again. 'He came round on Sunday and we had sex...'

Peter swallowed his beer the wrong way and spluttered.

'Are you okay? Then he asked me to come to the circus as he said he had a surprise for me. So I did, even though I fucking hate circuses. And then I see him carrying that Russian tart across a high wire. What a great surprise. And then later I see them kissing behind a caravan. And I'm dumped with Bodo while they go and have sex. I mean, is that nice? You know, I'm cool about who wants to sleep with who and if he wants to shag her that's fine. But to invite me over and then get off with her in front of me is not nice, is it?'

'No, that's not nice.' Peter was trying very hard not to laugh. He felt his airways contracting with the effort so he puffed on his inhaler again. It served her right. But it wasn't nice. Johnny really wasn't a very nice person. But with a body like that, hell, who cared about nice?

'Here, darling, have a cigarette.' He flashed a Marlboro packet towards her but she shook her head and pulled out a Benson's. 'So did you talk to him about it?'

'Yes, we talked on the way back. He said that we only had sex and that he could have sex with whoever he wanted. I said that I thought that he liked me. He said he did and that we were "very good friends" but that *Natasha* was special, someone he wanted to spend the rest of his life with. I asked him how the fuck he was gonna do that – on a fucking iron bed? He said they'd find a way. Then I said that I thought he'd made a mistake and if he hadn't then he shouldn't have invited me. But he just didn't get it.' She took a swig of beer.

'But, if she is that special, why did he have sex with you on Sunday?'

'Thank you, Peter. Exactly.'

Peter didn't tell her that Johnny had come home in a foul mood that day as he didn't want any more tears. But he bet that was why. Post-coital guilt. He used to get it if he'd ever been so drunk he'd slept with a woman. These days, he doubted he would be capable.

'Did he say anything to you?' she asked.

'No, darling. I've hardly seen him. He seems to be avoiding me.'

'But that's because you told him to move out,' she said.

'No I didn't,' Peter snapped.

'Well, that's what he told me on Sunday. He said that you'd told him to move out because he wouldn't fuck you.'

Peter laughed. Loudly. He didn't much care what he'd said: it was just slightly worrying when chunks of his life disappeared. Maybe the doctor was right. He wouldn't live to thirty. Then again if he'd only got four years left, he may as well enjoy them.

'So you still like him as well?' she asked.

Peter tugged on his cigarette. 'I can live without him.'

'Me too. He's trouble.'

That was the second time someone had said that about Johnny that evening.

She stood up and went towards the window. 'Can I open this blind? I love looking across. And maybe the clown is there.' She began to fiddle with it.

Peter yawned and uncrossed his legs. 'Better not. It breaks fairly easily. Mad, hey, listen, I've gotta sleep soon.'

'But it's not even morning yet. Don't you want to go out? We could try and find some nice men for a change.'

That seemed a drastic way of getting her away from the window. He was trying to have an early night.

'I'm not exactly dressed for going out, darling.'

Mad was still fiddling with the blind. She pulled one of the strings and the blind obediently opened its slats. 'Whoops,' she said.

Peter stood up and found himself gazing at Bodo, outlined by a dull, yellow bulb. This time, sadly, he was dressed. He waved across. Peter was about to raise his hand when he realised Mad hadn't seen him. She was still playing with the strings. Bodo began to wave frantically, making signs above his head at her. Peter pretended not to see him. How many men did she need? He could almost cope with them cannonballing their way across to see Johnny, but having Mad come round on a regular basis to wave at a clown would be too much.

'Come on then,' Peter said. 'I need a vodka and a nice man.'

She turned round to face him. 'Really?' Her face brightened for the first time that evening.

'Come to my room,' he said, and grinned. 'I have something for you.' Fuck the doctor.

Heidelberger Straße (East)

Johnny smoked a cigarette outside the red tent while he waited for the Saturday matinee to finish. The Berlin sky was as grey as ever, as if someone had put a lid on the city, slammed it into a deep freeze and forgotten about it for the winter. He could hear the finale music, so he knew it would not be long. His stomach knotted. This time two days ago he had been the one walking up there in the roof of the world, away from the Wall and checkpoints, in a space in the sky. He wished he were there now. But they'd all agreed it was too risky. He looked around him one more time as he stubbed out his cigarette. He didn't think he'd been followed. He knew he had to be careful. Bodo was convinced someone had trailed them in the park on Thursday night.

As the tent flapped open and the punters exited, some laughing, others dazed, Johnny mingled with the crowd. Some kids carried plastic plates on sticks, others balloons. He hopped over a rope to the back of the circus ground to look for Natasha. Perhaps after aerial practice, they'd be able to curl up together and hone their terrestrial skills as there was no evening performance.

'Johnny, there you are. I look everywhere,' Bodo called to him from outside a tent. There was a note of urgency in his voice.

Johnny hurried over and they went into the tent. Natasha was waiting. Her face beamed up at him. They hugged.

'I was making sure I wasn't followed,' he said to Bodo. He kissed Natasha and she squeezed his hand.

'Listen, you don't believe what I see Thursday night?' Bodo said, his painted eyes darting about excitedly.

'What? What?' Johnny felt his own excitement running up his arms.

'Alice.'

'Alice? I know you saw Alice. We were together.' His excitement slipped back down and out of his fingers. Alice was about the last person to excite him. On Thursday night she'd buzzed round him like a mosquito as they crossed back into the West, insisting that he'd made a mistake, that really he loved her. As if he didn't know. He'd thought Alice was a friend, that she'd be happy for him, but she wasn't.

'No, I see Alice from my apartment.'

Natasha gazed expectantly at him. He didn't know what the hell Bodo was on about.

'What? How?'

'I see Alice in apartment over the Wall!' Bodo announced triumphantly. 'And also, I think, your friend, the big American guy.'

'That's impossible,' Johnny said quietly.

'At half one.'

Johnny knew he meant half-past midnight. He was fairly sure Alice was still at Peter's at that time. It was possible. But that would mean that Bodo's apartment was opposite Peter's. Then he remembered the clown on the other side of the Wall.

'You're the clown? We saw you once. About a month ago. You waved to us?'

'A month ago? No, I don't remember. But maybe it was the Professor. There was one day after performance we come back to my apartment.'

Maybe.

'You live there? With Alice?' Natasha said. The tension in her body sliced him in half.

'Alice doesn't live there,' he explained. 'She was just visiting Peter, after we left you. It is Peter's apartment, the American guy, and I am staying there – and another couple of guys.'

Natasha mellowed while Bodo regained his painted smile. No doubt fantasies of a Wall romance with Alice vanished. Probably as well. Johnny suspected the feeling wasn't reciprocal.

'But I can wave to you,' Bodo said, beaming again. 'You know I think I see the American, but I wave and wave and he doesn't see me... *Wie heißt das?*' He turned to Natasha and said something.

'Deliberate,' she said.

Johnny remembered the blind down when he was there and Peter making some excuse to Alice for not opening it. She said she wanted to wave at the clown and he wouldn't let her. Could he have closed it deliberately? Surely not.

'So did Alice not see you?'

Bodo shook his head. 'No, she opens blind but she has her back to me.'

'I can't believe you live opposite,' Johnny muttered. Or that Peter hadn't said anything.

'Tonight we go and see,' Natasha declared.

'Why aren't you practising? What are you all doing here?' A voice spoke quietly behind them in German.

They swung round. It was the Professor standing in the entrance of the tent. Within minutes Johnny was gripping the taut fibres of the high wire beneath his feet. Up in the roof of the world he felt extraordinarily happy, as if he had left all his earthly worries packed in a bundle down below. He practised different walks, forwards and backwards. Natasha watched him until she was called away by her sister. The others burst out laughing when he did a goose step. He imagined himself stepping through the clouds, marching to nowhere; a lost soldier. A vision of an angel greeted him as Natasha flew through the air on the trapeze. He wanted to catch her but she was gone.

'Okay Johnny, we must train now.'

Johnny stepped off the wire. Natasha had to practise on her own, now that they could no longer do their act. She fell onto the safety net and darted up to the perch. She copied the same walks. Even the Professor laughed.

They practised hard for two hours. Johnny watched Natasha, his heart throbbing. She danced through the air and then lay down on the wire, suspended like a dew drop on a thread. She was beautiful.

'Na ja, besser, besser,' the Professor called up to her before yelling at Bodo when he almost didn't catch Zoyenka on the trapeze. Zoyenka yelled even louder.

Poor Bodo. He must be exhausted after clowning, juggling and flying, as well as being in love and Wall watching half the night. The Professor clapped his hands and made an announcement. This was followed by cheers of delight. Johnny looked at Natasha.

'We eat in his caravan,' she said, smiling.

Johnny didn't quite share their enthusiasm. Any terrestrial encounter with Natasha was looking less likely. Bodo took him to his caravan to wash in a bowl of lukewarm water. The caravan was old and small like the girls' but, unlike the girls', it was immaculate. Bodo talked all the time, mainly about Alice.

'I wish we not go on tour,' he said. 'I might never see her again.'

Johnny didn't like to say that he doubted it would make any difference: Alice would never come over to see him anyway. He wondered if Bodo and Natasha had slept together. Not that it mattered.

'I wish you weren't going as well,' Johnny said. 'End of September is a long time. Six months.' Six months without her. The thought of the days tugged at his heart. 'I want to go with you,' he added.

'It is not possible, Johnny. But you can ask the Professor.'

They went to the Professor's caravan. Although one of the bigger caravans, it was still cramped, smelly, noisy and hot. A couple of small dogs yapped at the new arrivals and sniffed around their ankles. A radio blasted out from the top of a little cupboard. The walls were coated with rugs, on which were tacked old faded photographs, newspaper cut-outs, medals and other circus memorabilia. An electric heater glowed under the table. Natasha hadn't arrived yet. The Professor, all grins and warmth, hugged him and ordered him to sit at the table. Johnny had never seen this sociable Professor before: it was as if the heat of the caravan had melted his edges. Today would be the right time to ask.

A glass of beer appeared before him, compliments of Hanna, the Professor's wife. She was in her forties, small, dark and round. Hanna hovered between a huge steaming pot and Johnny. He had never seen her before but she fussed around him as if she'd known him all her life. Her English was as limited as his German but they spoke with their eyes, hands, faces and photographs. She showed him that she was from an old circus family. Like him, she used to be a funambulist, but she fell on her thirtieth birthday and broke her legs in seven places. She was lucky to be alive of course.

Johnny asked her if she'd not worn a safety belt.

She had a belt but did not attach it as she had done the performance a thousand times before. She could do it with her eyes closed. But she lost her concentration for a fraction of a second and that was it: the end of her career.

'Have you never been on a wire since?'

She shook her head as she stirred the giant pot. Johnny saw tears in her eyes. She told him that when she broke her legs she also broke her balance. At least, that's what Johnny thought she said. A tear snaked down her face and dripped into the pot. The Professor slipped his arms around her waist and kissed her neck. Within seconds, she was laughing and telling him to stop.

'They were so good on the wire,' Bodo told him quietly. 'Maybe like you and Natasha.'

Johnny didn't reply. He tried to imagine what it would be like to be old, to look back on your life. It was hard: so much could happen in twenty years. So much happened in twenty days. All he could see was his life as a wire spanning an empty world to the horizon. He would have to walk that wire to be able to look back. Who knows where it would take him, where he would wobble, where he would fall. He didn't even know if the wire crossed the East or the West. Would he be kissing Natasha's neck in twenty years' time like the Professor in a caravan in East Berlin? Would he still be wire walking? He couldn't imagine a life without being able to perform but he knew that life, particularly circus life, came without guarantees.

Natasha and Zoyenka noisily entered the caravan and there were more hugs and kisses for everyone. Johnny tried to get Natasha to sit next to him but she sat opposite and rested her feet on his knees. He massaged her strong little toes. Zoyenka slipped in next to her sister and fell into a sulky silence. Another man, Thomas, the sharpshooter, came into the caravan, followed by another two male acrobats who were the Professor's sons. Johnny wondered how many people could actually fit in the caravan and around the table, designed for no more than eight. He counted thirteen.

Black bread, *Bulette, Bratwurst* and *Schaschlik* appeared and empty bottles of beer were full again. Everyone began talking, laughing, eating. Even Zoyenka smiled when she was allowed a glass of beer. The Professor squeezed in between himself and Bodo and slapped him on the back. He spoke to Bodo.

'He wants to tell you that you are the best wire walker he has met - after himself, of course!'

'Thank you. Ask him if there is any way I can go with you on tour? If I defect?'

The table around Johnny fell silent as if they had suddenly understood. The Professor looked at him, his dark eyes lined with concern. He said something to Bodo.

'He says you can not defect.'

So they had understood.

'Why not?' Zoyenka said.

'Yes, why not? This is what I've always wanted to do.' Johnny said, surprised by Zoyenka's defence. Natasha didn't say anything. 'I want to stay with you,' he added, looking the Professor in the eye.

The Professor dipped his eyes and began talking to Bodo in gunfire German. Others chipped in. As far as Johnny knew all the performers were German, except for Natasha and Zoyenka, who didn't seem to be understanding much either. Natasha slid her feet up and down his outstretched legs. He tried to catch her eagle toes again but they slipped away. Hanna called the girls over. They dipped under the table and went to help her. Whether it was coincidence or not, by the time Bodo spoke to him they had left the caravan to get more beer.

'I'm afraid I can not explain well. I do not think you understand the regime we live with. *Na ja,* it is very dangerous. We are not free. There are spies. Everywhere. We trust no one. You are mad to defect. They arrest you and, if they let you free and give you citizenship, you are forever watched. And, you never go back. We can not have responsibility. You know?'

Johnny looked around the table. Everyone was watching him. He took a sip of beer and met their gaze.

'I don't care. I want to perform with you. I want to be with Natasha. Surely I take responsibility for my life?'

The Professor shook his head and said something to Bodo.

'No,' Bodo said. 'They wouldn't allow you. We can not allow you.'

The words cut into his flesh.

'But it's not right,' he muttered. 'It's not fair. There has to be a way.' Everything was possible. Everyone else laughed.

'You know they teach people here that they are good and tell them that other people are bad. And when that doesn't work they build a wall. And then they tell people that they are surrounded by enemies and that they must watch their neighbours. This is not right. There is no way. This is why you can not defect.'

The Professor spoke to Bodo.

'He says that you must go to the circus in West Germany. There are many performers from the East. You know when they build the Wall many circus people are carried over in suitcases. Did you know? The old Berlin circus was finished with half here and half there. There was even someone who walked across the Wall on a tightrope. Can you imagine? But the Wall then was easier to cross. Now it is impossible perhaps. He says that the Wall will not be forever and you will meet Natasha again.'

The Professor and some of the others were nodding. Johnny didn't reply. They didn't get it. When? The Wall was going nowhere that he could see. Maybe in fifty years time but, by then, their lives would be over, their time together lost. There had to be a way. Maybe he could smuggle Natasha across to the West. But, even if he could, he knew she didn't want to leave her family.

The girls came back into the caravan with a crate of beer and everyone began talking again. Hanna dished out the contents of the pot. Johnny was not sure what it was but it looked like meatball soup. More beer flowed round the table and the earlier conversation seemingly forgotten. For Johnny, the rest of the meal felt like a last supper. They would be gone in three weeks – without him. He somehow doubted that he would ever be here, sharing their food, again. He clung to Natasha's foot. What were they going to do? Her toes gripped his hand. Several times she looked questioningly at him.

'When is your dance performance?' Bodo asked him.

Johnny was surprised that Bodo had remembered. He himself had almost forgotten.

'Next Saturday, 10 March. Two weeks before you go. And it goes on for a week. I really don't want to do it.'

Hanna said something to him. Bodo translated.

'She says after you dance in the air, it is hard to dance on the ground.'

Maybe that was it.

'You must do it,' Bodo said. 'I would like to see you dance.'

'I too,' said Natasha.

'It is sad that we can not go for the night,' Bodo said.

Even Zoyenka nodded.

By the time they had thanked the Professor and Hanna, hugged and kissed everyone, it was completely dark except for the ice crystals jostling the air, stabbing their faces.

Johnny desperately wanted to be alone with Natasha but he could feel time slipping between them.

'Can we go back to your caravan?' Johnny asked Natasha. Natasha, looking doubtful, pointed to her sister and shook her head.

'We can go to my place,' Bodo said. 'If no one follow us tonight. It is not far if we take a bus.' He winked at Johnny. 'Then you can wave to your American friend.'

Peter was the last person he wanted to wave to. Natasha pinched his arm. He slid it around her shoulders and pulled her towards him, shivering slightly. Bodo said something to Natasha about Zoyenka, who folded her arms and followed them anyway. Johnny thought she was acting strangely, but she was at that awkward age.

They walked briskly to Puschkin Allee and got on a battered old bus, empty aside from an old man with a bag of potatoes. They got out after a couple of stops and walked along Bouche Straße in the shadows of the dark Berlin houses. Bodo checked that they weren't being followed. No one could see anyone. Johnny could sense they were getting closer to the Wall. They turned off just before they reached it and crossed into what must be the other side of Heidelberger Straße.

Without a word, they followed Bodo through an entrance and across a courtyard, through another door and up some pitch-black stairs, which Johnny thought were just like the ones at Peter's. They reached the top as silently as cats hunting. As soon as they were in, Bodo shut and locked the door. They all felt their way through to the living room. In the dark the rooms were cold and empty.

'The doors have ears,' Bodo said. 'And there is no electricity tonight. Normally, I put on radio. I hope no one listens.'

Was the apartment bugged? Johnny made straight for the large window. The glow from the death strip pierced the apartment. He would be mad to want to live here.

'How come they have electricity,' he said, but he had been in the East long enough for it not to be a question. He stared above the arched lights highlighting the wire and concrete below. Bodo was right. There was Peter's flat, directly opposite. The blinds were up and the lamp was on in the lounge. It looked warm and cheery. He could not see anyone but he thought he could see the television flickering. Natasha came to join him while Bodo and Zoyenka lit some candles.

'That's where I live,' he said.

'So near and yet so long,' Natasha said. She sighed deeply. 'Where do you sleep?'

'My room's on the other side. You can't see it from here. That's the living room, the bathroom, Peter's room. And that's Michael's room.' He panned his finger across the building opposite.

They stood entwined in the dark, watching the other world like watching a silent film. The Western world flickering with life while the Eastern world remained in darkness.

'It is where you live, yes?' Bodo said, coming in with a candle.

'Yes. We will be able to wave to each other.'

'We make a secret code,' Natasha said.

'The guards find out,' Zoyenka said.

She was probably right, Johnny thought. Natasha snapped at her in Russian. Just then Peter rose from the couch and lunged towards the TV. He changed the channel and then came towards the window, yawning and stretching up towards the ceiling.

Johnny waved, even though he knew that Peter couldn't see him.

'Let me,' said Bodo.

Johnny, Natasha and Zoyenka stepped back and Bodo approached the window with his candle in his hand. A look of horror swept across Peter's face and within seconds the blinds fell down. Johnny and Natasha burst out laughing.

'You see?' Bodo said.

'I'm not surprised,' Johnny said. 'You must look like a ghost with that candle under your face.' Particularly if Peter were stoned.

'What is "ghost"?' Natasha asked.

'A dead person – come to life again.'

'Ah,' Natasha said. 'Listen, when we need to talk to you, we flash a light two times at 10 p.m.. Okay?'

'Okay,' Johnny replied. He would watch every night at ten o'clock. 'But then what?'

'Then you come and see me. I wait for you next day at the Friedrichstraße station.'

'Okay,' said Johnny. She made it sound so easy.

Zoyenka didn't say anything but Johnny noted, even in the dark, the look of disapproval on her face.

'Come on, let's look,' Natasha said, pulling him away.

There wasn't much to see. Bodo showed him an old-fashioned bakelite telephone with a receiver that sat on top, which he had only ever seen in films.

'Take it,' Bodo said. 'I must wait ten years for a connection.'

'I can't take it,' Johnny said. 'You might need it.'

'What? In my coffin?'

Bodo went over to the window once more and stared across the Wall. Johnny was about to join him but Natasha was leading him into a bedroom. Like the living room, it faced the Wall and the lights from below cast shadows onto the ceiling. They lay on the bed together and held each other tightly. The springs creaked and poked them through the mattress.

'I don't want to go,' Johnny whispered.

'I too,' said Natasha. 'You not coming with us?'

'The Professor says no.' Johnny knew as he said this that he was letting her down. 'But maybe I can come and visit you?'

She sighed and shook her head. 'No, too dangerous. The Professor is right. But perhaps I come back to East Berlin to meet you.'

They were both snatching at straws. Johnny kissed her but he felt as if he were falling not flying. He heard Bodo and Zoyenka talking in the lounge. Zoyenka sounded angry.

'You think better?' Natasha asked, after they have made the quickest love in history.

Johnny didn't know if she was serious. How could they make love in the shadows of death?

'Johnny?' Bodo called. 'It is time for you to go.'

'Okay,' he said.

They rearranged their clothes and joined Bodo and Zoyenka who were sitting at the candlelit table drinking beer. Zoyenka was frowning. Bodo had written a letter which he gave to Johnny.

'I have an idea,' he said, looking pleased with himself. 'Please will you give this letter to Alice.'

'Sure,' Johnny said, taking the letter and putting it in his pocket. He would go round early in the morning and slip it under her door. He didn't want to see her. 'If I don't get searched.'

Bodo shrugged. 'It is 10 p.m., you must go. Don't forget the telephone.'

Natasha spoke to Bodo. He nodded, but reluctantly.

'You come here next Tuesday? We have only matinee and we come after. We meet...' He turned to Natasha and they argued about where.

Johnny nodded anyway.

They made their way to Treptower S-Bahn. Johnny insisted on going alone from there. He hugged Natasha tightly on the platform. There was no one else around. The phone, cradled in his arm, poked them.

'See you soon,' he whispered as he opened the door of the train.

'Telephone me when you get to your home.' She laughed.

A Letter from the East

It was six o'clock when Alice banged on Peter's door, the letter still in her hand. She hoped Johnny would be at rehearsals. Her heart bumped clumsily inside her chest. Those stairs had almost killed her, even though she'd only had three vodkas and sixteen cigarettes all afternoon. And she had needed every single one. She knocked again.

The door opened. Peter stood there in his ladybird dressing gown and black fluffy slippers. He didn't look very pleased to see her, but she didn't care.

'Peter, I need to talk to you. Something has happened.'

'Hi Mad,' he said. 'What's up?' He held the door, barring her way from entering.

'I need to talk to you. I need to know what riggers are? Is Johnny in?'

'What? Is it important? I was just taking a nap.' He yawned.

'Yes, it's important. I have something I need to show you.' She waved the letter about. 'In secret,' she hissed.

Peter laughed. 'We're not in the East here, darling.'

You wait, she thought.

He sighed. 'Come on in, then. Johnny might be at some rehearsal. He's got some show or something soon.'

He led the way past Johnny's room, which was closed, through to the living room. Judging by the deep imprint on the sofa, it looked like Peter had been lying there watching the television. He crossed over to the window and closed the blinds.

'Why you doing that?' Alice couldn't help asking.

'In case you hadn't noticed, it's dark.'

'So, it doesn't have anything to do with Bodo living there?'

Peter visibly flinched. 'Who?' His eyes darted around the room as he sat down on the sofa. His fingers groped for his cigarettes. He grabbed one and threw the packet of Marlboro at her.

'Bodo, the guy we met with Johnny in Alexanderplatz. The clown I said I saw across the other side of the Wall from your window.' She hesitated before taking a Marlboro, but the situation called for a cigarette and she only had a couple of Benson's. She lit them both.

'He lives there?' he said, inhaling deeply, his hands shaking even more than hers.

'Yep.' Alice knew he was pretending.

'How do you know?'

Alice couldn't be bothered to explain. She just held out the letter.

'What's that? Let me see.' He snatched it from her and held it out at arm's length to read.

Dear Alice,

I am writing very quick when Johnny is with Natasha in my apartment. You know I live opposite the apartment of Peter - in the East of course. I see you on Thursday night after you leave us. Then Peter closes the blind. Johnny has the last show on Saturday 17 March. We want to go. I have one idea. I can put a wire across the wall to the apartment of Peter. Do you know riggers? I need 2 or 3 people to help rig the wires. I send instructions. If you can help, please wave the white flag to me from the apartment of Peter on Tuesday evening, 6 March at 11 p.m..

Johnny does not know about this.

I hope your beautiful friend Peter can help.

Your love

Bodo

'Well? What do you think, beautiful friend?' Alice asked impatiently. Peter stared at the letter incredulously.

'So that they can watch Johnny perform? They're mad. Tell them to go to hell.'

'Okay,' Alice said relieved. She hadn't really thought Peter would help, but she thought it only fair to ask him. It was his apartment. She certainly had no wish to help Johnny. But Bodo was quite sweet. And, as Peter said, didn't he have a right to see how miserable the West was? Besides, she had no idea what riggers were.

'Tuesday, that's today, when did you get this?'

'I found it this morning. Johnny must have delivered it.'

He hadn't woken her which was just as well. She never wanted to see him again after what he'd said after the circus. *'Natasha's special, someone I want to spend the rest of my life with. I thought you'd be happy for me.'* Get real, Johnny. And now she was being asked to help him/them spend the rest of their fucking lives together. Really. Mind you, if she were shot, then that would solve that little problem. Then again, it probably wouldn't as Johnny would never forgive her for helping. Whichever way, she lost.

Peter put the letter down on the table. 'I need a drink. Do you want one?'

She nodded.

Peter returned with two Beck's and a mirror with a couple of lines.

What a hero. Alice rolled a ten Mark note and did a line. She sniffed. Peter did the same, then sat on the edge of the sofa, and picked up the letter again.

'So Johnny knows that Bodo lives opposite?' he asked. He sniffed loudly.

'I would have thought so. Bodo says that Johnny was in his apartment. Hasn't he said anything to you?'

'No, but I haven't seen him since last week. Since we went out.' Peter went to the window and opened the blind. 'So Johnny doesn't know anything about them wanting to cross?'

'Apparently not. Why, you're not changing your mind are you?' she said, getting up and joining him at the window. All was dark and quiet. The glow from the death strip didn't quite reach the bright living room. It wasn't far across but it would still be madness. 'Do you think it's possible?'

'Who knows?'

'Do you know any riggers then?' Alice asked, jokingly.

'Not exactly, but I used to sail,' Peter said.

'Oh,' Alice said. 'Is that what it means?'

'Alice, is the education system in England that bad?'

'Yeah, it's that bad,' she snapped.

'Really. Rigging is anything that involves using ropes etc. but I guess it generally refers to sailing.'

'You used to sail?' She couldn't quite imagine him climbing up masts without breaking them.

'Yeah, I used to sail.'

His eyes floated around the room again. Surely not. 'What are you thinking?' she asked.

'Well, I'm thinking,' Peter said. 'It's their life, not ours.'

'Don't be daft, Peter. The guards are bound to see them or hear them.' It must be the drugs talking.

'Maybe, but look, the guards are down there. It depends how good they are. You've seen them perform at the circus – how good are they?'

'They're good, but it's a long way across.'

'It's not that far. It's only about ten metres. One guy walked between the top of the Twin Towers.'

'What Twin Towers?'

Peter sighed. Loudly. Alice thought it was because she didn't know anything. Well, it wasn't her fault. The education system in England was crap. Besides, he was about ten years older than her.

'You know the World Trade Centre in New York? The highest buildings in the world – 110 floors high.'

'Someone walked on a tightrope between two buildings?'

'Yeah, a French guy, Philippe Petit I think he was called. Ten years ago or more. You were still in diapers then.'

'I don't think so, Peter. I didn't know that, but we can't help them – what about that Russian tart?'

'What about her?'

'Well you don't just think they're just coming for the performance, do you?' Alice said.

'No, of course not, I'm not that dumb.'

'Well then, she'll want to move in with Johnny. And you.' Alice said, hoping this might put him off.

'I'll tell them to move out,' Peter said.

'And what if they're shot crossing.'

'Then she won't be moving in.'

Alice half laughed. 'Did you know that Bodo lived across there?'

'No, of course not. I have seen someone but I didn't know it was him. Now that we all know, then...' Peter drifted off for a while. 'Maybe we will help them.'

'What! Why? I don't see why we should. Couldn't we be arrested?'

'What for? If they were spies, then maybe. And, Johnny aside, as far as I know, it's never been done before, Alice. They've dug tunnels, crossed over in balloons, in the backs of cars... but never put a wire across.' Peter was getting excited. 'We'd be famous. We would go down in history, Mad darling.'

'Infamous, more like,' Alice said. But Peter had a point.

'Even better.'

They both stared at the black empty buildings opposite.

'I would need help,' Peter said.

Michael arrived back with a crate of beer and Peter asked him what he thought. He looked at them as if they were crazy. Alice nodded, eyeing the beer bottles, while Peter began a long explanation in German. Not understanding much, Alice took the crate of beer into the kitchen and stocked up the fridge. Then she handed out bottles to Peter and Michael and went to the window to stare across the Wall. Bodo's apartment was still hidden in the dark shadows. She tried to imagine them flinging a wire across and walking over the Wall, but the thought made her shiver. Michael was arguing with Peter about some technical point. She didn't understand what, but she understood that Michael didn't think it possible.

'Hey guys, what are we gonna do when Johnny comes home?'
They stopped arguing.
'Why shouldn't he know?' Michael asked.
Peter told him it would be a surprise.
'*Ja, ja*, big surprise, for sure.'
'*Willst du helfen oder nicht helfen?*' Alice asked, bored of not understanding.
'Okay, but I don't think it is good idea. It is dangerous,' Michael said. 'And I take no responsibility for the consequences.'
'Neither do I, darling.' Peter laughed, going into the kitchen.
Alice was surprised. So he had really agreed.
'Are we going to ask Hermann as well?' Alice called after him.
'We'll have to tell him. I don't think he'll be much help though,' Peter called back.

As Peter returned with a bowl of peanuts, someone opened the front door. Alice held her breath as the footsteps got closer.

It was Johnny in his DMs, black jeans, long coat and black wool hat.

'Oh hi,' he said. He took off his hat and ran his fingers through his dark hair.

Alice turned away, hoping no one would see her heart racing around the room. She wished she didn't feel so alive every time she saw him. She used to think that he felt like this too but she knew now that he didn't. Not that she didn't still think that they belonged together any more, only that she knew he didn't feel with as much intensity as she did. Well, any intensity at all actually. Passion came with a switch for Johnny. He could switch it on and a fire would run between them. They would burn for eternity, melt snow and ice; they would be the only two people in the world and when they made love they roared like a furnace. Then he would switch it off and while she lay awake shivering day and night thinking of him, of how they made each other feel, of how much she missed him, of how the burning hole inside her was eating away her insides, he would be crossing borders to other worlds, meeting other people, walking in the air, holding *her*... Maybe all men were like that. She didn't know. She'd never been in love before. If that's what it was.

'Have you come to wave at Bodo?' he asked her, coming to the window.

She turned and stared into his cool blue eyes. She couldn't believe he assumed that she even liked Bodo.

'Fuck off,' she said.

For once, Johnny looked taken aback.

Peter laughed and told her to behave herself. But she felt good, better than she'd felt for a long time. The burning had gone away for a moment. She turned back to the window and sucked on the Beck's bottle, amazed what two little words can do.

She saw Johnny step back in the reflection. Peter was asking him why he hadn't told him that Bodo lived opposite.

'I was only there for the first time on Saturday night,' Johnny said. 'I didn't know. Bodo said that he'd seen you and Alice on Thursday night but that you'd put the blind down on him. And on Saturday night as well. You remember?'

Peter said that he had no idea it was him. He'd thought he'd seen a ghost. Alice still thought he was lying. But what the hell.

She went into the kitchen to look at the clock: it was five to nine. They needed to get rid of Johnny. She went back into the living room and picked up some peanuts.

'I'm hungry. Peter, shall we get a kebab or something? We still have time before they come.'

Peter hesitated. Alice winked at him popping several peanuts into her mouth.

'Okay.'

'Who's coming?' Johnny asked Peter.

'Oh, just some *nice* boyfriends of Mad's. We met them at the Tunnel on Thursday night. She's promised to share them out. I'll go and get ready.'

'Okay, have a good time. I'm going to take a bath and crash,' Johnny said.

Peter and Johnny left the room together. Alice thought she heard Johnny ask Peter what he'd done to upset her now. As if he didn't know. She must be indeed mad to do anything to help him.

Peter came back and they went across the road to get a kebab.

'Do you always have to make me go out, Mad?' Peter said. 'Couldn't you have just said they were coming to my place? He wouldn't have stayed long with you there telling him to fuck off.'

'Maybe. But this way is better. Besides I'm hungry.'

'You're always hungry.'

When they got back, Johnny was in his room. Michael was still up, waiting. He told them that Johnny had been watching the apartment until about half an hour ago.

'Perhaps he was just waiting to glimpse her,' Alice said. 'So are we on?'

'Yeah, what the hell. It's their life.'

'Okay, have you got a white shirt or something, Peter?'

'I'll get a towel.'

At exactly eleven o'clock, they watched the light go on in Bodo's apartment. He wasn't on his own but with an older man, not *her*. It wasn't anyone Alice recognised, but they were talking non-stop and gesticulating wildly as they stood in the middle of the room in front of the window. They all waved to each other, then Alice improvised with a mop and a whitish towel and waved it around the lounge.

'Okay, Mad, I think that's enough,' Peter said. 'You're attracting more attention than a lighthouse.'

'No, I'm not,' Alice said.

Bodo and his friend were standing around a table. It looked like he was writing, and the other guy was pulling something out of a bag.

'Can the guards see them?' Alice said, peering down in the direction of the watchtower. It was quite a long way away.

'Maybe. They do have binoculars.'

'I know that.'

Bodo came to the window and mimed opening it.

'They want us to open the window,' Alice said, but Peter was already doing it.

'Shit. He's going to shoot us,' she said. The other guy was holding a bow and arrow in front of the window. She stepped back.

'He's not going to shoot us. He wants us to get out of the way,' Peter said.

'Oh really?' Alice said. She would never have guessed that. Peter was so stupid sometimes.

Michael opened the window. A blast of freezing air hit them.

'We go to the kitchen,' he said.

'What are they going to do?' Alice asked.

'They're going to send us something,' Michael said.

Maybe the older man was the one who shot the apple off that boy's head in the circus.

'Smart,' Peter said.

They retreated to the kitchen, where Alice helped herself to beer. She opened one for Peter and Michael as well. This was fun. The guys seemed really into it too. And the burning was still at bay. A single thud sounded from the other room. Then all was quiet. Michael looked out of the kitchen.

'Okay,' he said.

On the wooden floor was an arrow with a blunted head and something taped to its shaft.

134

'Show me, show me,' Alice said, as Michael stripped the tape off and spread five sheets of A4 paper on the floor.

Peter squatted down next to Michael and the two pored over the drawings and instructions. They were in German, Alice saw that much, and one of them was an intricate drawing of a room. It wasn't very interesting. She waved instead to Bodo who was once again hovering near the window. He stepped back, blew her a kiss and gave her a little wave. Ah, he was sweet really. If ever that fire died down, and if he didn't get shot, maybe he could have that date after all.

'So what is it?' she asked.

Peter and Michael gibbered in German. They weren't sure if next Saturday, 17 March would be enough time for them to prepare. Michael still didn't seem convinced that it was possible at all. Enough time? Over a week? She looked at one of the detailed drawings again. Dozens of squiggles trespassed the Wall and ran either side of the little balconies. A thick black line slid from Bodo's living room to Peter's bathroom.

'Why is it coming into the bathroom?' she asked.

'Because that's where they want the main cable fixed,' Peter said.

'What to a towel rail?' Alice said.

'Yeah, Mad, great idea.'

'Here we have to put a beam across on the floor at the same height as the window,' Michael explained.

'They don't want much, do they?'

'It is a lot of work,' Michael said, and sighed.

'But they have thought of everything,' Peter said.

'Maybe, maybe not.'

'How they going to get this thick black line across?' Alice said. Surely they weren't going to throw it.

'You see here.' Michael showed her one of the drawings. 'They will use a fishing line and then the cable will be attached to that. Then we must pull it across.'

'But how they going to get a fishing line across?' Alice imagined Bodo dangling a fishing rod over the Wall.

'Attached to an arrow. They'll shoot it across,' Peter said.

'Oh.'

'Someone's put a lot of thought into this,' Peter said.

They certainly had. Alice stared at the sketches of cables, rings and attachments. Each one with a separate note, presumably explaining how it was to be done. Impressive.

'What are these?' Alice asked, pointing to fainter lines heading for Peter's room.

'They're to support the main cable so that it doesn't sway.'

'Won't it be heavy? To pull across I mean.'

'Yes,' Michael said. 'And we won't be able to let it bend too much or it will hit the Wall.'

'But they know that.' Peter said.

'Maybe, maybe not,' Michael said again.

'I think they're waiting,' Alice said. Bodo was standing near the window. 'Do I wave the mop?'

Peter and Michael looked at each other, then at her. Peter nodded. Michael shook his head.

Crossing the Berlin Wall

Peter sucked on his inhaler as he ran around the apartment checking everything was in place. It was 5 p.m. Saturday, March 17. Johnny had already left for the theatre, Hermann was safely out the way in Köln. Only Michael and Alice to arrive. His hands shook but in view of the momentous event about to happen that wasn't surprising. Everything was ready – except for the horizontal metal bar that would join the two pillars in the bathroom, but that wouldn't take long to bolt together. He had followed Bodo's instructions exactly. The pulley system and reel worked. He lit a cigarette and checked again. The five sheets of paper were crumpled and worn out with checking. There was no way he could have missed anything. He opened the window for the thousandth time. The night was overcast, cold, but it didn't look like it would snow. They'd agreed to abort if it snowed.

He couldn't have done it without Michael, for sure. Not only had Michael been able to get most of the building materials from his work but had also helped, albeit reluctantly, drill into the walls and cement the metal rods in the bathroom. They had attached the metal bars next to the windows in his bedroom while Johnny was performing and hid them behind a curtain that Alice had acquired from somewhere. The steel pillars embedded in concrete in the bathroom were impossible to conceal, but they told Johnny that Hermann had a new project. Hermann, when told of the plan, had shrugged and said, 'I told you he was trouble.' But he'd agreed to spend hours in the bathroom contemplating the metal objects before disappearing back to Köln for the weekend. Peter made sure he'd taken his drugs with him as, if anything did go wrong, the police would be round for sure.

He sat down on the toilet. Ash fell onto the paper beneath the thick black line that linked East and West. If they did fall, it would be certain death. It was said the strip was mined. Even if it wasn't, the guards would shoot them if they were spotted. He hadn't had time all week to consider death, but now that all was ready he had a bad feeling. And the more he thought about it, the worse it got.

Michael wouldn't have got involved if he hadn't pleaded with him. Even Alice hadn't wanted to do it. Why the hell had he? He supposed it was partly because he wanted to prove that he could do it and partly because he believed in freedom. But, most likely, because he'd been high and thought that this might make him famous.

Mad rapped on the door. Peter shouted to her and went to open it. And, partly, because she'd be so pissed if the love of Johnny's life were here.

'Is he gone?'

Peter nodded. For once, she'd brought some beer. Amazing. She was also holding a slice of pepperoni pizza in her hand.

'Nice to see you dressed.'

'Hee, hee, aren't you funny.'

'I'm far too hungry and thirsty to be funny.' She stuffed the pizza in her mouth. 'Is everything ready?' she said between bites.

'I just need Michael to help me bolt up the bar in the bathroom.'

'Can I help?'

'No, I'll wait for Michael, thank you, darling. A slice of pizza would have been nice.'

'Oh, sorry, shall I go and get you one?'

'No, but you can open me one of those beers please.'

'Sure.' She went into the kitchen, clattered about in the fridge and returned with a couple of opened bottles.

'What'll we do if they're shot?' she said, handing him the beer.

'Not a lot we can do.'

'I guess not.'

They drank in silence. Then she said:

'You look better anyway.'

He grunted although he did feel better. A couple of weeks away from the Kiosk and a reduction in drugs and alcohol had helped, although that was about to end tonight as he had planned a surprise welcome party.

'I've got some really good speed,' she said.

'Oh good darling, that's just what the doctor recommended,' Peter said. She looked like she believed him.

'I wish I didn't have to go to this performance.'

'I got the same impression from Johnny.'

'Yeah, you said the other day that it hadn't been going very well.'

'I don't think he gets on that well with Sophie. Artistic differences. Johnny's vision is up there.' Peter rolled his eyes towards the ceiling.

'What a shame,' she said. She didn't seem at all interested. 'Well, anyway, I'll save the speed until later. I don't want to be buzzing and bored and have to sit still.'

'Where did you get it from?' Mad's speed was always good.

'London. A friend of mine sent it over in the post.'

'You were lucky they didn't find it.'

'It was inside a leather studded belt. The only problem was I had to cut into the leather to get it out.'

'How much did you get?'

'About an ounce. I need to sell some of it tonight as I'm skint. I've got half gram and gram packets.'

'On you?' Peter eyes opened wide.

'Yes, why?'

'Mad, what if something goes wrong tonight and the police come round and search us?'

'Oh fuck. I hadn't thought of that.'

'Well, maybe you should.'

'What about Hermann?'

'Hermann's not here. He's gone to Köln.'

'Oh.'

Mad promised to be back in twenty-five minutes. Silly ass. As she left, Michael arrived home from work. Peter inhaled in relief. He couldn't do this on his own. Michael had a Pilsner in his hand and a carrier bag full of beer. He staggered through the hallway.

'Michael? *Bist du besoffen*?'

'*Ich, ich, nein, kein… Scheiße.*'

Scheiße indeed. Peter tugged again on his Ventolin. Why the hell was he doing this? He toyed with the idea of walking out and leaving them to it but Michael dropped his bag, apologised and asked for a coffee. Peter shook his head and went into the kitchen.

Thirty minutes and two strong cups of coffee later, Michael put the finishing touches to the bar in the bathroom while Mad, who had returned precisely twenty-five minutes later, was keeping watch from the bathroom window. It was almost six o'clock.

'They're there!' she shrieked.

As Peter looked up, a light went off in Bodo's apartment. They were doing this in the dark. All week he had seen the shadows moving around the apartment, guided only by the light from the death strip.

'Okay, here goes. Open the window, Mad.'

She opened the window and they all left the bathroom, closed the door and lingered outside.

'Do we have time for a beer?' she asked.

'No,' Peter growled.

Within seconds, something thundered into the bathroom. A sharp ping ricocheted.

'I think it hit something,' Mad said.

Peter wished she wouldn't state the obvious. All the time. They waited a couple of minutes to make sure there weren't going to be any more missiles and then crept back to the bathroom, which was now covered in a web of fishing line. The arrow must have hit the metal pillars, got snagged around the shower rail and crashed round the bathroom before finally landing in the bath. Peter snatched it up and examined it. The fishing line was still attached.

'It's okay. Tell them it's okay,' he said to Mad, who was already holding the mop. He began to unspin the line. Michael helped him coil it onto the reel.

'Okay, now we can begin. What's happening over there?' he asked Mad.

'I don't know, I can't see them, Peter.' Panic had edged into her voice.

'If you can't see them, the guards can't either. We'll begin to reel the line in and see what happens. Michael.'

Peter felt calm, calmer than he'd felt for a long time. Adrenaline pumped around his body but he was in control. Helping people escape from the East was a good buzz. Michael began to reel in the line while Peter went to the window. He could just about make out the shimmering thread that crossed into darkness. He couldn't see the watchtower from his window but they may well be able to see inside Bodo's apartment. The thread glistened like quicksilver every so often.

'It's getting heavier,' Michael said.

As he said that the thread dived vertically towards the Wall.

'*Scheiße*, what are they doing?' Peter's heart raced up and down his body. 'Reel in quicker!'

Michael's hand steamed around the reel, his muscles pumping. Beads of sweat raced down his face.

'I think it's okay, the line is straightening.'

'I need a rest,' Michael said, panting.

'Okay, tell them to stop for a moment, Mad.'

Peter went to take over from Michael while Mad held up her hand. He began to reel slowly. Within seconds, he could feel his heart galloping like a herd of wild mustangs.

'It's coming,' Michael said.

'I should fucking hope so, darling. Never again.'

'It's here,' Michael said.

Michael came to give him a hand and together they reeled in the wire. The support wires were also taped on, which explained why the wire had been so heavy. The main cable was connected to a large metal safety clip which, in turn, linked to the fishing line.

'Okay, now all we need do is hook this into the V in the metal bar,' Peter said.

'It's good. And these, how you call, cavaletti wires?'

Peter nodded and shrugged. He didn't know what they were called but he sighed in relief as they clipped the main cable on. The cable was loose but it was up to them to tighten it. The correct tension would be crucial. But East and West were now connected.

'Can we have a beer now?' Alice said.

He ignored her again. They all wanted a beer but first they had to sort out the support wires that Michael was unravelling.

'Go to my room, Mad, and open the window.'

She did as she was told for once. Peter leaned out of the bathroom window. The support wires came off the main wire and needed to be anchored in his bedroom to the left. Bodo would do the same in his apartment but to the right. It was only about four foot from the bathroom window to the bedroom, but if he threw the wire it might fall. Or Mad might not catch it. They also needed to anchor the support wires through another window. They hadn't thought this through.

'*Scheiße*,' Michael said.

'How have they done it?' Peter asked. 'I can't see.'

'I don't know. I can't see as well,' said Michael. 'Perhaps we can tape to the stick?'

He meant the broom. 'We can try,' Peter said.

He got some tape, taped the wires around the bristles and then gave it to Michael to pass out the window. Peter went into his room and leaned into the forbidden zone. The broom danced around his hand. When he grasped hold of it, it swung out horizontally before he pulled it into his room. A split second later, a beam of light flashed up from the watchtower.

'Switch the goddam lights off,' Peter said.

The lights went out except for the hall light. Mad Alice and Michael crept into the bedroom. Mad looked scared.

'Mad, keep a lookout.' Peter attached the support wires with fingers that had taken on a life of their own. He hoped he hadn't fucked up. He clipped the wire onto the metal bar concealed behind the curtain. The search light flashed outside the window again. In all his years in the apartment, Peter had never seen it before. He had always been out when neighbours told him of flashing lights and flares fired into the night. Despite the stories, he had half thought that the watchtowers weren't all manned.

'Fuck, they are onto us,' Mad said.

Peter's sweaty hands gripped his inhaler.

'It is now impossible,' Michael said. 'They watch.'

'Well, can we have a beer now please?' Mad said.

'*Ja, ja*. Good idea.' Michael left the bedroom. Mad followed him.

Peter peered out of the window. He could just about make out the black line that joined East and West. It looked tauter than before, but maybe that was his imagination. The night had been blacked out again. There were no more flashes but, as Michael said, they must be watching. The apartment opposite hid in the darkness. They must have aborted the plan. Peter stomped into the living room, deflated. All that work. For nothing. Mad and Michael also stood in the dark, watching out the window, drinking beer. An open bottle on the coffee table beckoned to him. He had never made the connection before – Beck's. He drank thirstily.

'They're not coming, are they?' Mad said.

'No,' Peter replied.

'I tell you it was dangerous,' Michael said.

Yet still they watched in the dark, shivering, for thirty minutes.

Then Peter saw it.

A black ghost sailing towards them, a balancing pole anchoring it to the air. They all emitted several oh-my-god-mein-Gott. Peter ran to the bathroom. He could hardly believe it. The black shadow was getting larger and more tangible. Peter stood back. Whoever it was seemed to waver on the wire, the balancing pole dipping to either side like a seesaw. Peter forgot to breathe. Then, the figure steadied itself and continued walking towards him, albeit slightly above him as the wire was level with the window. The dark shape grew bigger every second but he wasn't sure who it was until he was nearly there. It was Bodo. Peter stepped back a little to give him some space. Bodo's right hand reached out to the top of the window as he slipped the balancing pole to Peter. My God, he had done it! Bodo had crossed the Berlin Wall. He stepped off the wire and through the window as if stepping out of an elevator.

'Welcome to the West,' Peter whispered, hugging him. In the half-light from the hall Bodo's blue eyes glistened. He was crying. Or maybe it was the cold.

'Thank you, Peter. I need to check the cavaletti. It is a little loose.'

Bodo hugged and kissed Mad, who was loitering in the hall, and shook hands quickly with Michael before darting into the bedroom to adjust the support wires. Peter went into the lounge with Alice and Michael and they all stared at the black line in amazement. Bodo called to Mad to switch on the living room lamp to signal to the next person.

'But what about the guards?' Mad hissed. 'They flashed the spotlight on us.'

'I think it is okay,' he said, coming into the lounge. 'They see something but not the wire. We switch off in one moment.'

Bodo went back to stand near the window in the bathroom. They all traipsed after him.

'She comes,' Bodo whispered. 'Please switch the light off.'

Alice ran back into the lounge but couldn't seem to find the switch. Peter thought she was pretending, but maybe not. He and Michael joined her and Peter clicked off the lamp and the three of them stared from the window into the darkness.

Peter clasped his Beck's as they all watched the next dark shadow climb slide out of the window opposite.

'Wow,' he said, watching the next person, presumably the Russian tart as Mad called her, stroll coolly across the Berlin Wall. 'They walk on a wire over the death strip as if they're cruising through the park.'

'It's her,' Mad spat.

More birdlike than human, she practically fluttered across the last part on tiptoes. She wore a black Russian fur hat, black gloves, thick black pants and a black jumper.

'Wow,' Peter said again. No wonder Mad was jealous.

Laughter resonated from the bathroom as she joined Bodo. They sounded as if they'd just got back from a party, and there seemed to be some debate as to whether a third person was coming.

'I need another beer, Mad,' Peter said, wiping the sweat from his face. 'Better get them some too.'

Bodo and Natasha burst into the living room, beaming harvest moon faces, flushed red from having performed the unperformable. Mad opened the bottles of beer with her orange lighter and held one in front of Natasha's face. Unbothered, Natasha passed it to Bodo, so Mad had to hand her another.

'Is that all of you?' Peter said.

'Yes, the Professor think he might come but he doesn't want to leave Hanna.'

Peter nodded. Hanna was presumably his wife, or dog, or elephant.

'And my sister too young,' Natasha added.

They kissed and hugged everyone, talking non-stop.

'This the wicked West German beer,' Natasha said, knocking back the bottle.

'Steady on there, Natasha,' Peter said, but she'd almost finished it. She wiped the remaining drops from her face and burped.

'Can I put the light on now?' Mad said loudly, and in English.

'No, I think they might see the wire,' Bodo replied.

'Well, it doesn't really matter now, you're here,' Mad said.

Bodo laughed and shook his head. Peter didn't know what he meant by laughing, but he didn't say anything. He wasn't in a rush to have the police storming around and sirens going outside. It would happen. But maybe not just yet. Let them enjoy a few hours first.

'It is almost seven o'clock. We must go no?' Bodo said.

'Soon,' Mad said, opening another bottle. 'There's time for another beer.'

'I can't believe you guys have just walked across that wire,' Peter said, once again staring across to the other side. Bodo's apartment was still in darkness but he thought a shadow flashed by the window.

'Was easy,' Natasha said. 'More easy than we think.'

'Thanks to you,' Bodo added. He turned to Michael and Mad and thanked them again too.

'Well, it was… a challenge,' Peter said. 'And I nearly dropped the broom with the what do you call them? Cavaletti wires?' He suddenly felt hugely relieved, and overwhelmed by what he had done. He had helped the first ever high wire crossing of the Berlin Wall! Now, he would, undoubtedly, be famous.

'Yes, we see. Also the guards.'

'I didn't think you'd do it. I thought it was too risky.'

'They look only twice at your apartment. They think it's just some mad Westerner.'

'But it was lucky they didn't see the wire,' Peter said. He imagined all the interviews, the photographs…

'Yes, it was lucky.'

'Imagine, you have made history!' Peter said. 'The first people to cross the Wall on a tightrope.'

'Well, there was one person in the early days of the Wall, but, *ja*, we are for sure the first since then.'

'Oh.' Peter felt momentarily deflated but then cheered up. The Wall was much harder to cross these days than in 1961.

'And we can not make public, of course,' Bodo added.

'Oh,' Peter repeated. Maybe not yet, but one day for sure. Then he would be famous. 'Is there someone still over there then?'

'Yes, of course. That is Thomas. He shoots the arrow. And Zoyenka, Natasha's sister. And the Professor. But he might have gone now. We can wave to them.'

They all stood there waving in the half light, drinking beer.

'You guys should really go or you'll miss Johnny's performance,' Peter said. It would take at least forty minutes to get there. 'Here, put one of these jackets on.'

'Okay, I want to see the face of Johnny,' Natasha said.

'So do I,' Mad said sarcastically.

Peter would quite like to see his face as well, but he had to be at the Kiosk.

'Are you not coming?' Bodo asked, putting on a long military coat belonging to Hermann.

'No, I have to work.'

'You must work much in the West,' Natasha said, choosing one of Peter's old donkey jackets that almost reached her knees.

Mad pulled an is-she-nuts face. Peter laughed and agreed. She looked slightly ridiculous in the coat, but she didn't seem to bother.

'Alice has promised to bring you to the bar afterwards for a beer. Okay?'

'Okay,' Bodo said.

They all fell silent as Peter opened the door of the apartment for them. He tried to imagine what it would be like to step into the forbidden Western world for the first time. He reckoned it would be a bit like stepping into the future.

Mehringdamm

Johnny and the other five dancers warmed up in the pre-war studio behind the stage, which also served as the dressing room. Thank God it was the last night. The show had got better after a disastrous first night but, even so, his heart wasn't in it. He had considered pulling out, but the dancers had demanded Sophie call an emergency rehearsal and change several sequences. Since then the performance had improved.

'Give it all you got tonight, eh Johnny?' Sophie said. 'There's gonna be some more reviewers.'

'Sure,' Johnny replied curtly. He stopped himself from adding that it wasn't his fault the reviews from the first night had been fairly crap, but this was her first show. She had done more than he had and it had been an interesting experience. But he wouldn't do it again.

He had no idea what he would do. He needed to stay in Berlin, even though meeting up with Natasha while she was on tour was not going to be easy. They had met for two hours at Alexanderplatz on Tuesday and walked aimlessly around. Bodo didn't want them to go to his place as he reckoned it was being watched and so they had nowhere to go, no way of kissing. They didn't want to draw any more attention to themselves. She had seemed distracted and he was reeling from performing for about ten people the night before. They had walked around the square, his already aching heart frozen by an ice cream. They promised to meet again next Tuesday. That would be the last time before she went on tour. Perhaps they could go to the cinema. At least it would be warm, away from the grey skies and they'd have somewhere to snuggle up. Maybe Alice had a point about the iron bed. He smiled. Maybe he should defect despite everyone's warnings: he knew that was what Natasha wanted. She seemed to think her father could help them. But it was too late to do anything for now.

'Okay, two minutes to curtain. Think we've got a full house, guys.'

He took deep breaths as he waited by the wings of the black stage. The taped Japanese drums started and he went in and crouched on the stage with two other dancers and concentrated his body and mind on the music and movement.

The hour long performance flew by. For the first time, the energy of the other dancers and the music pulsed in time, performing together. Even the lighting flashed down on them with more precision than other nights. The small auditorium was crammed with faces and, at the end, the sound of applause was louder than on any other night. As he bowed to the audience, he thought he saw Alice at the back, towering above the others. He'd be surprised, if it were her, as last time she'd told him to fuck off. Unless she'd come for the party afterwards. That would be typical, he thought, as he bowed again to his naked feet.

Backstage Sophie buzzed around like a bee in a giant flower. Thank you, thank you everyone, that was fantastic, but she couldn't help adding that she wished it had been like that from the beginning. Johnny ignored her and went to the decrepit shower in the men's toilets, where the tiles were cracked and the blackened, yellowish paint hung in slabs off the walls. He'd just soaped himself under the lukewarm water when Sophie appeared before him. He stared indignantly at her, but she didn't flinch at his nakedness.

'There's Alice and two others wanting to see you,' she said.

'Who are they?' Johnny asked. Any friends of Alice's were bound to be trouble.

'I've never seen them before. That's why I'm asking you,' Sophie said officiously. 'Alice says they're friends of yours, not hers, so I just wanted to make certain you wanted them. We've been asked to keep numbers down backstage.'

'Friends of mine? I doubt it. I'll be out in a minute.'

Johnny quickly towelled himself dry and put on his black pants, white shirt, waistcoat and laced up his DMs. He grabbed his leather jacket and canvas bag and headed back through the dark vinyl-floored corridor and into the main changing room, now full of people, friends of the performers, standing around drinking out of white plastic cups.

'They're outside,' Sophie said. 'Alice said she'd wait with them. I'd rather you got rid of them Johnny as it's kinda busy in here.'

Johnny nodded, dreading to think who was out there. He opened the door between the dressing room and stepped out into the corridor, stopped and blinked. Alice was talking to Bodo, while Natasha, in a large donkey jacket, was looking at the posters on the wall, cradling what looked like a black cat in her arms.

'What!' he squeaked.

'Hallo Johnny,' Natasha said, dropping the cat. It didn't move.

Barely able to speak, he opened his arms. Natasha slipped into them and he kissed her while Bodo slapped him on the back, warning him not to say anything. Johnny couldn't say anything. He was speechless.

147

This wasn't real, surely he must be hallucinating. But there was Alice frowning at him, smoking a cigarette, one arm folded, looking very real.

'I'm going to get a drink,' she snapped and strode into the dressing room.

'But. How? Why?' Johnny staccatoed in whispers. 'What's happened? How did you get here?'

'We want to see your show, of course,' Bodo said, grinning.

'Shush!' Natasha said. She leant up towards his ear. 'We tell you later.'

'It's okay, tell me now. No one here will say anything,' Johnny said.

'No,' Natasha hissed.

He closed his open mouth and waited while Natasha retrieved the furry lump on the floor which turned out to be her Russian hat. He squeezed her to make sure she was real.

'Ayah!'

They went into the dressing room.

'So who are your friends? Sophie said, approaching with a tray full of plastic cups.

'They're very special friends.' He unhooked Natasha and introduced her and Bodo. Sophie reluctantly offered them a plastic cup of Sekt. Alice came over carrying two cups and the little French girl, whose name he had forgotten, on her arm.

'So, tell me, what do you special friends do, Natasha?'

'Bodo is juggler. I am performance artist.'

'Really? Fascinating. What kind of artist?'

'Like acrobat.'

'Oh, I see,' Sophie laughed as Natasha nodded. 'What did you think to the show?'

Natasha didn't understand so Sophie spoke in German, but with the American accent it sounded almost the same.

'Was different,' Natasha said slowly. 'No laughter.'

The others didn't say anything. Johnny smiled. There was certainly no laughter.

'Guys! Where are you from? It's not circus, it's modern dance.'

No one said anything. Sophie didn't know who they were. How could anyone expect these people to admire dance on the ground when they danced in the air.

'Oh well, thanks for coming.' Sophie slunk away, frowning. 'Michelle? Are you coming?'

'Okay, I see you later,' Michelle, the French girl, said to Alice.

'She's the choreographer,' he whispered to Natasha.

'I say something bad?' Natasha said.

Johnny shook his head. 'The show wasn't great.'

Natasha and Bodo looked relieved.

'I thought it was good,' Alice said.

'I do not understand why their bodies not beautiful?' Natasha said. 'They do not even smile.'

'You don't smile to convey pain,' Alice snapped.

Natasha looked at him questioningly and Johnny was about to explain that it was all about challenging traditional concepts of beauty in dance, but he hugged her instead. Maybe she had a point.

'Come on, let's go,' he said. 'You have to tell me how you got here.'

Johnny had no idea where they were all going to stay. Peter wouldn't be happy, although Alice might let Bodo stay with her as she seemed quite pleased to see him. They would sort something out. The most important thing was that *Natasha was in the West*. The realisation lit up the world around him. No need for an iron bed now. No need to defect. They would be able to get married, find a circus to work in, set up their own company maybe. They would travel round Europe, even the States. One day they would have children and teach them to dance in the sky...

'I just can't believe you're here,' he said, kissing her hand.

'Are you ready? We have to go to the Kiosk,' Alice asked without looking at him. She loomed over Natasha, looking like she might head-butt her.

'The Kiosk? Why the Kiosk?' Johnny wanted to show them the bright lights of the city, not sit in some dingy bar with a load of piss artists. 'Let's go to the Ku'damm.'

Natasha and Bodo agreed immediately. Bodo added that he had waited twenty-three years to see the Ku'damm again.

'But you'll have time to do all that,' Alice said quickly. 'Peter's waiting for us.'

'Peter? What has Peter got to do with anything?'

'Without Peter they wouldn't be here,' Alice snarled, and split her plastic cup. 'And I promised him we'd go to the Kiosk after the show.'

Johnny felt his mouth open. He closed it quickly. Without Peter? How the hell had they got across? He couldn't imagine what use Peter could have been – beyond pouring tequila, he wasn't much good at anything.

'Perhaps we go to Ku'damm for five minutes, Alice, please,' Bodo said, flashing his blue eyes at her. 'It is still early.'

She sighed. 'O-kay. Come on then. See you later, Sophie.'

They all waved to Sophie and Benjamin and a group of their friends and left the theatre via a fire exit. Johnny hugged Natasha to him as they followed Alice's mass of red and black hair, which led them into the darkness that surrounded Mehringdamm, and down to the U-Bahn.

'Tell me, tell me,' Johnny pleaded with Natasha and Bodo, but they wouldn't – as if afraid the station were surrounded by spies. Alice marched along the platform, refusing to look at him.

They had the whole U-Bahn carriage on Line 7 to themselves. As soon as the orange doors shut, Johnny turned to them and opened his hands for an explanation. Natasha's little face beamed like a full moon. Bodo was looking at the U-Bahn map.

'I think Alice best to tell you,' Natasha said, swinging round one of the black poles.

Alice sat down on one of the new blue cushioned seats. Johnny stood in front of her.

'We rigged a high wire from Bodo's apartment to Peter's and they walked across,' Alice said, nonchalantly.

'What?' He really wished Alice wouldn't try to be funny, particularly at a time like this.

'That's how we did it,' she said. 'We spent over a week preparing – you didn't see as you were rehearsing. Bodo sent us all the details. Peter organised everything. I helped. It was to be a surprise for you. Don't know why we bothered, but there you go.' She turned and looked onto the platform at Möckernbrücke. No one got on.

'But, but, but...' He looked to the others for confirmation and they nodded.

'You walked across the Berlin Wall on a wire? That's impossible... It's madness.' The idea was insane. He collapsed onto the seat opposite Alice as Natasha perched next to him and Bodo sat next to Alice.

'Difficult, *ja*, but not impossible,' said Bodo. 'And not madness. We are here. It took a lot of plans. I first think about it when we are in caravan with the Professor. But we could not do it without Alice, or your beautiful friend, Peter.'

'But how?'

'They shot an arrow across connected to a fishing line. The wire was then connected to the line and we pulled it across,' Alice said, looking past him into the dark tunnel behind them. 'Well, Peter and Michael did mostly.'

'Michael?'

'Yes, he and Peter did all of the rigging. It took them ages.'

The train stopped at Kleistpark. Some elderly people got on and everyone fell silent. Johnny took Natasha's hand and held it tightly. He felt nauseous, unable to take in the risks she'd put herself through – so that she could be with him. They could so easily have been shot – look what had happened to him – and he'd only put a hand on the Wall. They could have plucked her out of the sky, blown her into the West in pieces. His stomach cramped at the thought and he looked gratefully into Alice's scowling eyes, but the side of her mouth turned up in disdain and she gave him a 'best of luck' shrug.

They changed trains at Berliner Straße to the Ku'damm. At every opportunity, Bodo headed straight for the plastic covered maps of Berlin with their pink fuzzy borders around the city. He pointed to places that no longer existed on maps in the East. Johnny watched Natasha's head flicking from side to side, absorbing the world around her. As they climbed the stairs that led to the Ku'damm, her eyes sparkled and her head spun round and round as she gazed at the bright lights, the shops, the cafes, the bars, the volume of traffic, the revolving Mercedes sign, the people, their clothes. She looked like a kid who had just discovered Aladdin's cave. He could smell the East on her hat. He was so happy that she was the one who'd defected. He would never have been able to live in the East.

'Wonderful,' Natasha whispered, gripping his fingers tightly.

Bodo shook his head, muttering, 'They lied to us, they lied to us,' as he and Natasha looked in the windows of KaDeWe. Natasha hungrily devoured everything she saw. 'Only rich people shop here,' Alice kept saying. They wandered through the Europa Centre lit by opaque round lollipop lights and mirrors. The Irish Pub was packed with American GIs. Alice showed them the giant water-clock, the green-gold liquid squeezing through the labyrinth of bubbles and test tubes as if it were in a futuristic science lab.

Natasha didn't say anything about the people wrapped in sleeping bags and cardboard boxes in the shop doors, at the exit of the Europa Centre, but he could see her registering them. Several people approached them and asked for *'Zigaretten bitte'* or *'Groschen'*. Alice took the brunt of the requests and happily doled out a packet of Camel. None of them gave money. Bodo kept sidling up to Alice, putting his arm around her at the slightest excuse. She didn't seem to mind.

Johnny treated them all to coffee and cakes in a patisserie – and brandy for Alice. Bodo fell silent as he munched through a chocolate gateaux and cream and sipped the fresh coffee. Natasha couldn't stop talking, almost simultaneously in German and English, her eyes darting from person to person, object to object. 'Like in a dream,' she kept saying, feeling the texture of a napkin. He wanted to ask them more about their crossing but no one seemed to want to talk about it.

'Come on, we should go,' Alice said, looking at her watch.

It was still before midnight.

'We go by taxi?' Natasha asked, putting some napkins in her pocket.

'Taxi! Taxis are expensive,' Alice began.

'Oh, in the East taxis very cheap.'

'Of course we can take a taxi,' Johnny replied, frowning at Alice. 'It won't cost much.'

They got in one of the large cream Mercedes taxis, smelling of the soft polished leather that covered the seats. The doors closed automatically, to the delight of Natasha, and they drove down Tauentzienstraße, past Nollendorfplatz, where Café Swing was still swinging. All the time Natasha clung to his hand, pointing at things with the other, careful that the driver wasn't looking in his mirror. She pointed at a couple kissing in a doorway, at a man walking his dog, at a group of kids ambling along, smoking and laughing, at two men with short hair, moustaches and leather pants holding hands, at the bright traffic lights, at a group of women dressed in short glittering skirts and swigging a bottle of something as they crossed the road. Johnny stoked her hand; she was much more interesting than the world outside.

Bodo also had his eyes pinned to the outside world but he no longer appeared to be looking. A sensory overload, Johnny thought. It must be even stranger for him: this was his city.

The roads became darker and emptier. Johnny wished they were going somewhere more glitzy for their first night. He doubted they would understand the concept of underground, the rejection of the beautiful capitalist West. They stopped near the Kiosk and Johnny opened the flaps on his bag and scrambled around for some Marks to pay for the taxi while the others got out. Hassan's money was coming to an end, but soon it would be spring and he would be able to start working in the parks. Maybe Natasha and he could put together an act until they decided what to do.

Alice led the way and buzzed at the door of the Kiosk. Johnny hadn't been since that night back in February during his first week in

Berlin. A badly edited memory of kissing Alice in the back room flashed before him. The door seemed to open by itself and, as they walked into the bar, the music faded and all the people, including Sophie, Benjamin and the other dancers as well as the Hungarian twins and Michelle, the French girl, stopped drinking, swung their heads in their direction, and began cheering and applauding them. Across the bar was a banner, *'Welcome to the West'* and there was Peter, arms outstretched, beaming happily. Johnny stood there uncertainly. He felt Natasha go cold. Even Alice looked taken aback. The pop of a champagne cork caused more cheering and a return to a normal Kiosk volume, although dozens of eyes still looked at them expectantly. No doubt Peter had told everyone how they had crossed over.

'This is for you,' Peter said, coming towards them with five glasses on a silver tray and placed it on a high round table. 'Hey you look like you need it. Was Johnny that bad?' He laughed. Peter was on form.

People donated stools for them and they sat as if in a space pod.

'Thanks Peter,' said Alice, grabbing one of the flutes, pouting lipsticked lips at him. 'I thought it was good.' She flashed one of her kill-men smiles at him.

'Did you not enjoy it?' Peter asked, handing out the other glasses to Bodo, Johnny and Natasha.

'Was good, but different,' Natasha said, inching forward a fraction. '*Prost* and thank you, Peter. A big surprise.'

'Well, it's not everyday you step into another world, is it?'

'No, no it's not,' Bodo said, joining in.

They began to talk about their walk around the Ku'damm. Peter, the consummate barman, magicked another bottle of champagne and refilled their glasses. Sophie came over and almost snogged Alice.

'Why didn't you tell us?' she demanded, looking from Alice to Johnny to Natasha. 'I wondered where you were from. Far out.'

'They were trying to keep it a secret,' Johnny said.

'Please don't tell. We have family in the East,' Natasha said.

'Oh, okay. But, hey guys, welcome to our decadent West. Is it really true you walked across a hire wire?' Sophie slammed her beer bottle into their glasses.

'Especially to see your show,' Natasha said, smiling.

'Heh, what a good incentive.'

Johnny didn't think that Natasha would know what an incentive was but she was grinning again. He desperately wanted to be alone with her. He squeezed her hand.

'So you're an aerialist performer as well?' Sophie said to Natasha. 'What kind of stuff do you do?'

'You want I show you?' Natasha said, knocking back her champagne. She could drink more than Alice given the chance.

'Yeah, I'd love you to,' Sophie said.

'What you want me to do?' She burped and laughed.

'Whatever you want.'

Natasha looked over at Peter, who winked at her. She took off the enormous donkey jacket and her hat. She scooped back her flattened dark hair and wound it into a knot. Johnny removed his bag from the table and put it on the floor beneath his stool. Then she asked everyone to hold onto their glasses as she raised a leg vertically onto the stool, stepped up and stood on her hands, gripping either side of the round two-foot wide table top, her legs scissoring the air. Her back rolled over her head and she pointed her toes and smiled at everyone. Then she lifted up her right arm and picked up a champagne glass, balanced only on her left arm.

'Awesome!' Sophie said.

Natasha gracefully bent over the table and arched backwards onto her stool and gulped at her champagne as if nothing had happened. Everyone applauded and whistled at her. Johnny touched her leg. She was truly fantastic. Another bottle of champagne appeared.

'Wow, Natasha, that's something else. Every bone in your body looks broken,' Sophie said. 'How do you do that?'

'I train every day from since I am three,' Natasha said

'Freaky,' Alice muttered.

Johnny frowned at them both. He didn't think Natasha would understand what they were saying, but Sophie and Alice had launched into a discussion about body mutilation, ballet and Chinese foot binding. Bodo desperately tried to follow Alice's conversation, agreeing anyway.

What should have been an evening of great happiness was tinged with a sadness Johnny couldn't quite put his finger on. Maybe it was him. He drank his champagne. It had been a long and momentous day.

'Can we go somewhere?' Johnny asked Natasha.

'We go back soon,' she said. 'To Peter. I tell Bodo.'

That was fine by Johnny. Bodo was still trying to talk to Alice, but she and Sophie were now onto big breasts and dance. Sophie, who had breasts, was insistent that dancers should not be one flat shape. Alice agreed and told Sophie that she was taking dance classes.

Johnny didn't quite see the connection – except for the breasts – but he smiled anyway. Alice was so young for her age.

Natasha said something to Bodo.

'We must go now,' Bodo told Alice. 'You come with us?'

'Where to?'

'To Peter's.'

'But Peter's here.' She looked confused.

'They're tired and want to rest,' Johnny said.

'But it's their first night in West Berlin.'

'We enjoy very much but now we must go,' Natasha said determinedly, pouring herself more champagne.

'Please yourself. But I'm not going,' Alice said to Bodo and turned back to Sophie. Johnny knew that Bodo wouldn't go without Alice.

'Bodo, we must go,' Natasha said, drinking the champagne.

'It's okay, Alice will bring him back,' Johnny said, picking up his ash covered bag from the floor. He couldn't wait to get out. He put his arm around Natasha.

'I think he comes now,' Natasha said.

Peter also looked pissed off when they told him they were going.

'Where are you going?' He sounded paranoid. 'Have another drink!'

Bodo, perhaps in order to diffuse the situation, began to juggle empty tequila glasses.

'Oh no!' Peter yelled.

Oh no, Johnny thought. Bottles were easy by comparison.

Bodo juggled two, three and then four. This time he caught even Alice's attention.

Johnny didn't know what happened next as he and Natasha slipped out of the bar. They walked a short way, hand in hand, and stopped before they got to the tunnel to wait for Bodo. A train thundered overhead.

'Why your friend still not like me.'

'Who?' Johnny said, knowing that she meant Alice.

'Alice.'

'Don't worry. She's not my friend any more. She doesn't like me.' He pulled her towards him and leant against the damp wall and kissed her.

'But she like you. Very much. Have you…' Natasha hesitated. 'Have you made love with Alice?'

Johnny didn't believe in lying. Besides, it wasn't a big deal.

'Yes,' he said.

155

A silence, as chilling as the aftermath of the passing train, whipped through the tunnel. 'It didn't mean anything,' he screamed after it. 'And it was a long time ago. Before I met you.'

But Natasha had already wriggled free and was walking back towards the Kiosk, where Bodo and Alice were coming out. She turned round, confused.

'I love you, Natasha,' he called to her. 'Come back. Peter lives this way.'

She turned round, smiling a tight, bitter smile as she walked towards and past him. Back under the tunnel, along York Straße, then Gneissenau Straße. Johnny walked beside her, Alice and Bodo a long way behind them. Or rather, she walked, he talked. He didn't know if she was listening to him or not. He pleaded with her on every slab of concrete he stepped on. He didn't understand why she was so angry: it wasn't as if he'd done anything really wrong. Love and sex were two different things.

They reached Hermannplatz and she still hadn't spoken to him. They walked down Sonnenallee, past Alice's apartment (not that he mentioned this) and still he talked. He told her how much she meant to him, how he hoped they would spend the rest of their lives together, how he hoped they would perform together, how she made him feel different to any other person.

'You must believe me, Natasha. I love you. Natasha.' He pulled her up as they turned into Heidelberger Straße and knelt down in front of her and held onto both her hands. 'I want to marry you. I want to be with you. Forever.' He looked up at her.

She sighed. 'Okay, Johnny, but where I come from we do not do this. This the wicked of capitalism. Now it difficult to believe you.' Her voice sliced up the Berlin night like the Wall. She walked away again, but he followed, head bowed. It had been a long time since anyone had spoken to him like that. There had been few rules in his life – apart from not getting caught. Now he was being confronted with the wickedness of capitalism, and he felt defenceless.

'I am sorry, Natasha,' he said, overtaking and pulling her towards him. They were almost back at Peter's. Surely she wouldn't leave him, now that she was here.

'How many women you make love with?' she asked him at last.

'Oh, I don't know,' Johnny said. 'Not many.'

'You do not know?' She sounded shocked.

'Four,' he said, lying for the first time in his life. 'The first couple of girlfriends were at college. They didn't mean anything either.'

She stared through him as he held his breath. Maybe she would want to believe him. As she nodded, he breathed again.

'So will you marry me?'

'I don't know, Johnny. I want to marry someone I believe. And it will be difficult for me on tour.'

'What do you mean?' Johnny asked, confused.

'I mean it difficult for me to have trust when on tour.'

'What tour?'

'The tour in DDR.' Her dark eyes flashed angrily at him.

He smiled at her as he smoothed back her hair from her flushed face.

'But you are here in the West now,' he said gently.

'Now, yes. But we go back.'

A stray asteroid must have hit the earth as he felt as if he were buried beneath rock. 'What do you mean? When?' he said, breathlessly, trying to find some light, some way out.

'Now, of course. We only come to see your show. And to see you,' she added, with an audible reluctance.

'But... but... but... I thought you were here to stay.' Even his voice sounded like a crushed stone, grating, pleading.

Natasha shook her head slowly. 'No, of course not. My sister waits for me. The Professor waits for me. I have my family.'

'And Bodo is going back too?'

'Yes, of course.'

'But did Peter and Alice know that?'

'Yes, of course. Bodo tell them we come only to see you.'

Bodo might well have told them, but they probably hadn't believed him. Johnny hung his head and felt his arms go limp around her back.

'But you've been drinking. You might fall,' Johnny tried one last attempt, knowing she would laugh at him.

She laughed.

Bodo and Alice were catching up with them. He must talk to Bodo, maybe he could persuade Natasha to stay? But Bodo stopped and kissed Alice under a street light. Johnny had a fleeting, unwanted flashback to when he and Alice had kissed under a Berlin streetlight all those months ago. As he and Natasha walked on, he heard Alice shouting at Bodo – no doubt she'd found out as well.

Johnny and Natasha slowly climbed the stairs to Peter's apartment, each one seemingly steeper than the last. The shock had weakened him. He showed Natasha his room – not that there was much to see – and put his bag down on his bed. She didn't say anything, but didn't seem very impressed. Then she showed him the bathroom, where they had rigged up the wire. Only after several seconds of staring out of the window could he make out the black line that joined East and West. That was impressive. The narrowest bridge in the world. If only they could keep it there.

They found Michael asleep on the sofa in the dark lounge. He opened a weary eye, looked at his watch and groaned. Johnny took Natasha into the kitchen and put some coffee and water in a pot. She would need to be alert if she were going to walk on a tightrope.

Alice and Bodo arrived.

'Can you believe it?' Alice shouted through to him. 'They're fucking crazy.'

Johnny didn't reply, but he heard Michael groan again. Natasha was gazing at him out of her large brown eyes, hurting. He sighed and kissed her on her forehead. She was right: she had her sister, her family, her life to think of.

'What's going on?' Michael said.

'They want to fucking cross back.' Alice laughed.

'*Na ja*. Good idea,' Michael said, yawning.

Alice came into the kitchen and, without looking at him or Natasha, headed straight for the fridge, humming to herself. Natasha whispered that she was going to the bathroom.

'What were you doing on your knees anyway?' Alice hissed at him as soon as Natasha had left, opening a bottle of Beck's.

'You wouldn't understand,' Johnny said, pouring out the coffee.

'Probably not,' she called back.

Johnny shook his head and handed out coffee to join Bodo and Michael who were standing at the window.

'We thought you were here to stay,' Johnny said quietly.

Bodo laughed. 'No, too many people know. Another time perhaps.' He winked at him. Johnny didn't know whether he was being serious or not, but he knew that his mind, as well as Natasha's, was made up.

All looked quiet on the strip below. Bodo began instructing Michael what to do when they'd gone. Johnny had no idea how they were going to pass the wires back without them hitting the wall. He heard his name mentioned but he didn't understand.

'Surely the wire will hit the death strip?' Johnny asked.

'Only the fishing wire,' Bodo said. 'We think that it doesn't set anything off.'

'You think?' The place was mined and alarmed.

Alice passed through the lounge, presumably to go to the bathroom, while Natasha joined them at the window. Johnny gave her a mug of coffee which she gulped back. He hugged her tightly, not ever wanting to let her go. He had a thousand things he wanted to say to her but he couldn't articulate them. All he could do was hold her, hoping his hands would say more than his words. Alice returned several minutes later. As she lit a cigarette, Johnny noticed she was wearing black lace gloves, as if waiting to plunge a knife into his heart.

'Okay, thank you, my friends,' Bodo said, hugging them all. 'We enjoy to be here with you. Are you ready Natasha? I just make final check,' he said.

Bodo kissed Alice before going into the bathroom. Alice followed him as far as the hall and stood with her back against the wall, drinking beer.

'Okay, everything is okay. Natasha, you go first,' Bodo came out into the hall and called to her.

'Don't go,' Johnny whispered to her in the dark.

'I have to,' she said.

'Then let me come with you?' Johnny said.

'No,' said Natasha. 'Not yet. We see each other Tuesday, at twelve. In S-Bahn station?'

Johnny nodded. She kissed him softly on the lips.

'You haven't answered my question,' he whispered.

'Johnny, you the first man I make love with. Does that answer your question?' She passed Alice without saying goodbye and went into the bathroom, where she stepped onto the window sill.

Friedrichstraße

'Please do this for me, Peter,' Johnny said, blue tears lapping at his eyes. 'I'll do anything you want.'

Peter loved Johnny pleading with him. The tables had, at last, turned. Just a little harder, Johnny darling, he kept thinking.

'Oh, really, Johnny, it's too much. I spent an entire week planning for them to come over. Everyone went to so much trouble for you – even Alice – so that you could get the love of your life over here. And then she fucks off back to tyranny and oppression. I mean, what kind of thanks is that? Really darling, I think you need to rethink this relationship of yours. It sounds pretty cold to me.' Peter didn't quite laugh at his own bad pun, but he was aware of a grin trying to stretch from one side of his face to the other.

It was Monday evening and he was still recovering from returning home at 1 p.m. yesterday, expecting his house to be overrun with reporters and police, only to find nothing. No sign of the circus or the equipment – except for the dismantled bar in the bathroom. Johnny and Michael had sorted it all out earlier. He couldn't believe Bodo and Natasha had gone. So much for the interviews and photographs, the fame and the riches. Not that he was bothered that they'd fucked back to tyranny and oppression, but he couldn't believe they'd taken such a risk just to see Johnny perform.

There was a trace of something that was keeping him nicely afloat. He wiped his nose, picked up his tobacco tin and sat down on the sofa to roll a joint.

'Please Peter.'

Johnny stood over him in his faded black jeans, DMs and studded belt. His brushed up black hair flopped over his pale face. Peter tightened his dressing gown.

'Why can't you ask Mad?' He yawned. 'I'm going to be way too tired to go to the East tomorrow. I need to rest.' He licked his Rizlas.

'Because Natasha knows I've slept with her and she's not too impressed.'

'Really? That's too bad.' He created the shit, he could live with it.

'And Alice wants to kill me.'

'Pity.'

'Please Peter. You needn't hang around. I'll give you a letter to give to her.'

Johnny's eyes looked like they might sink under the weight of the tears.

Peter lit his joint. 'What time have you arranged to meet her?'

'Twelve. Alexanderplatz. Upstairs on platform 1.'

Johnny had either lost his passport, or someone had stolen it on Saturday night in the Kiosk. It was possible that someone had stolen it – selling passports was big business in the East, but Peter knew all the people in the Kiosk that night and he couldn't imagine any of them stealing it.

'What did the police say?' Peter asked.

'Not a lot. I have to go to the Consulate tomorrow morning. I called them up to see if they would be able to issue me a temporary passport for tomorrow but they wouldn't. The earliest would be a couple of weeks.'

'That's not bad.'

'It's bad. Natasha will be in Dresden by then.'

However hard he tried, Peter just couldn't sympathise. His many trips trawling around hardware shops last week, trying to get all the rigging parts for Bodo, had made his legs ache. The hours spent arguing with Michael about how to interpret Bodo's instructions had made his head ache. And, as for having to put up with Mad coming round at all hours, well, that had been enough to almost kill him. Peter smoked his joint and looked up at Johnny. And for what? Hardly anyone even knew about the greatest crossing ever.

'Why should I, Johnny? What have you ever done for me?'

Johnny shrugged. The left side of his mouth shifted to one side, half smiling, half questioning. Peter hated it now when he did that.

'What do you want me to do?' Johnny said.

Peter sung quietly to himself, *Puff the Magic Dragon*... while waiting with a bunch of grumpy commuters for a U-Bahn at 9.15 a.m. the next morning. Even though he was off to the East he felt good. His black, curly hair shone in the windows of the arriving train and, dressed in his leather pants and long coat, he couldn't see his expanding figure. His lungs had started to breathe again and he felt alive. Johnny, the darling, had simply lapped at his pants last night.

He bought himself a *Tip* magazine and a coke when he changed trains at Mehringdamm. As he handed over a five Mark piece someone tapped him on the shoulder. He turned round and his good mood almost vanished.

Mad swayed in front of him, one arm draped over a man, who was shorter than her, with very long tapered sideburns, and wearing a leather jacket with tassels. Peter had never seen him before. They were both chewing like cows.

'What are you doing...' She paused. 'At this time in the morning?' Her mascara was smudged down her face and her lips were a rough pink.

'Oh hi there.' He couldn't be bothered to explain. Her dilated eyes zoomed in and out. He turned back to the woman serving him who looked like she was about to throw his change at him.

'We've just come from the Kiosk. It was another crazy night. You should have...'

'Sorry, darling, I have to go.'

'Oh. Where are you going? We'll come with you.'

Oh no you won't, Peter thought, and said quickly, 'I'm going to the East to tell Natasha that Johnny's lost his passport.'

Mad laughed, madly. 'I know he's lost his passport. But why are *you* going? Thought we'd agreed we'd done enough for him?' Her eyes accused him of betrayal.

Peter nodded. She was drunk but still razor sharp. He wasn't going to argue. The guy she was with looked like he might kill him. Little men were nearly always aggressive.

'I have a plan,' he said.

She nodded. 'Maybe you should tell her that he doesn't want to see her any more. Not that he can at the moment.' She laughed.

'Maybe I will,' he said.

'Good. That'll save us all a lot of trouble. Have fun.'

'And you be safe, darling,' Peter said, as she stumbled off the way he had come, dragging the guy with her. Actually, it looked like she might kill him. What a slapper. But how did she know Johnny had lost his passport?

He got on Line 6 and flicked through the magazine, trying to restore his good mood. 'Archaos' were coming to Berlin. That would be good. And 'Survival Research Laboratories'. They were awesome. He knew some of the machinists and technicians from San Francisco, so it would be good to see them again. It was a shame some of those machines weren't with him today – he could do with some backing in the East. *The Killing Fields* looked vaguely interesting, although probably very Hollywood. He also wanted to see *Brazil*. He flipped to the music section and there were reviews of John Lydon and the Pogues. He could read more later.

He got off at Kochstraße and walked towards the border with his magazine tucked inside his coat with Johnny's letter. It was another grey Berlin day. Sometimes, it seemed that the winter would never end and this year had been exceptionally bad. He used to revel in the cold darkness of the city after the shining blue skies and tanned smiling faces of California. It was the difference between day and night. But recently he wondered if it was wearing thin.

Johnny had told him it was much easier to cross at Checkpoint Charlie. So he was really pissed when the border guards confiscated his *Tip* magazine. Their grey-green stone faces, determined to change the world for the worse, completely ruined any remains of his good mood. Sadly, they didn't find the letter.

By the time he stepped into the East, his heart was pumping erratically and his hands trembled. He reached for his inhaler. The air, the buildings, the sudden darkness, everything was oppressive. He hated being here. He kicked at a loose piece of communism on the pavement. Oh well, he had a mission – for Johnny. Yet another one. He decided to risk the U-Bahn at Stadtmitte, where mangled red and white tape fluttered around the entrance and a bashed-up sign indicated some kind of maintenance work – but he went down anyway as it looked like it had been there since 1961. Only a couple of people stood on the platform, quiet, miserable, judgemental. They looked across at Peter, particularly at his leather pants and boots. Every time he tried to look them in the eye, they turned away. He wished he hadn't worn the leather, but he had half hoped he would be refused entry. Peter stuffed his hands in his coat pocket and shuffled awkwardly around a damp patch on the floor. Water dripped through the ceiling.

He felt the letter in his pocket and pulled it out: should he or shouldn't he? He slipped his finger into the envelope and the sealed paper popped up. He whipped out the note and unfolded it.

Darling Natasha,

I am sending this letter with Peter as I can not get to the East. My passport has either been lost or stolen – on Saturday night – and the Embassy will not issue me with a new one for two weeks. I am so sorry. I so much want to see you. I want to be with you. I even thought about trying to rig up the wire again but I can't do it alone.

Please can you go to B's and wave to me? I will be here all day waiting for you. You are the most special thing that has happened to me and I want you to know that I will love you and wait for you forever.

*All my love,
Johnny
xxx*

Peter felt his stomach lurch forward onto the train seconds before he did. Then he laughed. Oh really Johnny. That's a bit much. He'd only known her for a couple of months. Johnny was trying to save an already lost battle. They had had their chance and now one of them was going to get hurt if they weren't careful. He banged his head as he sat down on the almost empty train. Everything seemed smaller in the East.

He got off at Alexanderplatz and scanned the station as he thought about what to do. Several exits were walled up: he knew why. Hardly anyone remembered that there was another line, deeper than this platform that ran from West to West right under their noses. He looked for a trashcan, wondering where the entrances were – there must be entrances as the border guards got down there. He spotted a trashcan, walked up to it, casually tore the letter into small pieces and scattered them into the blackened container.

Natasha wasn't there when he eventually found his way up to the main station S-Bahn platform where they'd agreed to meet. At least he couldn't see her among the swarms of crushed and embittered faces.

He waited twenty minutes, thirty. He was just lighting his third cigarette, when he saw her fly out of a train door and flit down the platform like a feather carried by the wind. She stopped at the end of the platform when she saw him. He enjoyed the look of confusion on her face. She had no make-up on and her long black hair was tied back with a white ribbon. On her feet she wore off-white pumps without socks and her brown fur coat looked like it was inhabited by more creatures than just her. She slid slowly towards him, her brow creased, her small mouth serious.

Sow the seeds of doubt. Peter spoke to her in German.

'Johnny couldn't make it, Natasha. He asked me to meet you to tell you.'

'Why?'

'Because he says he's lost his passport.'

'He says?' Her frown deepened.

'Yes. He's gone to the Embassy this morning to try to apply for a new passport.'

'But when did this happen?' she asked.

'Saturday night perhaps.'

'But…' Natasha turned away, dipping her eyes to the floor.

'You should have stayed, you know,' Peter said. 'I couldn't believe you guys left.'

'I had to. My family…'

'Johnny said something about meeting you here in three weeks' time.'

'Three weeks?' Natasha shook her head. 'That will be impossible. We will be in Dresden.'

'Do you want me to give him a message?' Peter asked, looking at his watch.

'You go? I'm sorry, I don't know what to say.'

'Yeah, I can't stay long. He gave me a letter to give you but the passport controllers confiscated it. Together with my magazine.' Well, they could easily have done.

Natasha's dark eyes pierced him. He could smell the dried sweat on the fur.

'Confiscated? What does it mean?'

'They took it.'

'They take the letter? Was it addressed to me? What did it say?'

The smell was making him hyperventilate. He breathed hungrily through his inhaler, wishing he could snort it.

'I don't know. I didn't open it. But there was no name on the envelope.' He hadn't quite meant to worry her about the possibility of being arrested but too late now. 'I'm sure Johnny wouldn't write anything too obvious.' Then he remembered the reference to the wire: lucky it hadn't been confiscated.

Natasha looked deep into his eyes and sighed. Or, rather, she exhaled for about two minutes, almost inaudibly. He felt the warm breath on his hands and her dark gaze pierced him like knives. He tried to look sympathetic, but he knew it wasn't sincere. She knew too.

'Tell him… tell him I try to be here in three weeks, but I do not promise. It a long way from Dresden and we do not have so much time.'

'Okay, I will. And Natasha? Maybe it's for the best,' Peter said.

'Maybe.' She nodded slowly, her head getting lower each time. Her scalp was dusted with dandruff.

She turned away but, seconds later, spun round again. This time her eyes were deep muddy pools. Peter clutched his inhaler in his pocket.

'Has Alice something to do with this?' she asked.

'Alice? Well, you know they're good friends...' He coughed, implying more.

'Thank you for telling me.'

He nodded, feeling as if he'd just crushed an insect. She hobbled away from him, one limb less, a different creature than she'd been only ten minutes earlier.

Peter was about to call after her, but he turned and headed back the way he came as quickly as possible. It was for the best.

Zoologischer Garten

Time passed. Winter melted. But life in Berlin for Alice didn't change, except that she hadn't seen Johnny since that night they'd crossed the Wall back in March. She didn't care, hardly noticed. She had been having so much fun that she only realised that winter had passed when she got off the U-Bahn at Zoologischer Garten one Friday afternoon, dressed in her long black coat, and suddenly felt very hot as she made her way out of the station. She took off her coat and stuffed it in her plastic Bolle bag, angry that she'd dated her ticket in the machine and it hadn't been checked. Another two Marks wasted, but she'd been caught the other day with an unstamped five journey ticket and, although she'd played the stupid English girl and got away with it, she hadn't been in the mood to risk it again today. She'd only had two vodkas and you just never knew when the fat men in blue uniforms and peaked caps would line up on the platform before swarming the trains like the Gestapo.

She blinked into the blue world, fairly certain that it hadn't been that colour before she got on the train. She had a couple of hours before meeting some guy she'd met in Café Swing who had promised her a part in a film. He wanted her to come to his hotel, but she wasn't that stupid. He was fairly old with wispy grey hair in a ponytail, grey-blue eyes, and a beard and face that had been left out in the rain for too long. He had given her his business card and she had finally agreed to meet him at the Irish Pub in the Europa Centre at six o'clock today.

She took off her coat and crossed the busy roads, dizzy with people and traffic. The winter smell of coal had been chased away by diesel fumes, spicy sausages and Camel cigarettes. Across the road was the train station where she'd met Johnny all those months ago. A couple of tanks squatted outside the station, their guns pointing in the direction of the park, union jack flags on their sides. She decided to go for a walk in the Tiergarten – if she could find a way in without going to the Zoo.

She was glad she hadn't seen Johnny since that night as she'd done something hilarious, at least she thought it was hilarious – he would probably kill her. She'd been so pissed off when she saw him on his knees in front of *her* that when she got back to Peter's with Bodo, she'd put on black lace gloves, sneaked into Johnny's room and nicked his passport. Then, on her way home, she'd dropped it into someone's *Hinterhof* rubbish bin not far from Hermannplatz station. He'd never be able to marry her now, especially as they had gone back. The fools.

Served him right.

Served her right.

She'd laughed about it for days and was dying to tell Peter, but then she'd met him on his way to the East to give *her* a message from Johnny. Quite why Peter had agreed she had no idea. Johnny had probably offered him a shag. Anyway, she didn't care: she hadn't seen either of them for more than two months now. She had been to the Kiosk a couple of times but not even Peter was there. And no one had knocked on her door to arrest her.

As for Bodo, she hadn't heard a thing. He was cute, she liked him, but it was his decision to cross back over. She couldn't blame him, but what a lot of trouble for nothing. Before he left he had pleaded with her to come and visit him one day but she doubted if she'd ever see him again. Besides, they were on tour.

She walked past the entrance to the Zoo and followed a guy with a blue Mohican, dirty jeans, a studded dog lead around his neck and an Alsatian at his heels. He must be going to the park. The Mohican reminded her of Johnny when he first arrived in Berlin in January. In the days when he'd loved her.

She passed by the camels and over the river. Life slowed down in the park. Bicycles replaced cars and shoppers became strollers. The leaves on the trees muffled the city sounds. The guy with the blue Mohican headed towards a small group of people assembled around a tree. Alice took off her coat, sat on a bench and observed the world around her. It was pleasant and green. She really should visit the parks more often – there were enough of them in West Berlin. She pulled out a copy of *Tip* from the plastic bag and began to read an article about a group of artists in Winterfeldtplatz instead. They had created a new bar where you could sit on tree-like metal sculptures. It looked cool.

She paused from her reading and looked up into the green trees. There, walking barefoot on a rope slung between two trees about five foot off the ground, was a man in a top hat and tails. Butterflies dived into her stomach. It was him. It had to be. She got up and walked towards the crowd. For a second she thought she'd made a mistake: this guy was pulling funny faces, doing silly walks and things. The kids loved it. He even juggled on the tightrope. All the while more and more people stopped to watch. But then he looked at her. It was him.

Johnny.

The butterflies flew to her heart. He pointed at her, curling his forefinger towards himself. Within seconds she was below him, catching his top hat and, at his bidding, holding it out to the crowd as he walked from tree to tree, arcing missiles over his head. Several times he wavered but didn't fall. Then on a perch in one of the trees he looked up into the sky and swallowed fire.

The butterflies burned.

The crowd applauded and threw Deutsch Marks into the hat – notes as well as coins. Johnny bowed and jumped down from the tree. Only when the crowd started to drift away did he speak to her.

'Good to see you,' he said. 'You look great.'

'And you.' She couldn't believe she said that. 'Nice hat,' she added.

Johnny smiled his half smile with the left side of his mouth. 'I got it at the flea market. Did you come to see me?' he asked.

'No, I had no idea you were here. In fact, if I had known, I wouldn't have come.' Alice sat down on the grass and folded her arms.

He took off his black-tailed coat and laid it down for both of them to sit on. Underneath he wore black tights and a white sleeveless shirt. Dirt lined the contours in his feet. He offered her a Camel. Muscle pumped through his bare white arms like a model steam engine. She refused his offer and pulled out her packet of Benson's.

Several people came up to him and asked him if he was performing again today. He told them at six.

'Good performance,' she said when they were on their own. 'How long have you been doing it?'

'A couple of months. As soon as the weather got better. I had to start making some money.'

Alice nodded and lit her cigarette. Johnny lit his own.

'And you? What have you been doing?' Johnny asked.

'Oh, you know, the usual.' Why did she always have to be doing something?

'What about the play?'

'Oh, it kind of fizzled out. People wouldn't turn up to rehearsals... wouldn't agree on anything.' She tore at the grass with her fingers.

'It's hard to work with other people – especially when you're not getting paid. That dance performance with Sophie was difficult enough.'

'I thought it was good,' Alice said. His left arm brushed against hers as he raised his cigarette to his mouth. Her tummy tumbled over.

'That last night we pulled it together but it wasn't a good experience. I wouldn't do it again. Sophie asked me but I said no.'

'So what are you doing? Have you married that Russian girl yet?'

'Not yet. I haven't seen her. But one day...'

Envy stabbed Alice in the heart. She took a deep drag on her cigarette.

'How come she didn't stay when she had the chance? If she loved you,' she asked, turning towards him.

Johnny flinched. A wounded animal, she thought. Hm.

'She didn't want to leave her family,' he said, gazing across the park. 'Did you know I lost my passport the night they crossed in the Kiosk? Or someone stole it.'

'I think Peter said something about it,' Alice replied, now also staring across at the park in front of them.

'Well, I couldn't get across to meet her so I gave Peter a letter to give to her but it was confiscated by the border guards.'

'Really. Oh dear.' Alice tried to sound disinterested, hoping he wouldn't hear her thumping heart, imagining the muscles tautening like Johnny's moving arm.

'And now, I'm afraid something's happened. I've heard nothing from them for months.'

'What do you mean?'

'Well, her name, and my name, was on the letter. I think I even mentioned the crossing. I actually can't remember...' Johnny's voice trailed off.

For a moment, Alice felt sorry for him. She tugged on her cigarette. He was hurting. And it was all her fault for nicking his passport. But screw him. He'd hurt her too.

'I'm sure she's fine. No one knew about the walk did they, apart from us lot. Did Peter actually meet up with her?'

'Yeah, he saw her and gave her a message from me.'

'Well then.'

Johnny shook his head as he wiped his cigarette out on the grass.

'I don't know. You said you were watched in the East and Bodo was also very suspicious. Everyday I watch Bodo's apartment and nothing. It's as if they've disappeared.'

'I'm sure they're fine. You have a new passport now?'

'Yeah. I went back to meet Natasha three weeks later as we'd arranged but she didn't show. Peter told me she said she would. I waited for seven hours in the station.'

'Maybe she just couldn't make it,' Alice said, trying to ignore the layer of doubt settling around her. 'They're on tour, aren't they?' Maybe they had been arrested. Poor Bodo. And that would be her fault as well.

'Yeah,' Johnny said. 'They will be back at the end of September – if nothing's happened. I'm going to wait until then.'

'That's ages,' Alice muttered. A quarter of a year.

'Yes,' said Johnny. 'But not compared to the rest of your life.'

Alice didn't reply. To her, three months felt like a lifetime.

'Why don't you go to wherever it is they're performing?' she said.

'Because, if they are in trouble, I don't want to cause any more.'

She nodded and looked at her watch: it was quarter to six.

'What about you and Bodo?' Johnny asked her. Did anything happen between you two?'

'Bodo and me? I don't do iron curtain relationships.' She threw her cigarettes and orange lighter in her Bolle plastic bag.

'He liked you a lot.'

'A lot of men do, Johnny,' she couldn't help snapping, so she softened the edges of her words with a smile.

'Do you have to go?' Johnny asked.

'Kind of. I'm supposed to meet this guy about a part in a film at six.'

'What film?' Johnny asked.

'Oh, just some art film about Berlin.' She had forgotten to ask what it was about. 'I'll find out more later.'

'How long you gonna be?' Johnny asked.

'Dunno.'

'Can I take you out for a pizza later?' Johnny picked up his black hat and looked at the money. He must have made about fifty Marks.

Alice felt her eyes opening. She hummed uncertainly.

'No problem if you can't,' Johnny said quickly.

'No, no that's okay,' she said. 'I'll meet you about nine. Same place?'

'Sounds good.'

She left him counting out the Marks and she scurried back to the Europa Centre, trying not to skip. She had a date with Johnny! Just when she least expected it. She didn't feel like going into the dark Irish Pub now but Grey Ponytail was already there waiting alone at a table in the vast bar, drinking a pint of Guinness, looking very serious.

As she passed a waitress dressed in a black skirt and white blouse serving a group of American GIs, she thought about Bodo. She hoped nothing had happened to him. She didn't care about Natasha. But they were just on tour, she told herself. A band finished singing about a dirty old town and everyone clapped loudly. An American was trying to chat up a girl with long dark curls at the bar and he must have asked her where she was from as she shouted, 'Derry. It's Derry, not fuckin' Londonderry. I'm not fuckin' British, I'm Irish.'

Alice's hands felt clammy as she approached Grey Ponytail. She regretted meeting here. Her height and red and black hair and makeup felt incongruous against the background of beer mats and coquettish country Irish girls. But at least it was dark.

'Sorry I'm late,' she said, swinging round to sit down next to him, knocking the table with her bum. The Guinness slopped over the top of the glass. 'Sorry,' she muttered again.

'That's okay. I've only just got here as well. What will you have?'

'I'll have a large beer, thanks.' She wanted to ask for a vodka too, but thought that might give the wrong impression.

He ordered for her from one of the girls with overgrown dark hair and milk chocolate eyes.

'So tell me about your acting career?' he asked.

No foreplay then. 'Oh well, I went to East 17,' she said, trying to remember what Johnny had told her about it. 'And since I've been here I've done a couple of plays with a theatre group I'm part of.'

'East 17? Don't you mean East 15?' he said.

'Did I say 17?' She laughed and kicked herself.

'What about film work?'

'No, not much,' she replied, truthfully this time.

'Well, we can do some screen tests first, if you are interested? I have the equipment set up in my hotel room. It's not far from here. We can go there now if you want?' He looked at his watch. 'We have time.'

Oh right, Alice thought, her embarrassment vaporised. So it was another ploy to get her into bed. Men. All the same.

'What's this film about again?' she asked.

'It's kind of a documentary about life in Berlin. I'm aiming to capture various lives in a city divided by the Wall.'

It didn't sound very interesting to Alice. A bit too real. Documentaries were so boring. Even if it wasn't a ploy, she didn't want to do something that she didn't like or believe in.

'Have you got a script?' she asked.

'Not exactly. I work in images. The idea is for it to be more ad lib. I'm using various people from different sectors of society. For example, a Turkish immigrant family I have in mind, a German guy whose family is in the East, an American soldier and so on.' He supped his Guinness. A white line of scum frothed around his mouth like dried seaweed on sand.

The Irish girl brought her beer over and Ponytail paid for it.

'*Prost,*' Alice said. She drank thirstily.

He raised his glass. 'So what do you think?'

She wiped her mouth. 'Sounds interesting,' she lied. 'What role would I play though?'

'Well, as I said, it is going to be ad lib. But we would have a day in the life of Alice, or something like that, juxtaposed between other people's lives.'

Just a what? Hm. A day in the life of Alice. She wasn't sure if that was a good idea. She might regret it in the future. What if her parents saw it? They would keel over – if they hadn't already. Ponytail was looking at her expectantly. She drank back some more beer. She had a problem and she wasn't sure quite how to phrase it.

'I'm not sure. I'm interested in acting but you want me to act myself. Or, at least, I would be represented as myself when it might not really be myself.'

'Uhm.'

'You see the problem?'

'Not really – unless you have a problem with who you are,' Ponytail said, and smiled into his Guinness.

She resisted throwing her beer over him. Instead, she smiled back at him and sat up. She was taller than him.

'No, I don't have a problem with who I am. It's just not much of a challenge for me to be me,' she said, calmly, confidently. She was in control.

'Well, I would have thought it would have been a great opportunity for someone like you.'

Someone like her? What the fuck did he mean by that? She was losing her cool.

'How much would I be paid?' she asked.

'Only expenses, I'm afraid, and we need to begin next week. Anyway, listen, I have another meeting at seven. If you're interested, call me or come round to the hotel and I'll see what you look like on film. Okay?'

He stood up and offered her his hand. She touched it, unable to get rid of an unpleasant taste growing in her mouth.

'So how did it go with your film director?' Johnny asked, when he joined her at the pizza restaurant.

She was sitting next to the tropical fish tank watching a grouchy looking grey fish with whiskers open and close its mouth as if snogging the glass. She tapped its mouth but it paid no attention to her. She had waited three vodka and oranges for him. But, at least, the bad taste had almost gone.

'Boring,' she said breezily. 'And he kept asking me to do a screen test in his hotel room. I mean.'

'What kind of film is it?'

'He *says* it's a documentary about life in Berlin.' Alice lit a cigarette.

Johnny rested his head to one side on his raised arm and looked at her thoughtfully. She imitated him and he smiled. She was feeling much better.

'It might be interesting,' he said. 'Maybe, it is a low budget film and he hasn't got a studio set up here.'

'Well, next time I feel like sex, I'll go and find out.'

Johnny smiled. She loved to see the corners of his mouth broaden and curl up ever so slightly.

'It is really good to see you, Alice.'

She felt herself glowing and turned towards the fish tank so that he wouldn't see. She struggled to understand how he could love this other woman and yet still make her feel so good. An angel fish winked at her. Or maybe it was her imagination. She clearly imagined many things in life.

The Palace of Tears

Every night at ten he would gaze across the Wall at Bodo's apartment waiting for a sign. Every night. For six months. During the summer days he would make himself get up, go to a park, walk between trees, juggle batons, swallow fire and try not to think of the part of him that was missing. Sometimes he would see her small, dark, laughing face in the leaves and branches of the trees, in the clouds that drifted across the sky, in the reflection of the lakes in the parks, in the crumbling and bullet-pocked buildings, in the crowds that gathered below him, in the dark glass of the U-Bahns, in the shadows on the Wall. But it was only ever a fleeting fantasy which his memory carelessly dropped wherever he went. Wherever he went, he was always back at Heidelberger Straße by ten o'clock to stare at the darkening apartments as the night fell on the two cities, waiting. Just in case.

Every night, except once, in the beginning of June, when he had eaten with an Amazonian woman with long red and black hair, deep violet eyes, red kissing lips and charm as scorching and devastating as fire. Together they burned through pizzas, salads and sentences, drank wine, words and silences. They watched dancing angel fish through algae-tinted glass chase each other over white coral and coloured stones, their arrowed black fins following them like crested waves.

How come you don't love me? she had whispered. When we feel so good together?

I do love you but Natasha and I have something very special.

Then how can you love two people?

I don't know. Perhaps there are different kinds of love.

Perhaps.

Then, like angel fish, they chased each other through the streets of Berlin, up and down escalators, in and out of trains, along roads and across courtyards, until she caught him in a dark room. Safely anchored in her strong arms, he thought he would find relief. But touching her magnified every emotion a thousand times. He felt he would shatter into a million pieces. He wanted her, and for her to go away and to never see her again. In the shadows of the pillow he could see Natasha's tears. Why was he doing this? What kind of love was this? And then he fled into the night.

That was more than three months ago now. He had spent days searching out suitable trees in the parks so that he would never be in the same place for long. So that she wouldn't find him. She never did. Perhaps she had never looked. Perhaps she had left West Berlin. All that remained of their night together was a lingering aftertaste of warped misunderstanding, like burnt toast, as if a human fuse had blown.

Now, it was Monday, 8 October, and the cold was snaking into the city. He was still here, waiting. They had said the end of September. They should be back by now. If nothing bad had happened. But this night was no different, darker if anything. The same cold immovable glare from the death strip still glared at him. He could hear Peter moving behind him, calling him crazy, telling him that he was making himself ill, that his balls had shrunk to stewed meatballs and his penis resembled a mouldy carrot. Johnny blew a kiss in his direction and the abuse stopped. Peter was easy to satisfy – all bark and no bite.

And then he saw it.

A light in Bodo's living room. It was ten minutes past ten. Surely too close to be a coincidence? On-off. On-off. That was it. The sign he had been waiting for. But no one came to the window and, within seconds, the ghostly fresco returned. He stared and stared out of the window but nothing else happened.

As he lay in bed later that night he began to think he'd imagined it. Then, as he drifted into an uncertain sleep, he found himself passing through Checkpoint Charlie and taken into a secret room behind an interrogation booth. The door was locked behind him by a large, uniformed man with sharp, grey stones for eyes and a neatly trimmed, dark moustache which fringed his narrow pale lips. He was made to undress and stand naked under a single bulb while his interrogator walked around him, prodding him with a baton, asking him about his relationship with Natasha Barovskova.

I am the KGB and Natasha Barovskova is Russian, one of our citizens, he says, his moustache shaping his words. We know all about the daring highwire crossing in March. We let it happen because we thought it would be entertaining. We knew they would come back. But now you are planning something else, are you not? We know about your arrangements. We read the letter. We hear every conversation.

What arrangements? Johnny asks, confused. What have you heard? Even his letter hadn't said anything about their arrangements, had it?

Your juggling friend's apartment is bugged. Do you know that? But even if it wasn't we would still find out. Do you know that one third of all citizens in the German Democratic Republic are informers for the Stasi? They have the greatest surveillance network in the world. We, in Moscow, are a little jealous. But, of course, they share their secrets with us. Do you know, for example, there are hidden microphones and cameras in clocks, in pens, in briefcases? Wherever we want, we put one. Ingenious eh? We can even bug an apartment from three floors away without ever entering.

How? Johnny asks. Sweat trickles down from his armpits over his goosebumped skin.

How? The agent stops and stares at him out of those locked-up stony eyes, as if seeing him for the first time. He tuts. *That would be divulging state secrets. It is enough for you to know that we can. And we do. Do you know that we know everything about you?*

No, Johnny mutters. His right leg trembles in a way it never does when he walks between trees.

We know that your mother was born in East London in 1928. We know that she was a good time show girl in the West End, that she became pregnant out of wedlock, you say, at thirty-three with an officer in the British Army, with whom she had been having an affair with for five years. Did you know that he already had a wife and two children and you became a problem?

Johnny feels sick. How could he know so much? It's impossible. No, he shouts. That's not true.

Oh but it is true.

It was true. His mother had never spoken about him much – only that the bastard had disappeared in 1961, just after he was born. She had always said that they were alone in the world, that we are all alone in the world. But then a strange tall man had approached him after his mother's funeral and introduced himself as Donald Rye. He said that he was sorry for what had happened, that he had loved his mother very much, but circumstances had been difficult. He said that the world they lived in then wouldn't allow for illegitimate children and divorce was still taboo. Johnny had been too wrung out from his mother's death to really take in what this strange man was saying. The man slipped an envelope into his hand, patted his arm and told him to feel free to call him. Johnny had never contacted him.

But how do you know all this?

We know because it is our job to know. We deal in information. We know that you have a criminal record for theft. We know that your father gave you £2000 on your mother's death and you went to a drama school. Guilt money, I think you call it. We know everything about you, Johnny East. We know what you like to eat, to drink, who you like to fuck – as well as our little Natasha. Now, tell me, what are you planning?

Nothing, Johnny says. If you know so much, you must know that.

A sharp pain across his back. The agent had hit him with a baton.

You can't do that, he says.

Can't I? The agent hits him again, this time on his stomach.

Johnny tightens his muscles as the baton falls again. And again. And again. And again.

He awoke on his mattress, drenched in sweat. A bird was singing on his windowsill. It was morning. He got up, his body aching, and opened the window. The bird and its song fled as Johnny gasped at the chilled autumn air. He checked his naked body but there were no bruises. It had only been a nightmare. He shook his head. The face of the interrogator was beginning to blur, but he could still replay the interrogation. It was only a dream, he told himself over again. None of it was true. He went to take a shower and some paracetamol. Nothing would prevent him from going to the East today.

He held out his passport to the young border guard. It was a new passport with only one other DDR stamp in it, he had nothing to fear. The guard didn't look anything like the man in his nightmare. Yet, even so, he could feel sweat seeping out from beneath his arms and forehead as the guard stared at the photograph in his passport before looking up at him: stone-grey eyes. An eternity seemed to pass between them before the smooth, pale hand took a stamp, pressed it on the inkpad and transferred it to his passport and the blue visa showing the map of the Berlin that existed for him, valid until midnight.

Johnny walked into the East. He had never felt like this before; it wasn't like him to feel fear. Something had happened to her: he was sure of it. Because of him. Even as he walked through the dark, empty Berlin streets, he began to imagine cameras hidden in buildings, trees, traffic lights, an old clock with Roman numerals. He imagined he could hear footsteps behind him. He practised the breathing techniques he had learned at drama school but he couldn't quite smooth over the hiccup as he inhaled. This is not like you, Johnny, he told himself. It was as if he were still in his nightmare. Maybe Peter was right, maybe he was making himself ill. He had lost his balance and fallen off the rope a couple of times recently. He had put it down to a lack of concentration and tiredness but, maybe, he was unwell.

He reached Unter den Linden wishing he had taken the U-Bahn. It was still a long way to go. He crossed the road and kept on walking along Friedrichstraße. There were more people now, staring at him as if he had landed from Venus. He passed the library and followed the S-Bahn signs around roadworks, partitioned off by rusting metal caging that seemed to have been there for decades, until he reached the huge concrete and glass complex that formed Friedrichstraße station. A clock bordered by short lines instead of numbers told him it was almost midday. He began to hurry past the queues of people who shuffled to and from the station along the narrow pathway.

He peered anxiously into the station behind the Palace of Tears where he had first met Bodo. He blinked.

She was there. Standing patiently, waiting.

'Natasha,' he called, running to her, gathering her in his arms. He could hardly believe it: she was alive and well. She looked faintly surprised to see him. 'Natasha, my angel,' he whispered. 'I thought I would never see you again.'

'Stop,' she hissed.

Remembering where he was, he let go and they looked at each other. In the time that they had not seen each other, her dark hair had grown past her shoulders.

'You look shit,' she said, and laughed. 'Come on, let's drink coffee. But we must be careful.'

They hardly spoke as she led him over the river and along a quiet road lined with broken warehouses.

'Someone follow us,' she said.

They stopped while a young, short East German, with dark, greasy hair and wearing a denim jacket, passed them and pretended to look in a window. Johnny felt himself sweating again. The guy sauntered back towards them, casually, avoiding their gaze.

'You sell Levi?' he asked the pavement as he passed.

Levi? Johnny smiled, relieved, and shook his head. He was just a black marketeer guy.

'Change money?' he asked.

Johnny shook his head.

'Shame,' the guy replied. 'Next time you bring Levis.'

Johnny and Natasha moved on quickly.

'Where are you from?' he called after them.

'Excuse us, we have to go,' Johnny called back.

'He still follow,' Natasha said.

'It's okay, he's a long way behind,' Johnny said.

'Not okay. He does not want Levi.'

Johnny looked back again. The guy was carrying a bag. It wasn't a briefcase, more of a satchel, the old leather kind with straps wrapping over the top and a solid, flat bottom.

'Johnny, what we do?'

He could hear the tears in Natasha's voice.

'I don't know. I was so afraid something had happened to you. After what Peter told me about my note being confiscated...' Johnny pulled her towards him. He didn't care that they were outside a restaurant or that Levi was still watching them.

'Not here, Johnny. Better to wait until we go inside. It is more possible to be alone in the crowd.'

They went into the restaurant and stepped into the past. Gilded mirrors hung on each wall, glass chandeliers and rococo motifs adorned the high ceiling. A waiter wearing a starched white shirt, black waistcoat and trousers looked at them before scowling and showing them to a table near to one end of the restaurant, out of the way of anyone else. There were maybe a dozen other people, all very smartly dressed. A Beethoven symphony played in the background.

'Do you love me?' she whispered as soon as the waiter had gone to get the menu.

'Of course I love you. I love you more than anything. I have waited for you for so long, Natasha. Six months...'

They spoke without moving their lips.

The waiter returned with menus and Natasha ordered a bottle of champagne. Johnny couldn't help smiling at the irony that he could only afford champagne, a symbol of bourgeois lifestyle, in a communist country.

'But your friend Peter say when you lose your passport it is for the best. He say you like Alice.'

'He what?' Johnny felt fury spill out of his heart and into his voice.

'He say I should forget you.'

Johnny groaned. How could he have done that?

'I don't know what he said to you. Or why. But it is not true, Natasha. I have waited for you all this time on my own. I haven't seen Alice for six months and there was nothing between us anyway.'

'You sleep with her.'

The waiter returned with the champagne and told them to order. Johnny let Natasha order for him. He wasn't hungry. He'd just swallowed a thousand nails. The waiter took great pleasure in slowly rearranging the knives and forks and filling their glasses. All the time the nails dug deeper. Johnny took a gulp of champagne, hoping to blunt the pain.

'It was a long time ago,' he whispered at last. 'There is more to love than sex.'

'You think? She loves you.'

'I don't think so. We liked each other but, Natasha, we had nothing in common. Believe me, I love you. I waited for you for seven hours in April as we arranged, you know.'

'Okay, Johnny, I believe you. I tell Peter I do not promise to come to Berlin in June. We in Dresden. Was impossible for me.'

Johnny breathed in the heavy suspicious air. Peter had failed to mention the doubt.

'Peter didn't tell me that,' he said.

'I think your friend not a good friend,' Natasha said, her dark eyes searching the white tablecloth before staring through him.

'I think you're right.'

They drank the champagne and smoked a cigarette.

'He still there,' Natasha said.

Johnny knew she meant Levi. Sure enough, he was lurking outside the restaurant, his satchel pressed against the glass.

'Do you think he's watching us?' Johnny said. 'I had such a bad dream last night. I was interrogated by the KGB and, apparently, they know all about us.'

'It possible,' Natasha said.

The waiter arrived with a basket of stale bread. Johnny picked up a piece and pretended to eat it until the waiter had retreated.

'I didn't expect to see you today. There was a light on for only a few minutes and no one came to the window. I thought it might be a trick...'

'Bodo still in Leipzig,' Natasha explained. 'He tell me he ask one of the other acrobats to switch on the light. I think he ask him not to go to the window in case you not know him.'

Johnny nodded.

'I do not think I see you today, too,' she continued. 'I think you forget me.'

'I will never forget you.'

'Johnny, what we going to do? I miss you too much. Every night I think about you. I even fall from the high wire three times because I think about you. The Professor very angry with me.'

Johnny closed his eyes for a second. He didn't know what to say.

'*Schweinefleisch?*' The waiter hovered above them with two steaming plates.

'*Hier bitte,*' Natasha said.

The other plate landed in front of Johnny. Some kind of meatballs.

'I remember how much you like,' Natasha said. She smiled at him and at the waiter. To anyone else they could just be a normal couple eating lunch.

They ate without eating, going through the functions of putting food into their mouths, chewing and swallowing. Every so often they lifted their eyes from their plates and looked at each other, as if trying to swallow the space between them. If only they could swallow the restaurant, the man outside with a satchel, the Wall, the guards, the politicians, the men who wanted to change the world, the whole city, half the world.

Then, Johnny thought, their love might have a chance.

'I don't know,' he said, at last. 'I don't know what we're going to do.' He chewed and swallowed some more.

'Is it always this difficult?' Natasha said.

Johnny shook his head. How could it be? There were few people with a thirteen-foot high concrete wall and a death strip between them. If only she had stayed when she had the chance.

'I could not stay,' Natasha said, as if reading his mind. 'I promise Zoyenka.'

'It's okay. I understand.'

'But soon we return to Moscow. Zoyenka okay.' Her voice trailed off.

'When?'

'End of November.'

What she was saying? He shook his head.

'We did it once. The next time is easy.'

His nightmare flashed before him.

We know everything about you, Johnny East. We know what you like to eat, to drink, who you like to fuck – as well as our little Natasha. Now tell me what are you planning?

'It's not a good idea,' he hissed. 'It's too dangerous.'

'Why?'

'I don't know. It's just a feeling. I feel like we're being watched. Like they know. He glanced towards the window. Levi was still there.

'Johnny, they probably do. But I feel I die every day when I awake without you. If I fall then I die only one more time.'

He didn't know what to say. He wanted her to cross so much but he didn't want her to take the risk. If she fell, he would never be able to forgive himself. A loose nail dug deep into his guts. He was shaking his head.

'What?' she said angrily. 'It is my life. It will be fine. You paranoid.'

Maybe. Maybe he was being paranoid. They had done it before. It would be easier the second time. The waiter came and removed the plates. Natasha asked for coffee as the waiter poured out the rest of the champagne. They clinked glasses and she winked at him behind the waiter's back as she had done once after his first circus performance. He wanted her so much.

'To our future,' she said. 'Away from the Palace of Tears.'

To our future.

Kanal

Peter was making himself a cup of coffee on a grey October Friday afternoon when Johnny pranced into the kitchen and announced that they were going to do another high wire crossing. The carton of milk Peter was holding slipped through his fingers and hit the table. He quickly retrieved it, ignoring the white pool around the base, and poured some into his coffee. He had a feeling he was going to need it.

'You are joking, aren't you, darling?' he said.

'No, we have decided. This time it will be for good.'

'We?' Peter sat down at the table and clasped his hands around his favourite art deco cup. He slurped his coffee. It was strong, just how he liked it. He inhaled slowly, trying to keep his breathing steady. He looked at the sunflower clock. Ten minutes to eleven – way too early for a scene.

'Natasha and I – and, possibly, Bodo.'

'What about asking me?'

'What do you mean?' Johnny looked at him, surprised. He helped himself to some of his coffee. 'I'm telling you now.'

'I mean, don't you think it would be a good idea to talk it through with me and Michael, and even Hermann, before announcing that you are going to get us all into trouble?' Peter smiled as he clutched his mug, forgetting to exhale.

'Do you mind?' Johnny asked, turning his back on him to rinse a teaspoon under the faucet.

'Actually, yes, I do. I did it once for you. It took a lot of planning, a lot of stress, but I thought it would make you happy. And then they fucked off. Have you any idea how that felt?'

Johnny scraped back a chair and sat down at the kitchen table with him.

'Have you any idea how it feels to know that your friend lied to the person you love?' Johnny said.

'I didn't lie,' Peter snapped.

'You didn't tell me that Natasha couldn't promise to come from Dresden.' Johnny spoke harshly.

'She said she would try to make it,' Peter spluttered indignantly.

'What about the insinuations that you made about me and Alice?'

The bastard. He was going to need his inhaler soon.

'Natasha asked me about Alice,' he said. 'I said that you were good friends. That's not exactly a fucking lie, is it?' He coughed. 'Or even an insinuation.'

'I haven't seen Alice for months.'

'At that time you had. Fuck you, Johnny. I did you a favour by going to the East and meeting with that woman and this is the thanks I get. It wasn't my fault the letter was confiscated. Now you want more favours. Have you ever thought that sometimes you need to give and not just take all the time?' Peter grabbed his inhaler and blasted the salbutamol into his lungs. Johnny really should carry a health warning.

Johnny tilted his head to one side and looked at him. 'I'm sorry,' he said after a few minutes. He leaned across the table and put his hand on Peter's arm. He squeezed gently. 'I didn't mean to say that. I just didn't realise that crossing would be such a problem for you.'

Peter felt his anger subside slightly and his breathing stopped sounding like a blunt saw. Johnny had, at least, apologised. Besides, he had torn up and thrown away the letter for Natasha. He drank some more coffee and lit the cigarette that Johnny was offering him.

The problem was he really did think that crossing the Wall again was a bad idea. And he didn't want to have their deaths on his conscience for the rest of his life. Too many people knew about the crossing back in March. Why the hell had they gone back? Why take such a risk? He knew that people did all sorts of stupid things just to get a buzz but they didn't even seem to get that. Peter thought some more before he spoke.

'I think it's a really bad idea, Johnny. I would think it's almost impossible that you're not being watched. You've been over twice this week. I don't think you realise what you're doing most of the time.' Peter was about to launch into a lecture about the effective tyranny of the Stasi but he needed to calm his heart beat and his mind felt too clogged up with the morning. Never his best time.

Johnny sat and drank his coffee, more thoughtfully now.

'I know there are more risks this time.'

Just a few.

'But Natasha wants to take the risk.' Johnny paused before adding, 'We need each other, Peter.'

The remnants of Peter's wheezing turned into a loud, porcine snort. Oh really. He was overcome by revulsion. That smelly hybrid rubber-woman. Just the thought of it made his breath bitter. He tried not to imagine them making love in bizarre positions, reinventing the

Karma Sutra, and concentrated on the elegant but simple lines of his cup-mug.

'It's a shame you didn't know that before,' he said, unable to keep the bitterness out of his words.

'We did, but she had family commitments. It's hard. You don't choose love, Peter. Love chooses you.'

'Oh bollocks,' Peter said, not so much because he disagreed, more out of the bollocksness of the situation. And, besides, he did disagree.

'Please Peter. One last time. I promise this will be it.'

Peter stared into his ice-blue eyes. Johnny's hand stroked his arm. He sighed. 'When do you want to do it?'

'9 November. It's a Friday. Two weeks away. Please, Peter.'

Even after all these months, Johnny need only touch him and it was as if he had put a gun to his head, even though he knew damn well that any Johnny fix would be short-term and he would pine for weeks afterwards. But at such moments he had absolutely no control.

'Tell me you'll help?' Johnny whispered, still softly touching his arm.

Peter attempted one last stance.

'I'm just not sure it will work this time,' he said, hearing his own deep voice almost squeaking.

As Johnny removed his hand Peter felt the gun drop.

'But I don't see why not? Everything is still in place. It will be much easier than the last time.' Johnny stubbed out his cigarette with repeated stabbing motions as if it were an automatic shotgun. 'If you're that worried, maybe we could ask, what's her name, Frieda, to divert the guards' attention. Remember how she told us she stripped in front of them?'

Peter began to regain his strength. He, too, wiped out his cigarette and drank the rest of his coffee.

'Frieda moved back to Köln months ago. I'm not doing it, Johnny. It's different this time. Too many people know about the last walk. I would put money on the probability that you are being watched. They could be shot and I don't wanna feel bad about that.'

'How could they be watching me? Surely they would have stopped me by now?'

Peter immediately detected the doubt in Johnny's voice, which confirmed his decision. Even *he* thought he was being watched. Oh no, he wasn't going to be a part in this. Not even if Johnny appeared in his bed, naked. Not even if he kissed his nipples and nibbled at the hairs on his chest. Not even if he clutched his buttocks in his strong arms. Not even if his tongue forced its way into his mouth. Not even if he bent over forwards. Or backwards. Or any fucking way. He wasn't doing it.

'Okay then, I'll do it by myself,' Johnny said.

'Oh no, darling. This is my apartment.' Peter heard his voice bite.

Johnny sighed, got up and put his arms around Peter's shoulders. Peter felt the gun again, pressing into his forehead. He tried not to breathe in Johnny's soft skin.

'Please Peter,' Johnny whispered. 'You needn't have anything to do with it. If there are ever questions, I'll say that you didn't know. You can be out all night. I'll do it all myself. There's no need for you to get involved. Please?'

Peter forced his head from side to side. Johnny removed his arms and stepped away from him.

'Oh fuck you, Peter. Why not?'

'No, go fuck yourself. On a rolling donut, Johnny,' Peter screeched, pushing his chair out and standing up. He needed some air.

'So is that a no then?'

'I want nothing…' Peter waved and crossed his arms in front of him. 'Nothing to do with it.'

Ten minutes later, Peter faced the freezing Berlin day, clutching his inhaler in one hand and a woollen hat in the other. He stopped, breathing heavily, by the main door into the courtyard and pumped some more Ventolin into his lungs. At least he had resisted Johnny. The first time but not the last. That was it. Johnny was moving out.

He walked along the canal. The autumnal leaves splashed muddy colours onto the grey skies and the ground. He kicked at their soggy fish bone forms on the pavement. The cold snapped at his hands and around his neck. A young couple walked towards him, tucked into each other. He wished he had a man he could cuddle up to – for more than one night. He had still hoped that Johnny would love him. But it was never-never-never going to happen. He would give him a month's notice. Once Johnny was gone, he'd be able to let go and maybe meet someone else. Then again, two weeks would take them to November 9. He would tell Johnny that he wanted him out by November 9 at the latest, before they were able to cross.

'Hi stranger. Long time, no see.' A giant Medusa, with long purple extensions poking out of a black hood, spoke to him. She had a camera slung casually over her shoulder. It took him several seconds to realise it was Mad Alice or, at least, a version of her.

'Hi,' Peter said, stopping. 'I didn't recognise you for a second. Where've you been?'

'I went back to London for most of the summer.'

'How was it?'

'Fucking awful. It's so pretentious and there's all these twats running around with huge phones and wearing suits and drinking wine.'

Peter nodded sympathetically. He'd never been to London but, according to the Brits he knew, it suffered from capital syndrome. And Margaret Thatcher, who was even more dangerous than Reagan because she wasn't completely dumb.

'Where are you off to?' she asked.

'Just walking.'

She looked surprised. 'Peter, you never walk unless you have to. What's up? Want a beer?'

Peter hesitated, but then the possibility of bitching about Johnny outweighed enduring Mad's company. He agreed and took her to a nearby corner café, where he had once been on his way back from a club with some guy he'd picked up in Hawaiian shorts. He couldn't remember what happened to the guy, but he remembered they did good breakfasts. They sat near the window. Mad grabbed the menu.

'Hey, this looks good. I think I might have a breakfast.'

Peter realised that he was hungry as well so they ordered two continental breakfasts, except Mad wanted vodka in the orange. She had good ideas occasionally.

'I've never been here before,' she said, looking round at the posters of film releases on the pale blue walls. 'It's cool.'

The red and black poster dystopian image of *Brazil* caught his eye: he never did see it.

'Where were you going anyway?' Peter asked.

'I was just taking a walk, re-acclimatising myself to Berlin, taking some photos. I'm meeting someone later about doing some freelance photography work.'

Peter had to smile. She lied all the time. 'That's good. And what were you doing in London?' he asked.

'Oh you know. Signed on the dole like the other people without suits and giant phones and hung out. Acted in a play called *The Widow*. It was good but I just don't belong there. Do you know what I mean?'

Peter nodded. He didn't believe a word about the play but he knew what it felt like to not belong in a place. He also knew about the dole, something the Brits had that the Americans didn't. It seemed that anyone could live there without working. An American dream... Germany was the same. Better, in fact, as they paid you two thirds of your previous wage forever. If you were legal. They didn't know how lucky they were.

'So did you bring some good speed back with you?'

'Of course. And you? What have you been up to? Something momentous must have happened for you to be out on the streets?'

She laughed an annoying high-pitched girl laugh. Peter imitated her in his own double bass rumble. She stopped abruptly.

'Johnny wants the rubber woman to cross over again,' he announced dramatically.

'Oh fuck him,' Mad said. Her suddenly sharpened green eyes almost pierced him.

'That's exactly what I said,' Peter said. Well, he wasn't going to mention the rolling donut bit. She'd laugh.

'You didn't?' She laughed anyway.

'I did.'

'I don't believe you,' she said. 'He only needs to blink at you and you do what he says.' She continued to stare at him so hard he began to feel worn out.

'Well, not this time, darling,' he said. 'I'm not going through that again, particularly as he's been a couple of times to the East just this week. He's being watched and he knows it.'

Mad's dark eyebrows formed two hillocks over her brow, as if someone had drawn an ink painting of the horizon. She was irritatingly pretty.

'So when did he meet up with her? Last time I saw him he said that he hadn't heard from her and he was worried that she might be dead or in prison because of the letter that was confiscated from you. Or something like that.'

'They only met up a couple of weeks ago. Honestly, Mad, he spent every night throughout the summer watching the Wall. That's not healthy.'

Peter had no idea that she knew about the letter. But at least she didn't know that he'd thrown it away on purpose and he wasn't going to tell her in case she told Johnny. You never knew with women, particularly her.

'Not every night,' she said.

'Yeah, every night.'

'Not every night,' she repeated.

The vodka and orange arrived in tall glasses together with a basket of bread and butter. Mad immediately removed the umbrella and sucked on the straw.

'*Prost* Mad,' Peter said, touching her glass. 'So when did you see him?'

'A while back. Must have been the beginning of June. The night he wasn't Wall watching. He was performing in the park and he asked me out for a pizza. He told me how much he was missing her and then ended up in bed with me.'

Peter had been about to remove both the umbrella and the straw but, on hearing the latest Mad revelation, he changed his mind and found himself nudging the umbrella aside and drinking thirstily from the straw.

'In June? But that was after he got his passport back?'

'Oh yeah. He'd been over to the East to meet her but she hadn't shown up.'

'Then what?'

'What?'

'After you shagged him?'

'I went to London. He was fucking with my head, you know what I mean? I was kind of hoping he'd be gone when I got back. But it doesn't matter. I'm into photography now.'

Peter nodded. What a hypocritical bastard. Only a few minutes ago he'd accused him of making 'insinuations'. Turns out they were more than insinuations. Unless, of course, she was lying.

'He even said that he loved me. And her. I mean, you don't do that, do you?'

For once, he didn't think she was lying. 'That doesn't surprise me.'

'I haven't seen him since,' Mad said. 'And I don't particularly want to.'

'I'm going to tell him to move out when I get back,' Peter said.

'You're always saying that, Peter, and you never do.'

'This time I mean it.'

'When does he want her to cross?'

'November 9. It's a Friday apparently.'

'That's soon. Are you going to throw him out before then?'

'Well, I reckon I have to give him two weeks' notice. But I want him out by Friday, November 9 at the latest.'

Mad nodded thoughtfully.

'Who wants to cross?' she asked.

'Rubber woman and, he said, perhaps, your clown.'

'Bodo?'

Peter ah-hahd and lit a cigarette.

'The stupid bastards. Why didn't they stay when they had the chance?'

'Exactly.'

'So why do you think he's being watched?'

'He's crossed over so many times now, darling. And I would put money on there being spies within the circus, as well as in Bodo's apartment block. The Stasi know everything.'

'Ach! You've watched too many films,' she said.

'I don't think so,' Peter said, with more conviction then he'd felt for a long time. 'Whichever, I've had enough of him. I want him out of my life.'

'Fair enough,' Mad said, putting away her guidebook. 'Could be a good opportunity to take some great photographs though.'

November 9 1984

As he checked where the rigging was going, Johnny tried not to think about the young guy, a border guard, who was shot dead last week attempting to cross the Wall. Peter had thrown away Bodo's original plans, or he wouldn't give them to him, and he was petrified of making a mistake. He had met Bodo alone last Saturday on the platform of Treptower Park S-Bahn and they had discussed the details of the rigging behind newspapers. They had decided to cross at two in the morning to give him time to do everything on his own.

'It is a shame beautiful Peter will not help,' Bodo had said. 'It would be better to cross earlier.'

Johnny didn't say anything. Beautiful Peter had changed. Quite why it mattered to him that Natasha and Bodo should cross again was bizarre. He had huffed and puffed on his inhaler until sweat bucketed down his face, before slamming the lounge door, and every other door, and going out for hours. Then, when he'd returned, he'd told him to move out by 9 November. That was fine. He hadn't specified a time. They would be out by the morning.

'He does not tell on us, no?' Bodo asked.

'No, Peter would not do that,' Johnny said. Would he? No, of course not.

There was, in fact, only Bodo, Natasha and Tomas, the sharpshooter, who knew about their planned defection. Bodo had assured him that Tomas was a silent man who wouldn't tell anyone. Not that they had any choice. They needed someone to shoot the wires across and Tomas, at least, had done it before. Not even Zoyenka knew. Natasha was afraid to tell her. Her sister had been asking too many questions about them.

'She want to know where we go, when we next meet, everything,' Natasha told him. 'It is a bad world when you can not trust your sister and best friend.'

Johnny knew how much it hurt her. They were so close. By choosing to be with him she was giving up her sister and her performance partner, as well as her family, her past, everything she had known before. She was right: it was a bad world. Communism shouldn't be like this. Something had gone very wrong.

He had met her after Bodo in Marx-Engels-Platz and she was calm, ready. The entire circus had returned from touring and they were having a week's break before rehearsing for a Christmas show in East

Berlin. Zoyenka and Natasha weren't involved as they would be going back to Moscow at the end of November. Of course, he hadn't mentioned to either of them that someone had been shot dead crossing the Wall on 1 November, even though he could think of little else.

'Are you sure this is what you want to do?' he'd asked for the millionth time.

'I do not want to live without you, Johnny. I leave Zoyenka a note before,' Natasha said.

He felt her trembling in front of him as they stood on the edges of the busy square, as if electrical currents had been wired into her small body, making her quiver like a fish out of water. He slipped his arms around her but he couldn't stop her shaking.

'Are you afraid?' he'd asked.

'No Johnny. Not afraid. I love you.'

He hugged her tightly. She pushed him away and took deep breaths.

They had wandered across the bridge on Karl-Liebknecht-Straße, past the Dom on the other side of the Spree, and towards the Pergamon Museum. To Johnny, that day, the grand yet dark and gloomy buildings imposed a painful vision of state tyranny, as if buried deep inside the buildings themselves were the eyes, ears and bodies of the unseen and unseeable controllers of their destiny. He shook off the feeling, he was being melodramatic – East Berlin had that effect on you.

Before he left, Natasha touched his hand; a touch that sent shockwaves through his body. Their fingers gripped each other beneath their coat sleeves, danced, kissed, tied themselves in knots before unwinding and letting go. As they passed the National Gallery, he said, 'We must go there sometime.'

'I think it many years before we go there,' she said. 'They only ghosts in squares. The living more important. See you soon, Johnny.' She'd smiled, and they'd both turned and walked in opposite directions.

Johnny stopped pacing and looked at his watch. It was six o'clock. Soon was almost here. Thomas had agreed to shoot the arrow with the wires intact across into the bathroom at nine, when it was thought the guards changed their shifts. Bodo's apartment was still in darkness. The weather had been typically cold and overcast all day, as they had hoped. It meant that there would be no moon or stars shining on them. Bodo and Natasha planned to dress in black as before.

He opened the window and peered over the strip of West below him before the Wall. Caught in the shadows of the coned lighting, a Turkish woman, carrying half a dozen plastic Kaiser's shopping bags, called to two dark curly-haired children. The smells of the lignite briquettes, sizzling kebabs and *pommes frites* drifted through the night. The temperature was falling. Bodo had assured him that the wire would be well greased and couldn't freeze over, but what if it fell to minus twenty? But it couldn't. It was only 8 November.

Johnny closed the window and went into his room to pack. He had arranged a small apartment in Wedding for himself and Natasha. It was actually Sophie and Benjamin's flat but they were back in the States for a couple of months taking some dance workshops and only too happy for him to pay the rent while they were away. He had met them in the park last week when they had come to see him perform. The flat was basic with orange walls in the living room and no bathroom except for a turquoise toilet. It would be fine until he and Natasha figured out what to do next.

Anyway, he was glad to be moving out, Johnny thought, as he packed his clothes into his old rucksack. It was time for a new chapter. Natasha would have nothing when she came across. He didn't have much either: the West-East crossings had taken up most of his earnings from the park performances, but they would survive. They would have each other. And a new life.

He was alone in the apartment. Hermann was in West Germany and Michael usually went out drinking after work on Thursday nights. Peter had thundered out in another fit of temper when he had seen him in the bathroom checking the bars.

'You'd better fucking not, Johnny. I want you outta here by the time I get back from the Kiosk.'

'Fine by me,' Johnny said. Peter wouldn't be back until the morning. Did Peter think he'd changed his mind? Johnny had told him 9 November – perhaps Peter didn't believe that he would do it. It didn't matter. Peter couldn't stop him now – unless he called the police and he didn't think he'd do that. He momentarily wondered where Alice was. Bodo had asked about her but Johnny didn't know. He was fairly sure she wasn't in Berlin, thank God. West Berlin was too small to hide for long and he hadn't seen her since that crazy night in June. She was a beautiful girl and in another time maybe he could have loved her. But she didn't even come close to Natasha.

Okay. He was packed. Everything was ready. He made a large ham salad with potatoes – they would want something to eat when they arrived – and sat alone in the living room. On the television images of riots and confusion in Delhi jumped across the screen. The Indian Prime Minister, Indira Ghandi, had been assassinated yesterday by two Sikh security guards. He didn't understand much more. It belonged to another world, another story.

By the time he finished eating it was half-past eight. He still hadn't seen any sign of life in Bodo's apartment, not even a shadow. He tidied up the kitchen, then went into the bathroom, opened the window and checked again the pulley system and reel that joined the two metal pillars. He had no idea how but Peter had learned about rigging somewhere and he had to admit that he had done a good job. It was tried and tested. If anything went wrong it would be his fault. Not that it would, he told himself. Everything was going to be fine.

At nine o'clock he waited by the living room window. He could still see nothing but the curved lamps projecting cones of light onto the tubular tops of the concrete wall. All the apartments opposite looked deserted. As he lit a cigarette, he stared into the bright light and jagged shadows. Surely there should have been some sign of them by now? Maybe Peter was right. Maybe his nightmare had been a premonition. Maybe they had been watching him since April. Maybe Bodo's apartment was bugged. Maybe each visit he had made to the East had been monitored. Maybe they were fucked, whatever happened. Johnny felt himself being eaten from the inside.

Then he heard it – a metallic ping. Johnny wiped out his cigarette and leapt into the bathroom to find the arrow lying gracefully on the floor, a perfect landing. A surge of adrenalin coursed through his body as he checked the fishing line was still attached before switching on the main bathroom light. This was the signal that everything was okay. He waited a few seconds so that it didn't look suspicious, then switched it off and worked by the light in the hall. He attached the fishing line to the reel and began to wind it in. The line coiled neatly until he could feel it tautening. He stopped and waited. Tried again. It was still tight. They must have stopped for some reason. He waited again but no change. Maybe it had snagged. He snapped on the safety catch on the reel and went to the window.

'Shit,' Johnny said, jumping back to the reel.

The wire was hanging half way across the Wall, swaying slowly from side to side like a giant skipping rope. He reeled and reeled. No one had told him how heavy it would be. Within seconds, despite the freezing air creeping from the East into the bathroom window, sweat dripped from his forehead. Every muscle in his body expanded and his arms worked like pistons as he reeled in the last of the fishing line and the beginning of the cable. He couldn't believe Peter had done this. He could feel the heat on the reel as the cable got even heavier – if that were possible. He saw why: more wires were taped to the main cable. They must be the support wires. Still his muscles kept pumping until, finally, the reel groaned and refused to turn any more.

He unhooked the main cable from the fishing line and attached it to the V in the metal bar. He stood up, took a deep breath and reached for his cigarettes. His muscles ached, his hands trembled. Bodo's flat was still in darkness but no one appeared to have noticed the thick black line swinging between the buildings. Johnny checked his watch. Almost eleven. He still had plenty of time. He unpacked the support wires and lit his cigarette, staring at them in dismay.

Someone knocked at the door. A thousand visions flashed before him, nearly all contained the police. The only person he was half expecting was Michael, and he had his own key. He went towards the door and listened. Nothing. Then another rap.

'Who is it?' he called out in German.

'The fucking KGB,' a woman's voice replied in English.

No, it couldn't be. Alice? Shit. What was she doing here? What would Natasha think? She would see her from the East.

'I'm busy at the moment. Can you come back tomorrow?'

'Johnny, it's me, Alice, open the door, will you?'

He opened the door to be greeted by a stunning woman with long, purple and black dreads spilling from a black cap tilted kinkily on her head. He blinked. He didn't think he would have recognised her if he had passed her on the streets.

'Alice,' he said, lost for further words.

'Johnny,' she said, shivering. 'Fuck, it's cold out there. Peter told me what you wanted to do tomorrow. Are you still doing it? Is Bodo crossing?'

Tomorrow? So Peter really didn't know it was tonight. He hesitated. Maybe she could help him.

'Come in,' he said. He closed the door behind her. 'It's actually tonight. Peter wants me out by tomorrow. And, yes, Bodo is crossing.'

'Tonight? Peter said Friday.'

'It will be Friday by the time they cross,' Johnny said. 'Now you're here, would you help me with the wires, please.'

'No, why should I?'

Not her as well.

'As a friend, Alice, please.'

'You're not a friend, but okay.'

She followed him into the bathroom and immediately showed him how to wrap the wires to a broom and pass them through to the bedroom. In fact, they had everything in place within about an hour. All he needed to do was some fine tuning.

'Shall I tell them everything's okay?' she asked. Without waiting for a reply she switched the bathroom light on and off.

'Don't do that!' Johnny groaned.

'Why not?' Alice asked.

'In case the guards are watching.'

'Well we did last time,' she said sulkily.

'Things are different this time,' Johnny said.

Unbothered, she pulled out a bottle of Red Label Smirnoff vodka from her bag. She offered it to him and he took a swig. They lit up cigarettes in the hall.

'Did you hear about the guy who was shot trying to cross the Wall last week?' she said.

'Yeah.'

'I heard he was a guard. Dietrich someone.'

'Yeah. Let's hope the guards tonight want to defect as well.'

'I have a new camera. I don't suppose I'll be able to take photos, will I?'

Was she serious? 'I don't think so, Alice.'

'Okay, I only asked. So what time they coming?'

'Two o'clock,' Johnny replied. He looked at his watch. 'Another hour.'

She raised her dark, perfectly arched, eyebrows and looked at the nearly empty bottle. 'Well, maybe I'll come back in a bit.'

Johnny nodded.

'So, did you have a good summer?' Alice asked casually.

Johnny shrugged. 'It's been difficult.'

Alice hummed. Johnny could see she wanted to say more but she swallowed some vodka.

'But you obviously met up and she hadn't been arrested or anything so that's good, isn't it? And now you're going to spend the rest of your life together.'

Johnny shrugged again. He didn't want this conversation with Alice. His stomach felt a little calmer but it wouldn't take much to churn it up.

'What are you going to do?' she continued.

'Who knows. I have Sophie and Benjamin's flat in Wedding for a couple of months while they are in the States until we decide.'

'I didn't think you got on with Sophie,' Alice snapped.

Johnny thought it better not to reply.

She laughed. 'It seems to be hard for you to know who you like and don't like.'

Johnny checked the tension on the main wire and peered out of the bathroom window. The black line stretched above the wall like an umbilical cord. He thought he saw the wires in place on the other side. But it was dark. And cold. Bodo and Natasha would need to warm up properly. Everything still seemed to be calm and quiet outside. Unlike inside. He excused himself to Alice and went into Peter's room to check the support wires.

He heard her footsteps fade down the stairs and he went into the hall. The door was ajar but she was gone. He was tempted to close it so that she couldn't get back in but he knew Bodo would want to see her. Natasha would understand. He went into the lounge, sat down on the sofa and watched ARD with the sound turned down. He knew that they could see him.

The minutes moved slowly around his watch. In less than an hour it would all be over. He would be with Natasha forever. What was an hour compared to the previous eight months? He closed his eyes and could feel her heartbeat next to his. He imagined her looking out the dark window, watching him lying there, his eyes closed, his right leg crossed over his left thigh and his hands clasped loosely behind his head. 'I love you, Johnny,' she whispered. 'Not long now.' She was dressed in thick, black tights, a polo neck black top and black gloves. Her olive face was pale in the cold glare of the Wall but her dark, sad eyes burned with hope.

He could see Bodo standing behind her, both having their last private moments in the East, a world in which they had grown up and were about to leave forever. There would be no going back. They were having doubts and fears of the future. A tear formed in her eye and scurried down her face. She wiped it away. Bodo embraced her.

Johnny imagined them putting on the black balaclavas. They stretched out, breathing deeply, calmly. It was time for the last dance over the Wall. He projected a kiss onto her forehead, wished her luck and opened his eyes to the fuzzy grey lines on the television.

At one minute to two he got up, went into the bathroom and closed the door almost completely. This was it. A distorted square of light hung around the doorframe. He stood, waiting, heart pulsing, in the semi-dark. The air felt warmer outside, or maybe that was just his nerves. Seconds later, he saw the first black shadow stepping out of the window opposite. He held his breath as it glided silently towards him, high above the Wall, its extended arms dipping ever so slightly towards the death strip below. Behind him, he heard Alice enter the apartment, come down the hall and stand outside the bathroom. The smell of alcohol seeped through the square of light. He didn't turn round.

'It's going to snow,' Alice said, shivering.

'Shut up,' Johnny whispered. 'She's coming.'

Tiny white flakes appeared in the night and danced in front of the window. The shadow reached the middle of the wire, the most dangerous place. It stopped. Johnny could feel the vibrations from the wire. The wire was too loose. Shit. He could feel her absorbing the tremors. Or him. Natasha was supposed to be crossing first but the shadow looked too big to be her. Johnny forgot to breathe as the dark figure stood frozen on the high wire, suspended between East and West.

The Death Strip

Klaus looked at his watch. It was almost two o'clock and he desperately needed to piss. Of all nights. Earlier that evening when he and Heinrich had taken over the shift he had been warned that there may well be a violation on this post. This was the first time in almost a year that he had received a special warning. There had been other violations of the Wall recently. None that he'd been witness to but one of the perpetrators had been a guard. They'd been on duty together a few times in the past, as well. He vaguely remembered Dietrich as being careless. Now he was dead.

He turned and looked suspiciously at Heinrich but it couldn't be him. They'd been on a shift together before and he knew Heinrich as a serious and professional man – not someone who'd be dazzled by bright lights and lies. Heinrich stood gazing down at the strip of land to the north and the houses to the west.

How they knew there was going to be a breach, he had no idea. His commander had said that as *Postenführer* he trusted him to be alert and ready to protect the borders of the DDR. He had an excellent record to date, he'd added. Klaus felt proud of the trust invested in him but his nerves and the cold were attacking his bladder. Normally, he would call for the patrol but he didn't feel that he should at this moment. Instead, he squeezed his legs together and continued to focus on the tunnel of light to the south and the pitch-black buildings of the east. Nothing moved in the shadows.

He had been on this post before. In fact, he had been on most of the forty or so control points that protected the twenty-four kilometres of the city Wall. The dark, damp U-Bahn stations where the trains never stopped were the worst. Ghost trains full of glowing people whined through the tunnels like mirages from another world. Klaus didn't like being down there. He had bad memories of this post as well but he didn't think about them any more, and he refused to look towards the window that had once upset him so much.

He now knew that Heidelberger Straße was the narrowest stretch of the Berlin Wall. He also knew that it was every bit as fortified as the rest of the border. One step inside and an alarm would go off. Nevertheless, Klaus kept his eyes pinned to the strip of land below.

The only vaguely suspicious thing he'd seen was a bright light going on and off in an apartment on the fifth floor in the West about an hour ago. But, naturally, that happened. Somebody forgot something. It looked like a bathroom but as it was dark he couldn't be sure. A light was on in the next room and a television flickered. It was late but that was quite normal in the West. People in the East were more efficient with their energy and most people went to bed early ready for work the next day. Many people in the West didn't have work.

'It is going to snow,' Heinrich said, his back to him.

'You think?' Klaus said. 'Maybe.'

Heinrich didn't say any more. Klaus found himself looking up into the Berlin night. It was hard to see anything more than darkness: the lights from below blunted the sky. He remembered it had snowed ten months ago when there had been a minor violation on this post. That was the night he'd seen the wall stripper as well, the source of his bad memories. The message 'assholes' had upset him for weeks, turning his dreams into nightmares until, surprisingly, one day the entire unit had received extra education about wall strippers and how the women were paid by the capitalist west to corrupt the border guards. They had been shown slides of such women and one of them was his angel. There she was, only slightly blurred, naked with her snowball breasts and long, dark hair. His angel was only an angel in disguise. He had promptly forgotten about her after that.

Klaus stood up and down on his toes. He tried to think about something else other than his bladder. He was going on leave for three days next week. He couldn't wait to go back and see his family in Dresden. His mother and sister wrote to him almost every week. His mother was busy organising Christmas pantomimes for the children. Naturally, she had promised him his favourite *Käsekuchen* with cream and *Johannisbeersaft*, the thought of which made him cross his legs again.

'It's snowing,' Heinrich said.

Klaus watched the first furry snowflakes tumble through the air, gathering volume as they went. The Berlin winter had begun. Good, he thought. As soon as there's a covering on the ground, he would call the patrol. He checked his watch again. It was just after two.

'I don't think there will be any violations tonight now,' Klaus said, unable to keep the relief from his voice. He still couldn't imagine what it would be like to have to shoot someone.

'You can never be sure,' Heinrich said.

'True,' Klaus replied, afraid he'd been complacent. He put his binoculars to his eyes and watched the beautiful shapes of the snow crystals. As he lifted his binoculars higher a large dark shadow passed over the lens. Confused, he dropped the binoculars and looked up. There was nothing. Then, almost directly ahead of him, a large black cat crawled out of a window in the East onto a telegraph wire.

'*Mein Gott,*' he muttered.

The cat stood up on its hind legs and balanced on the wire, holding a pole in its paws. Klaus' mouth dropped open.

'What's the matter?' Heinrich said.

'There's something, someone up there! He is about to walk across to the West.' Klaus could hardly believe what he was saying. This was it. The violation he'd been warned off. His training took over as he pushed the alert button. He decided against firing the Very light pistol. The Commander would send the patrol round. He opened the middle window casement and aimed his machine gun at the man calmly walking high up between the buildings.

'A little higher!' he called to Heinrich, who was shining the spotlight between the dark buildings. The bright light burned through the whirling snowflakes and settled on the criminal. He was dressed entirely in black, including a balaclava. The high wire, not a telegraph wire, Klaus noted, led to the room on the right where he had seen the flashing light. He kicked himself for not reporting it.

'HALT,' he shouted into the loudspeaker. He heard his voice reverberating between East and West.

Johnny's heart stopped beating as the cone of light fell on Natasha. She was only a few metres away. This couldn't be happening. She froze. He leaned further out of the window and held out his hand. It hardly mattered if they saw him now.

'Come on, darling, you can do it,' he said to her. His voice echoed into the empty world below. Do what? Who was he kidding? Their guns were on her.

'Do what?' she whispered. Her words were blunted by the wool over her mouth but he saw the fear in her dark eyes.

Fuck. Someone please tell him this wasn't happening. Please let him wake up.

'Do your act,' he said, wildly.

Bodo, standing next to him by the open window, clutched his arm. He had made it. He had crossed first as he had been worried about the tension in the wire.

She crouched down on one leg, as she had done many times before in her performance, balancing the pole on her lap, elegant, submissive. She held out her arms in defeat.

'That's it, Natasha, you look beautiful.'

'She'll make it, Johnny. They can't shoot her like that,' Bodo whispered.

Indeed, the guards seemed as mesmerised as they were. They were watching the one and only Natasha Barovskova – the best aerialist performer in the world. A deep silence fell into the death strip. Natasha didn't move. Time stopped.

From behind him there was a flash of light. Natasha's hunted eyes glowed. Fucking Alice and her fucking camera.

'Don't!' Johnny shouted at Alice, hitting out at her.

Bodo's grip on his arm tightened. Johnny felt sick. Fucking Bodo. Why hadn't she crossed first? She would be here now. He put his hand on the quivering wire. It was the nearest he could get to her. She shook her head ever so slightly. He could see defeat in her eyes.

'Johnny. I don't think I make it,' she whispered.

'I think you should run,' he hissed.

'She can do it, she can do it,' Bodo was saying.

'I can't. I will fall. Or they shoot me.' Snow swirled around her like ash.

'Then go back! Slowly. Go back, Natasha. Please.' His voice wobbled.

'They shoot me still, Johnny.'

'No, please, Natasha. Don't do it. Please don't do this. Go back. Slowly. They won't shoot you. I promise'

Pain yanked at Johnny's body. He leaned towards the watchtower and held up both hands in defeat. '*Bitte*. Don't shoot!' he yelled. '*Nicht schießen*,' Bodo shouted behind him. '*Zurück. Nicht schießen!*'

She moved her leg up towards the wire again. Slowly.

The loudspeaker crackled into the Berlin night.

'*Sie geht zurück!*' Bodo called out.

Natasha stood up on the wire, her balancing pole dipping into the night. She would either need to walk backwards or turn around. She did neither.

A gunshot ricocheted.

Johnny's heart exploded. 'Run!' He held out his hand to her.

She took a step forward. 'Johnny!' she called.

But before he could reply, she was greeted by a torrent of bullets, ripping through the hole in the city.

She was blown off the wire. Johnny heard his own scream as she landed in the death strip. A black shadow in the white snow. Tears flew down his face. The snow around her darkened and his world collapsed.

'NOoooooo.'

'You got him, you got him. Stop firing,' Heinrich said.

Klaus stopped: his hands were trembling. Screams so loud he thought they might shatter the remaining panels of glass in the watchtower hurtled out of the fifth floor window in the West, followed by incomprehensible words in English. Relief seeped into his fingers. He had hesitated about shooting, afraid that he was shooting a surrendering man. But if he hadn't fired, the violator would have reached the West.

Heinrich positioned the spotlight onto the broken body that lay on the ground like a discarded doll. He had just missed falling on a roll of barbed wire. Snow was already beginning to cover him.

'Go down, I'll cover,' Heinrich said.

Klaus left the watchtower and went down to the strip, clutching his machine gun as it were a soft toy. A patrol vehicle had arrived and border guards were getting out of it and entering the inner wall, others were securing the apartment block on the East.

A man was still screaming from the window in the West. Klaus felt a sharp pain in his heart. Maybe it was a relative. The Wall had separated families as well as ideologies. But it couldn't be. They were shouting in English as well as in German. As he got closer, he saw that the snow around the fallen man was red. He was on his back, his right leg slung over his left shoulder. Klaus found the position disquieting, arousing even. Then he felt sick at the thought. He tried to breathe but his breath felt imprisoned. Blood was still leaking from several holes in the man's chest. Other guards reached the body first. A camera was flashing. More and more people from the West were screaming at him.

'He's still alive!' someone called.

Klaus stopped a couple of metres away while one of the patrollers knelt down and pulled off the balaclava. Long dark shiny hair tumbled out and glistening brown eyes stared up at him, only him. He went closer. Now the pain sickened him. The man he had shot was a young, beautiful woman. *Mein Gott.* Why? What had she expected? Klaus felt warm piss trickling down his leg.

'You pissed yourself,' she said. Her voice was soft, foreign, forgiving. She smiled.

Someone had gone to get a stretcher. Klaus could not take his eyes off her. She turned her attention to the window in the West where the man was crying for her. He must be her lover. Her eyes spoke a language he didn't understand. He was vaguely aware of confusion from the apartment on the fifth floor in the West. The man was trying to get out of the window. Others must be restraining him. A woman was shouting down in bad German to get her to a hospital.

Within seconds, the whole of the West had woken up and a thousand voices shouted down to him, calling him evil, a fascist, a criminal, a traitor, a murderer... *Murderers, Murderers...* Klaus bent down over her. She was so pretty. Younger than him, the same age as his sister perhaps. Her olive skin and dark eyes were framed by her long, loose hair.

'Why?' he said to her. 'Why did you do it? You broke the law of our country. You are a criminal.'

She smiled. She was almost completely white now, like a fallen angel.

'Maybe,' she mouthed. Or maybe he imagined it.

Murderers, Murderers...

Two medics carrying a stretcher arrived and tossed her on. She screamed in agony. From what he could see, it looked like her back and at least one leg was broken and her chest was one big, bloody mess. There was no way she could live for long. She clutched her heart. Klaus could only imagine the pain she must be in. He felt a tear storm down his face. How could she be a criminal? Her face was like the moon shining on him. She looked at him again.

'Tell Johnny I love him,' she whispered. 'But tell him he must be happy. That he must live his life. Please.'

Uhlandstraße

Johnny blinked at the grey eyes of the Consul as the man put the phone down, shaking his grey head. They were in an oak-panelled room in the back of the British Consulate on Uhlandstraße. The Consul sat behind a large wooden desk covered in green leather, he some distance in front.

'I am very sorry for your loss but I'm afraid there is little I can do at the moment, Mr East. I don't think you fully understood what you were getting yourself into. This is the Cold War, you know.'

Johnny crossed his arms in defiance. The last thing he needed was a lecture. It was nine o'clock in the morning. He hadn't slept, his eyes hurt, his mouth had dried up and he felt as if someone had drilled through his heart. He had seen her face: she had smiled at him, he was sure. She was still alive when they had thrown her into a military truck like a bin-bag. He had tried to get out of the window but no one would let him. Alice kept shouting at him to go to the Consulate. Behind him the apartment swarmed with police and MPs, asking questions, taking statements. Then Peter came back, out of his head, furious.

'Oh fuck you, you fucking asshole. I fucking told you not to do this. Get out of here, Johnny. I don't want to see you ever again.'

'It's not his fault, Peter,' Bodo pleaded in German.

'I don't care. I want you all OUT.'

Johnny picked up his coat. He didn't really want to see Peter again either.

'Where are you going?' some pious American official had asked.

He didn't know. Alice and Bodo got up to go with him.

'We're going to the Consulate,' Alice said. 'I have the photos. We could make real trouble for those bastards if we publish them.'

'I'm afraid I can not let you leave,' the police said to all of them. 'We will need to take you in for questioning.'

They were all taken to a police station and interrogated for the rest of the night. Johnny couldn't remember what he said. Peter wouldn't stop swearing at him. He remembered Alice yelling at the police that he was ill, that he needed a doctor. They were eventually released – except for Bodo.

'The British Consulate has already been informed,' the American said as he left. 'Whatever you do, don't speak to the press. If she is still alive, then it will worse for her.'

If she were alive. The Consulate had been his only hope. And now Johnny wanted to throw knives at this bureaucrat.

'I personally find it hard to believe you did what you did as if you were having a picnic in a park. I mean, for Christ's sake, stringing a wire between East and West and walking across it!' The Consul's head shook in disbelief, his grey eyes almost watering, his face ravaged by their Cold War.

'We did once before,' Johnny muttered weakly.

'You did it before? Are you insane? Had you any idea what you were doing? There is probably a file on you as long as Linie 1. No doubt every time you went to the East an extra few pages were added. Every step you took was probably monitored. They knew all about you; they knew you were planning something. They even appeared to know what day.'

Johnny didn't reply. He didn't want to hear this. He had heard it before in his nightmares. Had Zoyenka given them away? Tomas? Peter?

'*If* you go into the East, you will be arrested and, possibly, sentenced to twenty years. We will have no jurisdiction to help you. Is that what you want?'

'I want to know if she's still alive, that's all.' He felt his voice clog up. There was a hole the size of a U-Bahn line blown out of him. Emptiness. If spending twenty years in an East German prison would help fill that hole, then maybe it was what he wanted. He didn't know.

'We are doing all we can, Mr East. Unfortunately, information is sketchy. Your friend, Natasha Barovskova, was a Russian citizen which complicates things. Her father is in the Politburo. The KGB are involved.'

Johnny wasn't convinced that the Consul was telling him everything. His grey eyes had clouded over and he glanced towards the clock, his hands forming a pyramid under his chin.

'However, under the circumstances, Mr East, I think it very unlikely that your friend is still alive. We believe that she was hit several times in the chest. If she were still alive then they would have taken her to a hospital,' the Consul said. 'They may well issue a statement in the near future.'

'She *was* still alive when they carried her off in the truck,' Johnny said. 'She smiled at me for fuck's sake.'

'I'm sorry, Mr East. We are doing all we can to find out what happened to Natasha Barovskaya but please don't get your hopes up.

Even if she did survive there would be no chance of you ever meeting her again – at least, not while this bloody Wall's still around us. The West German police have been very considerate and no charges will be brought against you or your friends – even though there are grounds. The one that made it over will be able to claim asylum here. Although we still recommend that his defection be kept quiet. You never know.' The Consul stopped and stared hard at Johnny. 'I'm sorry, I really am. If I have any news I will contact you immediately.'

Johnny stormed out of the Consulate with parts of him leaking onto the grey slushy streets of Berlin. What use was a fucking Consulate if it couldn't find out the simplest thing? He only wanted to know if she were dead or alive. If she were dead, then maybe he could begin to mourn. If she were alive, then he needed to find out how she was. It looked like her back was broken. How could it not have been? She would be in a wheelchair for the rest of her life, but he could wheel her around the world. At least, they could be together. Oh what had he done? If only Peter had been there they could have crossed earlier. If only Alice hadn't switched the bathroom light on and off. If only it hadn't snowed. If only the guard hadn't looked up and seen her. If only she had crossed first. If only, if only, if only. If only he had refused to do it.

He remembered Natasha's words: 'I do not want to live without you, Johnny.' Now he had to live without her.

The cold in the air and the icy slush beneath his boots were having an almost soporific effect. Hope seeped out of the hole in his heart. He felt weak, weaker than he had ever felt before.

'Oh Natasha, what have I done to you?' He sunk onto the corner of Lietzenburger Straße and stared up into the grey clouds. The shadows of a dark machine gun straddled the sky as tears exploded from his eyes.

PART 2 – 2004

'It's gone but not forgotten. Fragments of *die Mauer* decorate mantelpieces and museums all over the world, but the city in which it was erected has done everything possible to obliterate its physical traces, if not its memory.'

Berlitz Travel Guide, 2004

Danckelmannstraße

When he finally left Berlin in January 1985, he swore he would never go back, even more so after the fall of the Wall in 1989. He had tried many times to contact Zoya, Natasha's sister, but she, too, had disappeared. It was as if the Sisters Barovskova had never existed. As far as he knew there had been no funeral, no demarcation between life and death, no end. As the years passed, he tried not to think about what had happened.

Which was why, on that Friday afternoon at the end of May 2004, Johnny stepped out of U-Bahn Sophie-Charlotte-Platz onto the wide and busy Kaiserdamm, a guidebook and map tucked under his right arm, a black jacket slung over his left shoulder and, what felt like, several thousand deathwatch beetles ticking slowly towards his heart.

He stopped, lifted his sunglasses, and found himself facing a police station sign, its distinctive green and gold emblem with the bear in the centre. He looked down, feeling slightly sick, and searched for Danckelmannstraße on the west side of the map. He checked where he needed to go, then put the Berlitz guidebook to the new, shiny, vibrant capital of a unified Germany in his bag. The U-bahn trains and stations hadn't changed, but he couldn't make sense of the new U-Bahn and S-Bahn map: more like the London underground than the old West Berlin network. As for the centre of Berlin – it was as if someone had thrown a metallic and digitalised dress over the old city. If he didn't know, he would hardly have recognised it. A high-tech city with a glass-roofed Government and a new currency. No more Deutsch Marks. No more barbed wire. No more guards. No more walls. No more Checkpoint Charlie.

But he did know, and he wasn't convinced.

It was a fancy dress. Beneath the disguise was the same city. He was almost sure of it. He checked his phone: no messages. He flicked down his sunglasses to shield himself more from the ghosts of the past than the sun and began to walk slowly up Kaiserdamm, away from the police station, past a shop, a café, Schlecker – a chemist's, a photo gallery, an Italian restaurant. He came to Kaiser's, the supermarket, its fancy white coffee pot proof that Berlin was the same city. He walked past as people came out carrying the same plastic ghost bags as they had done all those years ago, and found Danckelmannstraße. This was it, but he had thirty minutes or so to kill before meeting Bodo.

Penny, his old friend and now manager of his performance company for fifteen years, had nagged, flattered and threatened him in a Pizza Express near Covent Gardens last week.

'If you don't do it now you never will, Johnny. This...' She waved his notes for an aerial performance in Berlin, '... is fantastic. And it's time you faced up to the past. When I was there it was even difficult to work out where the Wall used to be. Berlin today is not the Berlin you knew. It's a great story – perfect for an aerial performance, you have fantastic performers and we can find you a venue. Besides, the EU grant won't sustain us forever, you know, and your money has gone. If this show is as good as I think it is, then this may keep us from telesales. Think of all the other performers. Surely you owe it to them? In other words, Johnny, this is crunch time,' she told him bluntly.

'Hm,' he said. He'd been working on the show for about five years, but he'd only really shown it to her out of curiosity. He wasn't ready to do it yet. 'I'm pleased you like it, Penny. But I need more time.'

'We don't have time,' she said, slicing up her pizza. 'What happened to you was a long time ago. You were a different person then. It was a different world. Go to Berlin and see for yourself. And you can speak to Henri while you're there. He's in Berlin at the moment. And that old juggler friend of yours – whatsisname? Bodo? I found his numbers on the net. You can give him a call. He will be perfect. Oh and I've booked a flight for you next week on Friday, and a hotel.' She rummaged through her bag and handed him a printed-out itinerary.

He glanced at it. Hotel Belmondo. It had sounded familiar even then. 'Oh Penny, is this really necessary?'

'Yes.'

'Okay, but no promises.' That was when he began to feel something burrowing towards his heart.

'Fine,' Penny said. 'In the meantime, I'll put an ad in the *Evening Standard* for anyone wanting a forty-three-year-old aerialist.'

She had been threatening him with telesales and bankruptcy for ten years now so he wasn't overly concerned. She exaggerated. If it were that bad, they could do a European tour with the material they already had. But fine. Penny had been a loyal friend and had helped him get his life back together when he had finally left Berlin all those years ago. And she had kept him from telesales until now. For her, he would go and talk to ghosts in Berlin. Maybe she was right. He had lived with the guilt and the horror for so long. But he couldn't finish his pizza.

His stomach somersaulted when he'd finally mustered enough courage to tap in one of the numbers Penny had given him for Bodo later that evening. He'd lost touch with everyone he knew from those days. They all reminded him of what happened and, when he remembered, a pain so great would shoot through him that he would stop breathing. In the early nineties, he had written to Bodo telling him about *The Flight Company*, inviting him to join if he wanted, but Bodo never replied. Out of everyone, he was most sorry he had lost touch with him, but Johnny didn't write again: a part of him was relieved.

Johnny had been greeted by a loud burp on the phone when he'd asked to speak to Bodo.

'Johnny? Johnny East? What a big surprise.'

'Bodo? Is that you? Long time huh. How are you?'

'*Ja gut*. Working in cabaret, you know. And you?'

'I'm good, Bodo. I'm coming to Berlin. I'm thinking of putting on an aerial show. Can we meet next Friday? If it goes ahead, I'd like you to be in it.'

'*Wunderbar*, Johnny! You come to Berlin finally. *Ja gut*.'

Bodo would be great in the show. Penny was right about that. *If he decided to go ahead with it.* They could do a double high wire juggling act at the opening. No doubt in his mid-forties Bodo wasn't quite as agile as he was twenty years ago, but Johnny reckoned he could still out-juggle anyone – even him.

'Why didn't you come to London? Did you never get my letter?' Johnny said.

'*Ja*, Johnny. I get the letter from you many years ago. But I can not leave Berlin. And then Alice comes.'

It had all begun with Alice. Her young, round face appeared before him, her lips pouting, red, kissing.

'What happened?' Johnny asked. Anything could happen with Alice.

'We live together for one year. Then she goes to England.'

'Why?'

Bodo paused. 'It becomes difficult. She wants to. She wants me to.'

'And didn't you go with her?'

'You know I wait for so long to get to the West Berlin. I can not leave.' He hiccupped. 'Shit vodka.'

Johnny had frowned. He couldn't understand why Bodo hadn't gone with Alice to England. He heard the sound of drinks being poured in the background and a high-pitched laugh. Surely Bodo didn't still drink like they used to?

'Where are you?' Johnny had asked.

'I'm at the club. You call me at work.'

'Oh, I'm sorry, I didn't realise. Do you have to go?'

'No, it is early.'

'I still have your phone, by the way,' Johnny said. 'The telephone you gave me in East Berlin. It's here in my flat in London. Do you need it now?'

'What phone?' Someone called to him in German. 'One moment, Johnny.' He shouted back and someone laughed in the background.

'*Ja*, it will be great to see you, Johnny,' he said. 'We have a good time. So many years. You come to my apartment in Danckelmannstraße after 3 p.m., *ja*? Before that I am at rehearsal.'

'Yeah, okay. What happened to your old apartment by the way? In the East?'

'*Scheiße*, Johnny, you lack news,' Bodo said. 'The DDR blow up my apartment, turn it to dust. Just after, in 1985. So no one could do what we do.' He laughed.

'They blew it up?' Johnny really did lack news. He knew nothing of what had happened after 9 November 1984. 'Shit. I didn't know that. I'm sorry.'

'It doesn't matter. I could never live there again, by the way. Too much memories, you know.'

'Yeah, I know,' Johnny said.

'I guess that's why you never come back to Berlin?' Bodo said.

'Yeah, I guess.'

'You tell me more when you come. But I don't know if I do your show. You know, I am not doing so much new work recently. Except for one new act with the knives.' He laughed again, a hollow ha-ha.

Johnny had smiled, remembering the first time he had met Bodo in East Berlin.

'And the past difficult...' Bodo's voice trailed off.

'Yeah, I know,' Johnny said. He had wanted to ask if there had ever been any news but he couldn't. They could talk about it in Berlin.

'And getting old.'

They were all getting old. He didn't perform much himself any more. He had decided that, whatever happened, this would be his last aerial performance. *If he decided to go ahead*.

He wasn't fooled. Even under these blue May skies on a street corner in Charlottenburg, the old British sector – not a place he had even lived – he could sense something of the murky past lingering in the air, surrounding him, pouring out of the Kaiser's white coffee pot, seeping into his skin. Despite what they all said, even though he couldn't see it, he could feel the old divided city. As soon as he had landed at Tegel earlier he felt it, as if his memories had leaked out and were trailing him like a bad smell. A Zeitgeist in its literal sense, a timeghost waiting for him, ticking by for twenty years. When the taxi had pulled up outside the Hotel Belmondo, he saw his younger self dancing past on a cold night in February 1984, illuminated behind a net curtain of snow. Alice's tall shadowy image waltzed by him, her long black coat flapping around her boots. She was laughing, swigging a bottle of vodka. Penny was right in that he'd never stayed at the hotel but he remembered saying to Alice that one day they would stay there. He hadn't been able to stay there for long – even a four-star hotel couldn't hide the ghosts.

He crossed the six lanes of Kaiserdamm and walked further up until he came to a small park, Lietzensee. On both sides of the path naked, or semi-naked, people sprawled on the grass, reading, talking, smoking, drinking beer and laughing. Johnny smiled to himself. That hadn't changed either. Dogs lolloped after one another, occasionally barking, bikes lay crashed out on their sides, wheels still spinning.

'Hey, *pass auf*!'

He swung off the path to avoid a pit-bull terrier pulling a woman on a bike. The young woman turned and smiled at him. Her long black dreadlocks, moon face and white teeth reminded him of Alice. He smiled back. She would be forty now. He hadn't seen her either for twenty years. She must have changed. He had stumbled on a review a few years ago of some sculptures in an exhibition in Norwich. She seemed to be doing well. He was pleased. He always thought that one day their paths would cross, but they never had. He wondered what had happened between her and Bodo, but he would find out soon enough.

As for him, there had been no one really special since Natasha. In the first few years she went everywhere with him, hovered over him while he ate breakfast, danced with him on the high wire, watched him as he lay in the bath, and curled up with him in bed. But when he went to touch her soft, olive skin, she disappeared and all he would hear was her voice. *'Let's do it, Johnny. What have we got to lose?'* As the years passed he could only see her face. Sometimes she frowned at him, sometimes she gave out her high-pitched silvery laugh. But even her face was fading. These days, he could only see her eyes. They had never had their photograph taken together so he had no way of seeing her whole again. Only Alice had taken photographs, and even if he knew where Alice was, and even if she still had the photographs, they weren't of the Natasha he had known.

He'd had other relationships, but they soon left him feeling cold. Then the cold would seep into the relationship and they would accuse him of being arrogant, selfish, uncaring, unable to commit, insensitive and/or a shithead. They were probably right on all counts. Instead, he had lived in the world she had shown him, high above the other world. At times, he wished it could have been different but it wasn't. He had done well for himself – considering. It wasn't easy to make a living out of performance but his had been the first aerial dance company in the UK. Thanks to Natasha, he had been able to offer something new.

He sat down on a bench and watched an old woman with long grey-white hair opposite talking to a plastic cup, the red and white Kaiser's plastic bag lodged between her legs. What would it be like to be old and alone in the world? It didn't bear thinking about. He checked his mobile: almost five to three. Time to meet the past.

Danckelmannstraße was lethargic, as if the silence and the heat were weighing it down. Cars lined both sides of the road, many of them Mercedes – with their logos poking out of the bonnets. He remembered when these symbols had been snapped off and worn like flowers. Maybe times had changed. The old Berlin grit-grey four storey buildings had been lightened to sandstone, some had even been painted bright yellow and pastel colours, and they basked in the street guarded by attentive rich-green plane trees trapped in concrete. The street seemed calm, peaceful: geraniums and marigolds grew from wrought iron railings around balconies. Johnny crept past cafés, an estate agent, a shoe shop.

An open entrance on the left revealed shaded buildings behind. This was it. Bodo told him that it should be open. Johnny looked for his name next to the buzzers but could not find it. He walked through into the large courtyard. A lone tree cast an imposing shadow over the rear house. He reeled as he passed some rubbish bins on the left, unsuccessfully hidden by an arch of ivy. Flies hovered noisily above the plastic containers. Some red and white tape trailed on the sticky floor.

Bodo had said he lived in a ground floor flat in the *Hinterhof*. Johnny guessed his apartment was the one with the dirty windows and half-open shutters. Strange though, Bodo's touring caravan used to be immaculate. A lone fly buzzed behind him into the dark stairwell. Inside was dark and dingy. Bodo's flat in the East had been better than this. He knocked at the door but no one answered. He checked his mobile. Ten past three. He tried to call and a faint purr responded from inside the apartment. This was the right place then. He knocked again and waited. Maybe he had been held up at the rehearsal. His only other contact in Berlin was Peter. Bodo had given him Peter's mobile number but he hadn't spoken to Peter for twenty years either. He didn't much want to start now.

He strolled back into the courtyard. A small old woman pushed past him with a shopping trolley. Johnny stopped her. Green eye make-up and thick mascara outlined her watery blue eyes, her lips were painted pink, and thick powder decorated her cooked apple complexion. For an instance, her eyes contracted like sea anemones in anger – or surprise. Johnny was at least two feet taller than her. He held up his hands, lifted his sunglasses and apologised in rusted German. He asked her if she knew of a man called Bodo Jongleur. He imitated throwing balls up in the air and pointed to his apartment. The woman snorted in disgust.

'Who are you?' she asked in a loud, theatrical English accent, incongruous with her shrunken body.

'An old friend from England. We were supposed to meet at three o'clock.'

'Then you are in the wrong place.'

He asked her if this was the address he had written down.

'*Ja*, of course it is.'

Johnny took a deep breath. It had been a long day, maybe he was more tired than he thought.

'Then this is where he lives,' he said patiently. 'He told me.'

'How did he tell you? Are you psychic?' The woman stared up at him, her anemone eyes locking onto his, challenging.

'He told me on the phone.'

'I think you make a mistake. Your friend Bodo is not here any more. Your friend Bodo throw the knives at himself.'

Johnny took another deep breath.

'Terrible,' she screeched. 'Such a terrible thing making a terrible mess. All over my yard. The *Hinterhof* still smells. Can you not smell it? And all the polices asking the questions of my tenants. So much trouble. And everything terrible. In such a nice neighbourhood. Your friend verrrry crazy.'

'Maybe,' he said, 'but where is he now?'

'Where? Where would you be with three knives in the head? Probably in the hell. He's dead of course.' The woman sounded triumphant, as if throwing down her trump card.

'But when? When did this happen?' It couldn't be true, Johnny calmed himself. Someone would have told him. The woman was insane.

'Last week, Saturday. They find the body near the green glass bin.'

She was senile. He had spoken to Bodo on Saturday. She couldn't mean him.

'*Ja, ja*. Saturday night, maybe early Sunday morning,' she continued. 'He goes into the yard to practise to throw the knives at himself. Better at himself than me. You know once I have the knife in my ceiling.'

Johnny would have smiled if he had not felt the blood drain from his lips.

'His poor mother...' she continued.

'He didn't have a mother. She was murdered by the Stasi,' he muttered.

'Just as well...'

He felt the beetles gnawing faster and faster. He needed something to hold onto but his hands were clammy, and he needed to get away from this madwoman. Could it be true? Could Bodo have had an accident? He said he was practising for a knife act. But how? How could he have done it on his own? Juggling knives were always blunted. Only weighted knives with razor sharp edges could penetrate a skull and jugglers never sharpened them as the weight would be affected. And three of them? The idea was insane. He tried to turn away, but his legs stuck to the courtyard floor and his head spun out of control. Time slipped backwards along a twenty-year slide as a green and white van pulled up outside the house. 'Polizei' was written on the side and the front.

'You must speak to them,' the woman said. 'They want to know more about your friend. *Guten Tag. Kommen Sie. Hier.*'

Johnny didn't want to speak to them, but the two men in green uniforms and black leather boots and holsters were walking across to where he was standing. It's all right, he told himself. They'll sort this out. There must be some kind of misunderstanding.

'*Guten Tag, Frau Übermann.*'

She launched into a long tirade. Johnny couldn't understand much: his German had never been very good. He stared foolishly at the police, who were now eyeing him with interest.

'You are the friend of Herr Kollender?' one of them asked him in a heavy accent.

'Herr who?' For a moment, hope hit Johnny with the speed of a bullet. 'Do you mean Bodo?'

The two police officers conferred with the old woman. Even Johnny understood that Bodo's real surname was, in fact, Kollender. In twenty years, he had never known that. They'd all called him Bodo Jongleur. His stage name, he guessed.

'*Ja ja*, Bodo Jongleur, that's right.'

'Yes,' said Johnny. 'I was supposed to meet him today at 3 p.m. but I have been told he is dead.' The word thumped in his ears. 'Is that true?'

'*Ja ja*, that is very true. Unfortunately Herr Kollender was dead last Sunday. Estimated time of departure is 2.00 a.m. Sunday 23 May. I am afraid …'

'Was it an accident?' Johnny said, his voice constricted by the heat. And shock.

'We are currently investigating the circumstances. We are waiting the post mortem. We must ask you some questions, Mr…?'

'East,' Johnny said. 'Johnny East.'

The two police exchanged raised eyebrows while one of them made a note of his name.

'Mr East. And perhaps you know how we can contact someone by name Alice Howard?'

He knew Alice's surname and it wasn't Howard. Alice Madison. 'Mad' as Peter used to call her. Although maybe she married? He couldn't imagine it, but it would be too much of a coincidence for there to be two Alices connected to Bodo.

'I know her but I don't know where she is. Why?'

'She contact us this morning with some information and now we must talk with her. But she does not respond.'

'What kind of information?' Johnny asked. But they wouldn't tell him.

Peter would know, Johnny thought, before the past whipped him, before he saw Peter coming back to the apartment in Heidelberger Straße, out of his head, screaming at him as he stood watching the now empty death strip while the police stomped through the apartment. *'Get out of here, Johnny. I don't want to see you ever again.'* And Alice standing there, looking on helplessly. She always said he would get his comeuppance. He deserved it, he knew. He had been an asshole to her. And to Peter.

The time bomb exploded and Johnny plummeted through the years. It made him dizzy, nausea twisted his stomach. Penny was wrong. It was not a different world. He was not a different person. It was not the right time and it never would be. He had to get out of Berlin. Now. It was not only a matter of facing the pain of the past but the pain of the present. What, in the end, had it all been for? He would get the first flight back to London and cancel the show. Sod the money, even the high wire acts. The other performers would find work. He would declare the company bankrupt and go and work in telesales.

'Perhaps you come with us and help with the enquiries?' one of the policemen said. He shifted his weight onto his right leg. His black boots shimmered in the afternoon sun.

Johnny didn't move.

'Ach! I thought you were his friend?' Frau Übermann snorted. 'You English have always the two sides of the face. And, you know, Herr Kollender owes me for last month rent.'

'This way, Mr East.' A gentle arm touched his.

A cold gust blew over him as he found himself propelled towards the green and white van.

'Next time you bring four hundred euros,' Frau Übermann called after him. 'Very cheap rent he had, *ja*.'

Kreuzberg

Black and white memories of Johnny and Bodo hanging out of his window, sobbing over the Berlin Wall, flashed in front of Peter as he sat outside the café in sunny Kreuzberg. Peter didn't remember much of the early years in Berlin but, every so often, he was haunted by memories so vivid, they could have happened yesterday. And returning to his apartment at 5 a.m. on November 9 1984 and finding it overrun with police, MPs, a red-eyed Bodo and a sobbing Johnny was the most vivid. All the more so because it was exactly how he'd imagined it would be. He shook his head trying to delete the scene. He had just finished his Friday shift and was exhausted, both emotionally and physically. Bodo's death had turned into a total nightmare.

His mobile sung *Paff, Der Zauberdrachen* and, temporarily at least, deleted the memories for him. He glanced at the unfamiliar number with a UK code. It could be Johnny – or it could be some cute man he'd met when he didn't remember. But it was more likely to be Johnny as he was about the only person he hadn't told since the police contacted him last Sunday with the news of Bodo's tragic accident, and lack of kin. He did not want to see Johnny, not then, not now, not ever. He hesitated. Maybe it wasn't him. He took the call.

'Hallo?'

'Peter? It's Johnny. I'm in Berlin and I've just heard about Bodo. Can we meet?'

The voice from the past was as resonant as a cello sonata.

'Johnny? Johnny who?' Peter tried to keep his voice cold but he could feel his heart sweating.

'Johnny East. We used to live together.'

'Hardly darling.' Peter let out a short rumble. 'You are a blast from the past. How are you? Listen, this isn't really a good time, Johnny…'

'It's important, Peter. Half an hour or so?'

Peter sighed loudly. 'Okay, I've just finished work and I was on my way to meet someone, but I can wait for you.'

Peter gave him directions on how to get to the café, snapped his phone shut and ordered another Warsteiner from Jason, a young German-American waiter. He was angry with himself. That had taken less than sixty seconds. Even after however many years Johnny still got what he wanted. How many years? Twenty. How quickly time ticked by. It rarely even ticked any more. Peter lit a cigarette and watched the setting sun as it hovered above the old grey Berlin buildings.

The café was in the middle of Kreuzberg, the once alternative fringe of Berlin, now the centre of the city. Yet to Peter it was still the old Kreuzberg with the familiar smells of kebabs spicing the streets. There was an air of serenity, a village-like feel, and the people sitting at the benches outside the café could be the same people from twenty years ago. An older woman with bright red hair was reading through a *Tip* magazine. Two girls with blonde dreadlocks and pierced eyebrows drank coffee and smoked. Down the other end of the wide street, some young kids, dressed in shorts and trainers, kicked a ball. A typical Kreuzberg scene. Only the cell phones, 'handies' as they were appropriately called in Germany, sang out a different era. And the fact that, behind him, two people were talking about Pluspunkt, the new tour of the underground Nazi torture chambers.

Peter inhaled his cigarette: when would Germany be allowed to forget its criminal past? No one mentioned Vietnam any more – and look what was happening in Iraq. Hell, politicians sucked. At least, he didn't live in America. The atrocities committed by his government today made even Honecker look benign. Although maybe all the post-Wall nostalgia was finally getting to him as well – there could be no denying that life had been miserable in the *Plattenbau*. Peter had always known communism was doomed to failure. Jason brought him his beer.

'Cheers darling. I need it.'

'Poor Peter. What an awful thing to happen. When's the funeral?' Jason asked.

'Who knows. The police won't issue a cause of death statement, which we need to book him into the crematorium. Dying in Berlin is a complicated business, you know.' Peter laughed. 'It's so much easier – and cheaper – in the Czech Republic.'

'But it was an accident, wasn't it?'

'Yeah, as far as I know. They are doing a post-mortem. I don't know why: with two knives in his head and one in his neck, it's fairly obvious how he died.'

Bodo had been practising juggling knives in the middle of the night, probably drunk, when he missed. He must have been drunk to miss three knives. Perhaps something or someone had startled him – distracted him for a fraction of a second? Apparently the third had hit the back of his neck as he fell forward, face first. Peter had always thought he was mad to juggle those things. Bodo used to boast that he had the knives sharpened to give an edge to the performance.

Jason squeezed his shoulder before going off to collect bottles and glasses from the opposite bench. He was cute – if only Peter were twenty years younger.

Twenty years. What had he done in that time? Drank an ocean of beer, smoked a forest of cigarettes, lived through the fall of the Berlin Wall and worked through numerous bars, cafes and unsuccessful relationships. He had nothing more to show other than an enlarged stomach and wheezy lungs. The thought was depressing.

Johnny had left Berlin at the end of 1984, just before they blew up Bodo's apartment block opposite. The dust and ash from the East had covered his apartment for months afterwards. No one heard from Johnny – or of him – for years. Not that Peter cared. Johnny had been nothing but trouble. Then a letter came to him for Bodo. Apparently, Johnny had inherited a load of money from an estranged father in the early nineties and set up his own dance company, or was it a circus?

Peter got the blame, of course – at least from Bodo. When they went out together, Bodo often ended up drinking vodka and then sobbing. 'If only you'd been there to help,' he'd stutter, 'maybe it wouldn't have happened.' But even now Peter wasn't convinced. Too many people had known what they were planning. He had warned Johnny. Johnny hadn't listened. Peter had even told him to get out of the apartment. Only they were to blame. He was only sorry that he had ripped up the letter to Natasha that day when Johnny asked him to meet her. But that wouldn't have stopped her from trying to cross.

Now Bodo was dead as well. He was sure it was a tragic accident, but if Bodo had committed suicide, he would probably get the blame for that as well. Bodo had called him on the Saturday night, only hours before he threw knives at himself, wanting to go out. Peter said he had a date. A lie.

'Shame,' Bodo said. Then he'd told him about Johnny coming over. That he wanted to do some show or something. He had sounded so pleased. He also said that Alice might come, too.

'It will be just like it used to be, Peter. Almost.'

On hearing the news, Peter thought he might take a vacation for a few weeks: anything rather than see Johnny and Mad Alice. He cringed. He would never know: if he had gone out with Bodo that night, would things have been different?

But he didn't believe it was suicide. Bodo had done well for himself in the West – particularly in the beginning. He had moved to Charlottenburg – to be as far away from the East as was reasonably possible – and worked the clubs and cabarets, mainly juggling, but he was awesome. Peter had seen him perform many times. He could juggle anything, but the knives were his speciality. The clubs loved him. He used to parade around the tables getting the clients to feel the sharpness of the blades. It was only after the Wall came down that Peter noticed a change in Bodo, but then they were all changing, getting older, disappointed. Peter was sure *he* was far more unhappy than Bodo.

The fall of the Berlin Wall. In the end it all happened so quickly. History had happened without warning, without authority. But he'd been there with Bodo on the night of November 9 1989.

As soon as he heard the confused broadcasts, both on ZDF and ARD, that East Germans would be free to travel immediately, he'd called Bodo.

'Ach, *'immediately'* in Stasi-speak means next year at the earliest – perhaps,' Bodo said, dismissively.

Peter agreed, but then the news spread through the city like wild fire that the borders were going to open later that night. He alone called about ten people and they all agreed to meet up at Café Adler at Checkpoint Charlie later. There was a real buzz in the air. Only Hermann and Michael remained unimpressed. Michael didn't believe it, while Hermann, a West German, wanted to help the border guards. 'We can't let those Ossis in,' he cried. 'We'll never get rid of them.' Too much speed had warped his brain. Peter managed to persuade him to run the Kiosk for him instead – although he heard later that he refused to open the door. In retrospect, Hermann had acted out what many subsequently feared.

Peter took a taxi and approached Checkpoint Charlie at about 10 p.m.. Hundreds of people were standing around outside the café and the Imbiss next to the Allied Hut.

'That's the end of the DDR,' the taxi driver had said, staring, open mouthed, at the crowds.

Peter thought that a bit strong. He had always known communism would fall but not then, not in his lifetime. They had lived with the Wall for so long: in those days it was almost impossible to imagine a world without it. But it certainly looked like something was going to happen that night. He had only hoped it wasn't going to be another Tiananmen Square scenario. As he walked closer, he could feel the cold dark air bubbling with excitement, expectation and champagne. Everyone seemed to be holding a bottle or a glass of Sekt. The guards, both on the ground near the customs and in the watchtowers, kept looking at each other as if unsure what to do. A young girl approached with a couple of glasses which she offered to them. They refused, but they no longer looked their usual sinister selves. No one knew what was going on. Hundreds of East Berliners queued patiently on the other side of the Wall, waiting to cross. The British and American military hovered around the Allied Hut.

The café was heaving with people. Little Willie, from the Kiosk, gave him a bottle of Sekt, which he shared with a British journalist who had a very cute ass crammed into tight black jeans. The journalist told him that all the border crossings would open at midnight.

'Just like that? After twenty-eight years?' Peter could hardly believe it.

'Who knows? But they're supposed to be issuing visas. Did you see the Schabowski Press Conference?'

'Yeah of course.'

'We reckon someone gave him the wrong announcement. Or, at least, no one had debriefed him.'

'He looked pretty horrified at what he was saying,' Peter said as he filled up their glasses.

'The 9th of November – a day to remember.'

It was only then that Peter realised it was exactly five years ago to the day when Bodo had crossed. Then, as now, he laughed out loud at the coincidence.

'What's so funny?' the journalist had asked.

For his cute ass, Peter would have told him, but then someone shouted that Bodo was juggling on the Wall.

'Hey, we must see this,' the journalist said.

He probably wouldn't have believed him anyway. The press had been prohibited from publishing anything about the escape and, to Peter's knowledge, there was still no documentation available at that time. Peter followed the journalist outside and there was Bodo juggling three Sekt bottles, perched on the Wall just to the left of the café, a border guard's cap tipped backwards over his long, white-blonde hair. A ladder had appeared from nowhere and people were climbing up the Wall, one by one, and straddling the concrete tube. The guards on the ground, now mainly hatless, watched uncertainly, both confused and bemused.

'Hey Peter!' Bodo called, having caught the bottles. 'Come on up!'

'No thanks, darling,' Peter said. There was no way he was climbing on that Wall. Even in those days, he had the balance of Humpty-Dumpty. And look what happened to Humpty-Dumpty on a three-foot high wall. Imagine what would happen to him on a thirteen-foot wall. The journalist left him and started taking photographs.

Champagne flowed as if from a spring in the ground. It was a miracle that he could remember anything, but the night remained crystal clear. Chanting began from both sides. A Stasi officer appeared to be talking to the border guards. Scenes of a bloodbath flashed in front of him and he could see the headlines, 'Thousands massacred at Checkpoint Charlie', 'The Cold War heats up', 'The DDR declares war at Checkpoint Charlie', 'Is this the beginning of the Third World War?', 'America threatens nuclear retaliation'. Or, quite simply, Bush the First, could just press the button.

It was perhaps a good thing that it was Bush the First and not Bush the Second. No buttons were pressed, no nuclear attacks launched, no bloodbaths, no displays of shock and awe. Just one awesome party. A wild night, even by Berlin standards. In fact, he might not have done much with his life, but he'd been there that night when the world changed. He had helped history reverse an unnatural order – Johnny hadn't.

Checkpoint Charlie opened at midnight and East Berliners, Trabants and Wartburgs started to cross for the first time in twenty-eight years. One of the first groups of pedestrians to reach the white line included the Professor and George, the bear, and Tomas, who he later learned was the knife thrower who had shot the arrows across to his apartment. George, the bear, took one of the few remaining guards' hats and put it on his own head. It somehow balanced on his ears and everyone cheered loudly as he crossed the white line – the bear being the great symbol of Berlin.

He and Bodo met them. Bodo couldn't stop crying. The night was full of tears, champagne and much hugging.

'Where's Johnny?' the Professor asked at one point.

But, of course, no one knew.

No one mentioned the rubber woman.

They didn't stay long or go very far. Several Westerners politely told the Professor that it was cruel to keep a bear in captivity.

'Take no notice,' Bodo said. 'They have some strange ideas. They care more about animals than people.'

Nonetheless, the Professor and George soon went back to the East.

After those extraordinary days, life in Berlin was never the same. Germany was still suffering from the hangover – even today. The yellow fumes from the Trabants hung over the city for years afterwards.

Peter didn't know what happened to George and the Professor. He never asked. Circuses with animals were not popular in the West. Bodo continued to live in Charlottenburg and work the clubs. Apparently, if he had stayed in the East he could have had a pension at thirty-five, but he had blown it by crossing the Wall. He drank a lot but who didn't. He shared Peter's love of music and, occasionally, they would listen to Marlene Dietrich together. When he was pie-eyed, he used to say how much he loved Alice and Peter would groan. The slapper must have left a plethora of broken hearts around the world.

Peter reckoned it must have been the early nineties when Bodo became more negative. Despite the redecorated *Plattenbauten* and the many opportunities for the East Germans, Bodo despised the new capitalist world, calling it a legitimate form of slavery. Bodo wasn't alone of course – there was a palpable tension between the *Neue* and *Alte Bundesländer*. Many West Germans began to regret tearing down the Wall as they were made to pay the *Solidaritätszuschlag,* the cost of reunification, while many East Germans were disappointed with their new golden life, which didn't even provide a secure job. Hell, what did they expect? Did no one realise the Wall fell because the DDR was bankrupt? The nineties was a tricky decade.

It must have been sometime in the mid-nineties when Alice came back to Berlin and moved in with Bodo; quite how or why was still a mystery to Peter. They must have kept in touch. She was older (as they all were), twelve years older, and no longer mad. On the contrary, she was painfully serious. She was still only twenty-nine which meant that in 1984 she must have been about seventeen. No wonder she had been annoying. But she was worse when she was older. She had done a degree in art or something and would talk for hours about redefining perceptions of everything. She left as suddenly and mysteriously as she had arrived.

'She's gone back to England,' Bodo explained, during another long and lugubrious night drinking vodka in the Kiosk.

'Why don't you go with her?' Peter asked

'I can't leave Berlin,' Bodo kept saying. 'Don't you understand?'

Peter didn't. Bodo said that he felt guilty for having survived. Instead of *her*. Crazy. More recently, since many of the Stasi files were in public domain, Bodo had tried to find out what happened to Natasha. Apparently, there was nothing on her. He found dozens on himself though. Of course, they had known everything. Oh well, no more guilt now. He was gone, away from it all. The ass.

'Peter?'

Peter looked up from the wooden table and saw the most beautiful man he had ever seen – at least, for twenty years. His stomach rolled over and over. Standing in front of him was the tall, dark, handsome stranger of his dreams. His skin was ever so slightly tanned, his short, dark, almost spiky hair glistened in the setting sun and the blue sky spilled into his eyes. He was wearing dark, loose trousers, black suede trainers with white velcro straps and a khaki sleeveless T-shirt, out of which hung muscular arms. A toothlike stone on a piece of leather hung around his neck and he still had the familiar earrings: a ring and a jet-black star-shaped stud in his left ear and another stud in his right. He had few lines for his age and Peter suddenly felt fat and middle-aged. He knew he had more lines on his face than a chicken's neck and gaps in his smile where he'd lost three rear molars.

He stood up and they embraced.

'Johnny darling,' he said.

'Good to see you, Peter.' He sounded as if he almost meant it.

'Do you want a beer?'

'Sure.'

Peter ordered another couple of beers.

'So this is where you work?'

'Yeah, I've been here for about six years.' Peter felt ashamed. He knew that Johnny would think he should have done more with his life. Then angry for feeling ashamed. Jason brought them two Warsteiners, which he placed on the bench on front of them with a smile. Peter picked his up and drank, without raising his glass.

'No more Beck's?' Johnny smiled.

'Sometimes. But not often. You know, there are so many good draught beers here now. Oh, hey, cheers.' He held his glass up.

'Here's to Bodo,' Johnny said.

Peter nodded as their glasses clinked.

Johnny drank thirstily. 'Yeah, it's good. It's a nice café. I remember coming here. It's strange, there are places that haven't changed a bit and places that I don't recognise at all.'

'Well, the Wall took up a lot of the city centre. But all they have constructed is a load of expensive shopping malls and offices.'

Johnny sat tall and upright opposite him on the bench. Peter couldn't keep his eyes off him – he looked gorgeous.

'You look very well,' Peter couldn't help saying, before kicking himself under the table.

'Thanks. So do you.'

Peter knew he was lying. Brits lied as naturally as butter melted on a summer's day.

'So have you been in Berlin all the time?'

'Pretty much.' Peter guessed what was coming next, so pre-empted him. 'I guess we're not all that ambitious, Johnny.' He smiled as he watched Johnny registering the rebuff.

'I didn't mean that,' he said quickly.

'I hear you came into some money,' Peter said.

'Yeah, my biological father, who I only ever met once, was killed on the M25 and left me fifty grand, so I began the company. It had always been my dream, you know.'

'Lucky you, darling.'

'Yeah, I was lucky in that respect. It's been hard work, but I don't know what I would have done otherwise. It's been my life. In fact, I was thinking of doing an aerial show here in Berlin this summer. That's why I'm here. I came to ask Bodo to be in the show.'

'So you're not going to do it now?'

'I don't know. I wasn't expecting to find Bodo dead.' He paused.

'Neither was anyone, darling. But, for what it's worth, I think Bodo would want you to do it.'

'Do you?'

Peter nodded. Johnny turned and ordered two more beers from Jason. When Johnny had turned back again, Jason winked at Peter, as if to say, he's cute. If only he knew.

'I had no idea what had happened,' Johnny continued. 'I only spoke to him on Saturday. I was supposed to meet him at three o'clock this afternoon. And when I got there an absolutely horrendous landlady told me that he was in the hell.'

'Ah, you mean Frau Übermann. The old hag asked me to pay the rest of his rent.'

'Next time you bring four hundred euros, *ja*.' Johnny imitated her German-English accent.

They smiled, an intimate moment that shook away the years. They drank their beer.

'So when did you last see him?' Johnny asked.

'A couple of weeks ago. But, like you, I spoke with him on Saturday.'

'Did you think he was okay?' Johnny asked.

Peter shrugged. 'Yeah, he was fine. As I'm sure you know he was working in a cabaret which he got fed up with now and then but, you know, we all have to make money.'

'Sure, but, well, do you think he was happy?'

'Oh Johnny. Who the fuck knows. Are you happy? Am I happy? What the fuck is happiness?' He grabbed his Marlboro. Johnny, of course, didn't smoke any more. He took a deep breath of smoke. 'He was looking forward to seeing you, I know that.'

Johnny tilted his head and turned up the side of his mouth in a half smile, a familiar expression that had always infuriated Peter. Jason brought then two more Warsteiners, giving Peter a couple of minutes to calm down.

'So, when's the funeral?' Johnny asked.

Peter snorted. 'We haven't got a cause of death statement which we need for the paperwork at the crematorium. They're still doing a post-mortem.'

'Are you arranging it all?'

'Not only me, the cabaret he worked at is also helping. It's just been a nightmare with the paperwork. I've helped contact people, but they've agreed to pay for it. They wanted to cremate him in the Czech Republic – as it would have cost a fraction of the amount, but I just know he will haunt me forever if I allow him to be cremated in the old East. He's in Ruhleben Krematorium. We decided on a humanist service and several old friends are going to do readings.' Peter switched his cigarette for the beer.

Johnny nodded slowly. 'Will there be many people there?'

'I think so. I've contacted quite a few and word spreads. I wasn't able to find the old circus performers. I haven't had time.'

'So he really has no family?'

'Not that I know of. He lived with his father in that flat in Treptow until his father had a heart attack, I believe. His mother had disappeared under strange circumstances. Bodo told me once his father spoke out against the State because her body was never found. He was dead within a year. Did Bodo never tell you?'

'Only that his mother was murdered by the Stasi.' Johnny hesitated. 'Did you contact Alice?'

'Yeah, I spoke to Alice. She's taken it real bad. She screamed down the phone and then became hysterical. Sounds like she needs professional counselling. I had no idea how upset she'd be.' It was awful. He wished he hadn't called.

'So she really did love him after all.'

'Well, they did live together for a few years which, for Mad, was quite an achievement. Well, for any of us, I guess. She changed, you know. As we all have. Are you with anyone?'

Johnny shook his head. Peter couldn't help but feel triumphant.

'Why didn't you tell me?' Johnny asked. 'About Bodo.'

'I had no idea where you were.'

'You could have found me on the net.'

'Johnny. I have been so busy. I couldn't remember everyone.' Peter knew he was hurting Johnny but he didn't really care. Johnny had hurt him in the past. Besides, he didn't have a computer and, even if he had, he wouldn't know what to do with it.

'I'm not exactly everyone,' Johnny said.

'Darling, I haven't seen you or heard from you in twenty years!'

'You told me you didn't want to see me again. You threw me out, Peter.'

Peter breathed in deeply as Johnny finished one beer and started on the next. Johnny used to be much more guarded than that.

'You know damn well I asked you to get out, darling, because I didn't want to be complicit in an act that could end in tragedy. Then, when I got back I found chaos and tragedy. What did you expect me to say? You were an asshole.'

They were silent for a minute. Johnny was looking at the table.

'Maybe. But can I ask you something?' Johnny said.

'Sure.'

'Did you ever tell anyone what we were doing?' Johnny asked.

Anger pounded into his heart. Peter knew they blamed him for not helping but now he was being accused of being an informer. 'Fuck you, Johnny.' He got up from the bench, banging his knee as he untangled his legs from the wood. What a skinny-assed prick.

'Wait, Peter. I'm sorry. I came to ask you for Alice's phone number. Please.'

'Why? Can't you look on the net?' Peter stood up tall, trying to hold in his stomach.

'I've already looked. I can't find her. Listen, she got in touch with the police.'

'What? Why?' Peter felt his chest thump loudly.

'Apparently, there's a letter from Bodo.'

'A letter?' The thumping stopped.

'What's the letter say?' he squeaked.

'I don't know. The police are investigating. They suspect he committed suicide. The knives had been sharpened and weighted at the sharp end. Did you know that?'

'He'd been sharpening his knives for years. I told the police that. But what does the letter say? Might there be an inquest?' Peter snatched his inhaler.

'I don't know. I guess it depends on what Alice says. That's why I want to speak to her first.'

Peter sprayed his heart with the inhaler as he found the number on his handy and showed it to Johnny.

Ku'damm

Johnny left Peter and wandered back to the Hotel Belmondo, feeling drunk after two beers. It was getting dark. The night clouds bandaged the reddish sky. The Ku'damm was buzzing. This part of Berlin hadn't changed much – except for there being more metal and glass structures looming over Karstadt, and Nokia, instead of Cinzano, was now illuminated around the top of the hotel. On the other side, there was a C&A, a Body Shop and hotels on top of hotels. He couldn't remember which were new. He took a shower and then went back out to find somewhere to eat. What a day. He had gone to Berlin to arrange an aerial show, found his old friend dead, practically been arrested and argued with Peter. He didn't care what Penny said. He was going back to London tomorrow. There were too many ghosts and now the police were involved. That wouldn't be good publicity. Two police officers had interviewed him in a small cubicle within their main office. They had been friendly but Johnny still felt an innate suspicion of police, especially ones with shiny boots and sunglasses. They wanted to know if he had any reason to suspect Bodo had committed suicide.

Of course, there were plenty of reasons. Bodo, in particular, had lived through terrible times. The past, *na ja*. But they'd never understand, they were too young. Johnny shook his head but they still wouldn't let him go. They wanted to know why Johnny was in Berlin. He told them he had come to ask Bodo to perform in an aerial show and that he'd spoken to him on the Saturday and he'd sounded fine. As for the knives, he shrugged. Bodo had told him he had a new act with knives. They asked about Alice. He said that Bodo had known someone called Alice and that they'd all been friends twenty years ago. At the time of the Wall.

'A long time ago, *nay*,' the young police officer echoed. 'And you have no idea where she is?'

'No.'

They'd copied his passport and asked him to leave his details before, finally, allowing him to leave.

He hadn't told Peter what the police had told him: that death hadn't been immediate, that he had died on the way to the hospital. Alone. With two scimitar knives in his skull and one in his neck.

He ordered some *Currywurst* from the Imbiss am Zoo and sat on the steps by the Gedächtniskirche. Only the kids break-dancing were different. As soon as finished eating he pressed her number. A child answered the phone. Johnny, taken by surprise, almost disconnected before telling himself that it didn't make any difference.

'Hello, this is Johnny, calling from Berlin. Is Alice there please?'

He heard the little boy shouting to his Mummy that it was Merlin. He smiled. He couldn't imagine Alice as a mother. A woman spoke.

'Hello?' she said.

'Alice?'

'Yes,' she said.

'It's Johnny.' He could hear her hesitating. 'Remember me?' he said.

'Yes, of course,' she said.

'I'm in Berlin. I came to see Bodo but, you know, what has happened?'

'Yes, I know.' Her voice broke off.

'I'm sorry, Alice. It's been a big shock to me, too.' He paused. 'You have a little boy?' he asked.

Her breath choked. 'Yes, David.'

'How old?'

'Five.'

'Wow. That's great. Are you married as well?'

'No, Johnny. I'm a single parent.'

'So your name isn't Howard?'

Her silence froze the phone.

'How do you know about that?' she asked.

Johnny explained that he had been asked to go down to the police station in Charlottenburg and that the police had informed him that they were trying to get hold of an Alice Howard.

'I called them when I received a letter from Bodo after he'd died.'

Johnny felt his stomach fall down. So, the police suspicions may well be right.

'Well, he'd posted it before the accident but the postmark was dated on the Monday. It kind of freaked me out and I called the police. Then I regretted it and gave them a false name. Why? What did they say?'

'Oh, they want to speak to you about it. They're talking about an inquest.'

'Well, I don't want to speak to them.' There was the old Alice. 'Don't give them my name,' she added.

'Of course not. I didn't say anything. What did the letter say?' Johnny asked gently.

'Just a letter, saying how much he loved me, how he was looking forward to seeing you and asking me to come over too,' Alice said, one word at a time.

He could hear the pain in every cracked word but he needed to know. 'So, it was not a ... a suicide note then?'

'No.' Her voice squeaked.

'Oh Alice, I'm so sorry.' Johnny didn't know what to say. 'Listen, Berlin is too much for me at the moment but I will come back for his funeral. I can meet you at the airport if you want? It would be good to see you,' he added. He meant it.

She sobbed an okay. He told her to call him if she needed anything and gave her his numbers. They said goodbye. He sat in one of the cafés on the Ku'damm and ordered an Irish coffee. It was only a few minutes later he realised it was the same café they'd sat in the night Bodo and Natasha had crossed over to see his performance. Natasha had been like a child in a toyshop, talking non-stop in German and English, munching a chocolate cake. Bodo couldn't believe that they had lied about the West. Johnny picked up the multi-layered napkin. He remembered the small, hard squares they used to have in the East. Like in a dream, Natasha had kept saying. Like in a dream.

Potsdamer Platz

'Look at the ghosts,' David said, pressing the tip of his small finger against the window of the aeroplane.

She peered over his blonde curls into the hazy blue skies and at the green fields below them. Tiny farm houses, small villages and wide straight autobahns decorated the model landscape. Wisps of clouds drifted by the window like lost souls. If only he knew.

It was the first time he had been on a plane. She hadn't wanted to bring him: a funeral was not exactly suitable for a five-year-old, but she had no choice as there was no one to leave him with now that her father was on his own. And, maybe, one day, he would be glad he had been there. Maybe it was time to tell him. He would find out sooner or later: he was a smart kid.

The funeral was tomorrow, Tuesday, 1 June, two weeks and two days after his death. Apparently, the coroner's report had taken some time. Partly, she suspected, her fault for calling the police.

She'd been in her flat in Norwich, chopping fresh coriander to add to a chicken curry, when Peter phoned her. He had never phoned her in England before – she didn't even know he'd got her phone number. Somehow she knew before he spoke that Bodo was dead. Her legs gave way beneath her when Peter told her what had happened. Those bloody knives, she screamed. She'd warned him time and time again. As she lay crumpled up on the floor, she was vaguely aware of him calming her sobs with platitudes.

'*Scheiße*. I'm sorry to have to be the one to tell you, Alice. It was a terrible accident. You know, those knives.'

He'd called her Alice. He never called her Alice.

Peter had ended the conversation just as soon as he could, promising to let her know when the funeral was. She didn't blame him. He, no doubt, had his own grief to deal with. Fortunately, David had been in nursery school when the call came.

'What's wrong, Mummy?' he asked when she met him later that day.

He'd looked up at her with such concern in his blue eyes that she'd burst out crying in the street. She picked him up and hugged him to her.

'A very good friend of mine has died,' she explained.

'Do I know her?'

'Him. No you don't. Although I very much wish you had.'

'Why didn't I then?'

She couldn't answer this. Because he lived a long way away. Because the time wasn't right. Because she was scared at how he would react.

Because he was always pissed. Because she didn't know he was going to die.

For days afterwards, all she could see was Bodo lying on the ground with blood seeping out of his head, alone. She felt as if someone had blown off a limb, only she wasn't sure which one it was. Sometimes it felt like an arm, other times a leg, at other times a hand. Her heart ached. David helped her: she had to keep herself together for him, but she was haunted by his simple question: why hadn't they gone to visit him? She had been busy with work; several big commissions over the last three years and what with teaching and juggling childcare since her mother died, it hadn't been easy. But that wasn't an excuse for not going.

Juggling.

Then she felt angry. Angry that he had never been to visit her. Angry that he had never really kept in touch or supported her. Angry that he drank alcohol to hide from the world. Angry that he was dead.

When she'd returned from taking David to the nursery on the Friday, four days after Peter had called her, she found a letter on the doormat. She recognised his writing immediately and the Berlin postmark. She felt sick as she opened the envelope. Had there been some terrible mistake?

When she read the letter she crumbled to the floor again.

Darling Alice,

I want to call you but it is 2am and I know you are angry with me because I'm a little drunk but I just want to say that I love you and that I always loved you since I saw you in Alex. You are a wonderful, strong and beautiful woman and I miss you.

My life is not quite how I imagine. The dream of a better world is just a dream and it is a high price to pay. There is something I never tell you: Natasha ask to cross first and I say no because I think it is more dangerous. I feel bad about that forever.

Did you know Johnny comes to Berlin? Will you come? It will be difficult to see him.

By the way, I am going to post this. Then I am going to practise my new act in the yard. One day I know I am going to have an accident. But an accident my darling Alice. I do not want you – or anyone - to think differently. The circus is a dangerous act.

235

I love you and remember me to David.

Bodo

For the first time in seven years, she crawled to the phone and called in sick to the art college where she lectured part-time. Then she called the police. He had committed suicide. The idiot. Just because he had made a wrong judgement twenty years ago. She needed to tell them. She didn't know what else to do. She should have called Peter. Or Johnny – if only she'd known his number then, or that he would remember her. She supposed she must have been in shock.

Not that it had been easy. How do you call the Berlin police from England? It wasn't an emergency so she didn't want to call 999. Interpol? She called several national numbers from the Yellow Pages and screamed in frustration when she was made to spend half an hour giving her name and address. She put the phone down, made a cup of tea and then looked online where she immediately found the Berlin police website and translated the page. She wrote down a number for Direktion 2, the local police station in Charlottenburg. At the top of the page were the words 'Resting Life'. A strange choice of words for a police website, but they had a calming effect at the time.

By the time she got through to someone, her breathing was steadier, her mind clearer. The woman she spoke to didn't speak much English and her German was not great any more. She said that she had some information regarding the death of Bodo Kollender. She had reason to believe he committed suicide. She thought the woman said she would get someone to call her back. As she spoke, her gaze fell again on Bodo's letter: *But an accident my darling Alice. I do not want you – or anyone – to think differently.* She gave a false name and phone number.

'How do you write that?' the woman asked.

'H-o-w-a-r-d.' Alice Howard, whoever she was.

She released the phone from her clammy fingers, still staring at the letter. Bodo had not been able to live with the guilt but he did not want anyone to know. She must respect his wishes. She spent the rest of that day petrified that Interpol would trace her.

At six o'clock, as she was making some pasta for David, the phone rang. She was going to ask David not to answer but he'd already picked it up. It was Johnny. It was strange to hear his voice after all these years. He sounded cut up as well. She lied to him about the contents of the letter. She was not going to tell him or anyone about Bodo's suicide. They had all suffered enough.

Johnny. It would be odd to see him again. She had been in love with him for so long and she had never felt like that again. Of course she had loved Bodo, but not that all consuming fire-love she used to feel for Johnny. It had taken many years to die down and even longer to go out. At times, she struggled to believe that she should feel so much and he so little. With time though, she had come to accept it. She concluded that in each relationship one person loved a little more than the other. She had loved him, he Natasha and Bodo her.

She had had no contact with him since West Berlin. They had all gone their own distraught ways. It was a terrible thing to have lived through. She still had the photos somewhere. Images of her being shot out of the sky. A fallen angel with broken wings bleeding to death on the snow in No Man's Land, surrounded by guards with machine guns. Natasha hadn't stood a chance. And yet she'd lived to witness her own death. Alice had seen her alive, eyes blinking. Who knows what had happened to her after they took her away. How long she had lived for? Johnny had tried to trace her but it was as if she had never existed. Those were still the days of the Cold War, even though she'd never thought about it then. The story remained untold. They were advised not to publicise it – for the sake of those involved in the East. Bodo's crossing was never made public.

Alice didn't go back for the fall of the Berlin Wall. It was too soon, too unexpected. She supposed, as with all of them, there had been a time for recuperation. She had needed to clean her life up: 1984 had whizzed into 1985 in an eternal winter, forever awake, forever dreaming of angels and soldiers, forever cold. It felt like years later, but it must have been only months, before she had finally got out of West Berlin and gone back to stay with her parents in Norfolk. It took her many years to get her life on track. She lived in London for a while in a bedsit, working in a shop on Regent Street, but London was big, expensive, trendy. She never liked living there. Then she ran away to Italy and fell in love with Florence. It was there she began painting and it was there she decided to return to England and go to art school.

When Alice had gone back to Berlin in the nineties, Bodo used to cry about had happened when he was pissed – almost every day. He would begin to sing songs he had sung as a Pioneer. 'The world needs you and you need the world, pioneer.' Then he would cry that the world would have been better without him. Alice hadn't known then that Natasha had asked to cross first. She used to try to comfort him but, after a while, it made her depressed as well. He drank her energy. For the second time in her life, she had to get out of Berlin.

She knew that in the nineties Johnny became the choreographer and director of the very successful *The Flight Company*. She read about him in all sorts of magazines and papers. She remembered some of the write-ups claiming he had 'fused dance with flight in an awesome display of aero-acrobatics', and her favourite: 'In this postmodernist world it is hard to imagine anything new but Johnny East has redefined the imagination'. She tried to see one of his shows once in London but the tickets began at twenty-five pounds and she couldn't afford it. She wondered if he ever married. She suspected not.

'We're going down, Mummy,' David said.

On cue, the air steward's voice told them to fasten their seat belts. They would be landing in about fifteen minutes. She picked up the easyJet in-flight magazine and flicked to Berlin and read that Berlin's debt level was around fifty billion euros. The price of change. No doubt that caused a lot of resentment – last time she'd been in Berlin, an invisible wall had grown around the city and the East hated the West for not living up to the dream and the West hated the East for draining them of Marks. But now, there must be a new generation who had never known the physical wall. It sounded like a great city. You could take a tour through secret sewers and torture chambers or ski at The Glacier. There were hundreds of clubs. She didn't recognise any of the names of them apart from Tresor. She and Bodo had been there once a long time ago. You could visit a graffitied section of the wall, along with a watchtower, which used to stand in this former no-man's land. That was all that was left of it. A tourist attraction.

The plane wheels unfolded and she peered again over David's hair, momentarily confused by the blue shimmering lakes and green forests. She often forgot how green Berlin was. Then she glimpsed a city of shining glass and metal. There was the old Fernsehturm, but rather than the threatening omnipotent red eyes watching them, it looked more like a silver cocktail stick poking into the blue sky. She smiled. The world had changed.

David began to cry as the pressure in the cabin hurt his ears. An air steward gave him a sweetie. Alice hugged him to her as he whimpered and sucked on his sweet at the same time. Not long now. Not long before she would meet the past. Her heart landed before they touched down onto the runway at Berlin-Tegel airport and rebounded as if on a bungee.

She pushed the trolley, complete with David at the helm, away from the baggage reclaim area and the hundreds of other trolleys and people, through customs and, suddenly, standing right in front of her was Johnny. All six foot of him, dark, tanned, slim, muscular. More conservative than he used to be in cotton pants and waistcoat, but in her flared jeans and dark red T-shirt, she was hardly the wild child she once was. She had to steer her way around some rope before she found herself wrapped in his arms.

She knew as soon as she touched him that she still loved him. The fire was still alive. Even after twenty years. He held her tightly and stroked her long dark hair. 'Johnny, it's good to see you,' she whispered. Their hands found each other and they squeezed each other's fingers before letting go. It was impossible to believe twenty years had passed. But she must be careful: she could not be hurt again. She moved away from him. He stared at her.

'Alice,' he said slowly, 'you look fantastic. And this must be David. Hello David.'

'Hello,' David said, before turning his face away, uninterested, and looking around the airport.

Alice smiled. David would not be disinterested for long.

'Hey David?' Johnny said.

'What?'

Johnny showed him a euro coin before whipping it behind his back and presenting two curled fists. 'Which hand?'

'That one,' David said, pointing to the left.

Johnny opened one, then the other, but they were both empty. David rushed around Johnny's leg to check that he had not hidden it. But he couldn't find it.

'Where is it?' he demanded.

'In your pocket, of course,' Johnny said, seriously.

David felt in his jacket pocket and pulled out the euro coin. He looked amazed and stared at Johnny in awe. Johnny winked at him.

'Wow. How did you do that?'

'Johnny is a magician,' Alice said.

'An ex-magician,' Johnny corrected.

She smiled to herself. She doubted it.

'I want to be an ex-magician,' David said.

She rolled her eyes in mock horror. Johnny laughed. A boyish, carefree laughter.

Johnny insisted they take a taxi to the Zoo. He talked to David, pointing things out on the way. There is no emotional space to be morose, nostalgic, angry or bitter when children are present and, not for the first time, she was glad of this. There was no mention of Bodo or Natasha or anything to do with their past. As they got closer, Johnny pointed out the station, the Zoo, the Kaiser-Wilhelm-Gedächtniskirche, the bombed church tower, the Europa Centre and Breitscheid Platz, where he used to juggle, and the U-Bahn Kurfürstendamm. There was Mövenpick, KFC, Berliner Morgenpost. But this part of Berlin was old now and the small panes of glass in the aluminium frames, once so modern, now seemed old-fashioned and run-down. In a way it looked how the East had looked in 1984.

'It still smells the same,' she said as they got out of the taxi.

He had booked them into the Hotel am Zoo. Alice had never stayed in a four-star hotel before. She remembered walking past it so many times in the past. But, even the hotel, she barely recognised.

They planned to go out for an early dinner, nothing too elaborate, somewhere they had never been before. They sat in the hotel bar drinking tea. Alice flicked through a new Berlitz guidebook Johnny had.

'Potsdamer Platz?' Johnny suggested, smiling at her. 'I haven't been there yet.'

'Sounds good,' she said. 'It was still a building site when I was last here.'

'Can we go on the U-Bahn?' David asked. He was fascinated by the white Us on the blue glossy signs since Johnny pointed them out and explained that a huge network of trains ran underground. But now he was fascinated by anything Johnny said.

They went down some steps to the U-Bahn at the Zoo.

'I can't get used to this map,' Johnny said.

They stopped to stare at the U-Bahn and S-Bahn maps in their hands.

'I know. The old green U1 is now the red U2 and it connects to the East. Remember Potsdamer Platz was in No Man's Land. All these stations were closed down when we were here. But it doesn't help that they've changed some of the names. Marx-Engels-Platz is now Hackescher Markt.'

'It's this way!' David shouted.

'I'm glad we've got a five-year-old with us,' Johnny said, laughing.

Alice smiled.

It was only six stops to Potsdamer Platz. The old orange U-Bahn hadn't changed, neither had the stations; they still had the kiosks in the middle and old tiled walls, but she could hardly believe the sight that greeted them once they got out at Potsdamer Platz – it was as if she had been transported to a different time and place. As she gazed up at the modern high-rise buildings, she noticed that where once some of the buildings were dressed in red, now they were dressed in images of buildings.

'Bizarre,' she said. 'There's nothing behind them. Only scaffolding.'

'They must still be deciding what to build,' Johnny said.

Then she recognised the clock by the S-Bahn and the little round green man in a bowler hat striding across the road on the pedestrian lights, which had always reminded her of a teddy bear – and the East.

As they walked through the Arkaden shopping centre, she tried to remember the black and white wasteland that was here but it was impossible. They crossed over the road and went into the Sony Centre. She looked in amazement at the cinemas and restaurants, and at the enormous concentric glass structure above them, striped with sails, creating an airy outside space, yet inside. Amazing. It really was another world. David clung to both her hand and Johnny's as they gazed at the high-tech world around them. Soft electronic music tinkled around them and water sprayed up from a pond not quite in the centre. Lifts glided up and down the glass and metal buildings.

'It beats even the Forum, doesn't it, David?'

'What's the Forum?'

'Oh, it's a new building in Norwich. Very modern, glass and metal. David likes going there.'

They ate at the Café Josty. Apparently, Johnny told her, it had been a haunt for artists and intellectuals in the 19th century.

'A bit like the Kiosk then,' she joked.

Johnny laughed. 'What happened to the Kiosk?' he asked.

'It closed down. After the fall of Wall. Peter never made any money.'

'I'm not surprised.'

She ordered the Berlin curry sausage and a pizza for David. Johnny ordered lukewarm goat's cheese on rocket salad with crispy bacon and a bottle of Cabernet Sauvignon. Alice couldn't help noticing that the wine cost twenty-two euros.

'I can't believe how much this has changed even since I was here,' Alice said, sipping her glass of wine, watching images of the trams in Potsdamer Platz before the Wall on the Sony screen. Neither could she believe how happy she felt, on the eve of Bodo's funeral as well. She swallowed the rising guilt and warned herself again of Johnny. They could be friends – nothing more. She would not be hurt again. It was good to have his friendship but they had had their chance together in life.

'What's changed?' David asked, his chin resting on the table.

She attempted to explain. 'There used to be land here, like an empty motorway, with a wall around it and watchtowers. There were guards and dogs. No one could go in.' Her explanation sounded surreal, unbelievable.

'Except for rabbits,' Johnny said.

'I'd forgotten about those,' Alice said. She'd forgotten so many things.

'Why couldn't anyone go in?' David asked.

'Because the city used to be separated. On one side lived people who believed in one thing and, on the other side, lived people who believed in something else. At least, their governments did. And they were afraid that one side would run away to the other. And so they built a wall to stop them.'

'That's silly,' David said, slipping off his chair.

She felt tears in her eyes again and blinked them away.

'You know I read in *Tip* that they're opening a hotel in the East like it used to be with drab wallpaper and pictures of Honecker in the rooms,' Johnny said. 'So a whole ideology and a way of life has become nothing more than a fashionable retro tourist attraction.'

Alice nodded but didn't say anything. The Wall had long been a tourist attraction, smashed up into tiny pieces (or other painted bits of concrete), glued to plastic mounts and sold for ten euros. There were model Trabants, fridge magnets of the old Berlin maps and she'd even seen mugs with her favourite green teddy bears striding around.

Johnny insisted on paying. They wandered around some more before taking the U-Bahn back to the Ku'damm which was still packed with shoppers and people eating and drinking outside the restaurants and cafés. It was warm, a balmy Berlin evening; a long way from the cold Berlin night when she had first met him at the station and they had walked to Nollendorfplatz and kissed in a doorway with the snow falling behind them under an arc light.

Johnny walked back with them to the hotel.

'Having kids kind of spoils any social life,' she said, as she prepared to say goodnight outside his room.

Johnny shrugged. 'Times are different.' He paused before adding, 'You could come and have something to drink in my room if you like? David can shout if he needs anything.'

She hesitated. She wasn't afraid for David but she was afraid for herself, afraid of being alone with Johnny. Afraid of what may happen. But she was older and wiser now. She knew how to say no. She would be careful. David was asleep before she'd even drawn the quilt over him. She kissed him goodnight and locked the hotel room behind her.

Johnny opened another bottle of red wine. Alice perched on the edge of the double bed. She wondered if he was seeing anyone. He was still gorgeous. She'd had a couple of disastrous relationships over the past five years since Bodo refused to come to England with her. Neither lasted longer than three months. She found out one was married in London with three kids after overhearing him talking on the phone. The other was a lot younger than her, an ex-student – not a good idea.

'It's really good to see you, Alice,' Johnny said quietly, as he poured the wine. He sat down on an upholstered chair opposite her.

'And you, Johnny.' She smiled. She was in control.

'It's ironic that Bodo has brought us all together again,' he said.

Pain stabbed her heart. 'Yes,' she said. 'Have you seen Peter?'

'Not this time. He's busy of course. It sounds like the funeral has been a nightmare to arrange.'

'How is he?'

'He's okay, I think. We only met up once for a beer when I was here a couple of weeks ago. We kind of argued. You know, about what happened.'

Alice was about to remind him that he had hurt Peter, as indeed he had hurt her, but it wasn't worth digging up dirt. Peter had known something bad was going to happen that night; something he didn't want to be a part of. He didn't want to feel guilty for the rest of his life. For once, he had been right. The guilt had killed Bodo. She could only imagine what Johnny had gone through. Out of all of them, Peter was the only one with a clear conscience.

'He looks a lot older, but then I guess we all do. Except you. You look great. You're forty, aren't you?'

'Thirty seven.'

Johnny looked surprised. Not surprising. She used to lie a lot.

'And you?' She knew how old he was.

'Forty-three. But that means you must have been only seventeen in eighty-four?'

She nodded and drank some wine.

'I'm six years older than you. I didn't know that.'

'Well, you didn't know everything then, did you, Johnny?' She smiled.

He smiled back. 'I guess not. I know you've been doing some sculptures for some big names in London though.'

'How do you know that?'

'I read an article in a paper a couple of years ago.'

She had only ever appeared in *Time Out* once – a couple of years ago.

'Yes, I have done some commissioned work. I enjoy it.'

'I always said you should go to art college. You know I still have that picture of a woman with wings you drew,' Johnny said.

'What woman with wings?' As she said that she remembered doodling in an old notebook and Johnny seeing it and telling her she should go to Art School. She didn't remember having given him anything though.

'I'll show it to you one day. Are you still working a lot at your sculpture?' Johnny asked, looking up at her.

'Yes, but not as much as I used to,' she said. 'There was a time when art was the most important thing to me. But not any more. David is more important. Your priorities change as you get older. Children change you.' She paused, wondering if he would ask her about David. He didn't. He just kept looking at her.

'How about you? Do you still perform?'

'Not so often. I did until I was forty. I actually wanted to do a final high wire juggling act with Bodo in this show but I've decided not to now. I'm not even sure whether to do the show,' Johnny added.

'Why not?'

'Because the show is about what happened to us, to me, in 1984, about the crossing. I spent years avoiding it but the story is perfect for an aerial show. After twenty years I thought it was time. I got a good grant, but then when I was here last week I didn't think I could do it. And with Bodo gone, I keep thinking maybe I should just let the past be. So I told the company I couldn't do it and now my financial manager wants to kill me. But now that you're here I feel better. What do you think?'

'I think Bodo would want you to do it,' she said, slowly, trying to erase the image of him lying on the ground with blood seeping out of his head. 'No one knows the story. I think they should. It is part of history. Berlin is a new world, it's not the world we lived in. That makes it easier for me anyway. Besides, you pissed me off but I wouldn't want anyone to kill you.' She grinned at him, vaguely aware that she was flirting. The lighting from the bedside lamps and a mirror light cast gave out a soft, orangey glow. The throw on the bed was silky beneath her hands. She was going to have to be careful.

He smiled back. 'It's not the world we lived in and yet, last week when I was here on my own, whenever I walked down a familiar street, I thought I heard voices from the past calling to me.'

Very careful.

'I think it's the grief. And the memories,' she said. 'But Bodo, at least, would want us to move on.' She couldn't speak for Natasha. She couldn't even say her name.

'Then I will think about it,' he said. He reached over to the dressing table and picked up the bottle. He poured some into her glass.

She would have a hangover tomorrow. But Bodo would forgive her, expect it even.

'Do you remember that boyfriend you had when I first met you?'

She shook her head. She'd had so many.

'You know the American? Tom was his name? Claimed to be a writer? We had a conversation about *Crime and Punishment*? You know, whether or not, someone can commit a crime and be able to live with the guilt?'

She vaguely remembered Tom but not him being a writer. She certainly didn't remember a conversation about *Crime and Punishment*. She frowned. Too much vodka.

'You know, the character, Raskolnikov, has to confess because of the guilt he feels. Well, sometimes, I feel like that,' Johnny said. 'If only I had said no.'

She nodded. Yes, she did remember. She had said that he was mad to confess. But it was hard to live with guilt. Johnny wasn't the only one. If she hadn't taken his passport, then he could have gone and lived happily ever after in the East and now they were one big family anyway. He still didn't know that she had stolen his passport. Would never know. Would things have turned out differently? It wasn't worth thinking about. And, in the end, guilt itself had proved as deadly as the original act.

'Are you sure Bodo didn't commit suicide?'

'Yes,' Alice lied. 'Of course. It was an accident. He was practising with weighted knives, the idiot.' Tears filled her eyes.

'Oh Alice,' Johnny said, coming over and sitting next to her on the bed. He put one arm around her. Then another. He held her tightly.

'It's okay. It's going to be okay.'

She tried to wipe her eyes but they filled up again.

'It's just such a waste of life,' she said.

'I know, Alice.'

She realised he was crying too. As once they had clung to each other under an arc light in the snow, now they clung to each other on a double bed in a warm hotel. But then they were young, free and full of life. Now they were surrounded by memories and dead lovers. She stared at his lips, trying not to remember what it was like to kiss them. She pulled away from him.

'I'd better go to my room, Johnny,' she whispered.

'Don't go, Alice. Stay here with me,' he said.

'No Johnny.'

He pulled her towards him again. She felt like a rag doll in his arms. He held her tightly and they rocked side by side, as if aboard a lifeboat in a stormy ocean. She looked into his glistening eyes. They were staring into hers as if seeing her for the first time. His short black hair looked playfully windswept around his face. They moved closer to one another and kissed. He tasted of tiramisu and red wine. His lips were soft, gentle, passionate. They made her swirl round and round. It had been a long time since anyone kissed her like that. Twenty years probably. She pushed him away.

'Johnny, I have to go. I don't want to be hurt again,' she whispered.

Ruhleben

Johnny spent the rest of the night before the funeral wide awake and wondering, tasting the memories of a forgotten passion, feelings he hadn't felt for twenty years. He wanted to make love with her so badly his body ached. Had he hurt Alice, who used to have so many boyfriends, that much? He wanted to say that he wouldn't hurt her again but how could he be sure? Something poked him in his heart. He wondered who David's father was. What a fool he must be to have left her, or maybe she left him? He would find out one day. There was no rush. But for the first time since he'd been back to Berlin, it was Alice's name, not Natasha's, on his lips as he listened to the hum of the air-conditioning and the distant sound of traffic on the Ku'damm through the double glazing.

He knocked on her door in the morning. She was ready, dressed in black trousers and a long burgundy velvet summer jacket, tapered in the middle. Her long dark hair glistened like beetles' wings. She looked gorgeous. David was wearing shiny page boy shoes. He looked serious.

'Hi, won't be a minute.' Her breathing was tight, her voice strained.

After a late breakfast of torn up pieces of croissants, ham and coffee, they left the hotel and joined another blue-skied Berlin day and headed underground to what was now the U2.

'Where is the funeral?' David asked.

'Ruhleben,' Alice said.

'This way.' David sounded more like a fifty-year-old than a five-year-old as he led them to the correct train.

As they passed Sophie-Charlotte-Platz, Alice's body shuddered. Johnny put his arm around her and she burrowed into his shoulder, her hair falling over her face. She was trembling. Of course, this was where she must have lived with Bodo. Alice said that he hadn't committed suicide, but he wasn't sure if she was telling the truth. If she wasn't, she must have her reasons. David looked at her, concerned. Johnny invited him to sit on his lap. He scrambled up and sat quietly, looking at Alice. Johnny grinned at him and pulled a euro coin out of his ear. This time he studied it seriously and put it in his pocket.

'Resting life,' Alice mumbled.

'What?'

'Resting life – Ruhleben. I'd forgotten what it meant.'

Johnny had never known.

They got out of the train and entered the leafy suburb and got a taxi to the crematorium, which was, in fact, just around the corner, past a garden centre, summer houses, a Lidl, a Burger King and McDonalds. A power station puffed ominously on the other side of the road.

They walked silently up the drive towards the *Feierhallen,* past the memorial plaques and flowers on each side. Johnny felt an ache in his heart as they neared the greening copper slanting roofs and lollipop lights.

Peter looked pale and stressed as he came towards the three of them unceremoniously. He was wearing black jeans, grey shirt and a black suede cowboy hat, and smoking a cigarette.

'Someone will be organising my funeral soon,' he said. 'I can't believe you're not allowed to smoke inside.' He laughed. 'It's a crematorium for God's sake. Hi Johnny. Mad darling, you look fantastic. Hello little boy.'

David held up his hand. 'Are you American?'

Peter shook it solemnly. 'I sure am.'

'Wow.'

'Gee Mad, where did he come from?'

'From me,' she said. 'This is David, my son.'

'But he's huge. I'm sure he wasn't with you last time you were here,' Peter said, staring at David.

'No, he wasn't.' Alice paused.

Johnny wondered if she was going to say more, but she didn't. Neither did Peter.

'You managed to contact a lot of people,' Johnny said, peering into the noisy hall where there were about fifty people seated. Most of them looked like they'd come dressed for a party rather than a funeral.

'We put a notice in the paper,' Peter said. 'I had no idea this many people would drag themselves out here though. We've had to upgrade to the *Große Halle*. There are people from London, Budapest, Prague, even New York. I reckon half of the old Kiosk lot are here. Sophie's here somewhere. Remember her?'

How could he forget. It would be good to see her. He had heard she was doing exciting things with dance.

'It should be a good party later. Shame he's gonna miss it. Have you decided to go ahead with your aerial show, Johnny?'

Both Peter and Alice stared at him expectantly. He hesitated but it was time.

'Yes,' he said.

'Do you want me to mention that your show will be in memory of Bodo?'

'Good idea, Peter. He would have liked that.' Alice sounded pleased.

Johnny nodded. Penny would be pleased as well.

'And Mad, can I have a word?' Peter indicated with a flick of his head that he meant in private.

'Look after David for a moment,' she asked Johnny.

Johnny walked away with David, who was concentrating on avoiding stepping on cracks. He wondered what Peter had to tell Alice that he couldn't hear. But he was pleased Peter had remembered the show – and had made him make up his mind. He seemed very much in charge. Johnny regretted what he had said the other week, accusing Peter of informing on them. He had no proof – only supposition. Some malign wind blew over him and, for once, he had spoken without thinking. It had been a traumatic day.

He went inside the hall with David, holding his hand. The memorial service was about to begin. They were to sit on the grey seats in the front, by the coffin. Upbeat circus music played loudly. Johnny didn't recognise anyone at first and then, slowly, the ghosts of the past revealed themselves to him. Hermann was there, looking paler than death, Michael was perched on a seat drinking a Schultheiss, and one of the Hungarian sisters was sitting on her own dressed in black. He didn't know which one: one used to have blond hair, the other raven. Whoever it was had grey hair now. There was Sophie, dressed in a long black coat, her head still shaved. She was with a couple of people he didn't recognise. An old man in a blue and white polka-dot scarf stood with his back to him in front of the hall by a table blooming with flowers. Someone from the circus? Two younger men stood either side of him. As they took their seats, Johnny recognised the old man as the Professor. He swallowed a lump that had grown in his throat. After all these years. He wanted to speak to him, but a woman in a black gown appeared and stood in front of a microphone on a lectern, head bowed. Behind her was a black and white image of Buddha in a garden. All fell silent in the hall except for the music.

Peter, Alice, and an older man, tanned with bleached hair, came in and sat next to Johnny and David in the front row. Johnny didn't know the man: he was wearing a dark suit and gold rings – the owner of the nightclub perhaps. The doors closed behind them. Alice burst into tears as she came face to face with the coffin. Johnny put an arm round her, blinking away his own tears, as she sat down. David sat the other side of him, still holding his hand. As the woman began to speak, Johnny looked up at the red kite flying away from the almost industrial painting high up on both sides of the wall. A symbol of hope, perhaps, a release from the grey landscape of roofs, factories and broken stones. A strange painting for a crematorium, but it took his mind off imagining Bodo lying there in front of him in that golden box with three holes in his head, his blond curls matted with blood. Instead, he imagined Bodo floating away on that red kite, away from the world that had failed him.

Johnny didn't understand much of the humanist service, but there were alternate bursts of laughter and silence. Other people gave readings. Someone from the back, in a purple feather boa, jeans and purple T-shirt, came forward with a book in his hand and broke the silence by tripping over the trailing feather boa. Rilke's 'Sonnets to Opheus' slid across the wooden floor.

'Darling, this is a funeral, not a circus,' Peter rumbled in English. Several people laughed.

As Johnny looked behind him, a woman slipped into the hall pushing a wheelchair. The face of the woman in the wheelchair was veiled in dark net and she was with a slim, petite woman in a monstrous hat, topped with a green bow, which tilted to one side like a flying saucer. During the demonstrative readings of Rilke, he felt as if they were staring at the back of his head, but when he turned round he saw just the dipped hat and dark veil.

Alice was biting her lower lip, a tear occasionally creeping down her pale cheek. Little David crossed and uncrossed his fingers, seemingly oblivious to the coffin in front of them and the strange assortment of characters crowding the crematorium.

Next, Peter got up to say a few words. His hands shook as he clutched a Marlboro packet in front of him. He cleared his throat and growled in German for a few minutes, during which he looked over at Alice several times. Then he switched to English.

'Not all here speak German so a few words in English to say that Bodo would have adored this audience. He loved to entertain and he was kind, generous, funny and one of the best performers in the world. He was a magician. The things he could juggle, darlings, you and I could only dream of...' Peter rumbled one of his charming bass laughs and people laughed. 'He lived through a difficult time and he, more than most, was a prisoner of his time. He had dreamed of a better world but the world he found in the West was not quite the one he imagined and even magicians struggle to change the world.' Peter paused and looked up at the congregation. 'Most of you probably don't know this but twenty years ago he crossed over to the West on a high wire in one of the most daring Wall crossings ever made. The story has never been told because back in 1984 we were warned that we could have gotten people in the East in trouble. But times have changed and in August there will be an aerial performance about this extraordinary crossing. Bodo was going to be a part of it but the performance will now be dedicated to his memory.

'His life ended in a terrible tragedy, a terrible accident, but he was practising the art he loved. The circus is full of excitement and risk. He loved both. His other great love and passion was his partner, Alice. And their child. They have been separated over the last few years but he still loved her very much. And I know he will be greatly missed by all of us…'

The world around Johnny blinked on/off. Something poked him again in his heart. David was Bodo's child. Why hadn't she told him? And why hadn't Bodo gone to the UK? He had loved her so much. Surely he hadn't left her to bring up David on her own? He looked at Alice but she was watching Peter who was making his way towards them, head bowed. Her hand reached across and squeezed his. A tear traced the lines in Peter's face.

The circus music started up again. It was time to say their final goodbyes. Alice sobbed. So did he as they passed the coffin one last time before the men in black would carry him to the furnaces. Goodbye Bodo. He had never cried so much as he had during the last couple of weeks – at least not for twenty years. Both he and Peter held Alice, held each other. Just before Johnny left the hall, he looked behind him again. The hats were gone. The wheelchair was gone. He shook his head. Too much of the past for one day.

Outside, in the bright warm sunshine, people he had never seen before came to hug Alice and pick up David.

Was he the only one who didn't know? Peter was giving out directions to the reception.

Eight of them squashed into a black van, including a couple of transvestites and Dietrich, the older guy with rings, who was the owner of the club where Bodo worked. The hearse-like van reminded Johnny of a guy from the past who used to drive around in one. Ollie was his name? The two transvestites, one with beautifully painted red finger nails, vied for David's attention. Johnny had never been to Norwich but he suspected that it wasn't like this. Dietrich pulled out a bottle of champagne and eight glasses from a cool box. As they drove out of the crematorium, Johnny thought he saw the woman in the hat pushing the wheelchair again. Then they were lost behind some trees. It couldn't have been: his imagination was playing with him.

'To Bodo!' Dietrich said, holding up his glass. 'And thank you, Peter, for your speaking.'

They all nodded, clinked glasses and drank to Bodo.

'He would have adored this,' Peter said, gulping back the champagne and wiping his mouth.

Alice smiled. Her eyes were red, but she had stopped crying.

'Thank you, Peter. And Dietrich. I appreciate all you have done,' she said.

'It was the little we could do,' Dietrich said. 'You know Bodo work for me ten years. We miss him.'

'At least he didn't suffer,' Peter said. 'They reckon he died quickly.'

They all hummed in agreement but Johnny couldn't help feeling that he had suffered enormously. There must have been a time, as he lay next to the bins with those knives in his head, when he realised he was dying and that he would never see Alice or his child again.

They arrived at the cabaret club where Bodo used to work. Johnny smiled to himself: only in Berlin could a post-funeral party be held in a chandelier-lit cabaret club. The waiters, dressed as clowns, gave out glasses of Sekt. Peter and Dietrich went to supervise the buffet and David was kidnapped by the two transvestites. Johnny was alone with Alice for the first time since the memorial service.

'I didn't know,' he said, 'that Bodo was David's father.'

'No one did. I only told David this morning. Peter guessed – otherwise I probably wouldn't have said anything.'

'Does David understand?'

'I think so. Of course it doesn't mean much to him. He never even met him.'

'But Bodo knew?'

'Yes, of course.' She paused and sighed heavily. 'He refused to come to England and I needed my parents to help me. He was always drunk or working. Or both. I decided to bring David up myself. I suppose I always thought that Bodo would change, apologise and come to England and we'd all live happily ever after. But, of course, life doesn't work like that.'

She spoke without tears now, watching David, who was having a silk cravat tied around his neck.

Johnny didn't reply. Bodo wouldn't go to England with Alice, the woman he adored? Drunk or working? This wasn't the Bodo Johnny had known. His brain flicked through image after image of West Berlin in 1984: Bodo juggling in Alex, Alice sitting with him in the East Berlin bars, snow, always snow, dark empty streets, searchlights, empty U-Bahn stations, running through the cobbled streets, across brown fields, rehearsing with Bodo in the warehouse. Bodo always asking, 'Will she be there, Johnny?' He recalled the last phone call with Bodo when he asked him why he didn't go with Alice to the UK. He said that it had taken him so long to get to West Berlin that he didn't want to leave.

Alice took a deep breath. 'You are not the only one to feel guilty. He blamed himself about... Natasha's death. He always regretted that she didn't cross first. He told me once that she had wanted to but he thought the wire too loose.'

More secrets from the past. And he thought he alone felt guilty.

'That wasn't his fault,' Johnny said.

'Of course. And neither was it yours,' Alice replied sharply. 'Or Peter's. Or mine. Or anyone's. There is no point in blaming ourselves for something that we can not change.'

She was right of course. What had happened had happened. It had been Natasha's decision to cross. She, perhaps more than any of them, had known the risks. He really shouldn't have said anything to Peter.

'Anyway, Johnny, I'll be back in a minute. I need to retrieve David.'

Seconds after Alice had left, Peter joined him with a bottle of Sekt and filled his glass.

'You knew about David?' Johnny asked him.

'No, I didn't. But he looks just like him.' He laughed. 'And Alice was here six years ago!'

Johnny nodded. He put his hand on Peter's arm and squeezed it. 'I'm really sorry about what I said the other week, Peter. Coming back to Berlin for the first time in twenty years and to be faced with Bodo's death, I don't know – the past just exploded in my face.'

'Forget it, Johnny. It doesn't matter.'

But he still sounded hurt.

Everyone was getting slowly drunk. A buffet table of cold meats, cheese, samosas, bread and pastries had been laid out. Sophie came over and they hugged. She hadn't changed much.

'So you learned to dance in the sky,' she said. 'I'm pleased. You've done really well. I've seen some of your work on the net – it's fantastic.'

'So have you,' Johnny said. 'I've read a lot of reviews.'

'Well, you know, it's hard having an independent dance company in America, but we're doing okay. I manage to pay my dancers and rent a studio and try to do a couple of new dances a year. You should come and watch. You can stay with us.'

Johnny nodded. Yes, he should.

'And I am so looking forward to this new show of yours in Berlin.'

'You'll come?' Johnny was surprised.

'You bet.'

Alice retrieved David, complete with bright blue cravat ('for the cutest little boy in Berlin'), and they grabbed a couple of samosas each. As Johnny was eating, the Professor arrived: the man who had changed his life.

'I'm just going to talk to the Professor,' Johnny said, squeezing Alice's shoulder and saying goodbye to Sophie, promising they'd be in touch.

'Oh, that's who it is,' Alice said. 'Of course.'

The old man wept when he saw him. He wrapped his thin arms around him, muttering his name, 'Johnny, Johnny, Johnny'.

Once more, Johnny felt hot tears pricking his eyes. 'It's been a long time,' he whispered.

'Too long, too long,' the Professor replied in German. 'My wife, Hannah, gone. Now Bodo.'

Johnny didn't know about Hannah. This was the man who had shown him his direction in life and, in all these years, he had never tried to find him. He wanted to explain why, how he couldn't cope with the past, how he didn't want to see anyone who reminded him of her. But it was as well the Professor couldn't understand. He knew now he should care about the living. He was pleased he had decided to do the show. He would dedicate it to Natasha and Bodo and history in general. And it would be the best show he had ever done.

'*Alles klar*, Johnny, *alles klar*.'

Peter and Alice came over. There were more hugs. Peter turned to Johnny.

'Did you know George was one of the first to cross Checkpoint Charlie and the first bear to cross over into the West?'

'Yeah?'

The Professor's glassy eyes twinkled.

'He was dancing on the Wall with a guard's cap on him. It was fantastic. You missed a great party, Johnny.'

Johnny didn't know that Peter even knew the Professor, let alone that he had been there in 1989.

'What happened to George?' Somehow it was easier to ask after a bear than people.

Peter spoke to the Professor in German.

'No one wanted to employ them in the West and the subsidies in the East ran out. George was old and no one could afford to look after him. He was one of the victims of Westernisation, I'm afraid.'

The Professor nodded gravely and said something to Johnny.

'What did he say?'

'He says that it's a bad time for them.'

'Is he retired?'

Peter spoke to the Professor again.

'Yes, he says his sons work for a touring circus but he lives alone in Kopënick. Hannah died of cancer two years ago.'

'Tell him I'm sorry to hear that and please ask him for his address. I would like to invite him to the show in the summer.'

Peter talked to the Professor while Johnny took out a pen and picked up a beer mat. Johnny thought he heard the words Zoya and Stasi but he wasn't sure and neither of them spoke to him. The Professor wrote his address and gave it to Johnny. Johnny promised he would write. They hugged once more. The Professor said he must go. His sons were waiting. Johnny watched as the lone figure in the polka-dot scarf glided gracefully out of the club.

'I can't imagine Bodo here,' Johnny muttered.

'He was an alcoholic,' Alice said. She sighed.

'What's an alcoholic?' David asked.

'Someone who drinks a lot,' Alice said, putting him down.

'Then everyone here is an alcoholic?' David looked up at them seriously.

Alice and Johnny laughed.

'Oh dear, Mad. How do you cope?' Peter said. 'Can't you teach him to do circus tricks or something, Johnny.'

Maybe, one day.

'I don't think so,' Alice said. 'We've had enough tricks. Anyway, Johnny, we're thinking of a memorial outside Peter's apartment on Heidelberger Straße. Where the Wall used to be and where … Natasha died.'

Johnny nodded.

'What's there these days?' Johnny asked, remembering only the dark buildings on the other side of the Wall.

'There's a park on one side, a Plus, some wasteland and a great big white Siemens building, or some corporate monster,' Peter said.

'Did Bodo know?'

'No, he would never come to my apartment.'

'Perhaps as well,' Johnny said, unable to imagine Heidelberger Straße without the Wall, even less with a Siemens building.

'The ashes have to remain at the crematorium but we could make something on the wasteland,' Peter said.

'I still have the phone he gave me from the East. He said once that he would only ever need it in his coffin. Maybe we should make a little shrine.'

'I don't know about that. He'll probably call us,' Peter said.

They smiled. Johnny was beginning to feel his head bubbling. Alice looked flushed as well. The Hungarian twin came over to talk to Alice. Johnny turned to Peter.

'Did the Professor say something to you?' he asked. 'I thought I heard Zoya's name mentioned.'

'Actually, he did. He said that he thought it was Zoya who informed on you guys all those years ago,' Peter said, his eyes glowing. 'Apparently, she had been seen talking to someone several times. Not me, you see.'

254

Zoyenka. He had wondered that at the time. He remembered Natasha complaining that Zoyenka wanted to know where they'd been, when they were next meeting, everything. She must have suspected.

'It's very possible,' he said. 'I tried many times to contact her but she disappeared. Did he say anything about Natasha?'

'No. No one ever heard anything. Bodo also tried to find out. He found plenty on himself but nothing on Natasha. They knew about the crossing – of course, the apartment had been bugged. You could go and see if there are any files on you.'

Johnny's eyes widened in surprise, not because of the apartment being bugged – he'd guessed that – but because he didn't know that the files were in public domain. Maybe, one day, he'd go when he had some time. He remembered the Consulate saying that there was probably a file on him as long as Linie 1. Alice must have overheard as she turned and looked at him.

The transvestite with the feather boa stumbled over and persuaded Peter to go on stage with him to sing Frank Sinatra's 'Fly Me to The Moon', one of Bodo's old favourites apparently.

Johnny picked David up and swung him round, landing him on his shoulders. Alice smiled at them. They watched Peter on stage swinging the microphone, and his hips, with the man in the purple boa. Peter dedicated the song to Bodo before unleashing his beautiful bass voice and flying them all to the moon. He was still good. Better than good. Johnny remembered Peter's idea of setting up an act together. What a shame they hadn't. Then he had an idea. Peter might forgive him then.

'He's good, isn't he?' Alice said.

'Yeah, I'd forgotten what a voice he had. I'm going to ask him if he'll sing in the show.'

'Good idea. He'll love it.'

That night Johnny invited Alice and David out for pasta.

'It's good to see so many people, so many old friends,' Johnny said, as they sat round a table in an Italian restaurant on the Ku'damm.

'Yes, it's very special to know people over so many years – even if you don't see them. And I'm glad you're doing the show,' Alice said.

'Yes, I think it's the right thing to do. By the way, do you still have the photos you took at the time?' Johnny asked.

'Yes, somewhere. I told you I would keep them for you,' she said, 'until you were ready.'

'I'm ready now. Can I have copies?'

'Sure,' she said. 'I'll have to dig them out. I often wonder what happened to the border guards. It must be a terrible thing for them to have to live with.'

Johnny didn't reply, but stared thoughtfully at the carpet. So many people had suffered. 'Terrible,' he echoed at last.

This time, Alice wouldn't even let him kiss her.

'No, Johnny, it's not right. Today was Bodo's funeral and, besides, you are too unstable. I need to know I can trust you.'

Maybe she was right. Only today, he imagined he saw Natasha in a wheelchair.

'But you do still like me, don't you?' he said.

'Of course, Johnny.'

He spent another sleepless night, trying to make sense of the last couple of days. The following morning he flew back to London and went straight to the office in Covent Garden, hungover and exhausted.

'You survived then?' Penny asked as he walked in. 'So are we going ahead with it?'

'Yes, Penny, we are. We are going to dance history in Natasha's and Bodo's memory and it is going to be the best show we have ever done.'

'Excellent Johnny. Then we have less than two months to get it on the road. And Henri says you are impossible and your designs are fucking impossible.'

Breitscheidplatz

'To be honest, I nearly didn't come. And I don't know if I want to see him, Peter. He didn't call me for two months! Even now he is a complete fucker,' a very mad Mad said, glancing over at David who was dipping his hands into the fountain.

He looked more and more like Bodo every time Peter saw him. He couldn't believe Johnny hadn't realised who the father was. Personally, he didn't do kids but, as far as kids went, he seemed quite cute. Unlike Mad, who was sharpening her claws like a wild cat as she flicked through the Mövenpick menu, even though they had already ordered. Peter glanced at his Marlboro. He might need one soon.

Johnny had asked him to meet Mad from the airport and bring her and David to the showground in the Tiergarten but she had wanted to stop at one of the cafes near the Europa Centre. He wasn't going to argue with her. He was just beginning to enjoy life again. At last, he was on stage where he belonged. Besides, it was another beautiful day and he had some free time. The square was the same as ever – packed with tourists, shoppers and buskers. A warm breeze fanned them.

'I thought he'd changed,' she said. 'I really did. He seemed so much more humble and nicer.'

'He's incredibly busy, Alice darling,' Peter said. 'It was so stressful in the weeks before the show opened. We were rehearsing eighteen hours a day and when Johnny wasn't with us, he was arguing with Henri about the set, or with Misha, the conductor of the orchestra, or he was with the performers, or having meetings with Penny. He just didn't stop. Everyone was so stressed but Johnny took the full whack. I couldn't have done it. I nearly told him what he could do with his cabaret songs. But the show is awesome.'

A waiter brought over a small beer for him and a cappuccino for Mad.

'So I've heard. There's tons about it in the UK and it's all over the internet. Even you're mentioned. You're famous, Peter! But you're not allowed to defend him.'

'I know, I know, darling. It hurts…' Peter laughed. 'But it is fucking awesome. And you know what? It's our story, our memories. Yours as well, Mad. And Bodo's. And David's. It's about time the world knew what happened in 1984.'

Peter drank some Diesel and lit a cigarette. He was down to three a day normally, although there was going to be a party later so that might mean a few more. Penny had organised it. He was praying Misha would be there. Misha, the conductor, was divine. Tall, dark, longish curly hair with huge round dark eyes as deep as Lake Baikal. And he talked in a deep voice with a thick Russian accent. He called him Pyotr. 'Pyotr, can you sing this a *be-it* more deep.' His voice would sink down into the ground. Oi. Even the thought made the hairs on his arms curl. He flicked his ash on the floor.

'So you're obviously enjoying performing?' Mad said.

'It's just the best thing that has happened to me,' Peter said, smiling into the sunshine.

'Well, you always were a natural performer.'

'Thanks, darling.'

'And you're not working at the café any more?'

'No, I quit the day after the funeral. I couldn't have stayed there any longer anyway. It was time to do something different.'

Mad raised her sunglasses and looked at him suspiciously.

'I'm pleased you're enjoying it. That's great.' She paused. 'So has he said anything about me?'

He really didn't want to get into this. Johnny hadn't said anything but it was fairly obvious he liked her. Always had. Sadly.

'I know he wants you to come,' Peter said. 'You know what Johnny's like, darling. He's not the best person at keeping in touch.'

Mad frowned. 'He managed to keep in touch with her – even when there was a fucking Wall between them.'

'Now, now. That was a long time ago, Alice.'

'I heard you guys talking about Natasha at the funeral. What were you saying?'

'We were?'

'Yes.'

'Oh, you mean with the Professor?'

She was nodding, waiting expectantly.

'Did Johnny not tell you?' Peter was surprised. But then if he hadn't spoken to her – for whatever reason. 'Maybe you should ask him?'

'I might not see him, Peter. So you may as well tell me.'

'Okay.' It wasn't a big secret, anyway. 'He said that uhm whatshername, the sister…'

'Zoyenka.'

'… that Zoyenka had probably grassed Natasha and Bodo. She had been seen talking to the Stasi, apparently.'

Mad nodded, looking relieved. She wasn't the only one. Peter had felt the world float when he heard. Or maybe that was the champagne. His only regret was that Bodo hadn't been there. They could have all stopped blaming themselves.

'And Natasha? What were you saying about her?'

'Nothing. If she did survive, she's never been seen again – as far as anyone knows. Nor the sister.' Peter put out his cigarette, deciding not to tell her about the woman in the wheelchair, who appeared at the show the first night. It was uncanny, but he was sure the woman looked like Natasha. He hadn't said anything to Johnny though. And she hadn't been back again. It may have been his imagination.

'Is he seeing anyone?'

'No, Mad. Darling, you don't understand, we haven't even had time to masturbate.'

Mad smiled at last. It was a relief to see some sunshine break through her cloudy face.

'So, are we ready?' He glanced at his watch. It was almost five. It was quite a walk and he had to do his makeup.

'No, Peter, I haven't finished my coffee. You go on if you like. I'm sure I'll find it, if I decide to go.'

'Oh Alice, Johnny will be very disappointed,' Peter said, beginning to panic. 'And I will be in trouble for not bringing you. Come on, you know you want to see him. He'll be putty in your hands. You'll be able to do with him whatever you want.' She was being a pain in the butt.

'Do you think?'

'I am certain.'

'But what kind of friend wants to be with you all night and then doesn't call for two months?'

'Darling, he's done much worse, remember?'

'I remember. That's why I don't want to see him. You know, when I saw him again, Peter, before the funeral, I felt that I still loved him. And, stupidly, I thought that he felt the same. I'm not going to be hurt again.'

Peter sighed. Mad would ruin his day if he wasn't careful.

'Alice,' he said. 'You'll never know what he feels unless you see him. You guys have to talk this through. You've come all this way, it would be madness not to. Besides, don't you want to see me in the show?'

She finished her coffee and inched her chair backward a fraction and folded her arms into the sun.

'I don't know, Peter. Some things never change, do they?'

Tiergarten

Time changes people, Johnny thought, as he left his hotel room, and his mobile, to stroll through the Tiergarten. He needed some air and to relax for a few minutes.

'Don't forget we have a meeting at five,' Penny called after him. She was like a tracker hound. She must have heard his door close.

'I won't,' Johnny replied.

He walked past the Zoo and thought about hiring a bike like all the rest of the performers who were staying at the hostel, but decided to jog. It was another warm day and children's cries and laughter bounced through the park. Families of picnickers and Turkish barbecuers dotted the patches of shrunken brown grass and cyclists whizzed along the paths. Two more weeks to go. Then they would all get a two-week break, at least.

The last month had been full on in Berlin, as had the two months before. The show had been an enormous success so far, thanks in part to the balmy nights, Henri's technical brilliance, Penny's managerial skills, his fantastic thirty performers (including the musicians and Peter) and, indeed, the rest of the team. Reviews and reviewers were appearing from all over the place, not only Berlin but also from London, the States, Japan, Russia, Hungary, the Czech Republic, Poland and Estonia. He had given so many interviews that when he spoke now he felt as if he was hearing a recording of himself. They all wanted to know how much was autobiographical? Did it really happen? Why hadn't it been documented? He had opened a minefield.

That didn't worry him: it was time someone knew the truth. But even in the shaded calm of the park, something else was causing his heart to leapfrog. Alice and David would be there later. Peter had gone to meet them from the airport. He looked at his watch: 16.09. They should be on their way. The Professor had also been invited to the performance this evening as well. And today was 13 August, exactly forty-three years since the building of the wall. Friday the 13th. Not that he was superstitious.

He had spoken to Alice only twice since the funeral. Once just after to thank her for the images she sent him and again a couple of weeks ago. Her voice had been ice-cold. Why hadn't he called or emailed her, she wanted to know. He tried to explain that he had been busy. 'A phone call doesn't take long, does it? Johnny, it's been two months!' He apologised and promised to get Penny to contact her with information about their tickets and accommodation. She had told him she wouldn't be able to come before 12 August and that she wasn't bothered anyway. The words slid along a glacier, rolling into him, knocking him over. She was right:

he should have called. It was just so hard. He had no time for any social life outside the company. He would make it up to her. He had to find a way for them to be together but, unless he gave up the company, or she joined, he couldn't think of a way.

He hoped the woman in the wheelchair wouldn't appear again, as she had at the funeral and, he suspected, on the opening night. But maybe it had been his imagination. He was under a lot of stress. Penny had insisted that no one had been there in a wheelchair and when he reached the place in the auditorium where he thought he'd seen her, she was gone. Yet still the question nagged him: was it Natasha? Could she possibly be alive? If it were her, she had made no attempt to talk to him. What would he say to her? Time changes people. Since meeting Alice again, he knew that even if Natasha were alive, he would not love her like he used to.

Not that she could still be alive.

A wind brushed against the trees, rustling the leaves. Johnny stopped, suddenly exhausted. He had run further than he'd thought: the Siegessäule, the golden woman with wings, was flying almost overhead. She had always reminded him of Natasha, even though it was Alice who had drawn her.

'Natasha, forgive me,' he whispered. 'I need to love again. It is time. Too many years have been lost. Goodbye, my angel.'

He waved to the golden woman and smiled to himself as he turned round. Maybe she knew.

It was almost five. The performance didn't begin until 9 p.m. but if he wasn't back for the meeting with Penny at the grounds, there would be trouble.

The enormous scaffolding came into view. Henri had almost been right in saying that his outdoor set for aerialists was fucking impossible until he'd come up with the suggestion of a midnight performance with everything built up around scaffolding and covered like a giant umbrella. Henri was being sarcastic at the time but Johnny knew that that was the answer. Not midnight, but a later performance, when it was dark or getting dark, with everything hanging on the scaffolding: lights, performers, multi-media. And it worked. The auditorium seated a thousand people and they'd been sold out every night. He would not have to work in telesales. But now there was something more important on his mind.

As he passed through the grounds he hunted for them, but he could not find them anywhere. It was still early, he told himself. He went into the rehearsal tent and headed to a small office where Penny, Henri and a couple of his lead performers were sitting waiting for him. Penny had a thick file on her lap and was twiddling a pen in her fingers. This looked serious.

'Okay, the good news is, everyone, that word has spread through the dance world and we've had requests for the show from festival organisations in San Francisco and Tokyo this autumn and Moscow, Prague, Budapest and New York for next summer. I told them we couldn't do the winter because of the cold.' Penny paused, waiting for the news to sink in.

It sank deeply. 'That's great,' said Johnny. It was terrible. What would Alice say?

'It's very great.'

'Fantastic,' Henri said. 'I've now got to reconstruct this monster on Red Square.'

But Johnny knew that he was pleased, really.

'I'm going to need help, Johnny. Someone beautiful, intelligent and very strong.'

'Okay,' said Johnny. He knew just the person. He had found a way.

'Can we tell everyone?' Dizz, one of the performers, asked.

'Later, I think,' Penny said, looking at Johnny. 'We'll make an announcement after I've sorted out a few more details.'

'Okay,' said Johnny.

'The bad news is that, even though we're sold out every evening and programmes, CDs and DVDs are selling well, we are barely covering costs.'

But Johnny wasn't listening.

'We need more merchandise,' Penny told him. 'T-shirts, postcards, pens…'

'Fine,' Johnny agreed.

Penny sighed in frustration.

'I'm sorry, there's something I need to do,' Johnny said, looking at his watch.

'Fine,' Penny echoed. 'I've just about said what I wanted to say. We can make the announcement at the party later. Okay?' She looked around.

Johnny nodded, got up and strode out, past the performers who were warming up in the rehearsal tent. He wandered around the grounds for a few minutes but he still could not see them.

'Johnny!' He heard little David's voice.

Relief seeped into his muscles. The little blond-haired boy was peering outside the refreshment tent. David rushed towards him and Johnny picked him up and turned him upside down. David giggled. Inside, Alice and Peter were sitting at a table drinking coffee and reading through the programme. Peter was pointing something out to her. He, at least, was happy. Alice's body was angular, defensive, angry, beautiful.

Her long dark hair was finely plaited in parts and she wore loose cotton trousers, a dark red T-shirt and red lipstick. Her indigo eyes glittered. She looked up at him. An ice-pick pierced his heart. She looked down again at the programme.

'Hello Johnny,' she said.

She didn't get up to kiss him. He kissed Peter, naked without his makeup. He still smelled of sherbert fountains and lavender. Peter rolled his eyes dramatically at him. He was in trouble. But he knew that.

He sat down with them. David came to sit on his knee, holding his ears. Even Alice managed a smile.

'Well, I hope you like the show,' he said, lamely. He didn't know what to say. Marry me, came to mind, but he knew she would tell him to fuck off. He looked into her eyes instead, asking her to forgive him. She pierced him again but this time she didn't look away.

'I'm sure I will. Who's performing you?'

'Someone more than half my age – a young Australian performer called Az. He's excellent.'

'You'll like Az, Alice,' Peter said, winking at her. 'Such a darling.'

Johnny pre-empted the next question. 'They're both excellent. Marie plays Natasha. Marie is actually from Dresden but has no memory of the Wall – she's eighteen.' Johnny spoke without feeling any pangs.

'Well, there've been good write ups in *The Guardian* and *The Independent*,' she said coolly.

'Yes, I've seen some. I know we're booked out for this show and we've been asked to take it to other cities: Moscow, Tokyo, San Francisco...' Johnny wondered if Alice would like those places. He wondered how she would like working with Henri.

'Awesome. Will I go?' Peter asked.

'Of course.'

Alice was quiet.

'Yippee. It's gonna be a great party later,' Peter said.

'Oh, I'd forgotten about that. I hope you'll come?' he asked Alice.

'Maybe. Your manager, Penny, has arranged a babysitter, but I'll see.'

Thank you, Penny.

Peter shuffled uncomfortably on his seat. He lit a Marlboro and began talking about touring around the world. Alice was nodding at Peter.

Johnny bounced David on his knee while staring at her profile, her slightly upturned nose, her long dark eyelashes against her pale skin. He loved the fine lines that sprang onto her face when she smiled and the small dimple in her cheeks. I love you, he said, without speaking. His knee sought hers beneath the table. As they touched, he got an electric shock. He pulled back and they looked at each other and smiled.

'Are you trying to kill me?' Johnny said.

She laughed.

'I reckon you'd be getting off lightly at that,' Peter said. 'Anyway, I'd better go and get ready, darlings.'

'It's only six o'clock – you have three hours!' Alice said.

'You try getting this old piece of garbage looking beautiful in any less.' Peter stood up, tall and confident. 'You guys need to talk anyhows. Come on, David. Let me show you the rehearsal tent. We can put some make-up on.'

Alice groaned but she didn't stop him. David scrambled off his knee and took hold of Peter's hand. A touching sight. Johnny smiled after them as they went towards the rehearsal tent.

'At least you've made someone happy,' Alice said.

Ouch.

'I could make you happy too,' he said. Ouch again.

'I doubt it. You haven't done very well so far.' Her sentences lashed him.

'You could give me a chance?'

'Why? Why Johnny? Last time we met you told me how much you liked me and then you didn't call me for two months – at a time when I needed a friend.'

'I'm sorry. It won't happen again.'

'How do I know that?'

'Because I want you to come with me.'

'What do you mean?'

'I want you to come on tour with me. I mean will you come on tour with me? I'd like to offer you a job, to help Henri, the set designer.' He paused as she didn't reply. He felt sick. 'But you don't have to... I'd still like you to come... I just thought you might be good at the job. I haven't quite sorted out the package but... would you be interested?'

'I'd be interested,' she said, at last. 'But are you asking me to come as a friend, lover or partner?'

'All three.'

'I don't know, Johnny. What about David?'

'He can come too. I'll teach him to walk the high wire.' He was talking faster now, urgently.

'What about school? He's due to start in September.'

'But Alice, he'll learn more in that year with us than at any school. Please say yes.'

'No juggling?'

264

'No juggling.'

'I'll think about it,' she said coolly. She paused before adding, 'By the way, Happy Birthday.'

'How did you know it was my birthday?' Johnny asked. He had told no one.

'Because you told me.'

'Twenty years ago?'

'Yes. Some things I never forget.'

But then she smiled at him and Johnny felt his stomach fall from a great height. He felt sea sick. It was those deep violet eyes. They spoke to him, told him that she loved him, that she had always loved him, that she wanted to be with him forever, that she had tried to tell him so many times in the past but he had never listened, that he was a complete and utter prick. He knew, he knew. But he was listening now. And looking. He would never stop looking.

'Have you thought about it?' he asked.

Her smile broke into a laugh. Then she leant forward and kissed him on the lips.

'Yes.'

'And?' He could feel something eating his heart. Those beetles must have got there.

'Yes.'

His brain buzzed with happiness. He was walking on air, high up above the world. He had forgotten how it felt to walk above the trees, to walk in the clouds. The peace and the quiet, the sense of complete contentment, of not wanting anything else in the world. He had thought he was too old to feel this again. But here he was, twenty years on, falling in love with the woman he had always loved. As he looked up above the park he imagined he glimpsed the golden woman with wings waving to him before disappearing behind the trees.

'Why you smiling?' Alice asked.

'Because I'm happy,' he whispered in her ear. 'Because some things do change.'

The Last Dance over the Berlin Wall
by
The Flight Company

In memory of Natasha Barovskova and Bodo Kollender who danced over the Berlin Wall in November 1984 and who showed me the way through the sky

Artistic Director and Choreographer
Johnny East

Cast members...

Klaus's eyes drift across the names of the cast, all the time struck by an unpleasant sensation that he sometimes feels in his dreams: a sensation that he hasn't felt while conscious for fifteen odd years, and he had hoped he would never feel again. It is a cold, clammy sensation, followed by a tightening in his chest and difficulty in breathing, as if he's swallowed an ice cream cone whole. As he stares at the walled-in umbrellaed scene in front of him with a very convincing replica of the 3.4 metre high Wall slicing down the middle of the stage, old apartment blocks on both sides and the watchtower on the left, the programme slips from his hands, off his knees and hits the wooden floor. Johnny. Johnny. That was his name. Could it possibly be the same Johnny?

'Are you okay?' Eva, his wife, asks.

'Yes, yes,' he mutters, bending down to pick up his programme. She couldn't have known about it. She knows that he guarded the Berlin Wall and she knows about 'an incident' but she doesn't know what happened. She doesn't know that he shot an angel. No one does – apart from those who were there. And who knows where they are now. He has no friends left from those days.

Eva said something about having read a great review of an aerial performance about the Berlin Wall in the Dresden News and what a super idea it would be to have a weekend in Berlin as a joint belated birthday trip for the boys. They could go to the performance on the Friday evening and then to the museums and wander around the capital on the Saturday and Sunday and be home by Sunday evening. It would be interesting for him, she added. He had been there, lived through it. He didn't ask for any details, didn't think it necessary. He had been reluctant to go for other reasons: Berlin is expensive and, in truth, he has little interest in museums – or theatre – and he didn't think the boys would want to. But Eva was insistent and, surprisingly, both Dieter and Sigmund thought it would be cool.

But there it is, on the front cover of the programme: a high wire act across the Berlin Wall. It is too much of a coincidence to be a coincidence. This is it. He is the man Johnny. The man who loved the angel he shot. The man who haunted him in his nightmares for twenty years. The man who caused his doctor to prescribe him with sleeping tablets for five years. The man who used to wake him up in the night because he pissed himself. The skeletons in the cupboard have slipped out and are about to fly before his eyes and make him relive the horror of twenty years ago. At last, he is to be punished for the crime he was ordered to commit. The pride of yesterday that is the shame of today. He sinks back into his seat and closes his eyes. Eva nudges him.

'Hey, you'll miss it,' she says.

He grunts. If only. He wants to say that he's already seen it but he knows she won't understand. He wants to get up and walk away but he can't get out: Eva and the boys are on his left and there are six other people on his right before the aisle.

Drumming, thumping like heartbeats, begins from the orchestra pit in front of them and spotlights flash on to performers dangling from ropes in the sky. Nine on each side. They whirl, twirl and tumble like snowflakes down to the stage.

They dance together as one synchronised performance representing popular dances of the twenties, thirties, forties and fifties. A tall man in drag sings a Marlene Dietrich song. Slowly, as they enter the sixties, the dancers' movements change until they become two very different acts. On massive screens at the back of the wall, jerky images of the building of the Wall and of soldiers shooting people trying to escape flash in front of him. A small, beautiful girl, dressed in silver, somersaults round and round a black and white world, while others juggle and backflip. The girl jumps on a trapeze and sculpts herself into kaleidoscopic patterns as if she were made of snowflakes. Klaus gazes at her in disbelief. Other performers climb the ropes, linked together like seahorses, and look over towards the West before diving down head first.

Then the lights set in the East and rise in the West. A young handsome man dances in a night club under bright colourful spotlights and mirrored balls. *When Two Tribes Go to War...* rumbles out of digital surround sound from enormous speakers. Klaus vaguely remembers listening to it on the American Forces station that they used to pick up illegally. The nightclub is full of the other beautiful performers, dancing, drinking, smoking. He can feel the auditorium moving as the spectators tap their feet. He looks at Eva and the boys. They are all in raptures. Sigmund is jerking his head forward as if he is trying to flip it off. And he isn't the only one.

He closes his eyes for a second and when he opens them, he sees himself climbing the watchtower, rifle in hand, together with Heinrich – yes, that was his name. He dances around the watchtower like Spiderman. Klaus frowns. He could never have done that. Like eagles they hunt the night sky, the red lights from the Fernsehturm flashing in the distance. Every so often they shoot at shadows on the Wall. He closes his eyes again but he keeps being shot at through the speakers. He feels his body jolt several times. Eva elbows him.

He suddenly needs to piss.

The Westerners visit the East and they meet up with the other dancers in Alex. Images of the drab concrete blocks and greyness flash before him. They dance together, showing each other different sequences. The Westerners have brought fire and they eat it like candy floss. High up above a fountain of white light, the boy and the girl dance a love dance and kiss. Then *he* comes along again and spoils their fun, pointing his gun at them and chasing them back to the West. From an apartment window high up in the East and a window in the West the two dance longingly, apart.

The boy visits the East several times but all the time *he* watches him from the Wall. As their love grows, Klaus' heart aches more and more, and the hole in his stomach grows bigger. Scenes of a circus in the East alternate with a modern dance show in the West, one in the air, the other on the ground. He knows what is coming. It is just a matter of time. He only hopes they won't include the scene with him peering into the Wall stripper's apartment. But how could they know that?

It begins to snow and the lights go down and the drum beat fills the park. A single spotlight falls on the Wall slicing the stage. A marksman, lingering in the window of the Eastern apartment, shoots an arrow across from East to West and a narrow wire shimmers in the night. The audience gasps as a man dressed in black steps out of a window onto the wire, a balancing pole in his hand. The man carefully makes his way across. A flashlight from the ground roams the sky but the man has stopped in the middle and is lying down on the wire. As much as he wants to, Klaus can't take his eyes off the stage. Don't look, don't look, he tells his double. This time he doesn't. The audience gives a collective sigh as the tightrope walker makes it to the other side. So one person did make it then? A man. If only the angel had crossed first. Perhaps it wouldn't have been so bad to kill a man? Klaus wonders what happened to him.

The lover hangs out the window and beckons to the girl. She steps out of the window in the East. She isn't dressed in a black balaclava and tights as she had been back then but in a long, white flowing dress that reaches to just above her ankles. She has long blonde hair as well. Even so, Klaus begins to feel sick. Everyone in the audience knows that something bad is going to happen. But only he knows how bad it had been.

As he looks up into the falling snow he sees her, of course, and aims his rifle. Powerful spotlights spin above the park, hitting the leaves on the trees and tunnelling cone-shaped burrows of light into the sky, almost reaching the stars. A dialogue begins with bass and drums and a siren cries out. The woman stops and stares at him, smiles at him. She sits down on the wire, defeated. Then she lies down, her balancing pole across her stomach. He aims his rifle and shoots her. But misses. She sits up and looks at him as if surprised. He shootsagainandagainandagain. She falls from the wire and spirals down to the stage on a spider's thread, like a leaf falling from a tree. And there he is. Photographic evidence flashes on the screens of his youthful back standing over the woman crumpled on the ground. He recognises the wet patch on his trousers and his hunched-over shoulders. As the bile in his stomach spreads up to his throat he closes his eyes and swallows. He listens to the music, a lone accordion and cabaret singer, sad, mournful, nostalgic. But then the drums begin again, determined, forceful.

He opens his eyes to find the Wall empty and unguarded. The other dancers have appeared from the East and they perform a dizzying display of aerial dance from ropes, trapeze and wires, ten metres above the stage. The Wall becomes invisible, an irrelevance, as the dancers fly through the night. Klaus gazes on with wonder. They are more like birds than people, creatures who belong in the treetops and in the stars above the park. It is not circus trapeze but more like modern dance in flight. It is truly fantastic. A visual feast which his hungry eyes and brain laps up for those last fifteen minutes, his role as executioner could almost have been forgotten. If it were not for the wet patch on his seat.

The performers twirl down to the stage and line up in front of the Wall. They bow to a stunned audience, who take a moment before to respond with wild applause and cheers.

'Eva, I have to do something,' he says, as soon as the performers have left the stage and the lights have come up on the auditorium.

'What? Wasn't that fantastic?' Eva says, still clapping. 'I've never seen anything like it. Didn't you enjoy it? You looked like you had your eyes closed most of the time.'

'I thought it was cool,' Sigmund says. 'So much better than the circus. But I'm glad I didn't live in the East in those days.'

'Me too,' Dieter agrees. 'Did they really shoot that girl?'

'No, of course not,' Eva says. 'It was a show.'

'But it says in the programme that it was based on a real event,' Dieter says. 'And loads of people got shot crossing the Wall, didn't they, Dad? Everyone knows that.'

'Naturally, some people died. I just have to do something,' Klaus says, getting up from his seat. 'I'll explain later, I promise. I'll meet you back at the hotel.'

'Klaus? What's going on? Ugh! Looks like you've sat on something.'

But he is pushing past the six people next to him. Everyone else seems reluctant to move.

He heads to where he thinks he has seen the performers retire to – a smaller tent at the back of the stage. He is stopped at the tent door by an officious middle-aged woman with glasses. A couple of police lurk around a rope preventing the public from straying into the performers' area. One of them has his eye on him. It is the times they live in. His short, almost cropped, hair probably does him no favours.

'I need to speak to Johnny,' he says in German. 'I have a message for him.'

The woman looks at him as if she hasn't understood. She calls a young man over who speaks to him. Klaus repeats his request and the man translates. This time she looks surprised.

'Who are you?' she asks him in English.

'Please tell her I have a message for Johnny. It is very important,' he tells the translator. How is he going to do this in English? He never uses the language. But Johnny must speak German.

'I'm sorry,' the woman says. She glances over at the police while the translator speaks to him. 'Johnny is very busy at the moment. Can I take the message?'

'It is personal.' Klaus sighs. He is going to have to play his last card. 'I used to guard the Berlin Wall. In 1984.'

She disappears into the tent, leaving him with the translator. Klaus isn't in the mood to make small talk so they stand in silence until a tall, attractive and very sophisticated man comes to the opening. He is with a small athletic woman with a shaved head. They hug and say goodbye with promises to meet later. She sounds American. So this must be Johnny.

'Johnny?' he asks, holding out hand. 'My name is Klaus. How do you do?'

'Klaus, what can I do for you?'

Klaus stutters in English that he needs to talk to him, in private. He feels his tongue trip over the words he never uses. But Johnny understands and leads him through the tent, under a trapeze, two high wires, past a trampoline and performers who are cooling down and talking excitedly, and through to a small room where there is a desk, computer and several chairs. Sitting on three of them are the cabaret singer, an old man and a beautiful woman with a little boy with white-blonde curly hair and deep blue eyes on her knees. The odd, sprightly old man is wearing a polka-dot handkerchief around his neck and tears are streaming down his face. He keeps muttering, 'wunderbar'. Johnny introduces them by name. The woman, Alice, stares at him out of eyes of indigo glass. He looks away. The cabaret singer, Peter, is German or speaks fluent German. The old man is introduced as the Professor.

'You can tell us anything,' Johnny says. 'We're old friends.'

Klaus hesitates. The old man is looking at him suspiciously and Alice's eyes are burning a hole in his tongue. His voice falters as he stutters that what he has to say isn't suitable for children.

After some discussion Alice insists on taking David to look around the rehearsal tent. 'I think I know what he's come here to say,' she says, giving him a faint, almost imperceptible, smile. Yes, she knows all right. The Professor also goes with them.

Once they have gone, Klaus takes a deep breath and speaks to Peter in German but looks at Johnny. The singer's deep voice fills the room as he translates. He tells Johnny that he was there when the woman he loved was shot down. Johnny flinches as if something hit him in the stomach. He tells him that he was with her when they put her in the military vehicle. That she spoke to him. She asked him to give Johnny a message. Naturally, for many years he was unable to and then, after the Wall fell, it seemed better to forget about it. He lived in Dresden and he had no idea who Johnny was. It is coincidence that he is here tonight. He pauses as the English echoes over his German.

Johnny closes his eyes.

'What did she say?' he asks.

Klaus understands and answers slowly in English:

'She ask me to tell you that she loves you. But to tell you that you must be happy. That you must live your life.'

The singer lights a Marlboro. This is followed by a silence, deeper than space itself. It is as if they have all floated off somewhere a long way away.

'Do you know what happened to her?' Johnny asks, eventually.

Klaus nods his head, then answers in German. 'We weren't told officially. We were never told anything but I heard she was dead on arrival at the hospital. Her chest was riddled with bullets.' He is going to add that her back was broken but there is too much pain in the room. The singer's voice now sounds like a beaten dog whimpering.

'How do you know that?'

'I knew one of the guards who travelled with her to the hospital. He told me.'

There is another long silence.

'You shot her, didn't you?' Johnny says.

Klaus looks down at the compacted earth around his black, dirt-smudged shoes. A tear drips from his eye and darkens the ground. He remembers the blood stains in the snow. He looks up and nods. Yes, he shot her.

'You're the guard in the photographs, aren't you? I recognise you now.'

Klaus continues nodding. Johnny pulls out a drawer and a pile of black and white photos. There are dozens of black and white frayed and faded images of him and the angel on the ground. She was just a child. In one of them she is looking at him and smiling. He thinks it was when she told him he'd pissed his pants. He feels sick again. Thank God they didn't use any of these in the show.

'Where did you get these from?'

'Alice,' the singer says. 'The woman who just left the room.'

So she was there. She had recognised him immediately.

'There was a time when I wanted to kill you,' Johnny says, closing the drawer. 'But all that is gone now. Times have changed.' He pauses. 'Thank you for telling me. It was important for me to know. I have spent so many years wondering…'

Klaus nods as the singer finishes speaking and stands up. The door opens and the old man, Alice and the little boy come in. Without a word, she goes and puts her arms around Johnny. The little boy looks questioningly at them all. It is time to go. He already has his hand on the door handle when Johnny calls to him.

'Klaus? I don't blame you, you know. It was a different world we lived in. We are all prisoners of our time.'

Klaus looks into Johnny's ice-blue eyes. It was true. He had been a prisoner of that time, forced to defend a world divided by words and ideology that mean nothing to most people now.

'I am very sorry,' he says in English, and walks out of the room, leaving Johnny and Alice silently rocking from side to side.

As Klaus passes underneath the trapeze, tears swing in front of his eyes but his heart leaps higher than it has in twenty years.

Acknowledgements

My thanks to friends who lived in West Berlin at that time, in particular, Alison Kelley and Mario Brandão, for sharing their memories and helping me remember mine.

A special thanks to Bill Horncastle for sharing his notes on Berlin, to Chris de Witt for his extensive photo gallery of the Berlin Wall and to Bob Biderman for his unwavering support and encouragement in helping me take some important narrative decisions, and for publishing the opening on www.visionsofthecity.com. Thanks, also, to Sofia von Mentzingen, Karin Seidel and Marie-Therese Hamacher for sharing their experiences of life in West Germany and Berlin in the 1980s, to Sabine Meier for her invaluable feedback, to Herr Fehzberg for information on Ruhleben Crematorium, and to Paul Tiefenbach for taking the time to correct my German. And to many writing friends and colleagues who have read and commented on this work throughout its many years in the making from Ian Nettleton and Ashley Stokes in Norwich back in 2001 to Penny Howson and Janice Russell in the Algarve in 2007. A final thanks to Anna Cassar for her detailed feedback and editorial skills, and to Beata Pozitiva for proof-reading the final version.

Background reading:

Berlitz Berlin Travel Guides
John Ardagh, *Germany and the Germans*, Penguin Books, 1987
Alfred Döblin, *Berlin, Alexanderplatz*, Continuum, 1999
Marianna S. Katonna, *Tales from the Berlin Wall,* Minerva Press, 1997
Christopher Hilton, *The Wall,* Sutton Publishing Ltd, 2001
Christopher Isherwood, *Goodbye to Berlin*, Minerva, 1989
Philippe Petit, *To reach the Clouds,* Faber and Faber, 2003
Peter Schneider, *The Wall Jumper,* Random House, 1983